HOME BODIES

HOME BODIES

Lethem, Ohio, Pop. 3,200

by Alicia Miller

illustrated by Ann McCarthy

THE ATLANTIC MONTHLY PRESS
NEW YORK
♦

Published simultaneously in Canada
Printed in the United States of America

Library of Congress Cataloging-in-Publication Data

Miller, Alicia.
Home bodies.

I. Title.
PS3563.I37418H6   1988   88-3414
ISBN 0-87113-186-2   813'.54

Designed by Laura Hough

The Atlantic Monthly Press
19 Union Square West
New York, NY 10003

FIRST PRINTING

For
Maudwynne and Henry Metcalf

I

On a July afternoon as hot as they come, when the river that runs through Lethem lies flat as a mirror (two sets of trees, two skies), and the katydids saw and saw as if they could sever this hour from the rest of the day, Katherine Watters pulls into Tano's Shop-Rite parking lot behind Main Street. She grabs a stray cart spookily touring the lot under its own steam. When she enters the store, a blast of air-conditioning stops Katherine in her tracks. Her system pauses uncertainly.

Will Katherine's body temperature stabilize, or will she keel over in Tano's Shop-Rite? If she does, will her dashing doctor husband show up to revive her? Would he use CPR or just tell her to quit horsing around and get off the floor? Could he wait while she staggered over and picked up some pea pods? Will Tano's, in fact, have pea pods today?

The store is packed. On hot days the whole town seems to congregate in the chilly aisles of Tano's, the coldest place for miles. Katherine tosses a loaf of bread into her cart and lingers by the ice cream long enough to hear two local real estate men in matching seersucker suits discussing the hotly contested Hamilton property. One greets her with a small, coy finger wave; the other winks. Katherine smiles and grabs half a gallon of chocolate eclair.

Will the Hamilton son manage to cut his sister out of the estate? Will the courts care that she's "born again"? Will they hold it against her that she used to hit the bottle and display rather conspicuous stress symptoms all over town? Would it militate in her favor that during these interludes she often impersonated Janis Joplin to a tee? Why are Tano's bananas always green?

Katherine pounces on the remaining pea pods. Waiting to have them weighed, she catches a glimpse of herself in the two-way mirror behind the vegetables. Her hair is especially weird because of the humidity, and there's a streak of mud on her T-shirt. She considers the possibility that the reflection isn't hers but some smudged, ghostly stranger's.

Will the tall woman with the peculiar hair ever find the image she seeks? Would it help if the mirror weren't tinted green? Will it be noted on her permanent record that she made an appearance at Tano's with mud on her shirt? Where exactly are these permanent records kept? And will the butcher have sole today or just that creepy monkfish?

She props a large box of raisin bran on the rack of her cart to conceal her muddied front. Not that anyone will notice. She's lived in Lethem so long, she might as well be part of the scenery. She tosses things into the cart, working without a list as usual.

The two pay phones, squeezed between the wine shelves and the deli corner, are busy. Katherine orders a dozen hot dogs and a pound of bacon and hears the caller closest to her, a man, say something about a phantom stock plan. This interests her less than the sudden plaintive outcry from the woman in tennis clothes on the other phone.

"Oh Fred, Fred. I can't get there today. Tomorrow, Fred, please." The woman is Adelaide Butler. Her husband is Ben.

Will Fred turn out to be merely a vet or a car mechanic? Or is Fred the secret lover of Adelaide, whose husband, a dentist, was recently spotted with a blond half his age? If Ben and Adelaide split, what will happen to their vanity license plates, DR 2TH and MRS 2TH? What precisely are the symptoms of nitrite poisoning?

Katherine wheels down an aisle and discovers the superintendent of schools in a powwow with the principal of the middle school and two school board members. They all greet her by name, fading back to let her by in an oddly graceful dipping and pivoting routine. She reaches behind the superintendent for a jar of peanut butter, and the little group gathers again without a ripple, almost as if choreographed.

Is social dancing about to stage a comeback in the Lethem schools? Will this replace computer literacy as the latest craze? Would the curriculum include break dancing as well as the waltz and fandango? Would handkerchiefs for sweaty palms become part of the boys' dress code? And is it true, as the ad suggests, that this new detergent will make her husband leap with joy over the brightness of the wash? Her husband *leap?* The *wash?*

Katherine stands in the check-out line gazing out the windows onto Main Street. Inside Tano's, it feels like the North Pole, outside, the Buckeye National Bank's digital thermometer registers ninety-five degrees. Heat shimmers up from the asphalt, giving the store-fronts down the street a quivering, dreamlike sense of movement. She rubs the backs of her arms and begins emptying her cart.

Just as she finishes, a red pickup truck barrels noisily down the street and slams to a halt in front of Tano's at the town's lone traffic light. She can't see the driver's face, only the way he taps the steering wheel impatiently. The truck trembles beneath him like a nervous horse. The second the light changes, the truck bolts left up Jefferson, bam.

Is the driver of the pickup fleeing justice? Racing to a fire? Could he be late for a steamy rendezvous? If so, will he be waylaid by the Lethem PD before he finds ecstasy, rapture, romance? Are there still such things *as* ecstasy, rapture, etc.? Does she have enough cash to pay the bill, or will she have to write a check? Stay tuned.

Several blocks from the center of town, the red pickup swerves abruptly down a winding drive and comes to a stop against the fence of the Rec Center pool. The driver switches off the engine and ransacks through the clutter on the passenger seat, tossing papers and tools and books to the floor helter-skelter until all that's left is an unsheathed bowie knife, two bills addressed to Midnight Blue, and a letter in a pale gray envelope. He eyes the letter, puts it in his shirt pocket, immediately takes it out, and throws it on top of the pile on the floor. He drops his head to the steering wheel.

He remains head-down for some minutes until a shrill cry from the pool rouses him. Only then does he gaze through the fence, lingering on the interesting legs of the lifeguard not twenty feet away. He resumes his search until he spots a small black book wedged between the seat and door. He whips through its pages until he finds something that satisfies him.

He wipes his forehead, climbs out of his truck, and leans against the fence, hoping for a breeze. No luck. The air is motionless, and the shouts of the children in the pool grate against his ears. Back in the truck, he drives slowly to the street where he peers out through the passenger window for so long, he appears to be casing the area.

When he pulls onto Jefferson, he holds the speedometer at twenty-five, the picture of nonchalance as he passes a gray car parked in the bushes with its radar aimed directly at him. The houses on his right grow larger and farther apart, immaculately tended Victorian homes built on a crest sloping up from the street, their front yards one continuous upsweeping lawn. Behind these houses, in the middle of backyards that roll down to the Dameron River, runs an alley entered from a side street half a mile farther up Jefferson. One house catches his eye today, a rambling white frame, all rectangles except for the small cupola. He studies the blue hydrangea crowding its foundations, the long first-floor windows, the porch roof, flat enough to set a ladder on. A low whistle escapes him.

Moving up Jefferson, he feels part of the heat, radiant, radiating the light that dapples the interior of his truck. He imagines the way the afternoon light falls in the white house, sees it playing over muted Oriental rugs, flaming the wood grain of antiques, spinning through chandeliers, cascading off silver. A breeze stirs heavy drapes and sets shadow-leaves swaying across Japanese wallpaper, shelves of leather-bound books. Everything is perfect, his to haunt.

He blows the hair out of his eyes and turns fast into the narrow alley, as if he could seize this vision by pressing the accelerator, lay hold of it by sheer speed. His truck chokes and belches, but he doesn't hear. Somewhere in that house he is listening to Mahler.

A few of the large houses on the south side of Jefferson have two fronts, one facing the street and an identical one looking down over the backyards and alley to the river beyond. These odd, double-fronted homes, built with paper mill money a century ago, pay tribute to the Dameron River. The builders buttered their bread on both sides; they knew where their fortunes came from.

Out of the back front door of the white frame house, Katherine Watters steps into the afternoon heat, ice cream safe in the freezer. She pauses at the top of the porch steps, shields her eyes against the sun, and sniffs.

DEODORANT SALES SKYROCKET AS
HEAT WAVE BLASTS AREA

She pinches off a browning geranium from a stone pot on the porch and tosses it into the hydrangea below. Tan and tall and heavily freckled, with astonishingly blue eyes and dark red hair, she looks younger than her late thirties. Something—her freckles, the loose-limbed way she moves—gives a sense of newness and youth at odds with her years.

She descends the steps and heads across half an acre of lawn toward the drive, skirting the orange two-man tent in her path. She stops now and then to pick up a piece of deadwood and sidearm it into the woods. By mistake, she hurls a long, twisted branch into a tree and watches it ricochet wildly back onto the drive.

DOGGED BY HEAT, SOUTHPAW SUCCUMBS TO
FUMBLITIS

The mailbox on the alley is jammed full and she slams it shut again.

JUNK MAIL BLAMED FOR HIGH INCIDENCE OF
POSTAL EMPLOYEE HERNIAS

She swats at a deerfly circling her head and turns left onto the alley's sticky asphalt.

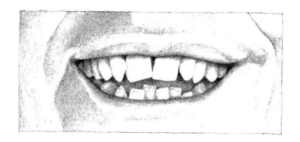

She hasn't gone far when a red pickup truck is suddenly upon her. She leaps aside as the truck squeals to a stop. The deerfly dives for her head again. "Damn," she mutters.

LETHEM MATRON DOWNED IN ALLEY,
FAMILY MOURNS

The truck backs up, and she glares at the driver, whose intense, preoccupied face rearranges itself into a knock-out grin.

"Hi," he says as if he hasn't almost run her over, as if he knows her. She has never seen him before and is caught off-guard by his familiarity, the way he draws the word out like a flirty joke. She examines his face again, yellow hair that hangs down over his forehead, dark eyes, pleasantly crooked teeth.

"You're dangerous," she says finally.

"I'm sorry. I guess I was going too fast." His voice is husky. He pronounces every sound so that she can even hear the *t* at the end of *fast*.

"You want to run someone over, you've got the right idea."

"Listen," he says, wide-eyed, "really. I'm sorry if I scared you." He smiles expectantly.

She waves him off and starts to leave.

"Wait a second," he says. "I'm a little lost. Maybe you can help me."

DRIVER ATTEMPTS TO TURN VICTIM INTO GOOD
SAMARITAN, THROTTLED BY SAME

She frowns.

"I'm looking for the Newcombs' house. Am I close?"

"Back there," she answers coolly, nodding in the direction she came from. "The second mailbox, the one with ducks on it."

"Thanks a lot."

"Don't thank me," she says. "Just thank your lucky stars Mrs. Newcomb didn't catch you going so fast. *She* would have executed a citizen's arrest."

"She's nuts, isn't she?" he says quickly. That voice again.

Katherine shrugs. He laughs. She thinks *reckless;* also, *brazen*. His eyebrows are dark, upside-down *V*'s, and he's younger than she thought at first, much younger than she is.

"It's amazing back here," he says. "I love this part of town, these houses. . . ." She finds herself not bothering with his words but only his voice—seductive, comical. Is he teasing her? Coming on? She stares at his arm on the edge of the open window, the way the blond hairs lie soft and golden. Unaccountably she wants to touch them.

WOMAN ACCOSTS STRANGER'S ARM,
THIRTY DAYS IN JAIL

She wonders how tall he is, probably not tall enough. The afternoon sun bears down like a weight. He stops talking, and she taps the side of his door. "Listen," she says, "I've got to run."

He settles his chin on his arm, "Run?"

"Run. You know, leave?" She is irritated and a little giddy. The heat.

"Ah"—he smiles—"but you do run. I've seen you out on Jefferson."

MYSTERY MAN APPREHENDED FOR
TAILING WOMAN JOGGER

"I used to run," he says, "in college. Sometimes I ran fifteen, twenty miles a day. I can't believe I ever did it."

She sizes him up in a different light. "Where was that?"

"Where was what?"

"The place you ran so much?"

"In the East," he says, looking over her head.

"Come off it," she says.

His face brightens apologetically. "Yale?"

"Well, it's a long way from here to New Haven," she says to cover her surprise. He laughs as if she'd said something clever, and she moves away, walking half backward. He doesn't turn around, but when she reaches his tailgate, she realizes he's been watching her in the side-view mirror. Their eyes meet. "Don't go so fast," she says to him in the mirror.

She walks off toward the bend in the alley, but she hasn't gone far when she hears the truck whining in reverse. She keeps right on walking until he's next to her.

"Maybe I'll see you again?" he says.

Things lurch, time shifts. She is standing under the front porch light. In the house beyond, her mother clears her throat, telegraphing parental vigilance. First dates. She'd always suspected adulthood was only a pose. Here was proof. "Who knows," she manages to say.

"What's your name?" he asks. She avoids his sharp, dark eyes.

YALIE MASQUERADING AS DRIVER OF PICKUP (OR
POSSIBLY VICE VERSA) SUSPECTED OF
X-RAY VISION

She sighs. "Katherine Watters. Now, really, I've got to go."

"Mine's Robin," he says, "Robin Hastings."

A child's name. It figures.

He is watching her closely. "You know," he says, "you really have the most unusual eyes."

She rolls them goofily to make it clear she doesn't fall for this.

"You *do*," he insists.

"So long," she calls over her shoulder.

"Bye," he answers, two syllables, almost three.

She hears his truck roar off and wonders, *Did I make that up?*

LETHEMITE AMBUSHED BY FIGMENT OF
HER IMAGINATION

She decides it's merely the heat. He was unexpected, that's all. Surprising. Also cute, she finds herself adding. Not to mention young. Still no one comes on like that—not to her, anyway. Most men she knows seem too tired.

The Edwards' Irish setter rushes out from the underbrush; a broken-stemmed daylily caught in her collar.

"Penny," Katherine says, leaning down to pat the dog. In the sunlight their hair is precisely the same color. "Penny, Penny." Penny licks Katherine's face. The dog's tongue is scratchy, its breath dreadful.

WOMAN FELLED BY CANINE HALITOSIS

"Oh, Penny," Katherine says. "Brush your teeth. Gargle. Do something."

His blond shoulder-length hair was normally straight, but today it flares out from his head in crinkly waves as if he's had a permanent. Yesterday, when he heard Bob Marley was dead, he put on the only Wailers tape he owned and, while it played over and over again, twisted his hair into dozens of braidlike tangles meant to resemble dreadlocks.

By the time he finished, he was Bob Marley's rhythm guitar, so completely had he been overcome by the incessant reggae beat. He was as close to stoned as he'd been for months. Far into the night Marley's message played on in his head: "total destruction, the only solution."

Doing his hair without a mirror hadn't been easy, but his tape player wasn't allowed in the bathroom. Anyway, he preferred his room, bare as it was, to the cold, white-tiled bathroom and its old-fashioned tub with menacing claw feet. He had to trade Elvin his last pack of cigarettes for the rubber bands, but this seemed an appropriate sacrifice for Marley, dead of lung cancer at thirty-eight. When he had finished his hair, he walked into the hall and found Elvin vacuuming. Elvin, the only black man for miles, was the guy who did all the shit work around the place. "That's one fine do, man," Elvin had said. Elvin was cool.

But this morning Ellen Wiggens, one of Dr. Krause's assistants, prevailed upon him to to comb his hair. "Maybe if you're going to town," Ellen said in her apologetic voice, "you should take those out. I mean, you wouldn't want to . . . uh, you know, take the chance of . . . like . . . giving someone the wrong idea." Ellen always seemed a little scared of him.

Today wasn't the day to make waves if he was going to do what he'd decided when Marley's words flashed on him: "Like a bird in the tree/The prisoners must be free." He was getting better at picking up messages.

Now, with a red bandana tied around his head, he no longer looks to himself like a Rastafarian pale face but still authentic, like someone out of Haight Ashbury—a phenomenon that occurred when he was in elementary school. He suffers deep nostalgia for times he never knew. Born too late.

Born to run, he thinks, pacing around his room. He'd just as soon keep his edgy boldness under wraps for a while. He sits down on his bed and concentrates on the wall for a time. Then from the nightstand he takes a pad of paper and a blue ballpoint pen that has "Buckeye National Bank: All Your Banking Needs" printed down its length in gold letters.

Dear Mom and Dad,
Moratorium on linear analysis here, so I'll keep comments on your latest letter to a minimum. It sounded (ho-hum) like all the rest, like they *dictated it to you with a gun to your collective head. (Is it true two heads are better than one? Better than seven or eight? Don't answer that.) Much as I get off on the idea of you two tearing your hair out—in your case, Dad, an increasingly diminishing possibility, ha ha—watch for coming attractions. Times*

are tough at Holly Hill. The Nosepickers are winning, but I'm going to make it. It's onward and upward for yours truly—
                                    Buddy
P.S. My knee is better.
P.P.S. My patron saint Shiva is putting up the good fight. Check out the weather lately if you don't believe me!

He reads the letter over and addresses the envelope. Then he begins another.

Dear Ms. Watters,
Maybe you don't remember me, but I was in your freshman English class a year and a half ago. I always wanted to tell you what an excellent teacher you were but I never got around to it till now. I hope it's not too late to reestablish contact with you. Since I was in your class, I've been doing some research in Freudian theory as it applies to the creative personality— particularly Vincent van Gogh's. I have formulated a potentially earth-shattering thesis on the subject, which time and space don't allow me to go into, but I'm certain my work could benefit from your critical analysis. I must break out of certain constraints, but you can expect a visit from me soon.
                              Your friend,
                              Kevin Newcomb
P.S. It's a little late, but I hope you didn't take the death of John Lennon too hard. He was a great man. I'll never forget how

much you liked that "interview" I did with him and Yoko for extra credit.

He folds this letter and puts it into an envelope on which he writes:

> Ms. Watters
> English Dept.
> Darke Hall
> Erie College
> Lakeview, Ohio

He sticks stamps on the letters, then rises from the bed and removes money and a small red notebook from his dresser drawer. He shoves these into the pocket of his jeans, along with the Bob Marley tape. From the closet he takes a worn khaki shirt and puts it on. Then, consulting Shiva, he determines that seventy-four is today's number. Pulling his bed and dresser away from the wall and positioning himself tightly in one corner, he starts inching around the edge of the room, one foot at a time. This is hard work, because his heel always has to touch the toe behind it. If it doesn't, he has to begin all over again. It's hard work, but of course somebody has to do it.

Harry Newcomb, home early to change clothes for nine holes of golf he can't conceive of playing in this heat, has been dawdling on the landing for some minutes, loafers in hand, looking out of the window and through the trees to the alley where his neighbor is talking with someone in a red pickup. The truck pulls off and she walks away until she's almost obscured by bushes, and Harry can see only her long legs, which seem to flash him some message before they disappear with the rest of her.

He's puzzled by this woman with the wine-colored hair who seems always dressed for some athletic event. He sees her running all over town; lately she runs in and out of his dreams, apparently having taken up occupancy in his sleeping mind. Harry can't understand it. He never would have pegged her for his type. For one thing, she's too tall.

He shrugs and starts down the steps, holding on to the banister, shoes in hand. Halfway down, he loses his footing on the highly polished stairs his wife refuses to carpet and bounces the rest of the way on his back, slamming into the love seat in the hall.

Torn between rage toward his wife and the shooting pains in his back, he notices that one of his flying shoes knocked a piece of veneer off the love seat. Hurriedly he shoves this into his shirt pocket and gets up slowly, head spinning, small explosions bursting in front of his eyes. He feels like a cripple.

"Harry!" his wife Irene calls from the kitchen. "What in heaven's name is going on?"

"Just testing your goddamn death trap," he replies, not loud enough for her to hear. He has fallen down these stairs three or four times. He wonders if she's trying to kill him.

Harry limps into the dining room where he meets his wife coming from the kitchen.

"What was all that racket?"

"Three guesses," he says. "Are you waiting for me to kill myself before you cover those stairs, or what?"

"Harry! You had no business on those stairs in your stocking feet. Those stairs are perfectly fine if you approach them properly."

"Properly! How's that? With pitons and a rappel? Suction cups?"

"Don't talk like that. Put on your shoes. You'll get your socks dirty."

"Not in this house, I won't," he snaps.

"What a nice compliment, Harry. It isn't often you remark on my housekeeping!" She smiles a too-sweet smile she knows gets his goat.

For a second he simply stares at her, feeling a trickle of perspiration run down his side. Irene looks so cool. No, not cool, dry. Dry as a bone. Her pink cotton dress is unwrinkled, her graying blond hair stiff. He notices she

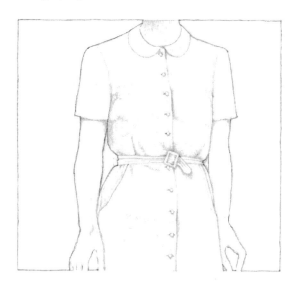

has a tiny smudge of lipstick on her front tooth.

"Come now, Harry, put your shoes on." Her tone of voice would be appropriate for a feeble-minded child.

"Right." He nods, not making a move. There's the sound of tires on the gravel drive.

"Oh!" she exclaims, "I'm so fed up with people being late! Tradesmen these days do nothing but dawdle. Please tell him to go away."

"Who?"

"For heaven's sake, Harry. The painter I told you was coming by. The one Ian recommended."

Harry can't remember anything about a painter. Maybe he is losing his marbles, he thinks. Twenty-five years of this could do it. And, of course, there's family precedent. Insanity inherited from a child.

"Oh, never mind," she says. "I'll take care of it." She turns on her heel and walks out of the room.

"Faggot," Harry mutters, thinking of Ian the decorator and the fortune he's costing. Between Ian's big ideas and Buddy at Holly Hill, Harry's preparing himself for Chapter Eleven.

He sits down wearily on a dining room chair and studies his shoes before slipping one on. Suddenly, up pops a vision of his neighbor stark naked, the outline of a bikini white against her tan. He sees, as clearly as if they were in front of him, her lovely freckled breasts, maroon-colored hair down there, more freckles. He'd like to count each one. This thought jars him. Freckles have always seemed to him like an imperfection.

The knock at the back door scatters his daydream, and like a man who has lost something valuable, Harry gets up and limps toward the kitchen, one shoe on, the other in his hand.

"Mrs. Newcomb?" a lilting voice says. What's this, another fruit? Harry wonders.

"You're very late," his wife says. "You said you'd be here at three-thirty, and it's after four.

"I'm sorry," the voice says. "I'm afraid I had a little trouble with my truck." Unctuous, Harry thinks, but maybe not queer. Who can tell these days? From the dining room doorway, he surveys the contents of an open pantry cupboard and briefly wonders why the two of them need three quarts of cooking oil, six boxes of bran, five cans of pitted olives. Who's she expecting, anyway? He reaches up and shuts the door against his wife's hoardings.

"Furthermore," his wife is saying from the back hall, "I asked specifically for a painter with experience. There must be some mistake."

"Oh, Mrs. Newcomb," the voice says genially, "I have a lot of experience, you'd be surprised. All the men who work for me . . ." His voice drops, low and intimate.

Harry's impressed with the way the voice is handling his wife. She invites whoever it is in, and enters the kitchen trailing a tall, lanky blond youth with broad shoulders.

"Harry!" she hisses, "for God's sake put on your other shoe." And then, sweetly, "This is Mr. Newcomb, Mr. Hastings. Mr. Newcomb seems to have a little trouble keeping his shoes on today." She laughs gaily.

Harry reaches out to shake the young man's hand, and looks up into a vaguely familiar face. Does he know this fellow from somewhere?

"How do you do," the young man says. His voice sounds completely unremarkable.

"Pleased to meet you," Harry returns, wondering why it is that his wife looks like a stranger and this stranger looks like someone he knows. "Excuse me." He leans down and helps his foot into his shoe. His back aches. "I was just on my way out."

"That's right," Irene chimes in. "Harry is on his way to play golf with a client. It seems a trifle warm for golf, but Harry goes the limit for Buckeye National! Lucky, lucky Buckeye National," she trills, no attempt to conceal her mockery.

Embarrassed, Harry mutters, "I'll be home around eight."

"You just take your time, dear, but don't forget we have bridge at the Daleys' at eight-thirty."

"Nice to meet you," Harry calls, walking out the side door and down the steps into the heat.

"Your clubs, Harry!" his wife calls. "Don't forget your golf clubs." Wearily he turns to go back up the steps, but the young man has already opened the door and is holding out his golf bag. His face is smiling, neutral. Harry suddenly recognizes who the fellow looks like: his son, Buddy. This rattles him. "Thanks," he manages.

"Have a good game," the young man says, again in a voice that sounds pleasantly normal, nothing like the voice that came to the door and broke down Irene's guard. Maybe he was imagining things.

He walks down the uneven stone path toward his BMW, parked in the shade, recognizing the red pickup next to it as the one he saw minutes before in the alley. Trouble with his truck? Harry lets it go. Still, he thinks, the boy must know his neighbor. Harry wishes he did. In fact, he's only spoken to her two or three times, the last time at Tano's in May, when one of her kids, the older one with glasses, had to point him out to her. She didn't even recognize him.

Harry starts his car down the driveway, braking at the garage so suddenly that the golf clubs sitting upright in the backseat fall forward, narrowly missing his head. He puts the car in park and enters the dark garage, going straight for a tackle box covered with a folded green tarp. He lifts the tarp and opens the box and is staggered to find that the pack of cigarettes he always keeps there has disappeared. He fumbles through lures and flies, pricking himself. In desperation, he dumps the contents of the box on the garage floor. The cigarettes are gone.

Damn her. She's found them again. He scoops everything back into the box and shoves it into the corner. He stands up, so furious that his head seems to be exploding. His back hurts too. In the house she's trying to kill him; out here she's trying to save his life. Why can't she make up her mind?

He slams the garage door and gets back into his car, jamming it into gear so that it leaps into the alley, narrowly missing the Irish setter from down the street who is tossing a chipmunk around on the edge of the road. Harry watches the dog slink off with the furry thing locked in its jaws, and thinks again of his neighbor. What in God's name is happening to him today: a dog reminds him of a woman, a perfect stranger of his son, his wife of no one at all.

He shakes his head in dismay. Sometimes he doesn't understand anything. He drives cautiously out of the alley. Sometimes he can't even remember what it feels like.

By the time she is halfway up the Edwards' driveway, Katherine is sweating and her hair is damp around her face. As she nears the house, she hears shouts from behind the screen of hemlocks along the pool fence.

Instead of continuing up the drive, she short-cuts through a bed of myrtle. Mosquitoes fly up with every step she takes, and she runs the last few yards to the pool gate.

LETHEM WOMAN FLATTENED BY VIRULENT
STRAIN OF INSECTS

Mona Edwards, lying in a lounge chair at the far end of the pool, lifts a thin arm in greeting. Katherine decides Mona has lost more weight. Ribs jut out skeletally between the top and the bottom of her black bikini.

VICTIM OF ADAGE "NEVER TOO RICH OR TOO THIN" FADES AWAY

Katherine enters the pool area just as her sons and Mona's boy climb out of the water. The three wave, then scramble over the fence and head for the house.

"Isn't this weather awful?" Mona calls across the pool.

Katherine nods but says nothing, and then, pulling off her sneakers, she executes a perfect shallow-water dive. The unheated pool feels like ice; she swims the length of it under water.

"You devil," Mona says as Katherine surfaces near the tips of Mona's scarlet-painted toes. "Where's your suit?"

"Home," Katherine says, turning away from Mona's feet.

"You're a nut, Kay. A real nut."

Katherine scarcely hears this. She is under water again, swimming. At the other end of the pool she executes a flip turn and, still under water, heads back toward Mona.

"Good gravy," Mona says as Katherine surfaces. "You're worse than the boys."

Tony Watters is twelve, tall and a little overweight. He looks studious in his horn-rimmed glasses, wet hair plastered to his head. His brother, Will, ten, is lean and freckled like his mother but has carrot-red hair. Scott Edwards is Will's age but small enough to be several years younger. The boys drip water over the Edwards' quarry-tiled kitchen floor. Only Tony notices, and the first thing he does when he reaches the sink is to hand a wad of paper towels to his brother.

"Here," he says, "Wipe the floor."

Will casually swipes at the floor while Scott hands Tony a large can of instant lemonade mix. Tony measures the mix into three red-plastic tumblers. His movements are deliberate, and the two younger boys try to hurry him.

"Ice," Tony commands. "We need ice."

"Jeez, Tony," Scott says, "just give us the lemonade."

"We must have ice," Tony answers. "This is a civilized country; we have ice in our drinks. Where do you think we are, Upper Volta?"

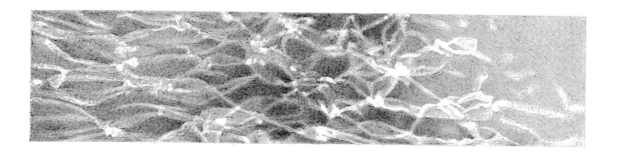

"Tony," Will groans. He tries to grab a glass, but Tony blocks the counter.

"Ice, you jerks."

"Shit," Scott says on his way to the freezer.

"*Re*tard," Will mutters.

Tony takes the tray of ice Scott shoves at him and places one cube in each glass, then a second, then a third. When he appears to be finished, the younger boys each grab a glass.

"Hold it," Tony orders. "First a toast."

Stopped before they can take a sip, the boys look up, impatient but faintly curious. Tony lifts his glass from the counter. "To the bride and groom, Lady Diana and Prince Charles!" He drinks. They watch him for a second before raising their glasses to their lips.

"Say it!" Tony booms.

"No," Will snaps. "This is stupid!"

"Just say it, Will," Scott says. "I'm gonna. I'm thirsty." He mumbles something, then takes a long drink. Will abruptly tosses his untouched lemonade into the sink.

"There, fag!" Will shouts. "I'm not *that* thirsty!" He turns and runs out the back door. Scott gulps down his drink and follows.

Tony shakes his head. "Little Willie and his tantrums," he says. He downs his own lemonade and mixes another glass, searching for some consolation. His brother's a creep, but even so, his feelings are hurt. He was just trying to have fun. Tony racks his brain—lemonade, Will, drain, sink. What was it his mother said to him yesterday? Loose lips sink ships? She told him that a sticker reading LOOSE LIPS SINK SHIPS was pasted next to the door of her kindergarten room, left over from World War II. So long ago, World War II, his mother at five. Hard even to imagine, except he's seen pictures, men in funny little helmets and leather jackets standing next to planes; his mother in an old-fashioned dress, knees knobby like Will's, her hair in braids. There is something he can't understand about time, how you can't get out of it. He never seems to change, yet all the while he grows. He can tell from clothes he wore last year, glasses he can't see out of anymore, hair he never used to have.

For as long as Tony can remember, he's been puzzled by how time works. He wants desperately to get behind it, to the past; or ahead of it, to the future. Once he told his brother that before they were born, they were still dead. Will cried. This still seems like a reasonable idea to Tony. Dead is hard, but not as hard as nothing at all.

"Tony!" His mother is calling him. Stupid Will, he thinks. It was just a joke. Before he leaves the sink, he stacks the glasses neatly. At the door, he shouts, "Coming!"

Walking across the grass, he spots his mother. She's fully dressed but dripping wet, and her bra shows through her T-shirt. He feels his face go red.

"What happened to you?" He says when he reaches her, wishing he could just ignore her and keep his mouth shut.

"The heat," she replies. "I was overcome. Let's go. Say good-bye to Mona."

"Thanks, Mrs. Edwards," Tony shouts

across the pool. Mona is arranging a red-and-black-checked beach towel on the fence.

"Oh, Tony," she says. "Don't be silly. Come back later if you have time."

His mother lingers behind, saying good-bye, and his brother runs on ahead. Tony waits for his mother on the edge of the drive. "What *did* happen to you?" he asks.

"I was hot. I took a swim."

"In your *clothes?* Why didn't you bring a suit?"

"I just didn't. I didn't expect to go swimming."

They walk to the alley in silence, Tony thinking about his mother acting like an entrant in some kind of wet T-shirt contest. She makes him nervous when she acts like this, like she doesn't know better.

"Next time wear a suit."

"Oh, Tony, don't be a drip."

"If I'm a drip, what are you?" He grabs the sleeve of her sopping wet T-shirt.

"Don't," she says.

"Don't *you.*"

"I embarrassed you," she says. "I'm sorry." She turns and hugs him before he can escape. "Poor kid," she says, laughing. "Poor deprived kid. Such an awful mother." She plants a big smack on his cheek, and he runs to the mailbox. By the time he has taken the mail out, his mother is ahead. "Hey, wait!" he calls.

He catches up. "I'm sorry, Neenee," he says. "You're really okay." Neenee always gets her, he knows. It's a name for her out of his infancy, from a lost language.

"Thanks," she says, smiling. "Thanks a lot."

"Now give me your sneakers, Nee," he says, wheedling. "Please. My feet are killing me."

"What is this?" his mother says. "First you insult me and now you want my shoes? You're really something."

But then, as he knew she would, she steps out of her sneakers. His feet have grown bigger than hers, he notices, and hang way off the backs. Nevertheless he shuffles ahead, leaving her to pick her way up the driveway barefoot.

When he reaches the lawn, Tony softens. He abandons her sneakers near a rhododendron bush and heads toward the house. Partway across the lawn, he drops the pile of mail to the ground, a marker to make sure she finds her way home.

Poised for departure, he waves to Mrs. Newcomb, watching him like a hawk from her back steps. She's one of those incredibly finicky women. Bored, nothing to do but worry about her house. Still, he wouldn't mind getting this job.

He turns the key in the ignition. A click, then nothing. He tries again—click—and again—click, not exactly the suavest exit in front of someone he's hoping to work for.

"Just a little trouble here," he calls as he runs around and lifts the hood. At the moment he'd like to shoot his truck.

Suddenly Mrs. Newcomb is next to him. "Hmmm," she says.

Bad enough he's no whiz at auto mechanics;

all he needs is her looking over his shoulder. He stares into the confusion of his engine. "Listen, Mrs. Newcomb, may I borrow your phone?"

"Come now!" she exclaims as if he's lost his mind. "Hop back in there and try to start it again."

Oh, great, he thinks. Mrs. Goodwrench. But on the chance he can wriggle back into her good graces, he humors her. Click. Click. Click. He gets out and finds her peering into his engine.

"I don't suppose you'd happen to have a rag," she says without looking up. He hands one to her, watching curiously as she pokes around as if she were taking inventory of his engine parts. Then, to his astonishment, she whips out the dipstick, wipes it off, and shoves it in again.

"You're down over half a quart," she informs him, displaying the stick. "Overdue for an oil change too."

For a moment he's unable to speak.

"Thanks," he finally says, "but look, you're getting your hands all dirty. Why don't I just call this guy who works on my truck?"

She raises her head and gives him an unsparing look, softened only a little by the strand of hair that has somehow come loose from her glued-on hairdo and now hangs over one eye. "You're obviously a person of little faith," she says. "And a very impatient one, to boot. Hold your horses."

Chastened, he remains quiet, afraid he's blown his chances of getting the job.

"What sort of trouble were you having earlier?" she asks.

"Earlier?" He has nearly forgotten. "Oh, earlier." He has to think. "The truck seemed to be, well, missing."

"Misfiring? Hmmm. When we get it running, you'd be wise to have your points and plugs checked. Also your valves and rings. It's none too tidy under here. By the way, did you notice any smoke from your tail pipe?"

He stares. He takes some time to say no.

She plunges her hand into a cluster of wires. "Ah," she says, bending lower. By now her hands are filthy and her cheek is streaked with grease. For a moment he can't locate in the person before him the fussy housewife possessed by her woodwork, or the woman who snapped at him on the phone yesterday.

When she lifts her head this time, she says, "Give it a try."

He hates to embarrass her even though he's sure he'll never see the woman again, but he gets into the truck and flips on the ignition. The engine turns over smoothly. "Mrs. Newcomb!" He scrambles out of the truck, "Mrs. Newcomb! You did it! Terrific!"

She pushes the hair out of her eye with the back of her hand. She looks much younger. "It was only a loose wire between your ignition switch and your starter," she says. "I'd say your most pressing problem at the moment is your muffler. Haven't you noticed? It sounds like there's a hole in it. You should have that taken care of right away."

He regards her with a kind of stupefied awe. Mrs. Newcomb, mistress of the secrets of the eight-cylinder engine.

"Well, then," she says, brushing off her hands.

"Thank you," he says, "Really. I mean, gee, you were just great."

"Hardly 'great.' Merely a believer that automobiles operate on principles that are fathomable. Anyone can master the basics. You only have to pay attention." She hands him the rag, and he smiles sheepishly.

"I'm proceeding on the theory you know more about painting than you do about cars," she adds.

"I do," he says, put in his place.

"Fine, then, I'll see you next Monday at nine."

"*Me?*"

"Young man," she says, "I think I'd know if there was someone here besides the two of us. Of *course*, you."

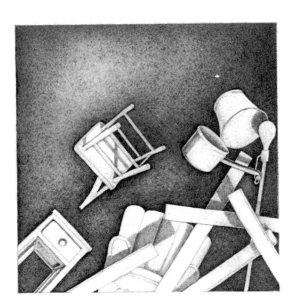

After he maneuvers his way around the edge of his room for the seventy-fourth time, Buddy shoves the furniture back and steps out into the hall. "Hey, Alex!" he calls.

From behind a closed door near the stairs, Alex shouts, "Wait a second!" Buddy ambles toward the closed door, chanting, "Be cool," as if it were a mantra. He tries the locked door.

"Hold on!" Alex yells from inside, "I'll be out in a minute. Go on downstairs. Tell Ruth I'm coming and she can sign you out. I'll catch you on the porch."

"Sure," Buddy says, and heads down the steps, hardly able to believe his luck. He wonders what Alex is doing behind that locked door—Alex, a graduate psychology student working at Holly Hill on some kind of internship, breaking one of Krause's cardinal rules about locked doors. Therapy for Alex's fellow summer intern, Amy Lovett? Whatever, it's the biggest break Buddy's had in months, maybe years.

At the bottom of the stairs he knocks on the frame of the office door. Krause's secretary, Ruth, pops her head out of Krause's office beyond. As usual, Krause isn't around. Probably out running. The old goat's an exercise freak.

"Hi, Kevin," Ruth says. "I bet you want your pass."

"You're right on the money as usual," he says. "What's a smart lady like you doing in a place like this?" Ruth's hair is turning gray, but she wears jeans and sandals and some kind of Hawaiian-looking shirt. She was at Woodstock, she told him once.

"Getting off on seeing people like you pull yourself together," she says, smiling and nodding so that her big silver earrings hop around. "By the way, where's Alex?" she asks.

"Right behind me," Buddy says. "He told me to get my pass and meet him on the porch, he'll be down in a minute. If you want me to wait," he adds, "I mean—" But his voice catches and he stops.

"Of course not, Kevin." She writes out the time on the pink slip Krause signed earlier and hands it to him. "Here you go," she says. "You have fun, now."

"Thanks, Ruth. Be seeing you." He takes the paper and turns to leave the office, knowing he'd better make tracks.

"Oh, Kevin, wait! Be a pal." Shuffling through the mess on her desk, Ruth locates a five and hands it to him. "Get me a pack of Marlboros, okay? I quit smoking again this morning, but it's not in the stars. I'm dying."

"Sure," he says, taking the money. Now he'll owe her money.

He opens the screen door and finds the big front porch with its cushioned wicker chairs empty, though the little TV on the table is on. He catches a glimpse of Merv Griffin and walks down the porch steps into the sun. The heat makes him feel like something heavy just fell on him. At the far end of the yard Elvin, his back to Buddy, is trimming the hedge. Slowly Buddy walks across the lawn in the opposite direction, heading for the woods as if he were looking for shade. A strange interior zinging noise almost stops him.

In spite of this, he makes it to the woods, where he breaks into a slow run, weaving in and out of trees until his breath comes hard and he begins to sweat. He removes the khaki shirt and ties its sleeves around his waist. If he can just make it to the cornfield adjacent to the woods, he'll be safe.

Suddenly he's aware that he's been counting his footsteps since he started running—389, 390, 391. As usual, this counting goes on without any help from him. He's sure he can make it. His spirits rise so high, his feet hardly touch the ground. He seems to fly. Then, sailing over a log, he trips and falls flat. The numbers fly out of his head, and in their absence he's suddenly frightened. What will his parents say? Where do they live? He's never even been to their new house. What if he forgets their address?

On his knees now, he realizes he's begun to cry. "Go back," someone says. "Go back." "No," he rasps, "No, no," and he pounds the ground. At that moment Bob Marley's voice washes over him, high-pitched, ghostly, a voice from the dead: "Like a bird in the tree, the prisoners must be free. Revolution." Over and over he hears it, lines from a stuck record. "Revolution."

Revolution: Somehow this gives him the strength to continue, and on hands and knees he crawls slowly at first, then faster, headed for the home he's never seen, sounds of revolution nearly splitting him open.

Someone sobs in the woods—not him, not him.

The blank page glows in the early-evening light. Nicolle Dundee is at it again. Irene Newcomb watches as the blue ballpoint pen glides across the page. She often wanders if she's merely a medium.

. . . perplexing, but Jennifer finally decided on the pale blue chiffon gown with its narrow rhinestone shoulder straps and a scattering of rhinestones across its tucked bodice. The color of the dress brought out the vivid blue of her eyes and lent the rich auburn of her abundant hair an unusual intensity. It showed off her trim figure to best advantage, too, clinging to her breasts and slender waist, flowing gracefully over her hips.

Stepping into a pair of delicate sandals, she turned to survey her image in the mirror. Satisfied with what she saw, she moved to her dressing table where she applied lipstick, blue eye shadow, and a touch of blush. There. Her hair caught the sun and for a second glistened brilliantly.

Suddenly she realized her heart was racing. What would it be like to see Lance Steel after six whole years? What would he think of her? The last time she'd seen him, she'd been a girl of seventeen, and Lance a happy-go-lucky law student. Since then everything had changed. Lance had married Veronica Gladstone, whose family was worth a fortune. Through her tears, Jennifer had read all about it on the society pages and resigned herself to losing him forever.

Yet even after all this time, the idea of Lance happily married caused a wrinkle to crease her smooth forehead. She mustn't allow herself to do this. Bygones were bygones; hadn't she told herself that a million times? Lance belonged to someone else.

Besides, look how her own life and the life of her twin sister, Jessica, had changed. Saved from ruin by their late aunt's husband, Calvin Lundin, here they were, far from their childhood home and the fire that had claimed the lives of their dear parents. She could scarcely believe the good fortune that followed so fast on the heels of such grave devastation. Yes, everything had changed, and of course she could now meet Lance without any of the old longing.

Jennifer surveyed the apartment's spacious living room. The coral-flame-stitched sofa and matching wing chairs glowed invitingly in the setting sun that flooded through the enormous windows. On the Lucite coffee table there was a tray of tempting imported cheese and a mouth-watering dip from an old recipe of her mother's. Long ago it had been Lance's favorite. Wine was chilling, more than enough for the four of them—her and her sister, Lance and his wife. She burned with curiosity to see if Veronica would be everything her pictures suggested. Did she worship Lance as Jennifer herself had?

At that moment the buzzer rang, and knowing Jessica was still dressing, Jennifer moved on anxious feet to the door. Speaking breathlessly into the intercom, she instructed the doorman to let her guests in. Then she paced back and forth.

"Jessica!" she called urgently at her sister's door. "Jessica, hurry! They're here!"

Jennifer's heart beat faster and faster as the

last of the sunset exploded in brilliant pinks and reds. Suddenly there was a tapping at the door behind her. She steadied herself, took a deep breath, and flung it open.

There before her, just as she remembered him, was Lance Steel. But he was alone! Where was his wife?

"Jennifer?" he murmured. "It *is* you, isn't it, Jenny?"

She nodded, unable to speak. His eyes swept over her, and she felt a hot tide rush to her throat and blaze in her cheeks. From his towering height he reached out for her with arms she remembered were strong and muscular under his impeccably tailored suit. Before she knew it, he was embracing the curves of her body. She felt helpless before him, trapped in old passions. Her knees gave way and she gasped. The last thing she remembered before she fainted was the crush of his powerful, hard—

"Irene?" Harry calls from the kitchen.

Irene's heart is pounding. Hurriedly she shoves the pad of paper into a drawer.

"Irene?"

"Coming, Harry," she calls as she rises from her desk. She almost bumps into her husband as she walks into the hall.

"My goodness," she says, frowning. "You startled me." She looks at him but has only the barest sense of recognition. A small bulge in his shirt pocket catches her eye.

"What's this?" she says, pulling out the piece of veneer she immediately recognizes as a chip from the love seat at the foot of the stairs.

"Something I found on the floor."

"It's from the love seat. You must have knocked it off earlier." Harry smells of gin, but she's in no mood to make a case of either that or the love seat now. She feels mildly disoriented. It isn't like her to lose track of time.

"I'll just take a fast shower," he says.

"Yes," she answers. "I made you a salad."

Irene slips by him and goes downstairs, stopping in the small lavatory to pat her hair and freshen her lipstick. Gazing in the mirror, however, she realizes it's not herself she's seeing but Jennifer. How peculiar. She wonders briefly what will happen to poor Jennifer next but pushes the question out of her mind. Nicolle handles these matters. Nicolle.

Irene sighs and smooths an eyebrow, her own, not anyone else's. The spell has vanished.

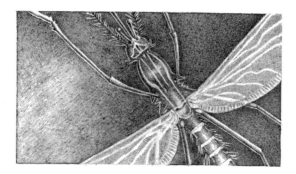

He walks for a long time before falling asleep under a tree. When he wakes, it's growing dark and mosquitoes buzz around his ears with a sharp electronic whine. The noise makes him frantic, like an itch he can't scratch, and he leaps to his feet, twirling around and slapping at his head.

But the mosquitoes keep after him. Finally he takes the khaki shirt from around his waist and ties it over his head so he can't hear. The land is rocky and treeless now, and he feels a little queasy. His makeshift headdress restricts his movements but presents him a vision of himself as an Arab sheikh. For a time he holds on to this but loses it to become the Virgin Mary. He finds himself near a dark and weathered barn. A star has led him here, and in the manger he will give birth to all the strangeness inside of him and be done with it for good. Joy to the world.

No.

He skirts the building as dogs bark in the distance: bloodhounds strain at their leashes, coming after him. He is a member of the French Foreign Legion. Stealthily he will make his way to the door of a house and say the code words, *Jimi Hendrix.* The people in the house will be expecting him. They will take him in and hide him until the war is over. He will go home a hero, confetti in his hair, medals, the works. His father will call him "Son," his mother will be humbled. A grateful nation will lift its arms.

No.

He decides he is lost but goes on, stumbling over rocks, seeing too late a barbed-wire fence, cows on the other side, their deep sounds calling out a message he can almost, but not quite, decipher. He will save them all. He, a poor shepherd boy. Free the village too.

No.

He is lost and knows it, and—486, 487, 488—what is it he's counting now? He has no idea, but as the sky blackens, he realizes that

he will have to pick which dream to dream before one picks him.

He descends a steep bank, staggering over rocks that clatter and shift, smelling dampness somewhere close by. Tree frogs stop their racket. He is cut off, at the edge of the world.

He is lost. He is lost, and this is one more test he is going to fail. Something sinister and taunting hovers over him as, one step at a time, he crosses a shallow creek, not more than a trickle. He clambers up the other bank, pulling himself over the top by grabbing two slender trees that loom white in the dark. He hugs the trees for support. He can't think. He can't think before or after him, and his head reels with emptiness. He wants to know where he is, what comes next, but the trees are mute.

He wishes himself a miracle, eyes shut tight, and when at last he opens them, he makes out, far in the distance, a glow in the sky. He imagines flames whipping in the wind, cries for help, searing heat.

No.

Not a fire, he tells himself. A city.

A breeze smelling of rain comes out of nowhere and he shivers. He takes the shirt from around his head and puts it on. Immediately he feels more like someone he knows. As he peers toward the faraway glow he notices in the middle distance tiny lights that appear and disappear, ghosts of shooting stars.

No.

Headlights, he understands. A road. He admonishes himself to buy this version of things for now.

He takes a deep breath and remembers what

he's doing. He kisses one of the trees and tells the other good-bye. He is far enough to hitch a ride. Hope overtakes him. In a hurry, he strides off, confident, taller. The counting goes on but doesn't matter. The glow in the sky stands between him and the numbers, holds back the dark. It leads him on toward the headlights that materialize out of nowhere, dim, and disappear. The glow helps him forget the pain in his knee.

Jesus, he thinks, maybe he can really make it. Him, Buddy. For once in his life maybe he can do something right.

menu for the dinner party Saturday, the shirts she forgot to pick up, the tent in the front yard that will make a spot if the boys don't move it. She checks herself and returns to things at hand, taking a sudden, deep comfort in her husband's familiar bulk.

She feels him begin to come and catches up. She is centered someplace far behind her eyes, a distance too remote to measure. All done. She tastes her husband's beard. For a second she has the illusion that this isn't David but instead Bill Unsser, a colleague with whom she had a small flirtation several years ago. For almost a year she made love to Bill Unsser in her head while she made love to her husband.

Once during that time she asked David if he ever thought about anyone else when they had sex. "Of course not," he said. Probably she would have answered the same way if he'd asked her.

Katherine and her husband, David, are making love in the cold stream from the window air conditioner. Katherine's mind wanders to odd details—the

"Oh, my God!"

"Shhh." Katherine cautions. "You're shouting. The boys. . . ."

He kisses her ear and rolls away. Katherine pulls up the sheet. Her face feels a little raw from his beard.

"Kitty . . ." He groans, but Katherine's too sleepy to answer, registering only distantly that he has gotten out of bed. She hears the bathroom light click on, water run, the toilet flush, but she can't bring herself to move. When David returns, she waits for him to switch on the light by his side of the bed and read one of the medical journals stacked there, but tonight he doesn't. Instead he strokes her back for a few minutes, then his hand falls. She is always amazed by how easily he falls asleep.

Katherine turns over on her back, suddenly wide awake. She tries to concentrate on the hum of the air conditioner, but her mind drifts to the phone call she received that morning from Bill Unsser telling her good-bye. His books were all packed, the movers were there. She wished him luck; the job was a good step up, and she was pleased for him. As they spoke, it occurred to her she might as well be talking to someone she hardly knew—strange when not long ago she would have been rendered manic by the sound of his voice. She tried hard to remember how intensely she had felt about him, but couldn't. Whoever she was then seemed to be missing from her current repertoire of personalities. "Cat," Bill always called her. Who was that? Katherine wills herself to go blank

and quiet, but a faint clank in the air conditioner troubles her. To block it she dictates:

Dear Ann Landers:

I never thought I'd be writing to you, but I have a question that bothers me. Is it all right to think of another man while I make love to my husband? Sometimes I think about a man I once came close (notice I said close*) to having an affair with. Other times I think of men I don't even know: the cute UPS man, who wears a gold chain and is much shorter than I am; my son's baseball coach, who owns a rainbow of polo shirts; the Dean of Students whose hair hangs over one eye and who can't quite pronounce his "L's."*

Don't get me wrong, my husband is swell (well, usually swell; certainly better than your average doctor), and we have been married fifteen years. But often my mind simply drifts. Is something wrong with me?

Curious in Lethem

Dear Curious:

No! If every marriage partner kept unfaithfulness on the fantasy level, the divorce courts would be out of business. I checked with my experts in this field, Dr. Emma Ripvoegel from the University of Oklahoma in Alva, and Dr. Chester Tittle from the Helping Hand Marriage Clinic in Boise, and they both agree that your

behavior, far from being abnormal, is
sexually healthy in every respect. "Marriage
is long; sex is short. We do what we can,"
says Dr. Ripvoegel.

Katherine turns over on her stomach and settles into a place somewhere between wakefulness and sleep. Outside of herself, she floats in the blue water of a swimming pool she doesn't recognize under an even bluer sky.

On the farthest edge of waking, the shrill ring of the telephone pulls her back. As she reaches for the receiver the memory of calls in the middle of the night when her husband was a resident and forever on duty sweeps over her.

"Yes?" she says.

"Mrs. Watters?" It's a woman's voice, familiar but not quite placeable.

"Yes."

"This is Irene Newcomb. I hope I didn't wake you."

"No, no. It's all right." What can the woman want now?

"I'm sorry I found it necessary to call you at this hour, but there's something I thought you should know."

"What is it, Mrs. Newcomb?"

"Well, Harry and I just drove past your driveway on our way home from playing bridge, and frankly, we couldn't believe what we saw!"

"What?" Katherine says. Knowing she will be made to wait, she attempts to catalog quickly the kinds of things that would interest Mrs. Newcomb: burning houses, masked bandits, flying saucers, crazed rapists.

"I'm afraid this sounds most improbable, but, well, we saw in your driveway—running *up* your driveway—as a matter of fact—a very large animal. Of course, it was dark, but I believe it was a riderless horse! A riderless horse heading straight for your house! Harry wanted to stop, of course, but I couldn't let him. He's no horseman, you know."

Katherine recalls the Harry Newcomb she spied across the ravine last week, decked out in what must have been his wife's floppy pink gardening hat. Cross dresser, maybe, but horseman, no. She stifles a laugh. A riderless horse. The Newcombs are persistently shocked by any suggestion of ruralness—heavy snows and septic tanks, dogs running loose.

"I have no idea what one does in a situation like this, but I myself . . ."

"Don't worry," Katherine says, "I'll figure something out. You were kind to call. I'll hang up now and take a look. Thanks."

"Dear," Mrs. Newcomb cautions, "take your husband with you. You never know what might be out there in the night."

Katherine eyes the large shape next to her. World War III could begin in this very bed and he wouldn't budge.

She pulls on a pair of shorts and a shirt. "Busybody," she mutters, feeling her way down the stairs. If there's anything in her driveway, it's probably only the Allens' pony from down the street who wanders off now and then, having figured out how to open the gate.

HOME BODIES / 27

The Newcombs wouldn't know the difference between a pony and a horse.

In the kitchen, Katherine turns on a light, then goes out the back-front door. The night is murky, pitch-black. Damn Irene Newcomb.

Dear Joyce Brothers:

I have a neighbor who seems to delight in pestering me with trivial complaints. Sometimes I get the feeling she spends most of her time thinking up ways to annoy me.

I realize you have more pressing letters to answer, but I'd appreciate knowing what's wrong with her, and how I can get her off my back. She makes me feel like a victim.

K. W.

Dear K.W.:

Although statistics show that eight out of ten Americans feel like victims, there is no indication that this is a preferred mental state. In your case there would seem to be ways to deal with your neighbor that will get you both off the hook.

In recent years it has become difficult for people to reach out to one another. Widespread narcissistic leanings have bred a pride in independence which unfortunately leads to loneliness. Singles bars are crowded because people hunger for closeness, emotional as well as physical.

Your neighbor may be reaching out for intimacy, love and approval. I urge you to react with more than feelings of victim-

ization. Why not take the time to spend a few minutes visiting each week? Involve her in one of your favorite activities. Perhaps you have more in common than you think.

Away from the house it's so dark that Katherine can scarcely maintain her bearings. She stops and listens, then walks in what seems to be the direction of the station wagon parked by the side of the house. The lawn is wet, and bits of grass cling to her bare feet.

She is almost dizzy with not being able to see by the time she reaches the big car. When she opens the door, the air inside hits her like a wave of hot breath. She reaches in and fumbles for the headlights. In their sudden glare the orange tent flares up, bushes materialize, trees, a corner of the house—all the familiar things that seemed to have abandoned the premises in the dark. She sees nothing out of the ordinary.

She switches on the high beam. In this wider light she catches a flicker of movement beyond the tent and makes out a large brown horse grazing near the middle of the lawn. The horse lifts its head slowly and looks toward the car lights, then just as slowly returns to its grazing.

As sorry as Katherine is to find Irene Newcomb vindicated, she is fascinated by the sight of the horse, and she sits for some minutes staring at it. Just as she is about to go inside to call, a pale shape emerges from the woods, a second horse, ghostly white, which casually joins the brown one on the lawn.

Captivated, Katherine gazes at the two horses until she remembers the battery. She gropes under the seat for the keys and starts the car. At the sound, both horses take off toward the deep ravine between her yard and the Newcombs'. She is left with only a vision of their tails, one light, one dark, streaming behind them.

For a minute or two she sits with the motor idling, then turns off the car, and, more sure-footed in the dark now, walks to the house. She calls the Lethem police from the kitchen phone and tells the dispatcher what she's seen.

"Fabulous," the dispatcher says. "We've been looking all over for them. Someone will be right there."

Katherine hangs up feeling a little dazed—whether from the hour, the bright kitchen, or the odd visitation of the horses, she can't tell. She isn't particularly fond of horses, yet she could have watched the two in her yard all night, could have stood secret guard over them until daybreak. She must be more tired than she thought.

After only a minute or two a car comes slowly up the drive. She goes out to talk to the policeman.

"They were here just a few minutes ago," she tells him. "They went off toward the ravine."

"You've heard of wild-goose chases?" the policeman says.

"Who are they?"

"They're from the horse show down the hill. They belong to some guy from Michigan who claims they're worth a quarter of a million bucks. If they're worth so much, you'd think they could keep them locked up. Every year during this show it happens—a couple of those damn horses get loose."

"Look!" she says. The horses are back, moving from the bottom of the yard up the lawn toward the house.

"Good," he says, reaching into his car and relaying this information over the squawking radio. When he's finished, he says to her, "Now if they'll just stay put long enough for us to get a van and someone who knows what to do, we're all set."

"How about some coffee," she asks.

"Thanks."

She walks to the house and sets water to boil on the stove, then steps back on the porch in time to see both horses raise their heads. At that moment she hears what they must have heard, the sound of a truck. The horses don't move a muscle as a pickup pulling a trailer crunches up the drive and stops. The driver climbs out of the truck and walks toward them.

Katherine is twenty or thirty yards away and

can see only that the driver is tall, with a visored cap set back at a comical angle, its bill pointing almost skyward. He moves steadily in on the horses, who seem not to notice. Several yards from them he stops and makes a low sound that Katherine can barely hear. Almost immediately the dark horse walks over to him. He deftly slips a halter over its head and leads it to the trailer.

The man walks back toward the white horse who, at his approach, rears and paws the air. Taking one slow, processional step at a time, the man starts toward the horse, who skitters around missing the orange tent by inches. The man raises his arm in an ancient hieratic gesture, and suddenly the horse freezes.

For some minutes the man and horse stand utterly still, twenty feet apart. At a point when it seems to Katherine that they have both turned into statues, the man whistles—four eerie notes that make her catch her breath with their strangeness. The sound transforms the horse; it glides across the grass to the man and allows him to drop the halter over its head. All done. Katherine finds herself covered with goose bumps. Thunder rumbles.

Come now, she thinks, what's going on? Can her life be so dull that a man and a horse tax her system? Enough of this, she tells herself. She doesn't even like horses.

Dear Doctor:
What exactly are goose bumps? What causes them?

K. W.

Dear K. W.:
The condition you refer to (the medical term for which is horripilation) is a bristling of the skin so that it resembles the flesh of a plucked goose. This reaction dates from primitive times when human beings were covered with hair. As the follicles stood on end, the hair spread and heat loss was decreased. Obviously cold is the major cause of goose bumps. Fear is another, as is overstimulation. In the Middle Ages it was thought that goose bumps were induced by wantonness and sexual hysteria. Now, of course, we know better.

By the time she has carried the coffee outside, the truck and horse trailer are gone. "Who was that?" she asks the policeman.

"Some friend of the man who owns the horses. At least he was quick."

"It was queer," she says.

"Queer?" He shrugs and takes a sip of coffee. "Your lawn's probably a little torn up," he tells her. "That white one nearly got your tent too. I hope no one's in it."

"No, not tonight. My boys sometimes, but no, it's empty."

He finishes the coffee and hands her the mug. "Thanks," he says. "By the way, I gave that guy your name. I hope that was okay."

"It wasn't really me," she says. "It was Mrs. Newcomb next door. She saw them and phoned me."

"She doesn't miss much, does she?" the policeman says, shaking his head.

"You know her?"

"She's a steady customer. A couple of weeks ago she had burglars."

"Burglars? In *Lethem?*"

"Raccoons," he says, chuckling. "Raccoons in her garbage cans."

"That figures," Katherine says. "Well, thanks for coming."

She watches the police car turn around and disappear down the drive. Lightning slashes the sky. It begins to rain. By morning, she thinks, all traces of the horses will be gone. Already she can hear herself telling the story to David and the boys, making jokes about Mrs. Newcomb and her riderless horse, laughing at the cartoonlike angle of the stranger's cap.

She won't tell anyone, of course, how the man stirred in her some dreamy sense of recognition, mysteriously promising something, but what? The things that go on in the night. She feels like she's wandered into someone else's dream.

The rain is coming down hard, and by the time she reaches the porch, she's soaked. She turns off the lights, and, heading up the stairs, composes one more letter.

Dear Miss Manners:

How does one go about thanking two horses and a strange man for a midnight thrill?

Puzzled

Dear Puzzled:

You certainly piqued Miss Manners's curiosity at the same time you posed a knotty question of etiquette. Unfortunately you do not describe the exact nature of this thrill, nor precisely what your involvement may have been. In most instances Miss Manners advises a cheerful note sent promptly after the event. In your case (and bearing in mind that I do not know the particulars), it might be the less said, the better.

Katherine drops her wet shorts and shirt to the floor and climbs into bed. Almost immediately she is asleep.

Seven cars pass, long stretches of time between them. His store of confidence is almost depleted by the time number eight stops.

"Need a lift?"

"And how," Buddy says, getting in. His knee throbs. He can't see the driver's face, but the car smells new. On the radio, violins are playing "Strawberry Fields." Buddy isn't sure how to interpret this.

"You going far?" the driver asks.

"Near the city," Buddy answers. "Lethem?"

"Sure. I can drop you on the Interstate right outside there."

"Thanks."

The driver lights a cigarette, and in the flame from his lighter worlds dance, flicker, veer off. Buddy hears his name.

"Cigarette, buddy?"

"Yeah, thanks." The driver passes him a pack of cigarettes and a lighter.

"Help yourself. The cigarette lighter in this car doesn't work. A month old, and the lighter's kaput."

Buddy takes a drag on the cigarette and begins to shake. "Detroit," he manages to say. "They'll get you coming and going."

The man doesn't reply, and they drive for a while in silence.

"You wouldn't believe what just happened to me," the driver finally says.

It's me, Buddy thinks. He can't believe he captured me so easily, not even a fight. Buddy's heart catches in his throat. Someone in the car, not the driver, says, "What happened?"

"Listen," the driver says, "Is there some reason you're shouting?"

Buddy remembers that Krause had told him he raised his voice when he felt anxious. Concentrating hard, he lowers his voice to what seems little more than a whisper. "Sorry,"

Buddy says. "See, I work with the deaf. I guess it's a habit."

"Nothing personal. For a minute I throught maybe *you* were deaf."

"No, not me." Is this a trap he's fallen into?

"Like I was saying, it's hard to believe what happened to me today."

"What?" Buddy actually whispers, and hoping to correct himself, he tries again. "What?"

"I didn't mean to make you self-conscious."

"No problem." That feels about right.

"Well, what happens is, I'm up in Buffalo for a sales meeting. I go up every month to the home office. Anyway, on my way back, I get the idea of stopping to see my aunt, who lives a little south of there. I call her to tell her I'm coming, but nobody answers. I don't know why, I decide to go, anyway. So I drive up to her house about seven o'clock, and nobody's home. A little kid comes up and says, 'You looking for Mrs. Prentice?' That's my aunt, and I tell him yes. So he says, 'Well, she's over at such-and-such's,' and he gives me this name— Reed, I think it is. He says his mom and dad are there too. So I think I'll run over and surprise her. I ask the kid where to go, and he tells me. It's a small town, but God Almighty, when I get to where the kid said, I find out it's a . . . Wait. Just guess. What's the worst thing you can think of?"

Buddy has lit another cigarette and is studying the flame from the lighter to see if it will tell him something.

"I mean the worst, the very worst."

"Fire," Buddy says. "The house was on fire."

"Hell, no. The *worst.*"

Buddy searches through his mind, but all he can think of is his mother. "I give up," he says, and flicks the lighter again.

"It was a funeral home! My aunt, she's dead! I mean, can you believe that? Just dropped dead all of a sudden. I was out of town and nobody could reach me. So here I am, I go to have dinner with her and wind up at her funeral! Doesn't that beat everything? I used to be real close to her too. I even lived with her for a summer when I was small, after my mother died."

"Hey, that's too bad about your mother," Buddy says. You lose your mother, he thinks, you lose an enemy. You lose everything.

"This is my aunt I'm talking about. My mother's been dead for thirty years."

"Yeah. I'm sorry about your aunt too." Buddy gazed ahead of them and sees oncoming headlights blur as rain hits the windshield.

"The worst thing was, I had to act like I knew what was going on."

Buddy wishes the man would stop talking. He wants to tell him he doesn't care. Instead he takes another cigarette and says, "Just like in real life, huh?"

"I don't know," the driver says. "All I know is, my aunt's dead."

Buddy has a brainstorm. "You feel bad," he says. Krause would say something like that.

"Damn straight, I feel bad. How the hell would *you* feel?"

"You wonder how other people would feel in your shoes?"

"Hell, no. I *know* how they'd feel."

"Bad," Buddy intones. "Really bad."

Silence.

"You say you teach the deaf?" the man asks after a while.

Buddy hears the driver speak, and for a second he doesn't know where he is, let alone what the man is talking about. He flicks the lighter several times. The man's story has made him feel strange, turned around. He wishes he hadn't heard it or could somehow erase it. Like a tape. Like time.

"I've got a watch," Buddy says suddenly. The driver turns his head and glances at Buddy's extended arm.

"One of those chronometer ones, probably. I can't see much in the dark."

"It's special. It goes both ways." The driver turns his head again, but Buddy is watching the windshield wipers go back and forth, trying to recall just why he's telling the man about his watch, when Krause has told him that his theory of time has nothing to do with what Krause called "real time." Krause suggested Buddy try to keep the two straight.

"Sure," the driver says.

"It goes backward sometimes. If I work on it." He remembers why he wants the driver to know about his watch. "Maybe I can do it now. I mean, make it so that soon it will be a year ago or even a week ago and your aunt will be alive."

"Listen, bud, I'm tired," the driver says, "I'm too worn-out for jokes. Besides, you're yelling again."

Buddy drops his hand back into his lap,

aware that the thwack-thwack of the wipers is being counted: 123, 124, 125. He shouldn't have tried to tell the man about his watch.

"How'd you get into teaching the deaf?" the man asks after a while.

"My parents. They're both deaf. A lot of people are deaf."

"That must have been rough."

"The breaks," Buddy says, no longer very interested in this conversation.

They approach a lighted intersection, and the driver shifts in his seat, checking Buddy out. Buddy does some checking on his own and sees the man's face clearly for the first time. He looks like nobody at all, Buddy thinks. The car sweeps down a ramp to the Interstate, and Buddy leans his head against the door and shuts his eyes.

"Where exactly is this school you teach at?" the man asks after they've traveled a while. Buddy pretends to be asleep so he won't have to answer. The glass feels cool against his forehead, and he counts the intervaled seams in the road.

The man fiddles with the radio and finds a lot of static and some classical music before he turns it off. Buddy hears the glove compartment open and feels his sore knee nudged. If it's a gun the man is getting out, it's okay with him. He wouldn't miss much if he were dead.

Buddy waits but hears only the crackling of cellophane—a pack of cigarettes being opened. For a moment he is disappointed; he could have used a helping hand. He imagines himself

in a casket, wearing a black velvet suit, looking peaceful.

Buddy sleeps on that. In his dream a woman comes up to him, a woman he can't see but recognizes as the driver's aunt. She tells him things he knows are true, even though he can't hear her. She grips his shoulder and he grabs her arm tightly.

"Hey! Let go!" the driver is saying in a rough voice.

"Huh?"

"Let go my arm!"

Buddy releases the arm and opens his eyes.

"This is yours, anyway, buddy. This is where you wanted out."

Buddy fishes around for some clue to where he is. The light is bright, fluorescent. The rain has stopped.

"You said Lethem, didn't you?"

"Oh, yeah," Buddy mumbles, remembering.

"You're there. It's just down this road. I gotta get going."

"Thanks," Buddy says, pressing down on the door handle.

"You better take it easy, buddy. You were sort of moaning back there in your sleep." In the blue light the driver looks green.

"It was your aunt," Buddy tells him as he gets out of the car. After the air-conditioning, the steamy air hits him like a wet towel. Before he can ask the driver directions, he's gone. Buddy watches the car turn back onto the Interstate, and then speed off. Hello, goodbye.

Still caught in sleep, Buddy stands in the center of the deserted road and looks for something that will tell him which way to go. Finally he spots a sign on the other side. His knee is stiff, and he limps as he crosses to the white wooden sign on which a red-jacketed figure on a horse jumps over a curlicue.

WELCOME TO THE VILLAGE
OF
LETHEM
POPULATION 3,200
BIRD SANCTUARY

Make that 3,201, he says to the sign. Painfully he moves out of the lights and heads down the dark road, not sure where he's going or why, but only that it's okay with the driver's aunt, who still seems to be with him. 3,202.

A misty rain begins falling, fine and light. "Put up your umbrella," he orders the old lady. She is wearing black lace-up shoes. "Watch the puddle," he cautions.

Just the two of us, he thinks, and then laughs into the night, a laugh that seems a little odd and creepy.

Just the two of us
We can make it if we try
Just the two of us.
You and I.

This sounds so nice, he sings it again.

"You and me," his mother's voice corrects.

"You and I," he tosses back, amazed at his boldness. He slams his fist into his other hand. "Take that and that and that," he says. "And this: I brought along a friend, a stranger's aunt,

deader than dead." He smiles to himself. The old lady nods.

"Hey, Mom," he yells into the night. "I'm home!"

Robin dashes through the parking lot but he can't outrun the rain. By the time he's reached his truck, water streams from his hair. He wipes his face with his shirttail. Some arrangement he's had with the world is all out of whack.

On the slick winding road, he swerves to miss a raccoon and reflects on Jake, his old riding instructor. Until tonight, Robin had thought of Jake as someone whose life he'd passed through a long time ago. He never dreamed Jake would have such a different version of things.

Jake turned up in Lethem this week for the horse show and invited Robin for a late dinner with his newest wife, Dee—wife number three or four? Robin had seen Jake only once or twice in the last six years, but the minute he saw him tonight, he could tell Jake had been hitting the bottle pretty hard. His words were deliberate, his eyes slow. He looked thicker, too; older; no longer handsome. Like no one Robin remembered.

The phone call about the horses came at the beginning of dinner, right after Jake showed Robin and Dee a picture from his wallet—a frayed black-and-white photograph of Robin at fourteen clearing a jump on Duncan's Dream. Robin was surprised Jake carried it around with him, and even more surprised when he saw the long blond hair that streamed out from under the rider's hard hat. He looked like a skinny girl.

"Weird," Robin said, studying himself ten years ago. He handed the picture back to Jake and touched the back of his neck, bare now, as it had been for years. He couldn't remember how it felt to have hair that long.

Jake stared at the photograph. "You were going somewhere, that's for sure. I told you about him," Jake said to his platinum-haired wife. "He could have made it to the Nationals, but he quit." Robin wasn't prepared for the bitterness in Jake's voice.

"I thought I knew you," Jake went on, "but I guess I had you pegged all wrong." Jake looked almost haunted. Robin shifted uneasily in his chair and played with his salad.

"Honey," Jake's wife said, "he was just a kid."

Jake waved his hand. "Well, I didn't get it then, and I don't get it now. He walks away from me, that's one thing. So then he goes four years to college and here he is now doing what? Painting houses and running someone else's stable. Christ, if I'd known he wanted to go back to horses . . .'"

"Jake," Dee cautioned.

"Well, it beats the hell out of me," Jake said, and took a long drink.

Determined to ride this out, Robin said, "It's fun. At least I'm on my own, and you wouldn't believe the people I meet. Anyway, maybe I'll strike it rich."

"You're planning to strike it rich painting houses?" Jake asked sharply. "That's a good one. Jesus." Then, turning to Dee, he said, "The reason he's here, he came after some girl. Some snooty girl with a rich old man. I met her once; she acted like I wasn't there. She acted like *he* wasn't there. Now the latest I hear, she's taken off."

Neither Robin nor Dee said a word. Jake looked around the table. "Our Robin," he said, "a house painter. And all because of some girl who's gone. Make sense out of that, somebody, will you?" Jake's face was scarlet, and he was talking too loud.

"Calm down, Jake," Dee said.

"Listen, you think I'm out to get you?" Jake said almost soberly, looking directly at Robin. "You're wrong. I just don't want to see you wasting your life. And I don't want to be someone you can blame when you wake up one day and find your life's nothing but a bunch of screw-ups, full of people you've disappointed, people like me who've invested plenty in you. . . ."

At that point the waiter interrupted with the phone call for Jake. After he was gone, Robin breathed for what felt like the first time all night.

"I'm sorry about him," Dee said. "He means

well. He doesn't want to see you hurt. He thinks of you like a son."

"Me?" Robin said. That wasn't exactly his own interpretation. They sat for a few minutes in silence before Jake came back, red-faced and angry, with the story of the missing horses.

"I'll go," Robin said, so relieved to have a reason to leave that he nearly took the tablecloth with him when he jumped up. "You stay here and eat your dinner. I'll get one of your trailers and drive around. They can't be far from the polo field."

Jake sat down. He looked dazed. "Sure," he said. *"You* go. Show me your stuff."

Robin stared at Jake for a second, then let it pass. "I'll call you as soon as I know something," he said, and left. He felt like he'd just been let out of jail.

He drove to the nearby polo field and hitched up one of Jake's trailers to his truck, pausing only long enough to tell Jake's frantic groom to stay put. At the police station they sent him over to the house on Jefferson. He'd been too preoccupied at the time to make much of the fact that the horses turned up in the yard of the woman he'd met only that afternoon. This was odd, but not any odder than everything else that had happened that night.

Now it's late, and he's tired, though not so tired that he isn't pulled up short by the sign in front of a bar near the town limits, one of those illuminated things on wheels with a flashing arrow on top.

GALA WEDDING BREAKFAST
SEE PR CHARLES AND LADY DI

SAY I DO ON OUR GIANT TV!
FREE GLASS CHAMPAGNE! 7/29 STARTING 6 AM
AT SKIP'S BAR

He shakes his head. It takes all kinds.

Past Skip's, his headlights pick out a solitary figure limping along the side of the road. Robin notices the headband and long blond hair and sees that he's talking animatedly to himself. A burnout, poor guy. Still, the hair reminds him of his own in the picture Jake passed around earlier, and eyeing the straggler in the rearview mirror, Robin ponders the peculiar ties that bind us to strangers, the missed connections that distance us from people we think we know.

At the dirt road he turns right off the highway where the stable he calls home looms in the dark. He parks his truck and greets the two large yellow Labs who come bounding out of the barn. Hurriedly he checks the horses up and down the long aisles, then he switches on the light in his own room. On his bed lies a fat white cat who opens her eyes lazily. Beside the cat is the mail he tossed there earlier. He turns his back and walks into the bathroom.

When he comes out, the letter from Jannie he hoped would somehow disappear is still there. He tears open the pale gray envelope and reads it quickly. The same old thing in her squat, back-slanted writing. The letter doesn't quite say how nicely she's doing without him, but might as well.

He reads the letter a second time before crumpling and tossing it into the wastebasket, pivoting even before it lands to fling open the door to his closet and deliver a terrific punch to the battered side wall. Plasterboard gives way, and a microsecond later the pain begins in his knuckles.

The cat leaps off the bed and crouches by the door. "It's all right, Ariel. It's okay." He picks up the cat and turns off the light. With the cat cradled in his arm, he looks through the window and out across the darkened fields, sucking his knuckles, wondering if this is what it feels like to be crazy.

He stands at the window a long time, overcome by an absence so profound, he almost loses track of himself. After a while he lies down on the bed, shifting the cat to the center of his chest, stroking it with both hands. The rain starts up again, harder now, drumming loud on the roof. He thinks of unshed tears. He knows better, but just for a minute he lets himself go the distance.

I t's the wine, Harry thinks as he tosses. He sleeps on and off, but so fitfully that it's more like an imitation of sleep. His heart races, his stomach churns. He grows angrier and angrier with Phoebe Daly and her sangria. He'd wanted Scotch but wound up with Phoebe's dark red concoction, orange slices floating in the pitcher as if she'd tossed in the breakfast garbage. He needs an antacid.

They lost at bridge as usual. He had downed three glasses; he was thirsty as hell. The foul-tasting stuff surged through his system like poison. He hates playing bridge, and Irene knows it.

Harry wills himself to get up. He drinks two glasses of water, takes a swig of antacid, and returns to bed, his head pounding. Chilly, he pulls up the light blanket, but in seconds he's too hot. Next to him, Irene sleeps undisturbed. He wants to wake her, say, "You and your friends. Look at me."

But he can hear her ask, "How many martinis did you have after golf, Harry?"

Nothing escapes her, except when she's asleep. She went right for the piece of veneer in his shirt pocket. Who knows how she spotted it? She should have been a detective. Better yet a spy. Put that poor guy—what was his name, Philbrick?—to shame. Three lives, hell. She could manage more than that. Irene Newcomb, secret agent. Everywhere at once, doesn't miss a trick. He used to think she kept such close track because she loved him. Now he knows better. She's trying to drive him nuts.

He sleeps for a few minutes. He is running across the golf course, chasing someone. Abruptly he is in his office and the phone is ringing. He can't understand why Sue doesn't answer it. What's a secretary for? "Spends half her time in the ladies' room," someone mutters. Himself, he realizes as he opens his eyes.

Harry gropes for the phone, drops the receiver, leans over the bed to retrieve it. Jackhammers blast away in his head. He manages to grab the receiver, and only then notices that it's growing light outside. His eyeballs ache.

"Hello?" he says. His voice sounds thick.

When he hears Dr. Krause on the other

end, things leap into focus too sharply. He hears his son's name, hears "runaway." Oh, no, he thinks. Jesus, poor kid. Hears words from some distance: "state police . . . up all night searching . . . stay put, he may turn up at home.

"Be calm if he does," Krause counsels. "Don't overplay the tough stuff, but let him know you're not pleased with what he's done." Krause continues, trying to comfort. No signs of self-destructiveness lately. Probably feeling a little adventuresome. Could be one of his pranks.

Harry sighs heavily into the phone, promises to stay in touch, hangs up. He lies back in bed, wide-awake. Some things you wish you'd never heard. He had invested so much hope in Holly Hill.

He gets out of bed again, Irene still fast asleep. Let her sleep while she can. The news seems too awful to pass on. He swallows two aspirin, washes his face, brushes his teeth. Then he goes back to bed. The clock says five; he shuts off the alarm. Irene had wanted to get up early to see that wedding; she can watch the reruns later. What's a wedding thousands of miles away in the face of Krause's call?

He lies back in bed, feeling used up. You try and you try, and you don't make any headway. You get so discouraged. My God, you don't know.

He imagines pouring his heart out to the woman next door. The whole thing's too complicated to go into, he tells her. He's not right in the head, he's sick. Among other things, my son hurts himself. Started off drinking Mr. Clean. Came and told us right away. Almost knocked us off our pins. Next he tried to eat a crystal wineglass. Dishwasher detergent. A handful of aspirin. Never enough to do himself in, but enough. Poor kid, he only made it out of the kitchen once. That was to shoot his knee full of BBs with the air rifle I kept to chase away squirrels.

It breaks your heart, Harry confides to his neighbor, mangles it. Your own flesh and blood. You're never sure what's next, only that it's something awful. After a while you don't know who to feel sorrier for, the kid or yourself. Even in this kook world, admitting your son is a nut isn't easy. And just when you think you're accustomed to it, something else happens to knock the wind out of you. You look at strangers, no matter how bad off they are, and you envy them. And then there's the guilt, he tells her. Even though you know you might not deserve it. It shadows you like a ghost, one more thing driving you into silence. Thousands of dollars and nothing seems to work. You clam up. My wife: I wonder who she is sometimes, it's been so long. Being brave takes too much out of you. But the loneliness is terrible, so bad that you try not to take stock. You feel frail, depleted, like you're living on a low-cal diet of feelings, hardly enough to survive.

Harry's neighbor is a good listener. She understands it isn't his fault. Tears spring to his tired eyes. He lets them come. He hasn't opened up in so long, he's amazed even to imagine himself doing this.

He wants her to know it's not Irene's fault, either. Irene may be different, he tells his neighbor. Some people probably find her a little eccentric. But she's not crazy, though God knows why we both aren't after everything we've been through. A strong woman, determined, intelligent; but everything goes haywire under this kind of strain.

I miss her, he hears himself telling his neighbor. I miss my wife. This thought rocks him. He's never put it into words before.

He pulls himself back to five-fifteen A.M. The facts are these, he thinks admonishing himself. My kid is a nut case. My wife is no one I know. I'm spilling my guts out to somebody I made up.

And yet he feels as if he has found the voice he thought he lost. Maybe it's not as late as you think. After all, in the six months since Buddy left, the two of them have formed some unspoken hope of being normal again, of stealing back a life.

Now this.

The room is light and he's exhausted. At least his head feels better. A couple hours sleep and he'll be okay. Then he'll talk to Irene.

He slides toward sleep, snagging all the way on thoughts of Buddy. Where can he be? But no. He won't let himself think about that now. Time enough when he wakes. What's a few more hours, anyway? For whatever's coming next, they'll need all the sleep they can get.

"God, Kay, it's all so romantic, I hate to see it end." Mona sits on a stool in the Watters' kitchen, staring at the small TV. Her knees are drawn up, and her tennis shoes are hooked behind the stool's top rung. "I still can't get over how pretty she looks in hats. Do you remember hats, Kay?"

Katherine, her back to Mona, finishes pouring herself a cup of coffee. "Unfortunately, yes."

"I used to love hats. I thought they were sexy. When I was fat, I wore them all the time. Those big Scarlett O'Hara things, even those little Jackie Kennedy pillboxes. I have a feeling hats will be making a comeback soon."

KNOW YOUR NEIGHBORS: MONA EDWARDS,
JEFFERSON AVENUE

We caught up with busy Mona Edwards not long ago in a neighbor's kitchen, where she was watching the end of the royal wedding proceedings. Mona, founder and director of the Lethem Rec Center's popular weight reduction/exercise program, Take It Off!, also finds time to have a finger in the pie of almost every civic organization worth tasting. Most recently she organized the bang-up Fourth of July fireworks display at the high-school football field.

At the time we spoke, she was discussing one of her many interests, fashion, and predicted that hats would soon be back in style. (Take heed, all you fashion-conscious gals. Mona can spot a trend a mile off!)

Over Mona's pigtailed head, Katherine watches the royal couple at the door of the train, waving, smiling. She has the jitters from drinking coffee.

"It is now four forty-five London time," the announcer is saying, "and Prince Charles and his bride are preparing to depart from Waterloo Station for Hampshire to begin their honeymoon at Broadlands, home of the late Lord Mountbatten."

"Wait," Katherine says, "Turn that thing down."

"It's your door, I think."

Katherine sets down her coffee and walks into the hall.

"I've got to get going," Mona calls to her. "I'll be late for tennis."

Katherine makes out a tall figure through the

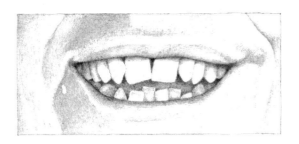

screen door. His back is turned, but at the sound of her step he swivels around. Katherine recognizes him not once, but twice.

"It was *you.*"

"If that's Scott," Mona calls, "tell him to get in the car. He's got swim-team practice."

"It's not Scott," Katherine yells over her shoulder. And then to the person on the porch she says, "Excuse me. Come on in."

He smiles and steps into the house. He is wearing white overalls and a red T-shirt. There's a drop of yellow paint near the tip of his nose.

"Listen, I just dropped by to thank—"

"What is it about you?" she says, interrupting. "You look different."

"I do?"

"You do."

"Well . . ."

"Well, it's puzzling, is all. First I don't know you and you almost run me over. Then some strange person comes to round up the horses that, naturally, are all over my yard at midnight, and I don't recognize you. Now I do, and you look different." She feels the caffeine.

"What can I say?" He grins. "It's me."

"If that's not the boys," Mona calls from the kitchen, "are they out there? Do you see them?"

"Shout up the back stairs," Katherine suggests. "Maybe they're up there."

"Listen," he says over the sudden din of rock music that momentarily blasts above them, "you have company, you're busy. Maybe I should come back later."

"Oh, no, it's okay. My neighbor and I were just watching the end of the wedding festivities. Come on in." She leads him through the hall, but he stops before they reach the kitchen.

"Your house," he says, and seems troubled, "it's . . . it's not what I expected. I mean, from the outside it looks like it has all these rooms, but it's so open." He eyes a wall of paperbacks. "I thought it would have a lot of antiques and things, but it's . . . well, modern-looking. What do you call it?"

"Spare?" she suggests. "The infirmary look? We knocked a lot of things down. We were after space."

"Everything's white," he says. "You must really like white." He seems vaguely disoriented.

"Wait a second," Katherine says, poking her head in the doorway and surveying the empty kitchen. "Let me see if she needs help. Here, have a seat. That's the honeymoon train standing in the station," she tells him, pointing to the TV. "Turn the sound up if you want." Upstairs a vacuum cleaner roars.

She darts around him and starts up the back stairs, only to find Mona coming down. The red plaid ribbons tied around Mona's brown pigtails and the dim light of the stairway make her look like a twelve-year-old.

Active for the past three years in Take It Off!, Mona herself lost over forty pounds on a strict diet regimen which she says she wouldn't recommend. "It was awful." That's why she decided to organize Take It Off!—"to help people like me learn to eat the proper foods. After all," she continues, "by zeroing in on the source of your hunger—anxiety, sadness, what have you—most people can refocus how they deal with food. One of TIO's goals is to teach people the difference between real physical hunger and plain old bored mouths." Slim at one hundred and two pounds, Mona obviously learned her lesson well.

"Nobody's upstairs," Mona says, "except Charmaine. And she thinks Scott and Will went off on the minibike."

"Well, they can't be far." Katherine steps back into the kitchen with Mona and introduces her to Robin. Mona squints at the train on TV and says, "Hasn't it left yet?"

The three of them watch the silent TV as the small train moves slowly away from the camera over a maze of crisscrossing tracks and switches. For a second it seems to be caught between the intricate network of rails and an overhead canopy of wires that zigzags in all directions.

"Lord," Mona says, "just look at that. How do you suppose anyone could navigate their way out of that place?"

"A fitting end," Katherine remarks. "All that other, it was fairy tale. This is real stuff."

"What is?" Mona asks.

"Confusion, complications," Katherine says. "A zillion routes, all of them tricky. Hot wires, who knows? You go too fast and wham! It's curtains."

Robin laughs.

"Excuse me," Mona says, "but what's so funny? What *are* you talking about?"

"Life, Mona," Katherine says.

"Oh, for heaven's sake," Mona says. "They'll live happily ever after. Anyway, it's just a train. Trains were so civilized."

Travel ranks high among Mona's interests. She and her husband, Sam, who manages his own natural resource investment firm, have been in fourteen different countries together.

"I like the U.S.A. best," Mona admits. "It's nice when everyone speaks the same language." Although she prefers trains, she now usually goes by plane. "How I miss trains," she muses. And then with typical enthusiasm adds, "Remember those wonderful Pullman porters?"

"Maybe so," Katherine says, "but there aren't any trains anymore. Not unless you count Amtrak, and the only time I was on an Amtrak, it was eight hours behind schedule and smelled like a humidor."

"They're supposed to have nice trains in England," Robin offers cheerfully.

"Ah, England," Katherine says, " 'This happy breed of men, this little world, This precious stone set in the something sea . . .' "

" 'Silver,' " Robin offers. " 'silver sea, Which serves it in the office . . . of a wall . . .' I'm not sure what comes next."

" 'Or,' " Katherine takes over, " 'as a moat defensive to a house, Against the envy of less happier lands. This blessed plot, this earth, this realm, this England.' "

"Wow," Robin says. "You're amazing! You really *do* know it, don't you?" Katherine blushes in spite of herself.

Mona is unimpressed. "Oh, I can't stand all you readers," she says, picking up her purse. "By the way," she adds, "are you having something painted? I mean, is he—are you—a painter? Or are people your age dressing like that again?"

"I really am a painter," Robin says, smiling.

"Among other things, we suspect," Katherine murmurs.

"Seriously," he says, "I like to paint. I like doing things you can stand back and admire." Mona seems puzzled. "I'm a painter," Robin says, "really, no kidding. As a matter of fact, I'm going to be working for your neighbor, Mrs. Newcomb."

"Good grief," Mona says. "I hope she's nicer to you than she is to the kids around here. She and that husband of hers . . ."

"Spare him the details," Katherine says.

"And these are *nice* boys I'm talking about, Kay's and mine. She acts like they're juvenile delinquents or something. Speaking of which," Mona says, glancing at the clock, "I've got to corral Scott and get a move on." She slings her purse over her shoulder.

"It was nice meeting you," Robin says.

"Wait," Mona says earnestly, "I'm not sure I get this. I mean, it's none of my business, but who are you, anyway?"

"Mona keeps close tabs on us," Katherine volunteers.

"I mean, are you a student of Kay's or something? You knew that poem . . ." She throws up her hands. "Oh never mind. I'm just being nosy."

"Actually," Robin says, "I stopped by to thank Mrs. Watters for the horses. The owner really appreciates—"

"*Horses?* What horses?"

"It's a long story, Mona," Katherine says. "I didn't have a chance to tell you, but we had a couple of horses wandering around the neighborhood last night. They got loose from the horse show."

"Oh, my Lord!" Mona says. "I wish you'd told me earlier. That's a big load off my mind."

"It is?" Katherine says.

"Well, I hate to talk about it, but at first I thought poor Penny had lost her insides or something."

"You *what?*"

"Honestly, Kay. At the bottom of my driveway. I was ready to take Penny to the vet when I decided that couldn't possibly be hers. I mean, there's so *much* of it. It's so . . ."

"I'll clean it up for you," Robin says.

"You're sweet. Right by the red mailbox. You can't miss it."

Mona dotes on her Irish setter, Penny, and her Abyssinian cat, Koko, who'll be nineteen years old in October. "Pets do a lot of good in the world," Mona feels. Last Christmas, as President of Lethem Save-A-Pet, Mona donned a Santa Claus outfit (size petite!) to conduct an auction of stray cats and dogs, the most successful fund-raising event in Save-A-Pet's history!

"There's Scott," Katherine says, pointing out the window.

"I'm going to nab him while I can. Does Will want to come?" Mona heads for the door.

"I'll ask him," Katherine says as the three of them step onto the porch. "Let me get this straightened out." She says to Robin. "I'll just be a minute."

"Take your time," he says. Six-three, she wonders, six-four? He really is very tall.

"Good-bye, Robert," Mona says from the lawn. "Thanks a million for you-know-what."

"It's Robin," Katherine corrects quietly. "Robin, not Robert."

Robin? Mona says incredulously. "You mean that big handsome person is named Robin?"

Kay nods.

"Sorry, Robin," Mona calls, emphasizing the last syllable. He smiles and waves, and the two women move toward Mona's maroon Volvo. Scott is already in the backseat, and Will, after a "Please, Mom," hops in next to him.

Mona turns to Katherine and says in hushed tones, "Aside from his name, he's kind of cute. God, Kay, you forget about young men until you see them up close."

Katherine is astonished. She and Mona never talk this way. Their relationship is light and neighborly, restricted to practical matters.

"I don't know how you teach. I couldn't stand to be around people that age—boys, I mean—very long." Mona fiddles with her keys and looks off into the woods. She laughs nervously.

"Of course you could," Katherine says. "You get used to it. Anyway, when you think how young they are. And dumb. Even the smart ones don't know much."

"Who is he, Kay? Really."

"Really? I haven't the faintest idea. I met him yesterday in the alley by mistake. Then he turned up last night to pick up those horses."

"And this morning he's on your doorstep. Maybe he's giving you the rush." Mona winks.

"Please."

"I'd watch my step if I were you," Mona says as she climbs into the car.

Katherine shakes her head, wondering what's come over Mona. Too much wedding, she decides. Romance on the brain.

"I hate getting older," Mona says suddenly. Her uncharacteristic intimacy jars Katherine again.

"Don't be silly," Katherine says quickly. "You're not old, look at you!"

"From a distance, sure, I look okay." Mona sighs.

In spite of herself, Katherine can't help noticing the way the skin is beginning to sag under Mona's eyes, little lines becoming creases. "You look swell," Katherine says.

"Don't I wish," Mona replies. "Of course, I'm a human pygmy for every face cream on the market!"

Guinea pig, of course. Katherine laughs.

"Oh, Lord," Mona says, "Maybe it's just the idea of being forty-one. Some days my life seems awfully dull. With Sam away all the time . . ." She twists her mouth. "The other day I realized I've been married half my life."

This whirlwind of activity, born and raised in southern Ohio, attended college for two years before marrying her childhood sweetheart. "I've known him since I was fourteen," she confides. "He's like one of the family."

"Listen," Mona says, "don't pay any attention to me. I snuck a little ice cream last night. Processed carbohydrates make me goofy. Between that and getting up early to see the wedding, I'm not myself. I'll play tennis and snap out of it."

"Have fun," Katherine says.

"Okay, see you later." Mona pulls her car out, then turns around to the backseat, apparently talking to the boys. Katherine watches as the Volvo heads straight for a big oak on the edge of the drive.

"Mona!" she shrieks.

At the last possible second Mona swerves. Then she waves and toots her horn, and the car disappears down the hill. Katherine shakes her head.

> That's Mona Edwards, Lethem's own dynamo, a mover and shaker, one of our town's most effective doers, an energetic inspiration for us all—your neighbor on Jefferson Avenue.

"Gee," Robin says as Katherine walks up the porch steps, "I thought for a second there she really had that tree. You've got some doozies for neighbors, Katherine."

He laughs, but Katherine can only stare at him. No one ever calls her by her real name. Her knees feel a little queer, and she sits down in the nearest porch chair. He towers above her, all smiles.

"Have a seat," she finally manages, and he sits down on the glider, gazing at her with a kind of rapt anticipation.

"Well," she says. She can't find her place.

"You teach," he says, as if this were a fascinating piece of information. "That's just great. Where do you teach? What do you teach? Tell

me." Rattled, she wonders what he's really after.

Suddenly Tony roars over the crest of the drive on the minibike.

"You've got another visitor." Robin sounds disappointed.

"No," Katherine says, immensely relieved. "That's Tony."

"Tony?"

"Tony, my son."

"Nobody knows," Charmaine sings softly as she irons a white skirt, "No, nobody knows." She fools around with the line a few more times, shoots a spray of steam toward the ironing board and slaps the iron down.

> *Nobody knows*
> *The troubles I seen*
> *Nobody knows*
> *But Jesus.*

She sets the iron on end and turns the skirt around, raising her rich contralto, marred only by being quite flat.

> *Nobody knows*
> *The troubles I seen—*
> *Glory Halleluiah.*

She stops. Beside her on a table is a small transistor radio turned low. A rapid voice says,

"Mother Sister Light! She will save your soul, she will wipe you clean, she will lead you on the path to love, happiness, and peace of mind—debt-free. Just pick up the phone and call . . ."

Charmaine begins to sing again.

"Hey, Charmaine. You ready now?" Tony comes up behind her. Charmaine jumps and drops the iron to the floor, narrowly missing her foot.

"Sweet Jesus!" she says, hand over her heart. "What you mean sneaking up on a person like some kind of ghost? You want to kill old Charmaine? Shame on you, Tony Watters!"

"I'm sorry," he says, picking up the iron and handing it to her. "I just came into the room, is all. I didn't mean to scare you." He is carrying a bottle of Coke. He turns on the TV and throws himself on the couch.

"Whew!" Charmaine says, fanning herself with her hand. Tony doesn't look up. She turns off her radio, and the two of them watch the noon news for a few minutes. Charmaine finishes the white skirt and then spreads a striped blouse over the ironing board. On the television is an overturned car. Charmaine wads the blouse up again.

"Whew!" she says louder, fanning herself with more vigor. Without taking his eyes off the television, Tony says, "What's wrong?"

"Hot," she says.

"It's not so hot. The guy just said it was only eighty-two. That's the coolest it's been for over a week." He picks up his Coke.

"I got my own hot waves," Charmaine says. "Lord!"

"What's that supposed to mean?" he asks idly.

"The change," she mutters. "Nothin' you'd know."

"You want my Coke, right?"

"Sweet baby," she says. "I wouldn't take that Coke for all the world. Run down and get me one of my own like a good boy."

Tony groans.

"Listen to you," she says, taking the striped blouse out again. "With your legs so much younger than mine!"

Slowly he gets to his feet.

"And a sandwich too. How about it?"

He descends the back stairs to the kitchen, where he finds his mother cracking eggs into a bowl. "What's that?" he asks.

"Eggs," she says, not bothering to look up.

"No kidding." She turns her head in his direction, but her eyes aren't focused. He takes bread and cheese and peanut butter out of the refrigerator and sets them on the counter.

"Take me to town after lunch so I can get those Nikes. Will you?"

"What?" she asks.

He follows her to the stove, watching as she pours the eggs into the pan and makes an omelet. He repeats the question.

"Tomorrow," she says.

"Before that," he presses, but she merely shakes her head and slides the omelet on a plate.

"Can I have some?" he asks.

"It's for him," she says, nodding toward the porch.

"You mean, *he's* still here? How come?"

"He's eating lunch," she says. "I invited him."

"You never make *me* omelets for lunch."

She butters toast. "You never fix me cheese and peanut butter sandwiches, either," she says without looking up.

"You wouldn't eat them," he says. "Anyway, that's different. It's just for Charmaine."

"Well"—she shrugs—"this is just for . . ."

"Horse Man." He snickers.

She pours a glass of milk.

"Hey," he says, "isn't there a high school in the city called Horse Man?"

"Horace Mann," she says. "Horace, two syllables. Mann, two n's."

"Is that supposed to be a person?"

"Was," she says, putting the milk away. "A nineteenth-century American educator, the father of coeducation. The one who made it possible for you to go to school with all those cute girls."

"Gag," Tony says.

She moves faster now, putting silverware and a napkin on a tray. "Why don't you do something constructive this afternoon?" she says as she picks up the tray and heads across the kitchen. "Like, put the tent away. It's making a spot on the lawn." She starts out the kitchen door.

"Wait," he says.

She turns around and looks at him, but he can tell she's not really paying attention. "Did you want something?"

"I'm not going to put the tent away," he says. "Maybe I'll want to sleep there tonight."

"Well, just move it to the woods or some-thing. Don't forget we're leaving for Michigan Sunday." She walks out of the kitchen.

"Wait a second," he says, but this time she doesn't stop. He hears the screen door slam behind her and the Horse Man say, "Katherine, you shouldn't have gone to so much trouble."

Katherine? Tony thinks. *Katherine?* How weird can you get? Most people call his mother Kay, except for his Dad, who calls her Kitty. Then there's her father, who calls her Kate, and her mother, who calls her Sister, which makes him and Will giggle. But nobody calls her Katherine.

He screws the lids back on the peanut butter and jelly jars. Spotting a box of Ho-Ho's, he puts three on the plate, along with the sandwiches and a peach. Anyone would know better than to call his mother Katherine.

Charmaine is hanging the blouse on a hanger when he enters. "It's not a ghost," he announces loudly to her back, "it's me." She switches off the iron and heaves herself onto the couch.

"My, my," she says, taking a sandwich. "Thank you."

Tony joins her, and the two of them eat in silence, watching the end of the weather report.

"You want those?" Charmaine points to the foil-wrapped Ho-Ho's. "I don't need one." Tony nods. She puts her peach pit on the edge of the plate, opens the Coke, and takes a long drink. Sighing, she leans her head back against the couch.

Tony eats the Ho-Ho's, and after a while

Charmaine sits up and says, "You going to play today? It's about that time."

"I forgot," he says. "Wait." He gets up and goes across the hall to his room, returning with a small paperback, *The Original Lucky Dream Book*, edited by Professor Zorro. The book was a present from Charmaine on his tenth birthday. His mother would murder them both if she knew about it.

"Did you have a dream?" she asks as he leafs through the book.

"No," he answers. "You?"

"Just about my mama. I don't feel lucky today. I guess I'll just play her name."

Charmaine's mother's name was Addie. Charmaine plays Addie almost every day but never wins with it. She did win playing Will's birthdate last year and gave Will a silver dollar. Tony himself has never won, but playing gives him and Charmaine something to talk about. Also, it's a secret from his parents, like having a private life. If he ever does win, he'll give the money to Charmaine to keep for him till he grows up.

"I think I'm hot today. Lucky, I mean." He

doesn't want her to start up on hot flashes again.

"Yeah?" she says, suddenly more interested. "You got a hunch?"

"Maybe," he says, skimming down the page. " 'Horse, Horse (dead), Horseshoe, Horse (white) . . .' "

"I want three-four-two," he tells her, deciding to stick with plain Horse. "And box it."

"You know," she says thoughtfully, "that might just be. 'Cause of them horses in your yard last night. Your Mama told me this morning. That's almost as good as a dream. Lord. Maybe I'd better play that one too."

"And this," he says, running down the list of men's names. "Five-seventeen. Box that one too. Fifty cents on both. No, a dollar."

"What's that five-seventeen?"

"Horace," he says.

She looks puzzled. "Horace? Who's that?" She goes to the phone.

"Nobody," he says. "Just a feeling."

"I guess I'll cover that one, too, just in case." She dials the phone and speaks into it, so low he can't hear her. After a minute Charmaine hangs up and returns to the ironing board.

"You know," she says, "my auntie had a neighbor by the name of Horace. He wore a big diamond ring. He seemed like the nicest man, turned out to be some criminal. Went to jail too. But we might get ourselves lucky, who knows?" She turns on the iron and pulls a pair of khaki pants out of the bundle.

"You ready to sing," he asks her.

She nods. He plugs the cord of the microphone into the tape recorder.

"Say when," he says, holding the microphone out to her.

She takes a swig of Coke and tests the iron. It sizzles.

"When," she says.

Will Watters and Scott Edwards make their separate ways down the side of the ravine that divides the Watterses' yard from the Newcombs'. Will is the more cautious of the two, and he tacks right and left, stopping frequently to watch Scott running full steam ahead down the slope. Scott's blond head bobs as he skims over rocks and scrub and the spongy footing of seasons of dead leaves. Though it's the middle of the afternoon and the sun is hot, the light in the ravine is shadowy and dim. The creek that normally trickles along its bottom is high from the previous night's rain.

At the bottom of the ravine the boys cross the creek on a fallen log and face a steeper incline. Climbing the Newcombs' side, they pull themselves up by grabbing on to small trees. Halfway up, Scott tosses a stick down to the creek below, and they watch as the water sweeps it along toward the river.

Near the top, Scott digs around in the leaves until he finds the rope that, months ago, they secured to a root of a large beech tree on the edge of the Newcombs' yard above them. One at a time, Spider-Man fashion, they walk up the incline, clinging to the rope until first Scott, and then Will, reaches the base of the

beech whose tangled, aboveground roots offer footing.

Carefully they peer around the tree until they have an unobstructed view of the side of the Newcombs' house, not more than ten yards away across a strip of lawn. Though the house appears deserted, they can see that a door on the screened-in porch is open to the inside. The boys duck down and confer, then stand up again and wait in silence. Nothing happens.

Finally Scott tosses a stone toward the second-floor windows above the porch. It hits a screen and bounces to the porch roof with a clatter. The boys duck down, laughing, until Will gets himself under control and stands. Scott hunches over, still snorting. Will kicks him sharply, and Scott rises to see the dim figure of Mrs. Newcomb standing in the doorway linking the house to the porch.

"Buddy?" she calls uncertainly. "Bud? Is that you?"

The boys exchange looks. Scott winds his index finger slowly around his ear.

"Bud," she calls when she reaches the door to the yard. "If that's you out there, just stop all this, please, and come on in. You're safe."

At this, Scott starts giggling and drops down, but Will doesn't move a muscle. "Bud?" she calls, and appears to gaze directly at Will. He is terror-struck until she turns away. "Let's get out of here!" he whispers to Scott. "Something funny's going on."

From the other side of the porch, Mrs. Newcomb calls out, "No more games, Buddy. I know it's you."

"Chicken," Scott mutters to Will, and

stands up just enough to reach in the pocket of his jeans. "She's just flipped, is all."

"Don't," Will says as Scott sets out the cherry bombs he's taken from his pocket. "C'mon, don't." Will reaches behind him for the dangling rope, ready to leave.

"Fucker," Scott hisses at him. "You leave and I'll tell your Mom about those cigarettes you stole."

Will lets the rope fall, and suddenly both boys are distracted by the sound of car doors slamming in the Watters' driveway, not far behind them as the crow flies. An engine starts up, then another, and Charmaine calls, "Bye, Tony. You be good, y'hear?" Where the drive dips, Will sees two red splashes through the trees, the red truck and his mother's red Rabbit, both headed for the alley. His mother must be taking Charmaine to the bus.

"Gimme the matches, quick!" Scott says. Reluctantly Will hands over a pack of matches from his pocket.

"I'll light, you throw," Scott tells him. Will shakes his head.

"*You* throw," Will whispers, and grabs the matches back. Hurriedly he lights the tails of three cherry bombs. Scott tosses these toward the Newcombs' porch as Will lights the rest. The first of them explodes with a loud clap that bounces off the other side of the ravine in a deafening echo. Scott throws the last, and the explosions follow in noisy succession—bang! bang! bang! Before Will knows it, Scott has grabbed the end of the rope and is gone.

Will reaches behind him for the swinging rope, but by the time he catches it, everything is too quiet, no bird noises, nothing. He's afraid to move.

"What in God's name is going on out there?" Mrs. Newcomb cries.

The words are hardly out of her mouth when the air fills with a new sound, something so loud that at first it seems only jumbled-up noise. Will inches his back up the tree trunk far enough to see that Mrs. Newcomb is looking out of the porch door, searching the sky.

Gradually the sounds floating over the ravine into the Newcombs' yard, over Will, practically paralyzed against the tree, over Mrs. Newcomb, whose twisted face is riveted heavenward, unscramble:

> . . . *Halleluiah!*
> *Glory Halleluiah!*
> *Since I laid my*
> *Bird on down,*
> *Lord.*

The voice ascends from a wavering quaver to a near shout.

> *Lord!*
> *Lord!*

Then it falls.

> *Lord.*
> *Since I laid*
> *My*
> *Bird*

On

Down.

There follows a second of loud, recorded silence during which neither Will nor Mrs. Newcomb moves. Then the voice resumes in another key, softer this time, no longer singing of laying down birds but of someone named Grace, and lost-and-founds. It is the saddest sound Will has ever heard.

Suddenly Will knows the voice. Caught between Charmaine's singing and Mrs. Newcomb's horrified expression, he understands a lot of things but not why the sight of Mrs. Newcomb's face frightens him so.

Only then does he notice her long white gown. She looks like a ghost, or the Bride of Frankenstein. As Charmaine's voice switches to a faster paced song, Mrs. Newcomb shakes her head and slowly closes the porch door.

Will takes off like a shot and falls in a terrifying, almost headfirst, tumble down the hill.

Buddy moves cautiously along the edge of the creek. The woods around him seem like the middle of nowhere, but the river's at his back. He knows where he is. Twenty-four hours as a fugitive from justice and he's doing pretty well. Amazing, in fact.

While paying attention to his footing, Buddy contemplates the way he'd gutted it out last night, doubling back after he reached the town to sleep near the Interstate in a barn. It was a big, dark place with dozens of horses. The rain made a terrible battering noise on the roof. He'd about lost it in the noisy pitch-dark but miraculously had prevailed over the old night-dreads. Also over two big dogs who might have eaten him if he hadn't picked right up on their karma and pretended to recognize them from another life. He'd surprised himself by waking up alive and walking unaccosted into the morning sunshine.

Buddy considers other personal victories— lifting a New York Yankees cap from a pickup by the barn and tucking his hair under it. Afterward, passing for a Normal, for nobody in particular, in that bar full of air head women glued to the six-foot TV screen. They were watching Prince Charles's enormous nose, ooh-ing and aah-ing over Lady Di, drinking champagne out of plastic cups. Not one of

them noticed him wolf down a bowl of stale pretzels.

And afterward, sauntering outside only to find himself being offered a ride to town by some guy with Michigan plates who stopped because he'd thought—from the hat, he said, from his build—that Buddy was somebody else. That caught Buddy off-guard for a second before he found himself delivering an attack on George Steinbrenner he couldn't believe he had in him. For a bona fide case, he was doing okay so far. (The idea that all that was behind him flickered across his mind. He let it go, superstitious.)

But look how he'd finessed his parents' gingerbready little town. It was almost as Hicksville as the place he'd just split from if you didn't count the Mercedes and Porsches (seventeen and six). And on top of everything else, locating his parents' house with the speed and ingenuity of Perry Mason. Hitting the right side of the street, finding the alley in the back, having the brains to wait for the mailman's Jeep and follow at a distance till he found the right mailbox.

Something puzzles him about the mail, though, this Nicolle Dundee who's getting a bunch of letters, in care of his mother. The name sounds like a stripper's and makes him think of big, heavy, oversize tits. He hasn't thought about tits for a long time. It's kind of refreshing. A number of things are going right, but he knows better than to think about this too hard. That's when the shit always hits the fan.

The woods are suddenly pierced by a clatter of small explosions. He throws himself to the ground, certain that someone is shooting at him. Facedown in a pile of leaves, he barely has time to think before the sky fills with a mutilated version of Aretha Franklin's "Amazing Grace." This could be part of Their Plan, he thinks, then corrects himself. No. There has to be some explanation. Nothing is going to mess with his head today. Not even the off-key voice grinding out another chorus:

Through many dangers, toils and snares
I have already come
'Twas grace that brought me safe this far
And grace will lead me home.

Take the best of what gets laid on you, he cautions himself. Forget the phantom voice coming down from the trees. A radio or a tape player. Forget that somebody thought this was worth playing. Listen to the words. After all, maybe grace—whatever that is—got him through the night and cleaned him up inside.

At that moment he's startled by a rustle of leaves and the sound of something whizzing past. One of Them? By the time he looks up, no one is there. Getting to his feet, he brushes that idea away and starts up the steep hill to his left. He has a tough time finding handholds and hasn't gone far when he hears a crack above him and a boy tumbles right into his arms, throwing him off-balance so completely that both of them fall together. They slam into a log near the creek bank and stop abruptly, the kid piled on Buddy's lap like the two of them were riding a sled.

Buddy's knee hurts. So does his rear end. In spite of this he feels unaccountably buoyant at the prospect of company. He becomes the picture of calm collectedness.

"It's like this," he says, helping the bewildered boy to his feet. "Guns go off. Someone plays hymns in the woods. People fall from the sky. None of it bothers me." He smiles.

The boy, freckle-faced and red-haired, looks at him as if he's just seen a ghost, and makes a jump for the creek. Buddy catches his arm and pulls him back.

"Hey, man. Don't leave yet. What's happening? You always have crazy scenes like this around here?"

In the tumble, Buddy's New York Yankees cap has fallen off, and his hair now hangs to his shoulders. He picks the hat up from the ground and sets it on the boy's head. The hat sits low, almost to his eyes, so that the boy looks slightly deranged.

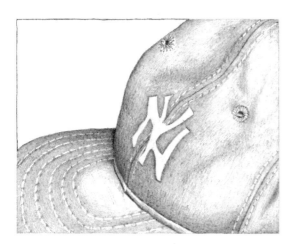

"Your thinking cap," Buddy says, bowing gallantly.

"No," the boy says, struggling to get away.

"Oh, come on, what's going on? Is that the Newcombs' house up there on top? Are they celebrating or something? Speak." He tries to grin in a comforting way. The boy shifts the baseball cap to the back of his head and stares at him.

"Who are you?" the boy asks nervously.

"That's a long story," Buddy answers. "How about if we swap?"

"I think I'd better get home. My mom'll be looking for me."

"Don't worry, it's cool," Buddy reassures him.

The boy looks uncertain. "It is?"

"Sure. Have a seat. Tell me what you've been up to lately." The way he says it sounds just right. Even so, Buddy's surprised when the red-haired kid actually sits down next to him on the bank of the creek. This makes him feel like a person who knows what he's doing, a big brother maybe, someone like that.

"So tell me," Buddy says, leaning back on one elbow, "what's your name?" All he needs to complete the picture is a long stalk of grass to chew on.

"Scott Edwards." the boy answers. "What's yours?"

"Wally," Buddy says, out of the blue. "Wally Cleaver."

"Oh," the boy says. "You look like a hippie."

Buddy melts. In all his life he has never been so flattered.

Through the shady Sunday morning streets of Lethem, the Watters family heads out of town. In the backseat of the station wagon, Will twists a Rubik's cube. Next to him, wearing the earphones of a small radio, Tony stares out of the window to a tune so loud that a tiny, annoying version of it is audible in the front. His mother gestures for him to turn down the volume, and the car becomes silent except for the clicking cube. Katherine searches in her purse for her sunglasses. Her husband, David, drives.

David is a large man with an appealing dark-eyed gaze and a face still open and boyish in spite of his graying hair and beard. Twice in the past week David was told he looked like Kenny Rogers. This caused him an unusual burst of self-concern, and he told Katherine that he was thinking of shaving off his beard and that starting the first day of their vacation, he was going on a three-day, grape-only diet. (Leave it to a doctor, she thought, to fall for that one.)

This is the third departure for Michigan the family has attempted in the last half hour. The first time they went back home to get the green book bag Katherine had left behind on the porch. The second time was for the large sack of grapes she'd left in the kitchen. David never complained. Katherine herself has a headache now, perhaps from the wine the night before, and she could do with a few more hours of sleep.

"Okay," David says as they pass through downtown Lethem for the third time, "what did we leave this time?" His voice is good-natured. He smiles often.

Will doesn't answer, and Tony can't hear him. Katherine yawns and says, "Let's pretend nothing."

"From the looks of this car, that's easy," David answers, eyeing the area behind the boys, full of suitcases, garment bags, snorkeling masks and flippers.

"We look like the what's-their-names leaving the Dust Bowl for California," he adds.

"The Joads," she says, leaning against the door. Katherine thinks David could have pulled off even that trip without breaking a sweat. He's unflappable, one of life's steady customers.

Most of the time their differences don't seem to matter. Though Katherine goes to great lengths to hide it, she labors under a burden of twitches and nerves—she regards them as temperamental tics, or sometimes, in the face of her husband's impassivity, personal flaws. When she suggests aloud that she may be on the verge of nervous collapse, David invariably tells her to relax—not much comfort but something she's used to after fifteen years.

Sometimes their differences get her down. Last night after the dinner they'd had, for instance, she had a sinking spell over one of David's radiology partners, Alex Friar. Alex has always delighted in baiting Katherine. She tries to avoid it, she tries to avoid *him*, but the previous night she couldn't, and she'd fallen into a ridiculous argument with him over the ERA. Not that the subject of their debates mattered anymore. By now they had nearly a decade of arguments behind them—Vietnam, Watergate, the ethics of radiation therapy, capital punishment, you name it.

"If I never see that man again," she stormed when Alex and his wife left, "it'll be too soon. He's dreadful!"

"Face it, Kitty." David smiled. "He's nuts about you. Besides, you love it."

"I do not!" she countered, "I hate it. I hate it that I don't know better by now, and if you want to know the truth, I hate it that you always sit and listen to us like you're laughing!"

"Kitty, I'm not laughing. I just enjoy it, is all."

"Couldn't you ever say anything? Couldn't you agree with me once in a while? I mean, I *know* you don't agree with him, but you just sit there!"

"You take pretty good care of yourself," David replied, smiling at her.

"*You!*" she declared, shaking her head. She began pitching things into the dishwasher. He came up behind her and put his arms around her, but she shrugged him off.

"Don't you ever want to get mad?" she asked when it became apparent he wasn't going to leave.

"About what?" He appeared genuinely curious.

"Oh, David," she wailed, "doesn't anything matter to you?" David didn't bother to answer. Instead he went into the dining room and returned with the dirty wineglasses.

"I only argue with Alex because everyone else is so boring," she said petulantly. "I mean, after all, how long can anyone talk to the Bergsons about bird-watching, for God's sake? Or the Tibbets about their wretchedly perfect children? It's dismal."

"Well," David said, "if the subject here is boring people, we could always discuss the Erie College English Department. Now there's a bunch of live wires."

"Just forget it," she said. "That's not the point."

"Well, then, what is?"

"I don't know," she said. "I guess just once I'd like to see you get exercised about something." She slammed a pan down on the counter.

"Now?" He grinned lewdly, pretending to twirl the end of his mustache. "In the kitchen?"

"Oh, for chrissake," she said, banging the dishwasher closed. "I'm going to bed."

"I have a few more things to put in the car," he called after her. "I'll be up in a minute."

"Well, I'll be asleep," she nearly shouted. Fair warning.

"Okay, good night," he said, unperturbed. "But, Kitty? Hey?"

"What?" she barked from the top of the stairs.

"That was a good dinner, one of your best."

For a second she wanted to scream.

earing the entrance to the Interstate, Tony shouts, "Look, Mom. I bet that's where the Horse Man lives." Because of the earphones, his voice is unnaturally loud, like a deaf person's.

Katherine merely nods. She'd studied the large barn from the road yesterday and now gives it only a casual glance, enough to see the red truck in front.

"Who's Horse Man?" David says as he turns onto the Interstate.

"Just the guy who came to pick up the horses the other night. I told you."

"How come you're calling him Horse Man, Tony?" David asks, lifting his eyes to the rearview mirror.

"He thinks it's clever," Katherine says.

"He's neat, Dad," Will says eagerly. "On Friday he showed me how to fix the brakes on the minibike. I forgot to tell you."

"You mean, he's been around again?" David asks Katherine. She feels a small twinge, a certain speeding-up of things.

"He comes all the time," Will offers. "He's nice."

"If he's that nice," says David without a trace of irony, "I'll have to meet him."

Katherine concentrates on the car ahead of them, finally making out the bumper sticker as David draws closer.

I'D RATHER BE SMASHING IMPERIALISM!

She weighs this as an alternative to her present situation and rejects it.

"He is nice," she says after a minute or two. "What there is of him."

"Who are we talking about now?" David asks.

"Tony's Horse Man," she replies, sorry to have brought it up.

"What do you mean, 'what there is of him'?" He looks over at her.

"He's just young," she says offhandedly. "You know, not quite all there yet. His parents died when he was small. He was raised by relatives."

"What did you say his name was?" David asks.

"Robin Hastings," she answers, and sighs.

SAVE AN ALLIGATOR. SHOOT A PREPPY!

David sets the car on cruise control and stretches his right leg out until his foot touches hers.

"He used to have a Honda 500," Will announces. "He knows all about motorcycles."

Katherine pulls her foot away and sits cross-legged. She takes a pack of gum from her purse and, after unwrapping a stick for David, passes it to the backseat.

"Thanks," David says, and pats her knee the way he might pat Will's.

DECADENCE: A WAY OF LIFE

"I'm going to try to sleep," Katherine says.
"Sure, go ahead."

"Wake me if you want me to drive," she adds.

"Look, Dad," Will says, thrusting the Rubik's cube into the front. "I got two sides."

"Not bad," David says. "Now keep it up. Watch your corners."

Katherine shuts her eyes, troubled again over the previous night. Sometimes David's abiding unruffledness disheartened her. Secretly she entertains visions of shouting matches, knock-down drag-outs, after which they would fall into each other's arms. Yet she can't think of a more unlikely sparring partner than calm, reasonable David. They married when she was a twenty-two-year-old grad student, David a twenty-four-year-old medical student, and their life has flowed with an almost uncanny tranquillity. Mostly she's grateful. Still, part of her suspects there must be more to marriage than reasonableness and calm.

"Mom?" Tony booms.

Her eyes fly open for a second.

IF YOU DON'T LIKE THE WAY I DRIVE, STAY OFF THE SIDEWALK

"Shh," David says, "She's trying to sleep." Tony doesn't hear, and Will finally delivers the message by shouting across the backseat.

Is it struggle she longs for? Danger? Surprise? Lately she wonders if the price they pay for tranquillity isn't higher than she admits. On her part it seems to involve keeping the lid on, battening down hatches she's not sure were meant to be closed. The idea that there's *more* seems to lurk around the edges of her life like an apparition.

She opens her eyes. "Do you think I'm greedy?" she asks her husband.

"Greedy?" he says, and frowns.

"Tony's the one who's greedy," Will pipes up from the backseat. "He said I could listen to his radio, and now he won't let me."

"What makes you ask?" David says.

DON'T FOLLOW ME. I'M LOST TOO!

"Please," Will whines, "C'mon, Tony, give it to me."

"After lunch," Tony tells him.

"Let's eat," Will says. "I'm starving."

"Have some grapes," Katherine says.

"Yecch."

"Hey, that's a good idea," David says. "Hand me a bunch of grapes, Will, would you please?"

"I thought you were going on a diet," Will says, passing his father a large bunch.

"Grapes *are* my diet. Just watch. Soon I'll be a shadow of myself. You won't recognize me." David laughs and pops a grape into his mouth.

Katherine rests her head against the car

window. She dozes off and wakes up half an hour later. Her headache is gone, along with her crazy misgivings. She was just tired, she thinks.

"I have to go to the bathroom," Tony announces. His voice sounds normal, and when Katherine turns to look, she sees his earphones on the seat next to him. Will has fallen asleep.

"Me too," Katherine says.

"We'll need gas in about twenty miles. Let's wait. Can everyone wait?"

DUCK HUNTERS DO IT IN THE WATER!

"When Will put the tent away," Katherine says to Tony, "did he find that hunting knife Scott lost?"

"I don't know. Do you want me to ask him?"

"Let him sleep," Katherine answers.

"He's not asleep. He's just faking. Aren't you, Will?"

Will groans a little dramatically and rubs his eyes with his fists. "How much longer till we get there?"

"A long, long time," Tony says in a menacing voice.

"Don't tease, Tony," Katherine says. "I just wanted to know, Will, did you find Mr. Edwards's hunting knife when you put the tent away?"

Will nods.

Something makes her say, "You *did* put the tent away, didn't you?"

He lowers his eyes and shakes his head.

"You mean, you *didn't* take the tent down?" Katherine's voice rises. "Oh, Will. That's not like you. You said you would. What happened?"

From someplace near the floor Will, who is nearly folded in half by now, releases a small "I forgot."

"For*got!*"

"You know, Will," David says evenly. "When we ask you to do something, we depend on you to do it."

"Yeah," Tony adds.

"I'd appreciate it if you'd stay out of this, Tony," David says. "It's not the tent so much, Will. The tent will probably be okay. It's that you didn't do what you said you would."

"I forgot," Will says, louder this time, so that Katherine catches something funny. At that moment, however, her bladder's all she can think of.

"Listen, David, I've really got to go. Can't we stop up here?"

"Fine," he says. And then to Will, "I think you should know, Will, that if this kind of thing happens again, your minibike days are over for a while. Do you read me?"

"That's right, Will," Tony says. "One more slip and it's back to the old Schwinn. Ha!"

"That'll be enough, Tony," David says.

"I'm dying," Katherine announces.

"Me too," Tony says, thrusting his head over the front seat.

"I'm going as fast as I can," David says, pulling up an exit ramp behind a green van.

NOW THAT I'VE FOUND MY IDENTITY, I'M ON
THE LOOKOUT FOR A GOOD FANTASY!

Katherine crosses her legs. "Check that," she says to David, pointing to the van's bumper sticker.

He grins broadly. "I've already found mine," he says, squeezing her knee.

"I'd settle for a toilet myself," she says.

"Where are we?" Will rises from the floor of the backseat.

"Nowhere, dummy. Can't you see?"

"My stomach hurts," Will says wanly. Abruptly he gags, and there's a dreadful splashing noise.

"The window!" Katherine screams. "For God's sake, open the window, Will!"

Will tries throwing up out of the window but isn't very successful.

"Get me out of here!" Tony shouts as David pulls into a gas station. "Get me out of this stuff!"

"Hold on," David says.

The second the car stops, Tony bolts, and David jumps out and opens the door for Will. "Come on, buddy," he says to the child gently. "Come on." Tears stream down Will's ashen face as his father leads him away to the men's room.

For a minute Katherine can't move. She feels slow and witless. The task she will inevitably rise to seems distant—a poor, unfortunate stranger's, not hers. Dully she stares at the RV ahead of them as it pulls away.

ARE WE HAVING FUN YET?

Katherine gets out of the car. She pretends she didn't see this.

II

. . . childhood home was tragically de-
stroyed by a raging fire that took the lives of
their parents and left Jessica and Jennifer pen-
niless orphans. Their mother's late half sister's husband, Calvin Lundin, the famous
financier whose sprawling empire spanned the
globe, flew to their side in their hour of need.

Though the twins had only seen him once
before—and that when they were small—Calvin proved as kind and helpful as a trusted old
friend, steering them through the dark days of
the funeral and the harsh realities of their
father's debt-ridden estate with a wise and
sympathetic hand. When the twins repeatedly
tried to express their gratitude, Calvin refused
to listen. He was the only relative they had in
the world, he pointed out. It was only natural
that he would be eager to help them.

Nicolle Dundee writes lickety-split. She
wouldn't have a son who apparently has disappeared from the face of the earth, or a husband
who hasn't thought about her for years. Her
house wouldn't be crawling with painters,
sending her from room to room like a fugitive.

Thus Jessica and Jennifer were hardly in a
position to say no when Calvin (he insisted
they call him by his first name) urged them to
leave their native New England and return
with him to Southern California. They would
enter the world of high finance and be his
special assistants.

"Special!" Jessica scoffed later when the
twins were alone. "How special can we be? He
can't even tell us apart!"

"Now, Jessica," Jennifer said. "Don't be
harsh." Ever since the girls were children, Jessica had been sharp-tongued and willful. "He
has been so good. In time he'll learn who we
are." As usual, it was left to Jennifer to
smooth things over.

"I'm the one with the mole, right here," she
told Calvin one day when the two of them
were alone. She pointed to the back of her left
hand.

Calvin Lundin smiled. "You're the one with
the twinkle in your eye and the sweet disposi-
tion," he said quietly. "Your sister, well, you
two may look identical, but the minute she
opens her mouth, your sister—"

"Please!" Jennifer said, interrupting, "don't
say a word against my sister."

"On the contrary, my dear. I have always
been fascinated by women who speak their
minds."

Jennifer cringed. The possibility of friction
between her sister and Calvin Lundin did not
bode well.

Nicolle wears a long white satin peignoir
when she writes, not unlike the one Irene has
on now, except that Nicolle's would have a

flattering frame of marabou feathers around the neck. Unfortunately these make Irene sneeze.

Before long, the twins found themselves transplanted to Los Angeles where Calvin presented them with a luxurious condominium overlooking the Pacific, stylish new wardrobes, and the promised jobs. Even Jessica couldn't find fault with Calvin now, though she often told her sister how much she missed the East.

For some time things went smoothly—no matter that Calvin still seemed to have trouble knowing which girl was which. The work was demanding, and the twins had little time for anything else. Somehow their tragic past seemed less horrible in the bright California sunshine.

Slowly, under Calvin's patient tutelage, the girls began to gain mastery over the intricacies of the business world. After almost six months of their mentor's careful guidance, months punctuated by little else besides an occasional weekend aboard Calvin's eighty-five-foot yacht, *Taurus,* Jennifer was surprised to hear him announce it was time that the twins tasted more of life than business. They deserved better company than an old man. (Though Calvin—fit and handsome—didn't seem exactly old. Even Jessica once admitted to her sister that she found him rather dashing!)

Calvin was persistent. "Get out into the world," he advised. "Look around! Live while you're young!" His deep-set eyes flashed with wisdom. "All work and no play makes Jack a dull boy!"

Irene yawns. The words come in spite of her. It's Nicolle, of course; Nicolle, who, if she paused, would probably reach for a French chocolate or ring for her maid to bring her a cup of tea. Then again, she might gaze beyond the bouquet of yellow long-stemmed roses (sent daily by a secret admirer) on her Louis XIV desk, out through the expanse of her penthouse windows to the towers of the teeming city. Irene finds herself staring blankly at a Douglas fir now. Nicolle, of course, wouldn't know a fir from a pine.

After a few moments the paper beckons. Nicolle's pen, twenty-four-karat gold and slim, makes Irene's blue Buckeye National Bank ballpoint all but invisible. Irene watches with detachment as it touches the page, under a power hardly her own.

At these words Jessica gasped, but to Jennifer's great relief said nothing. The twins had discussed this very subject between themselves. Jessica had insisted she would never recover from the loss of her fiancé, Rick, in a mountain-climbing accident during their second year of junior college. To Jennifer's certain knowledge, her sister had spurned the overtures of Rick's friend, Barry Barnes, and refused even to date the handsome Dr. Smythe. Rather than enter the whirlwind world of dating and parties, Jessica vowed she would lead a cloistered life dedicated to repaying their father's debts.

When on one occasion Jessica had hinted to Calvin Lundin her dedication to the dead Rick, the older man tried to console her by speaking about his marriage. He and his wife,

Della, had meant the world to each other, for they were childless. When Della so unexpectedly passed away, his life nearly collapsed. Not until he reached outside of himself, he continued, did he once again believe life was worth living. Jessica—and Jennifer, too—would find someone just as he had, but they must give themselves a chance.

Both girls were startled by Calvin's mention of this mysterious someone, for they had never known him to have a date and were not aware he had any close friends. They had seen pictures of the beautiful Della—he had five or six in his office—and had assumed her loss was still fresh enough (she had died only a year before their parents) that there was no one else in his life.

Though Jennifer burned with curiosity, she was much too polite to pursue the matter, and Jessica did not seem very interested. Since Calvin volunteered nothing more, Jennifer accepted this as a secret he was entitled to. Still, the question was never far from her mind. Who could it be, this . . .

Irene rubs her eyes. Below her in the yard, bright yellow goldfinches crowd the thistle feeder. As she watches, a disturbance sends them flickering away in a golden explosion. She considers the empty, swaying feeder for a time, then reluctantly returns to the paper.

. . . "someone"?

"You are young, my dears," Calvin told the girls one weekend, continuing his campaign to get them back into the social swing. They were on the deck of the *Taurus*, sipping bouillon from blue-and-gold Meisen cups, all three

of them bundled in Jaeger lap robes against the chilly wind that blew off Catalina. "Broken hearts mend. Time heals all wounds."

These words of wisdom he addressed directly to Jessica (he seemed to be getting better at telling the two girls apart), whose eyes under their silken lashes flashed stubbornly. Jennifer held her breath, afraid of what might come next. Blessedly Jessica remained silent.

As for Jennifer, she did not share her sister's determination to remain isolated. Lance Steel had made her aware of that. The previous week, when Jennifer saw him and, to her horror, fainted in his arms, reviving after he had left to find her sister hovering worriedly over her, she realized that she was drawn to life, to life and to the future. She *was* young, wasn't she?

Lance Steel! The thought of him sent a tingling through Jennifer's limbs, a delectable, languorous sensation that took her breath away. She blushed with shame. After all, Lance was a married man! Her feelings were reckless and all in vain. Yet in spite of herself she felt alive to him . . .

"Mrs. Newcomb? Mrs. Newcomb? Are you in there?"

"Just a moment, please," Irene says as she stuffs the white peignoir in the closet. She smooths her shirtdress and pats her hair, then hurriedly goes to the door of the small upstairs room she's been relegated to that morning, taking a second to settle her face, holding her eyes open wide, sucking in her cheeks. Lately she has found something attractive about the idea of gaunt cheeks. When she was young, her round cheeks gave her a sweet, cherubic look. Now they make her face look a little puffy.

Biting the inside of her mouth, she opens the door to see Robin Hastings, arms folded across his chest. Gazing far up into his dark eyes, she finds herself giving him a dreamy, sunken-cheek look. It isn't the first time she's responded to his youthfulness in this manner. "Yes?" she finally says, "what is it?"

"I'm sorry to bother you, but I wanted you to know we're leaving now." He smiles down at her, a charming smile. No one has smiled at her like this for years, and it utterly disarms her. "The ocher paint for the den won't be mixed until late this afternoon," he says, "so we won't be back today. Plus, you should know that both bathrooms upstairs are wet. They'll be dry by tonight."

Irene allows herself to stare at him wistfully, pulling hard at the insides of her cheeks, nodding slowly. "Of course," she attempts to say without releasing her cheeks, but to her horror, a strange sucking noise emanates from her mouth along with the words. She pulls her cheeks back in again, pretending nothing has happened.

He tilts his head toward her with a look of concern. "Is anything wrong?"

"Certainly not," she says, abandoning all efforts to minimize her cheeks. She feels a fool, suddenly aware of how he must see her: a middle-aged woman, shapely but plain, her face puffy under permanented, colorless hair on its way from blond to gray.

She gazes down at her shirtwaist dress. It occurs to her that she looks less like herself than she does her own mother. Stunned, she says, "I must do something with my hair."

He leans toward her again, his forehead creased. "I beg your pardon?"

Mortified, she manages to say, "Nothing. It was nothing."

"Well, then," he says, blinking rapidly, smiling stiffly, "I'll see you tomorrow."

She follows after him along the upstairs hall, trying to regain her composure. As he reaches the stairs she calls him back into one of the newly painted bathrooms and asks a sensible-sounding question about the paint on the molding. She must cover her lapse of a few minutes before.

"Sure it's oil-based," he says. "I always stick to oil-base in bathrooms."

His cheerful answer sounds forced.

After his departure, Irene wanders through the downstairs, wondering what in the world has come over her to have exposed herself to a perfect stranger—a tradesman, no less, a mere boy. In the living room, she makes her way around furniture draped in sheets of plastic, and floor lamps huddled in the center of the room, without noticing the disorder. She stares out of a drapeless window for a moment, then makes a beeline for the stairs.

What she sees in the full-length mirror on her closet door confirms everything she read in Robin Hastings's eyes. She looks old. She looks like her mother. From her low-heeled pumps to her rigidly set pale hair, she could almost *be* the woman she remembers regarding with pity twenty-five years ago. "How sad," she recalls

1 13

thinking. "She's plain as a pot, life is over for her."

It hadn't been, of course. Irene's mother had proved her wrong. But it's she, herself, Irene wants to think of now, not her mother. How in the world had she come to look so old and plain? How did she lose track of herself so completely that a stranger had to deliver this message? Irene shakes her head and sits down on the edge of the bed, safely out of mirror range.

Irene considers herself a simple person, not tricky, certainly not vain. Her life would be unremarkable if not for her son's illness. After a few minutes she asks herself what else she has besides Buddy—whom nobody may have, who may be gone for good this time. Well, she has Harry, she guesses, but Harry has ignored her for so long that she often wonders if there isn't another woman, or if she, herself, has become invisible. And really, the only remnant of the woman her husband married Irene can locate now is the angry, overly fussy creature she would rather not be.

She sighs. She doesn't often entertain depressing thoughts. She had waited for things to change—for Buddy to recover, for Harry to notice her. But until she discovered Nicolle, Irene had never thought she, herself, could change. Today, though, in a young stranger's eyes, she saw the need to. She's tired of being invisible.

Irene goes back to the mirror and asks herself what's to be done. Well, certainly she could do something with her hair. The color, she notes, is awful. It makes her think of oatmeal stuck in the bottom of a pan. Her makeup is the same she's worn for thirty years; her dress a latter-day version of those her mother used to wear.

As she shakes her head in dismay her eyes light on her ankles. Inspired by that small vision of beauty, she undoes the top buttons of her dress. With her buttons undone, she feels a small sense of abandonment, a tiny surge of hope.

Suddenly there's a flash of blinding sunlight from the cupola on top of the Watterses' roof across the ravine. Peering through the trees, Irene sees nothing out of the ordinary. The Watterses are out of town. Perhaps it was merely the movement of branches in the breeze. Then again, maybe the Watterses returned and someone just opened a window in that small, round room of theirs. If that's the case, she'd better steel herself for more pranks from those tiresome boys.

But because Irene is a conscientious neighbor in spite of the treatment she's received from the Watterses, she dials their number.

The phone rings and rings. She must have been seeing things.

Irene pulls the small Lethem phone book from the drawer, turning to the yellow pages. She runs her finger down a list of beauty shops, trying to recall the name of the place she's heard so much about.

"Lewis and Clarke." That's it. "A personalized expedition into your beauty potential." Irene wrinkles her nose with distaste but finds herself dialing the number. The first appointment, she's told, isn't for over a week. Irene says she'll take it, then patiently spells out her name, N-I-C-O-L-L-E.

She hangs up the phone and waits for the self-reproach that's bound to descend. Oddly enough, she's struck instead with a rush of anticipation. A new me, could it possibly happen? For a second she catches the wild promise of change: Buddy coming home; Harry taking notice of her; the painter walking in and stopping dead in his tracks.

Irene quickly retrieves her notebook from the guest room where she had left it. Sitting down, she scans the page. The breeze from the window is cool on her neck. She touches the undone buttons of her dress. Suddenly she sees Robin Hastings's startled face when he encounters her transformed. With uncommon energy the blue pen moves across the page.

. . . as she had never been for another man. The mere thought of him made her heart hammer. He'd awakened something that lay buried deep inside her. She had known a number of men—boys, really—but none who had stunned her into arousal like the tall, muscular Lance Steel with his laugh-crinkled brown eyes and his handsome, perpetually tanned face under its cap of sun-streaked blond hair.

The memory of their first kiss so many years ago sent hot flames of longing through her body even now. After all this time she could still taste the way his tongue had plundered her innocent mouth, still feel the length of his thigh, hard against her body.

Then suddenly Jennifer remembered Lance's wife, and the whole world seemed to come crashing down around her. Without meaning to, she let out a tortured cry, blessedly lost in the din of the rising wind. How could she go on? she wanted to wail to the darkening sea. Must she live with this hopelessness forever? Tears brushed her cheeks as she made her way to the boat's railing. A storm was brewing.

"It's all right," Jessica said, coming up behind her and taking Jennifer's hand. It wasn't the first time the twins had read each other's thoughts. "It's all right," Jessica repeated calmly. "I have a plan."

Tony stands on the dock watching the motorboat head toward the middle of the lake. His brother drives, wearing the moth-eaten New York Yankees cap he dug up someplace. His father waves and Tony waves back.

He's glad he stayed behind. He fished with them yesterday and the day before. He can sit still for hours on land, but he's itchy and restless after five minutes in the boat. Besides, this year he can't stand to look at the fish. He hates to see the perch squirming, gasping for breath, turning dull before his eyes. He doesn't want to watch things die.

Tony lies down on the wooden dock. The August sun is warm on his face, and he begins to see brilliant yellow lights inside his eyeballs. He tries his trick, of seeing his own eyes staring back at him when his eyes are closed, like he might have a second set of eyes on the insides of his lids. But the light is too bright and his eyeballs ache from the effort.

He flips over on his stomach and hangs his head off the edge of the dock, watching the water lap at the pilings. He wishes he had something to do. If he goes into the house, his mother will probably make him clean. Either he's forgotten what happens to her when she gets here, or she's worse than usual this year. Maybe it's because his grandparents and aunt and uncle are coming, and his mother wants to show his grandmother how neat she can be. They should have brought Charmaine.

His mother is all worked up over this stupid house. She runs around glaring at things, going after crumbs and sand. It's awful. Yesterday he thought they would have to take her away when Will spilled a bowl of Spaghettio's on the hall carpet. In fact, she did go off somewhere by herself until dinnertime. His father ended up calling a man from town who came with a machine and cleaned the whole rug. The carpet still smells. When his mother finally returned, his father told her she was too upset, she was

letting everything bother her. That made her angry, and she told him she never wanted to come back to this house.

Tony hopes they never do. It's not much fun here anymore. He used to like it; in fact, he almost cried last year because he didn't want to go home. This year he's wanted to go home since before they got here. This year the only people his age around the lake are girls, and all they do is lie in the sun and talk about boys and clothes and boobs. They talk about boobs a lot—not in front of him, of course, but he's overheard them. Only Melissa Rice from Chicago has any, though, and they're not much. For boobs, Tony thinks, they ought to see Miss Carol Ann Drumley, his English teacher. Hers are so big, they look like the ones in the *Playboy*s Scott Edward steals from his father and rents out.

Miss Drumley's amazing. He sat in her class all last year spellbound most of the time, staring at her big, loose set of bazongas, trying to imagine how they looked under her clothes. He doesn't think she wears a bra, but he's never spotted her nipples even though he did extra-credit work just to get up close. Why do some nipples stick out?

Tony sits up quickly, hand over his crotch. It doesn't seem safe out here in the open dreaming of Miss Drumley's tits. Even though no one's around, you never can tell. Some people might be able to read his mind—and from a distance, too, who knows? He dangles his feet over the edge of the dock, watching the way the water magnifies them until they're about size fourteen, somebody else's big feet. After a few minutes he scans the lake for the boat but can't find it. Then again, maybe he can't see the boat for the hovering vision of Miss Drumley's knockers. Will calls them balloons. Will doesn't know Miss Drumley. If he did, he wouldn't talk like a baby about them.

Tony decides to compose a paper for Miss Drumley in his head. That way he can feel near her without exactly thinking about the other thing. Maybe he'll tell Miss Drumley about his summer vacation, practice up for the boring theme she'll probably assign the first day of class.

"My summer vacation this year in Michigan was a real mess," he begins. He knows right away she would say not to use *mess*. "Look it up in your thesaurus and find a better, more descriptive word," she always says. "Enlarge your vocabulary," she urges. (Mammary glands is what his father told him they were called. Glands! Ick.)

"My summer vacation this year in Michigan was not much fun. To start with, my brother got sick all over my new radio and earphones. My mother tried to clean it up, but it was totaled. We ended up throwing it away in a trash bin on the Interstate.

"My Dad told me he would get me a new one when we went home. In the meantime he said I should pay more attention to people for a change." (38-D, one of the boys in his class guessed, but Tony thinks it's more like 40 or 42.) "My Mom said what she always says, that I should read.

"As you know, I'm a big reader. These are the books I brought with me: *Catcher in the Rye, A Day No Pigs Would Die,* and *The Old Man and the Sea.* But reading isn't a substitute for listening to the radio. I mean, they're two different activities." (Once at the Lethem Library, Tony saw Miss Drumley bouncing around in a T-shirt and jeans. She was with some guy who had a black mustache.)

"Anyway, that wasn't a great way to start the trip. The whole backseat was wrecked, and I had to ride for two hundred miles squished"—he wonders if they feel like Jell-o; they can't be real hard and flop around like they do—"between suitcases in the back of the station wagon while my brother rode in the front with my mom and dad. The smell was repulsive.

"When we got to my grandparents' house on Pelham Lake, which is near Traverse City and only a little ways from Lake Michigan, everyone was relieved but not for long. My grandmother is very strict about keeping this house clean. She is like that about her house in Winnetka, too, but here it's a lot harder because there's sand and because this house is shut up half the year. Anyhow, my mom opened a kitchen drawer and found mouse droppings. I had to spend practically a whole day helping her clean out the kitchen while my brother and dad set traps all over the house.

"The second day we were here, one of the traps, a little box with a spring, had about ten mice in it. My mom refused to cook dinner, so we went into town to a restaurant my dad likes. He watched us eat because he's on some diet. My mother kept shaking her head.

"My dad and I went canoeing around the

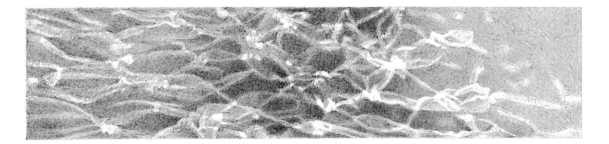

lake. I like to canoe, but sometimes I get uncomfortable with my dad because he's so quiet. If you want to know the truth, I think he likes my brother more than me. I think he thinks I'm strange because I don't like a lot of things he does, like fishing and football. He never gets mad at me, though.

"My mom is different from my dad. When she's not up here in Michigan acting like a maniac about cleanliness, she talks a lot and is funny. My brother and I have these conversations where one of us takes the part of Penny, our neighbor's stupid Irish setter, and the other one talks for our poor old dog Venus, who died last year. We pretend Penny goes to retarded classes or that she's a hooker. She's always asking Venus for advice. Anyway, the point of this is that when my brother and I have these conversations in weird voices, it bothers my dad that sometimes my mom joins in. Yesterday, for instance, I heard him tell her he didn't think it was 'appropriate behavior for a mother'! My mother said, 'How would you know?' He didn't answer. If he talked more, I wouldn't have to imagine what's on my dad's mind. Now I always imagine the worst. Some-times I wish I'd wake up and things would be different, that my Dad would talk a lot and we would be like a family on TV."

Tony has lost track of Miss Drumley now, having taken some inner turn he didn't intend. He pulls off his shirt, removes his glasses, and eases himself into the lake. The water is cold, and he can't bring himself to go all the way under, so he hangs onto the end of the dock, shivering.

A screen door slams, and blurredly he sees his mother coming across the lawn toward the dock. In the peculiar view he has of her, framed between the mossy underside of the dock and the black water, she appears by stages, feet first, then legs, then everything else but her head. Her footsteps pound onto the dock, and when she's nearly to the end, he pulls himself up and shouts, "Boo!" In that moment, unguarded, she looks all wrong; she looks lonely or something, not like herself.

"Tony!" she yells. "You nearly scared me to death! I thought you were a ghost. Why didn't you go fishing?"

Tony dives underwater. He surfaces and swims as fast as he can away from her. When he finally stops and turns around, she is motioning him in, yelling. Reluctantly he begins swimming back, doing a slow breaststroke so that he hears her when she shouts, "I said, do you want to drive to Traverse City with me? I need some groceries I can't buy here."

He keeps on swimming. "Well, do you?" she calls. "Maybe we could find a store that sells Walkmen. Hurry up if you want to come." She must know he's heard, because she turns around and heads for the house.

He wants to tell her he hates her for letting him see her that way, for making him feel confused. He imagines screaming, "What's going on?" then realizes that's the last thing he wants to know. What he wants is the whole thing out of his mind, gone like it never happened.

Tony picks his way across the mucky bottom of the lake. "Wait up!" he shouts, not wanting to blow the chance of a new radio. He races down the dock and grabs his glasses. The fuzzy world comes sharply into focus. He was seeing things, that's all.

"Wait for me, Mom," he yells, "Hey! Wait up!"

The roar of jet engines wakes him. The tail end of a dream skids away as he scrambles for his bearings in the dark. He huddles on the floor for protection, under siege from above. He stiffens at the idea of capture, but the creak and groan of something close by distracts him. Eyes shut, he reaches out to touch a smooth, slick surface. Recognition hits him, releasing a high-pitched cackle, his own, barely audible against all the other sounds.

He is in the kid's tent. The noise is the wind. Things are crashing crazily overhead. If he's safe, it may be only from his pursuers.

Before the thought of safety can sink in, the danger outside reaches down and blows open the door flap, sending a high-velocity barrage of leaves and twigs that strikes him so sharply, he feels the sting through his jeans. He ducks his head as the tent billows around him, threatening to fly away.

The sounds grow louder, and he tucks his head between his knees in the grip of new terrors, a whirling, flapping anarchy of sensations, the world turning inside out and screeching. A deafening crack, earsplitting noises; then the reverberation of something crashing to earth so fiercely, he's thrown on his side. He curls into a ball, trembling, and waits for the pain that's sure to follow.

But nothing happens. Instead the roaring stops as abruptly, as if someone has shut it off. Rain begins—big, slow, heavy drops thumping on the tent roof. Shakily he gathers himself to his knees and crawls toward the opening. An enormous fallen tree blocks his way. He snakes around it, amidst jagged roots twisting upward against the yellowish night sky.

He heads out of the woods, skirting fallen branches some thick as trees. Circling the house, he notes the absence of lights down the front yard slope.

He lifts the basement window he had jimmied open the day before, and slips through. The space is too dark, black. A drain gurgles,

shriek. Drugged crazies shout down a nurse; a droning psychiatrist smirks. Fat policemen tell him terrible things he must do. Richard Nixon belches. His high school homecoming queen points at him, convulsed. Everyone he has ever known is here, laughing at him. Their laughter is terrible, knives sinking into his flesh, the laughter of death. He leaks away as someone hollers, "Jesus! Jesus!" He is rot and sickness.

A fire engine's siren slices the night. The sound quiets his laughter. He is invisible now, dead. From nowhere a vast light shimmers, bursts wildly, and draws him in.

Forewarned by the emergency weather bulletin, Mona guides her groggy son, Scott, down the basement stairs and settles him on a blanket against the northwest wall. The wind howls menacingly.

She runs back upstairs to fetch the old cat, Koko, from under her bed. Penny follows at her heels, rump twitching queerly, panting as if she were in heat. Mona stops in the dining room and takes a small white box from the bottom drawer of the buffet. Carrying the cat and the box, she dashes back down to the basement, hurried by the rattle of windowpanes and the scrape of branches against the house.

Sam is out of town as usual, and as the wind roars around the house she can't for the life of her remember where he is. Only this morning she attached his neatly typed itinerary to the refrigerator door with a magnet, but now she can't think what it said.

She takes a flashlight from the shelf over the

water drips. He imagines walls thick with bat-mouthed creatures ready to attack. His heart slams crazily. Something crashes to the floor. He swivels around to find the end of the stair rail jabbing his thigh, and he takes the wooden stairs fast, one hand in front of him, the other on the rough wall. He rans blindly into the door at the top and bangs it shut, prepared to find sanctuary in the downstairs hall.

But something is all wrong, and he begins trembling uncontrollably. Wracking sobs shake him, and he falls to the floor weeping. In place of shelter, every nightmare he has ever had descends on him in a torrent of hallucinations. The world mocks him, the world laughs. He puts his hands over his ears, but the laughter grows louder. His parents snicker across a breakfast table, enemy children twice his size dryer and sits down next to her son, wondering where Sam can be. Finally she fixes on him in a candlelit restaurant in Paris, though of course he isn't in Paris. She pictures him breaking open a crusty roll and spreading it with sweet butter. Vichyssoise appears, cold and thick as a milk shake. A salad with walnuts and rounds of incredibly dry goat cheese. Salmon, sliced thin as paper, under a delicate lemony sauce flecked with truffles. While his family and house are being sucked into the sky, Sam considers dessert: chocolate mousse, double chocolate torte with caramel icing, profiteroles dripping with fudge sauce. Her mouth waters. Why couldn't he be here, where they need him?

A high whistling begins, and the cat struggles in her arms. She leans across her son and opens the door of the broom closet, dropping Koko inside and shutting the door.

"What is it? What's going on?" Scott asks sleepily.

"Nothing," she says. "A storm. Go back to sleep."

The two bare bulbs above them flicker and go out. Flying gravel hits the windows, and the wind booms loud enough to wake the dead. The noise is terrifying, the loudest she's ever heard, yet as she fingers the string of the white box she feels calm.

She puts the box on her lap. Her son sits up suddenly and clutches her right arm. Offended by his wakefulness, Mona sets the box next to her on the floor.

A metallic crash pieces its way across the screaming wind, then something hits the floor above them.

"What was that?" Scott shouts.

"Go to sleep!" she yells back. The house is falling down. What can she do? Penny paces the basement floor whining.

Mona inches the string off the box with her left hand, trying not to rattle the waxed paper. For a minute or two she simply feels the contents, running her fingers lovingly over the smooth surface of the raised, connected triangles, tracing the ridges between. Pretending idleness, she counts the triangles, reaching sixteen and then discovering one loner in a corner like a gift. She closes the lid but then opens it again, touching, stroking. Her heart speeds.

She smuggles the odd triangle into her mouth, fondling it with her tongue. The candy melts in a thick, syrupy sweetness that sends her into a tailspin of rapture. She breaks off another and slithers it around in her mouth, then another.

A deafening clap of thunder splits the air close by, rocking the house. Scott tightens his grip on her arm as she closes her lips on another triangle, caressing the piece between her tongue and the roof of her mouth, feeling sharp edges melt to roundness before slickly disappearing down her throat. Her pleasure is so acute, it erases everything—the raging storm, Sam's absence, the demands of her son, even her recent preoccupation with the sagging skin under her eyes. All of it disappears like magic, in a bliss of chocolate.

"I smell something!" Scott shouts. Mona sniffs for fire, but he tugs at her arm and moves his face close to hers. "It's chocolate!" he screams. "You're eating chocolate!"

She shoves a triangle of chocolate into his mouth. "You tell anyone about this and I'll murder you!" she yells. The wind dies in the middle of her sentence, so that "I'll murder you!" fills the silent basement.

"Have another," she says by way of apology, and forces a piece into his hands. She pushes the box under the blanket and turns on the flashlight. She feels Scott's eyes on her and turns away.

As if nothing has happened, she gets up and lets the cat out of the broom closet. Scott scrambles to his feet and grabs the flashlight from her, bolting up the stairs along with the dog. As a punishment, Mona makes herself finish the rest of the chocolate, chewing quickly, not even tasting it.

Overhead, Penny yelps and Scott shouts, "Mom! Mom!" But Mona doesn't rush up the stairs. Instead she gropes her way to the tiny lavatory next to the broom closet and lifts the

toilet seat. She sticks her finger down her throat and throws up neatly, in an efficient act of absolution.

She flushes the toilet, then rinses her mouth. An altered Mona, brand-new for the time being, goes determinedly up the stairs. With a measure of equanimity that impresses even her, she surveys the wreckage, calms her son, and makes a tourniquet for the foot Penny has gashed on glass from the shattered dining room window. While Scott checks the upstairs, Mona wipes up the worst of the blood so nothing will set while they're at the vet's. By the time Scott returns, she has clipped the dog on a leash and found her purse.

The three of them venture outside. A gentle rain is falling from a queer yellowish sky. In the distance, down Jefferson, sirens wail over the darkened town. They pick their way across the littered lawn until they come to the pool fence. Scott shines the light on the water.

"Jeez!" he exclaims, "It's wrecked. The whole thing's ruined."

The pool is clotted with leaves and branches. The broken spokes of the table umbrella bob from side to side. The diving board is missing.

"Don't worry," Mona says cheerfully. "It just needs cleaning out." She takes his hand comfortingly.

Scott turns the light on the drive, and they see a tree lying across the roof of her Volvo.

"Good God!" she says.

"Mom! It's totaled!"

"Oh, for heaven's sake," she says, and then in a confidential tone, "You know, I never liked that car. Besides, its tires were rotten."

"But, Mom. How are we gonna get Penny to the vet?" Scott wails. "She'll bleed to death!"

"Let me think," Mona says.

"This is really gross," Scott says wanly, playing the flashlight around the yard. "It's like everything fell down. I wish Dad were here. Where is he, anyway?"

"*I* know!" she says. "We can get Kay's car. I saw her keys yesterday when I took in their mail. She wouldn't mind if we borrowed it. Look, get one of the pool towels from the bushes."

"Excellent!" Scott runs to get the towel.

With the lame Penny between them, they start down the drive. The place is a terrible mess, but Mona's spirits rise with every step. They will have an adventure on this dark, stormy night, and then something more, but for a minute she can't quite think what. Nearing the alley, she remembers: it's the Jamoca Almond Fudge ice cream pie in the freezer that she may have to eat for purely practical reasons if the power doesn't come back on. This is such a wonderful thing to look forward to that she hardly notices the wreckage. She is busy imagining the chewy frozen-fudge fluting that edges the crushed-sugar-cone crust.

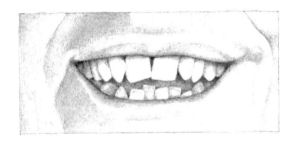

"Robin!" He can't place the woman's voice.

"Yo!"

"Where are you?"

"Up here, in the loft. Who is it?"

"Me. Carol Ann. I came to find out if Minkie's okay, but I can't see a thing."

"Hold on," he shouts. "I'll be right there." He centers the bucket under the leak in the roof and jumps down from the hay. Descending the loft stairs, he shines the flashlight every which way. Seen in pieces like this, the barn looks strange, as if the insides shifted around during the storm. At the bottom of the stairs he catches her white shirt in the light. The fabric looks fiercely bright, her breasts large and loose underneath it. They always astonish him.

"Carol Ann," he says, "what are you doing out on a night like this?"

"I tried to call, but the phones are down." Her heavy, dark hair is pulled back from her face, and she isn't wearing any makeup.

"Where's Ben?" he asks. Ben's a landscape architect Robin met when he first came to Lethem, an old acquaintance of Jannie's. Carol Ann has lived with Ben for longer than Robin's known him, but Jannie didn't like her for some reason.

Robin's firsthand knowledge of Carol Ann Drumley is limited: She is stacked, pretty in an Indian-princess way, and teaches at the Lethem Middle School. The few times Robin's seen her with Ben, she's been quiet, vaguely mysterious, the kind of woman you could imagine entertaining certain ideas about if she weren't attached. When she comes to the barn to ride, Carol Ann is all business. She never hangs around to chat, like most of the other women.

"Ben's away," she says. "Are the horses all right?"

"Everything's fine. It was crazy for a while with that wind, but the only damage I can find is a little leak in the roof. Here, let's go look at Minkie."

As they enter Minkie's stall the horse looks over at them calmly. Carol Ann coos and rubs the horse's nose. She takes a carrot from the back pocket of her jeans, and Minkie chomps down on it. Carol Ann nuzzles the horse's neck, her back to Robin, off in a world of her own.

It occurs to him that she wants to be alone with the horse. "Just give a yell when you're ready to leave and I'll come back with the light."

"Thanks," she says. In the flashlight beam, her eyes look sad.

"Are you okay, Carol Ann?" he asks hesitantly, stopping at the stall door.

"Sure," she says. There is no particular weight to her answer, and he walks on out, shutting the stall's half door after himself. "I'll be around," he says, and then remembers what he'd meant to ask. "By the way, did you come through town?"

"It's a mess," she says softly. "Half the bag factory blew into the river. Mill Road is blocked off." Her voice is uncertain. He examines his shoe with the flashlight. "The power's out everywhere, I guess," she adds.

"A lot of trees came down." Minkie shifts and snorts.

"Is your house okay?" Robin asks.

"The Weber grill blew off the porch. I can't find the top anywhere. All the lawn furniture disappeared." Robin imagines pieces of domestic life floating over the treetops.

"Nothing is ever there when you need it," Carol says.

He can't conceive of her needing a grill or a lawn chair that much. Not tonight, anyway.

"Oh, I'm sure they'll turn up," he tells her. "They're probably just in your neighbor's yard."

"It's Ben," she says, and her voice cracks. She begins to sob. He doesn't know if he should leave or stay and, for lack of anything better to do, flicks the flashlight off and sticks it in his back pocket. In the dark the barn feels more familiar. He waits uncomfortably for her to stop crying.

She sniffles loudly. "Excuse me. I didn't mean to do that. Her name is Constantina," she tells him in a flat voice. "She's a sales rep for Mars."

The planet? The God of War? The candy bar?

"He met her at the laundromat. She admired my underwear, he told me. That's how they got talking."

Robin tries to imagine Ben in a laundromat but has trouble. The improbably named Constantina, however, he can see: she would be tall and gypsy-dark, Greek or Italian, with a wide mouth. She would look like Carol Ann, only more so. Ben told him that he always wound up with women who looked like Carol Ann.

"Then the grill blew away," she says. "Ben gave it to me for my birthday."

"I'm sorry," he says. "I didn't know anything was wrong."

Like a ghost, she floats across the stall until he can feel her standing close to him on the other side of the wooden door. He gets a whiff of alcohol and perfume.

"I shouldn't have come," she says. "I'm going home." She pushes the door open and steps into the aisle.

"It's so dark," she says in a small voice. "I'm all turned around. Where are you?"

He reaches for the flashlight and turns it on, but after a second her hand covers his and she turns it off. "Leave it off," she says. "I know where I'm going now." She removes her hand, and they walk down the aisle. He feels imperfectly suited for whatever he should be doing, consoling or comforting her. What can he say? Something seems fishy about her coming here like this; about the Laundromat story too.

Halfway to the barn door she stops and touches his arm. "Hold me," she says, pressing herself against him. "Please." He's caught completely off-guard and thrown by her slightly boozy breath.

"Please," she says again into his neck, and stirred into arousal, he puts his arms around her in spite of his better judgment. Her breasts push against his chest; her knee slides between his legs.

"Carol Ann," he says, on the verge of giving way. Some remnant of sense pulls him back.

"Listen," he says, "Ben . . ." He pauses. "I mean, I'm sure things will work out. Maybe Ben is just, you know, going through a phase. Maybe you should go home and sleep on it. Ben . . ." Robin wants her but not like this, not with her shaky and desperate and not quite sober, and not without knowing what's going on. Besides, there's Jannie.

"Ben!" she says. "Don't give me Ben. I throw myself at you and you think of Ben! Oh God, men! If you want to know the truth, I didn't plan this. I came out here mostly to ask you what I should do." She is so close to him, he can feel her breath warm on his neck.

"What *should* I do?" she repeats. "Can you tell me?"

Robin realizes she regards him as the village expert on broken hearts. Is that what Jannie's departure has reduced him to? "You just hold yourself tight," he says, trying to disentangle himself from her arms. This time she moves away.

"That's *it?*" she asks, "That's all you can tell me? I thought you'd have more to say than *that!*"

"Look," he begins, not sure what comes next. "Ben will be back."

"He won't be back," she says flatly. "He moved out this afternoon. He's gone."

"Are you sure?"

"Yeah, I'm sure," she says.

They reach the door, and Robin gropes for the handle. Before he can open it, she takes his hand. "Let me stay with you."

He can't think what to say.

"Did you know I used to be married?" she

asks abruptly. "For three years. Then my husband ran off with some guy. I mean, after three years of this relatively normal life, it turned out he wanted to be gay. I thought nothing would ever shock me again after that, but I was wrong. Everything shocks me. It shocks me that Ben left. It shocks me that I came out here tonight. It shocks me that you turn out to be . . ."

"What?" he asks nervously.

"Dumb," she says.

"Dumb?"

"Dumb, yes. You act like you know a lot, like you understand things. But you don't. You come on so warm, and then you just stop. Like now. Like a brick wall. You know what you are? You're misleading. You're like a mirage." Her voice wavers and she sniffs.

"Mirage?"

"Oh, come off it," she snaps indignantly. "You've been flirting with me for months. Even Ben's noticed."

He's staggered. What's she talking about?

"You know what I think, Robin?" She yanks the door open. "I think you're a big phony!" She walks outside, stumbles, then rights herself. "Goddammit," she mutters.

"Are you okay?" he asks, turning on the flashlight.

"Terrific," she says, banging her car door shut. She starts the engine, turns on her lights, and takes off down the drive. Her tires squeal when she hits the street.

He shines his flashlight up into the low, murky clouds. It feels like the sky just fell on him.

The rain and wind wake Katherine in the middle of something, less a dream than a thought: a flicker of wide shoulders, delicate wrists. She wonders at this invasion; it's one thing to have thoughts of him pester her days, but this is quite another. Nipped by a guilty conscience, she feels swift, wide-awake.

She slips out of bed and, in atonement for this new private life of hers, pads diligently from room to room, shutting the windows of her in-laws' summer house.

The eerie clang of the flagpole's halyard follows her, and a foghorn on Lake Michigan half a mile away groans mournfully. She knows the house by heart, yet bumps into furniture, walks into walls. She considers the idea that the house is on to her. Still, she refuses to turn on the lights, convinced she is safer under the cover of darkness.

On the way downstairs her mother-in-law's face rises before her.

"I always knew she had it in her to be something of a slut," the white-haired woman says. "Do you know what she's up to now? Making up to a *house* painter!"

"I am not making up to him!" Mooning, perhaps, she thinks dreamily. Those shoulders, that blond hair.

Her father-in-law joins his wife. "Our David has never been anything but unfailingly loyal to you. What is it you're after?"

"My God," she imagines herself saying. "It was only a thought!"

Her mother-in-law says, "There's a name for women like you."

"What?"
"Cradle snatcher."
Katherine cringes.

As the rain gusts against the windows she retraces her steps through the house, wiping up the floors with a towel from the downstairs bathroom. They find her again in one of the guest rooms.

"You see?" her mother-in-law says to her husband. "Rags aplenty, and *look* what she's mopping the floors with!" She shakes her head. All along she's known the worst.
"Oh, leave me alone!"

Katherine peers out a window, trying to make out the lake beyond the front yard. The only thing she can see is the ghostly white shape of the motorboat leaping at its mooring. The incessant clanging from the flagpole reminds her of monsters dragging their chains in dank dungeons, lunatic scientists.

She carries the sopping towel with her down the stairs, perversely enjoying dripping water on the pale, wholly impractical carpeting. She goes to incredible pains to keep this house as neat as her mother-in-law's fanaticism demands. In the last week the effort has nearly driven her mad.

Yet aside from the housecleaning obsession, her mother-in-law has few tangible flaws, Katherine has to admit. The woman is abidingly, correctly pleasant. For a cold woman and the wounded mother of an only son, Katherine thinks to add.

She tosses the heavy towel in the direction of the washing machine. Now that she's finished barricading the house against the wind and rain, she pulls out a chair and props her feet on the edge of the breakfast table. She wants to be alone. Almost immediately, however, her figmentary in-laws join her. Guiltily she drops her feet to the floor. Too late.

The white-haired woman struggles to contain herself. "Such a dreadful worry for poor David," she sputters to her husband. "But what can we expect from someone who never even wipes off the canned goods she brings from the store, or rewraps the meat she puts into the freezer? A person who would put her feet on the table!" She shudders.

Her father-in-law looks grave, as if he's just lost a ward full of patients. "We must be philosophical, Charlotte," he tells his wife. "After all, she is the mother of our grandsons, poor boys."

Katherine has had enough. She leaves the table and goes quickly upstairs, stubbing her toe on a table leg in the hall. Limping, she shuts the bedroom door firmly behind her and climbs into bed.

After a while she decides she's shaken them and closes her eyes, off-duty. Abruptly things flutter and fall as he appears, descending from above like a giant bird. Enfolded in his strong, young wings, she discovers lost memories, shimmering possibilities.

She is about to swoon when her in-laws materialize next to the bed, eyeing her arrangement clinically. The rain pounds; wings beat against the night.

"Bug off," Katherine tells them.

But it really doesn't matter. For the moment nothing can touch her. With the giant bird swooping her up once again, she is Leda.

Leda? Katherine almost says aloud. Did she think *Leda?* Even for her that seems a bit much. She dismisses everyone and everything and goes to sleep.

Buddy curls on the floor of the Waters' dark hall, dazed by a fierce inner light. He speeds dizzyingly fast through shimmering corridors that burst into flame as he approaches. Everywhere he looks, sparks, glowing arcs, fiery cascades—all radiating from him. Dazzled by his power, Buddy understands: *He* is the light! *He* illuminates the world!

Suddenly, a terrible noise eclipses the light. Buddy flattens against the wall and opens his eyes to see a pale circle of light—not his—dance jerkily through the door. A voice sings:

. . . and I've come to say
Bananas have to ripen in a certain way.

The bearer of the ghostly light narrowly misses stepping on him. They've come for me, he thinks: This is it.

Yet something is wrong. They've sent someone too small for the job, a woman or a girl. He could crush her light, crush her too.

. . . in a salad
You can eat them in a pie, aiya!

Keys jangle. His heart pounds. He is much bigger than she is. He could . . .

No, No, No!

Buddy slumps against the wall. A refrigerator opens, a foot taps. "Kay, how could you?" the voice says. "Nothing to eat but this ratty wheat bread!"

His confusion mounts. Footsteps come toward him. The light plays on the wall, then turns, followed by two thin legs. The door slams. Silence.

Buddy is lost, not certain what he's seen. After a time he can't remember seeing anything except his lost fire-trip, an aching memory that caroms him toward emptiness.

Darkness smothers him. Voices shriek at him. He has forgotten how to breathe. In a bolt of terror, he is on his feet, fleeing up stairs that climb and stop and climb again. He must get back to the light. Only the light can save him from the airless, screaming void.

Abruptly there is a door and then more stairs, steep as a ladder. Panting, he reaches the top. He looks out on spots of light, points of flickering crystal—not much, but he breathes.

Then, in the strange round room he seems to remember from a dream, he drops to the floor and holds himself tight, staring at a sky that strains with stars. Buddy rocks himself. He rocks until there is neither light nor dark, only vacant space-less sleep.

He's in a stall near the door when he hears the car. At first he thinks Carol Ann is coming back, but when he looks out, he sees Katherine Watter's Rabbit. He can't imagine what she's doing here, but the idea picks him up a little.

He starts out of the door, only to hear, "Yoo hoo, Robin! Is that you?" The voice isn't Katherine's, and he feels momentarily let down. Who in the world says "Yoo hoo"?

"Right!" he says into the dark. The sky has begun to clear. Stars are popping out here and there.

"Thank God! You have no idea what I've gone through to get here!" The voice belongs to that nutty woman from Katherine's house. What was her name? He shines his flashlight ahead of him and sees pink ribbons, a pink shirt, the woman's speedy skinniness rushing toward him.

"It's Mona Edwards, Robin," she says. "I know it was crazy of me to come, but my husband's out of town."

Oh, no, he thinks, but manages to say, "Mona! How nice to see you."

"Listen," she says, "I've been going out of my mind. You have no idea."

"Well!" he says, eyes bright, smile fixed. She must be old enough to be his mother.

"I thought if you knew so much about horses, you might know about dogs too. Wait."

Relieved, he follows her to the car where she lets a big Irish setter out of the backseat and grabs the dog's trailing leash.

"This is Penny, Robin," Mona says. Robin is ready to shake hands with the dog, hug it. "Penny got hurt in the storm. She stepped on some glass." Robin sees that one of the dog's front paws is wrapped in a bloody kitchen towel.

"Hey, there, Penny," he says, stooping down. Penny leaps up, moaning and yelping. Breathlessly Mona tells Robin about finding the twenty-four-hour pet clinic closed because of the storm. After that she drove to her pediatrician's house.

"The big jerk kept telling me he didn't know the first thing about dogs. I told him, 'Oh, go on. Just pretend she's human,' but he couldn't. He's a real turkey, I always knew it." Mona says everything in a hurry, so that Robin wonders if she's on speed. Maybe that's why she's so thin.

"I was going to switch pediatricians, anyway," Mona rattles. "He's always been a pain. His name is Hetherton. Don't ever go to him," she cautions, "no matter how badly you need a pediatrician. Remember that." She is very serious, and Robin promises not to. By then she's off on something else, breathlessly telling him what a time she's had.

"Lord love a duck," she says with a sigh. "Everything is a total wreck. I'm worn to a frazzle. The bag factory nearly blew away, and oh, yes, a tree smashed my Volvo. My husband is out of town. Did I say that? Anyway, I had to borrow Kay's."

Mona is one of the daffiest people he's ever met. Still, there's something about her that's kind of cute, especially for someone that old. Her high-speed nervous chatter makes him want to sit her down and say, "There, there." He doesn't remember her being so small, though. In the dark she could be a little girl.

Suddenly the lights in the barn flicker on. Things fall into place as he and Mona blink. "Light," she announces, and sighs. "That's something. On a scale of nine to ten I'd give this night about a thirteen for being a disaster."

Robin strains for sense, smiling down at her all the while. "You're so tiny," he says for lack of anything else.

"Don't be fooled by what you see." She laughs. "I'm a rotunda at heart."

He leads her into the barn where he unwraps the dog's paw and removes the bloody towel. He asks Mona to hold Penny's paw off the ground while he gets a first-aid kit.

"Hurry," she implores. "Penny gets hysterics." He runs into the office, grabs the first-aid kit, and then dashes back in time to see Penny leading Mona in a peculiarly drunken-looking three-legged dance. "I should get my son to help," she calls from behind the twisting body of the dog. "He's dead asleep in the car."

Robin assures her the two of them can handle it. He removes several slivers of glass way up between the pads of the dog's foot. Penny squeals nervously all the while.

"Oh, you're wonderful!" Mona exclaims. "I'm so glad I came. Thank you. Dear, dear Penny, what a friend we've found!"

Robin squeezes a big blob of antibacterial ointment over the dog's paw and wraps it up in gauze. Already the bleeding has stopped. When he's finished, he stands up and wipes his hands on his jeans.

"Honestly," Mona says a little bleakly. "Would you believe it? Most of the big adventures of my life involve pets. What a soap opera!"

Robin kneels back down to secure the end of the gauze that Penny has begun to unwrap. He considers *All My Puppies, The Dogs of Our Lives, As the World Barks.* He is smiling when he stands up.

"Good gracious, you're cheerful," Mona says. "You smile more than anyone I've ever seen." His smile broadens automatically, and for a split second he wants to tell her he isn't really cheerful. He just knows how to smile.

"I don't know how to thank you. Maybe I'll make you a cake or something. Do you like chocolate?"

He tells her he loves it, though actually, he doesn't, and they walk toward the barn door. When they reach it, Robin lifts up the large door he had closed during the storm. A breeze streams in, cool and fresh.

"May I ask you a personal question?" Mona says suddenly. He nods, afraid to imagine what's coming. "Have you ever thought about having your teeth straightened? I mean, you'd be an absolute knockout if your teeth were straight. You ought to talk to Kay. She knows all about things like that. Dentists, doctors. If her husband had been home, I wouldn't have been racing around tonight over this poor dog!"

Robin runs his tongue over his teeth. This is his night. He's a flirt and a phony, and now his teeth need straightening. The teeth part is true,

he concedes. Maybe all of it is true. What does he know?

"And, oh, heavens! I forgot to tell you," she says. He wonders if he has bad breath too. "Your driveway. It's just littered with vegetables!"

He lets Mona guide him across the parking lot. "Look at that!" she says.

He shines his flashlight over the gravel drive where zucchinis, cucumbers, and tomatoes are scattered around like a crazy salad, some of them squished by Carol Ann's and then Mona's car. He guesses all this must have blown across from his neighbor's garden down the road.

"You'll have quite a time returning all that," Mona says, shaking her head. This wouldn't have occurred to him, but she's probably right. He'll pick it up tonight and take it down in the morning. He scoops up several zucchinis and a tomato. The zucchinis are rather large. Robin hands one to her.

"For me?" she says. "Just what I need! When they're this big, you stuff them," she says brightly. "They're a good source of Vitamin A," she adds. He gathers up as many vegetables as he can carry and carts them back to the red car. Mona lets the dog into the backseat, then opens the trunk for Robin.

"You've been fabulous," Mona tells him as she gets into her car. He puzzles again over what makes her move so swiftly and how she gets away with the zany things she says. Maybe she's not too bright, he considers. Maybe she's lost a few bolts along the way.

"Really," Mona is saying, "Don't ever let anyone tell you you're not a sweet, kind, generous person after this."

He demurs awkwardly, and she starts the engine. "Well, Kay will be home in a couple of days." Her son's sleeping body falls against her, and she pushes him so that he slumps back against the door. "Thanks again. Toodle-ooo!" She waves a skinny arm, and in the shadowy light from the barn he watches her weave slowly down the driveway, trying to avoid the vegetables.

What a night! He feels as if he's been racketing nuttily for hours to the staccato rhythm of Mona's voice. He wonders if she goes great guns like this all hours of the day and night. He wonders what he would have done if she'd been Carol Ann. He will never know exactly what had been on her mind. He should probably be kicking himself for not seizing the day.

Now he's tired. On Mona's goofy scale of nine to ten he decides he's a twenty, in favor of unconsciousness.

He switches off the barn lights. He'll worry about the vegetables in the morning.

Harry wakes to a clear, wind-tossed day. Surveying the clutter strewn about his yard—the branches and leaves, his recently installed long-range TV antenna—he's surprised to see a child's small plastic wading pool resting peacefully atop a sea of daisies, an improbable sky-blue shipwreck. He gazes at it for some time before turning away from the bedroom window and heading for the shower.

An unfamiliar cake of soap, redolent of coconut, sends him on a swift tropical journey—swaying palms, brilliant sunsets, dancing girls half naked in the velvet night. He rinses well, but the smell of the soap lingers sweetly.

Halfway into a white shirt that the Lethem

Laundry has laminated front to back, he has a brainstorm: He'll stay home from work today. After all, he hasn't taken a day off for a long time.

Discarding the stiff white shirt, he dresses in old work clothes. He walks quietly out of the bedroom, leaving his sleeping wife behind. Downstairs, he stops to put on a pot of coffee, then goes out for the paper. The yard will take him longer than a day to clean up. Still, the sky is so blue, he looks forward to tackling the job.

At the mailbox he glances across the alley toward the river. The willows droop heavily, unbothered by the storm, but something in this vista is changed. He realizes his neighbor's large wooden swing set is gone. He wonders what it clobbered when it landed. Maybe he'll look around for it later so he can return the missing swing set to her. *That* might impress her, him lifting the big clumsy timbers, dragging them to her door. Would she notice him then?

He shakes open the paper: HUNDREDS HOMELESS AFTER FREAK WINDSTORMS RAVAGE AREA— AT LEAST 7 DEAD, MANY MISSING; ABSENCE OF CONFIRMED FUNNEL-CLOUD SIGHTING DISPUTES TORNADO THEORY, METEOROLOGISTS SAY; BRIDGETON MAN HURLED ½ MILE IN CAR, LANDS UNHARMED—FOUR FLAT TIRES AND A DENTED FENDER.

Folding the paper, Harry starts back up the drive, suddenly dogged by thoughts of his son. Everything these days leads back to Buddy. Could he still be in the area? Was he out in all that weather? Is he even alive? Though Harry has talked to Dr. Krause several times a day for the past two weeks, more and more it seems they might be discussing some fabrication of their joint imaginations. The police have turned up nothing. Ditto for the private detective Krause called in, and the search parties around Holly Hill. What more can they do? Agony every time he turns around.

Yet something in the breeze off the river makes Harry think it might be possible, at least for a while, to ease the staggering burden. He remembers the man in the joke whose golf partner dies on the third hole. Terrible, people say when the man reaches the eighteenth hole. How did you do it? Three wood, drag so-and-so, the man answers. Seven iron, drag . . .

Harry smiles, lugging thoughts of Buddy the rest of the way up the drive. For a minute, standing on his back porch, he feels a peculiar sense of communion with all that's left standing in the world, a hint in the morning air of better things to come.

In the quiet kitchen he pours himself a bowl of cornflakes and loads the top with sugar, skipping the sour grapefruit juice Irene always presses upon him. He reads the sports news and skims the business section, fumbling in vain at the empty pocket of his shirt for a cigarette, as he does at least forty times a day. Finishing his second cup of coffee, he looks around for his briefcase. He wants to check his calendar to see what he'll be missing.

But his briefcase is not where he left it on a kitchen chair. Everything downstairs has been moved around and shrouded by the painters. Finally he spots the briefcase in the living room, on top of a plastic drop cloth that covers a chair. As he reaches across a coffee table for the briefcase, the pile under the drop cloth tilts precariously. Harry watches everything under the plastic slide slowly to the floor. He considers simply taking his briefcase and walking away, then stoops to pick up the whole mess.

Lifting the drop cloth, he restacks at least a dozen magazines, several copies of the weekly *Lethem Record*, and an abundance of unopened third-class mail. An envelope boldly asks, "Do you want all the luck, money, happiness, and good fortune life has to offer?" Harry rips it open and reads from a phony piece of parchment:

Friend:
An ancient God reached across 1,000 years to give me this Medallion of Good Fortune layered in 14K gold and set with a genuine diamond! Can a supernatural Medallion of ancient origin bring you all the Success, Luck, Happiness and Joy that it brought me?

Harry shakes his head at the long-winded questioner. Isn't there a law?

He selects another envelope, conspicuous for its plainness. "Enhance your sex life within three days!" he reads. "A revolutionary new device!" Only $13.99 and it's his.

Harry isn't surprised to find that it's addressed to Buddy. So are all the rest: the ads for crotchless underwear (edible or not; your choice); a six-volume encyclopedia of mysticism; a thousand and one ways to get rich in your spare time; a badly reproduced letter that

begins, "So you want a mammoth penis, who can blame you?"

Jesus, Harry thinks, crumpling the last letter. The kid is on everybody's nut list. Disgusted, he dumps the mail into a throwaway pile.

He rounds up loose grocery coupons, recipes torn from magazines, and at least two dozen catalogs. The contents of a manila folder spill out in a flutter of pastel papers. Piles within piles, he thinks as he begins picking these up, dismayed by this newest stash of odds and ends. He'll have to say something to Irene. It's not like her to be such a pack-rat.

A magenta scrawl covers a pink sheet of paper. He reads.

Dear Nicolle,
I loved your Samantha. There are a lot of similarities between she and I except I've always been afraid of horses and I've never had a boyfriend like Rex. I've never had a boyfriend at all, if you want to know the truth. What I do is live with my mom and work in this stamping plant and everyday I hate to get up. Your book mady me feel better tho. Please write more soon.
Your friend,
Agnes Belkin

Puzzled, Harry reads from flowery aqua notepaper.

Dear Nicolle,
Just thought you'd like to know that Nicolle (after you!!!) Shannon Bickerstaff

was born on June 26th at 6:28 pm. She was 20 inches long and weighed 6 pounds 14-½ oz. When she was born she was bald but now she has a little blond fuzz. Would you be her honorary godmother? Answer back soon.

> *Sincerely,*
> *Mrs. Todd Bickerstaff*

Harry next picks up a piece of lined notebook paper.

> *Dear Nicolle,*
> *Last year my husband got layed off and two months later he was killed in a motorcycle accident. About that time, my brother's trailer burned up with him in it. Then I lost a breast. Truly, I thought my heart would never mend. This week, though, I read* Winter Heat *and began feeling a little better. Why don't you write about someone like me next time, only have her luck change, like maybe mine will? Thanks for listening.*

> *Donna Jean Pilcher*

This one makes Harry feel dreadful. He raises his glasses and rubs his eyes, for a split second registering a strange inner vision of the lost breast flying through the air, chased by his neighbor's swing set, the twirling TV antenna, the wayward blue wading pool. The Bridgeton man gazes down in horror as he and his hurtling car bring up the rear. Somewhere in all this is Buddy too. The world can fly away; nothing holds anything down.

These letter writers and crackpot mail getters go on looking for miracles, solutions that will change their lives. What failure of reason permits this? What insane optimism? In the dusky living room Harry experiences sudden goose bumps. He should have gone to work.

But who is this Nicolle these people are writing to? he wonders.

> *Dear Nicolle,*
> *You set me to dreaming about when I was a girl and we had horses. Now I am old and crippled up with arthritis . . .*

> *Dear Miss Dundee,*
> *I am thirteen and in the eighth grade and my parents are very strict. Can you tell me how . . .*

> *Dear Nicolle,*
> *I am a nervous wreck and am turning to you for help . . .*

> *Dear Nicolle,*
> *What will Samantha do now that she's married? What happens next?*

Always a good question, Harry concedes. Still, he has no idea whose mail this is or what it's doing in his house. All he knows is that it threatens to ruin his day. He gathers up the letters, twenty or thirty of them, and shoves them into the folder gingerly, feeling as if he's handling shreds of strangers' sad lives: death, defection, helplessness, maiming. Just get rid of it, he tells himself, wedging the folder into the middle of the stack of catalogs. Get it out of sight.

"Good Lord, Harry!"

He jumps at Irene's voice.

"I thought you'd gone to work! Whatever are you doing sitting on the floor? The painters will be here any minute."

Hoisting himself to his feet, Harry says, "I was looking for my briefcase, and I ran across this junk mail. What are all these letters doing here? Who's Nicolle? Is this a joke or something?"

Irene's mouth drops open. For once she appears speechless. He wonders what he's done now. He's prepared to tell her to forget the whole thing—what's important, after all?—when he notices how strange she looks standing there in the shadows of the stairwell, not like her usual efficient self. She looks lost and very young, fragile in an almost-forgotten kind of way.

"Irene?" he says, "what's wrong?"

She moves backward unsteadily and sits down on a step. She lowers her head into her hands. Harry can't ever remember her doing this before, and it touches him. The thought crosses his mind that maybe this is it: Here she goes. Funny, he always figured *he*'d be the first one to crack.

"Irene?" he says moving toward her, feeling as if the worst is already over and he is merely going through some necessary motions. He hunkers down next to her. "Talk to me, Irene," he says.

"Those letters," she finally says into her hands. "They're to me. I . . . I'm Nicolle. I should have told you a long time ago. I *was* going to tell you before income tax time, not that the money's been much, but." Lifting her dazed face, she tells him in a soft, faraway voice he hasn't heard for years about discovering Nicolle, writing *Winter Heat,* coming up with a success on her very first try.

At first Harry thinks craziness might have been easier to swallow. At least he's had practice there. Still, he doesn't know whether to laugh or cry. Irene writing romances! Should he be pleased that she's found a vocation, or depressed that she's joined the ranks of crotchless underwear salesmen preying on the downtrodden and brainless?

"Really, Harry," Irene says. "I had every intention of telling you."

He tries to put an intelligent look on his face, but it's not easy.

"Oh, Harry," she says gratefully. "I was so afraid you'd laugh. Thank you, at least, for not laughing. Thank you." Her voice, unusually gentle, makes him think of a white flag fluttering in the breeze.

"I've thought about this a great deal," she says. "I've come to the conclusion that it doesn't really hurt anyone. Of course, I do realize that for me it's an escape, a crutch." She lowers her eyes.

A fleeting image of his neighbor passes through his mind. For some reason he can't for the life of him remember what's supposed to be wrong with a crutch. Then Irene puts her arms around him, the last thing he expected.

"It's so hard sometimes," she says softly. "So lonely." Tears spring to his eyes. Still squatting, he hugs her in return, catching the scent of coconut again. It's been so long since they did anything more than embrace dutifully—sex like a chore to be gotten over with, like shaking hands. Longer still since they tried to comfort each other, as if they'd both been afraid that might be the fastest way to break. Now here they are. He's not sure why. He's not sure of anything at the moment except that Buddy has been like a wedge between them, driving them so far apart that they've come to this: private lives, secrets, imaginary friends.

"I've never told you this," she whispers as though reading his mind, "but for a long time I hated him for ruining our life. But lately . . . lately I've begun to understand it's not only Buddy; it's me as well. Us."

"I know, I know," he tells her, and he does know, but he's not certain he wants to think about it. His thigh muscle begins to quiver. He can't stoop like this much longer.

Irene evidently notices, because she pats the step and says, "Here, sit down." Gratefully he unbends and joins her, stretching his cramped leg out in front of him, flexing his ankle.

"Well," she says hesitantly, "aren't you going to tell me how you feel about this Nicolle business?"

He's not sure what he feels, and right now it's Irene who occupies his mind. For years she's been brittle and hard to take. Now she seems suddenly gentle, warm. Has she changed? Or has this Irene been here all the time, along with all the other Irenes? Buddy's not the only one who alters from one minute to the next. But something holds the rest of us together that doesn't hold him, some thread of continuity, maybe only imagined. Why should he be surprised that Irene seems different, or that Irene is Nicolle? Nobody is really ever who we think they are.

"To tell you the truth," he finally manages, "I'm amazed. You could knock me over with a feather." Aware of straying from the subject, he adds, "But tell me, what do you do with all those letters?"

"Why, I answer them, Harry, what else? I know some of them are pathetic, but I try to be kind. If they ask, which they occasionally do, I even tell them a little about me."

"You tell *strangers?* Really?" He never would have expected this.

She shrugs. "People you don't know feel safe. That's all."

Of course, he thinks, you can be anyone you want to with strangers and not suffer the consequences. Only the long hauls get you. Still, maybe they're all that matter in the end. How long can you carry on with ghosts, or made-up neighbors, and not go nuts?

She squeezes his hand. "Harry," she says. "Oh, Harry." She sounds almost like she's claiming him. And though he's not sure he's reclaimable at this late date, or that she won't change her mind and disappear again for years, he suddenly wants this to be true, wants it with all his bedraggled heart.

"Irene," he starts to say. A knock at the back door interrupts him.

Irene gives him a quick peck on the cheek. "I'm afraid the painter is here." Reluctantly she gives up his hand and heads for the kitchen to answer the door.

Left alone, Harry wonders if he made this up. He sighs heavily and follows Irene into the kitchen in time to see the painter brandishing two of the largest zucchinis Harry's ever seen.

"Hi," the painter says brightly. "Look what I brought you!"

"My land!" Irene says.

"By the way," the painter says, "I found the top of your grill in the bushes outside."

"The top of our grill?" Irene asks. "But we don't even own a grill."

The painter seems puzzled. He sets the muddy-green zucchinis on the table. Harry studies the elephantine vegetables, one of which must be a foot and a half long and has a lump at one end. Suddenly all he can think of is the mimeographed letter: "So you want a mammoth . . ."

Harry begins to laugh. The laugh rises from deep inside and shakes everything loose in its path. There's no stopping it. Harry clutches the back of a chair, his eyes spilling over. He's

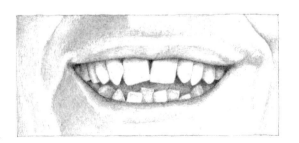

helpless. He sneaks a look at Irene, expecting to find her glaring daggers at him. Instead she's laughing too. Not as hard as he is, but she's laughing.

"Don't mind us," Irene says to the painter between giggles.

The young man eyes them both as if they've lost their marbles. What's with this kid? Harry wonders through his laughter. He comes in lugging these freak vegetables . . .

Heaving with laughter, Harry reels from the room. He has to get away from that knuckle-brained painter and his damn zucchinis. He staggers through the dining room, nearly doubled over. He's breathless and his chest aches. He's laughing like a maniac, but he feels great, better than he has in ages. If he doesn't die laughing, there may be hope.

In the small round room amid the treetops where the late-afternoon sun flickers through the leaves, Buddy crouches on the floor, oblivious to the whine of chain saws outside. He is intent on rewinding the tape he found downstairs. After listening to it ten or twelve times, he's decided that it's definitely a sign from his people (whoever they are), not something from the other side. The tape holds his mission. Only the question of timing remains unclear.

The tape has allowed him to grasp some hold on himself, but his nerves feel singed. From time to time he shuts his eyes, weary from seeing too much, too far: the end of everything and afterward—ashes floating down on silent lunar planes.

Shiva has been with him all day and now dances in the corner, garlands of skulls clacking, hair on fire. Buddy has tried to get his attention, but Shiva's too busy to notice.

Buddy returns to the tape, convinced he's on the verge of a breakthrough. Punching the play button, he strains again to crack the code. After female singers struggle raggedly to end a song, a quick male voice begins.

"Are you sick, depressed, can't hold your tears? Plagued by bad luck, broken dreams? Do evil shadows hound you? Hard times have you low? Well, search no further. You have found the help you need in the loving hands of the Reverend Mother Sister Light.

"This woman of God has been looking for you, and you have been looking for her, even if you didn't know it. Phone 555-5959, or stop in now at 6800 Candlepark, across from the K-Mart. She has saved the most important people in the world, and *she can save you!*"

(Organ music swells.)

"Mother Sister Light! She is the candle in your darkness. Her wisdom burns for you. Call now. Satisfaction guaranteed. Let the light of Mother Sister Light shine in your life!"

(Voices sing, "Let it shine, shine, shine.")

"The Reverend Mother Sister Light has the answer to your burning question. She's waiting for you. So drop in at 6800 Candlepark, or phone 555-5959. Mother Sister Light—she will tell you what you want to know *before you utter a word!*"

("Call on me," voices sing, climbing up the scale. "I am the light!")

The recording stops abruptly, but the tape reels on. After a moment of silence a phantom voice says, "When." More silence, then the tape ends.

The small round room is hot, and the heat seems to come from inside Buddy. He is burning up as he rewinds the tape. Nothing else holds his attention for long—not the heat, not his patchy beard, not his smell or his ragged clothes.

He rewinds only part of the tape and plays the ending with the critical, dangling "When," listening three more times until it is clear what he must do. Shutting off the tape recorder, he rises unsteadily to his feet. For good luck and

bravery, he cocks his finger at the roof of his parents' house, takes aim, fires. The house explodes in slowest motion. His mother and father are sucked out headfirst, launched into the sky on their way to a distant orbit. Someone laughs. Leaves whisper in the wind. His parents' house still stands; this was only practice. Shiva quickens his dance.

Buddy descends the narrow stairs, no longer afraid. He doesn't care if someone else is in the house. He's invisible. An old trick, learned when he was young so his parents couldn't see him.

He enters the bedroom where he saw the phone earlier. He's on the right course. These are his friends. He will be helped to a final answer, helped without uttering a word.

Buddy dials the number and holds his breath. Nothing he will ever hear again may be as important as what he listens for now. In the middle of the fourth ring, a deep voice answers.

The voice draws out the word; the message burns a path right through him, empties him of air. Noises roar in his ears. On the verge of dropping the phone, he thinks to double-check.

"Repeat what you just said." Buddy's own voice is hoarse. It's a terrible effort to speak.

"What Ah said, precisely, was 'Yes.'" The voice sounds impatient, not very friendly, but Buddy knows this is just an act. "Now, if you callin' for Light, fire away, buddy."

Buddy gasps.

"We ain't got all day, you know," the voice says.

Buddy can't speak. He feels like he's been hit by an avalanche. Finally he manages to say into the phone, "Now? You mean *now?*"

"You got it. Now or never."

Buddy lets the receiver drop and runs from the room.

T he low sun fills the living room with dazzling orange light. Pausing in the doorway on her way to the kitchen, Katherine notes the overlit family scene before her: mother, father, two children.

This might be any August sunset of the past thirty years at the Pelham Lake house except for a few alterations—the age of the principles, their size, their clothes. It can't go on forever, Katherine thinks. Someone should record this slice of vanishing Americana, complete with its Edwardian observances (who dresses up in a summer house anymore, for instance?). She imagines TV cameras positioning themselves, an interviewer approaching.

I: Tell us about these people.
K: Why me?
I: Why not you?
K: Well, I'm not really one of them. My truth is a little slant.
I: Quick. You're on. Roll 'em!

(The cameras would pan around the room, pausing on the unremarkable but expensive furniture, not the kind anyone in his right mind would put in a house that's closed up over half the year. A fireplace of white-painted brick at one end of the long room; at the other, beyond the grouping of sofas and wing chairs, a sturdy wooden bridge table. Bookshelves where odd bedfellows nestle: J. P. Marquand next to Kahlil Gibran, Tennyson next to the American Kennel Club *Book of Dogs*, several Hemingways by a running foot of Nancy Drews.)

    Katherine clears her throat.
    That's my husband, David, she would say to the interviewer, the one kneeling on the hearth starting a fire. There's a chill in the air tonight.
    Behind David, on the arm of the wing chair nearest the fireplace, is his mother, Charlotte. Notice how she leans down to say things into her son's ear a little coquettishly. She loves secrets, yet I suspect she may be simply telling him how to do his job or admonishing him not to make a mess. He doesn't seem to mind.
    As you can see, Charlotte is tall and slender. When she stands, her bearing is regal. She considers good posture essential. "Stand straight as a ramrod," I've heard her tell her grandsons, and with great seriousness, too—as if she believed standing straight might shape them up morally.

(Charlotte bends out of the sunlight as she talks to her son. When she pulls back from him, white hair becomes a brilliant aura. For a second the woman seems far too vivid. She leans toward David again; out of the sun, she is once more herself. Charlotte does not put a hand on her son's shoulder as one might do in her situation—for balance, for intimacy, simply for emphasis. Would the camera pick that up, the way she seems to hold herself back?)

Charlotte is a handsome woman, permanently tan from playing golf regularly for almost fifty years. She is sixty-eight, and her golf scores would be decent for a player half her age. Charlotte is now as devoted to golf as she once was to her children and her hospital volunteer work. She smiles often, quickly and automatically. Since she's a perfectionist, she's often in a state of disappointment. You can detect this in her fast-fading smile and her eyes, which sometimes go blank. Charlotte talks about people not being "like us," and her most crushing insult is that someone is *déclassé*.

Charlotte projected great ambitions onto her son and would be thoroughly pleased with his accomplishments were it not for me, his wife, whom I believe she secretly regards as an interloper. I do not take this personally; it comes with the territory. She treats her grandsons, Tony and Will, with strained pity. Her efforts to herd them along to the Episcopal church have been greeted with stupefied looks and a lack of enthusiasm. Has she written them off? She wouldn't admit it, of course, but then she rarely says what's on her mind.

Behind Charlotte is David's father, Clayton. His hands are folded on his knees, giving him an uncharacteristic look of serenity. Clayton is a doctor (eye, ear, nose, and throat) who, at seventy, still practices. He wouldn't know what to do without his work. His wife has pressed him for years to retire to Florida. This tension between them, like so many other things, is not publicly discussed.

Clayton is engaged in a halting conversation with his daughter Bitsy who's sitting on the couch. He doesn't appear to notice she has to look right into the sun to talk to him. She's shielding her eyes with her hands.

(The camera would show Clayton is very distinguished, rosy-cheeked and fit. Through the comb lines of his white hair, you can see that even the top of his head is tanned.)

Bitsy is thirty-five, four years younger than her brother David. She is compactly built, and her long dark hair is pulled off her face with a single barrette. Bitsy seems to be listening to her father, but more likely she's daydreaming, bored as she often is when she's not around horses. Bitsy owns four or five, and has ridden horses all her life.

For a number of years, she has run a program of equestrian therapy at a small private mental hospital near her home, and she attaches great spiritual weight to a person's intimacy with horses. It's not difficult to imagine Bitsy, whose avid, lifelong preoccupation has been with four-legged creatures, dealing with people who aren't right in the head.

Her mother heaved a sigh of relief five years ago when Bitsy married her husband, a divorced but otherwise respectable polo-playing doctor. All along, she feared Bitsy would run off with a stable boy, a mental patient, or, possibly worse, remain single. Bitsy is seven months pregnant now, though her rust-colored shift, patterned with horse heads, hides her condition.

I used to think every family would turn out to be strange up close. The families of my friends invariably became comfortingly queerer the better I knew them—flawed and human as my own. Little things—the unmar-

ried uncle who lived in the attic and tippled, the grandmother who talked to herself night and day, the younger brother who went from school to school "misunderstood"—fascinated me. But, frankly, the only thing particularly odd about this family, which has dragged golf clubs and tennis rackets and horses in vans to this summer house for so many years, is that there's *nothing* really strange about them. I used to search for some chink in their armor of blandness, but that was wishful thinking. This is no armor, this is it. They don't talk, not seriously. They don't get angry. Duty, not love or pleasure, seems to motivate their gatherings. They circle around one another so politely that the point seems *not* to connect.

I: Finish the room before we lose the light.

That's Bitsy's husband, Neil Wellend, Katherine would continue, there at the bridge table leafing through a *Sports Illustrated.* Neil is an orthopedist, a tall, slightly beefy man who always seems drawn along by his wife like a huge child. For some reason I suspect Neil of having some fabulous secret life. In the years I've known him, he's frequently seemed ready to make a pass— like one of those boys from college who, when they finally struck, would have you on top of the coats in the guest room before you knew it, and say peculiar things in your ear.

I: Aren't you forgetting someone?

K: My husband, you mean?

I: Cough up.

David stands up in front of the crackling fire. Since he shaved off his beard last week and lost a quick eight or ten pounds, he looks younger, almost boyish.

"Three cheers for the fire starter!" Charlotte Watters trills. "This is more like it."

Katherine rouses herself. Enough of this silly business. She ducks down the hall into the kitchen and decides not to worry about these people whose overlapping visits were engineered by Charlotte for the sake of reunion.

"Hey, Kitty!" Before Katherine can back away, Neil, Bitsy's husband, has his arm around her and is squeezing her shoulder. "What's up with you?" he asks. "I was watching you back there. You looked gloomy."

"Neil, how could I be gloomy with all our loved ones around the hearth?" He kneads her shoulder, then moves his hands toward her neck. Usually he gives her the creeps, but tonight his touch feels so good that she wants to ask him to keep it up.

"You're tight," he says.

"Don't I wish," she answers, pouring nuts into a silver bowl.

"Here," she says, handing the bowl to him.

"What am I supposed to do with this?" he asks. She's given him a task that's beneath him, woman's work.

"Run it into the living room, will you? I've got to get something out of the oven."

"Kitty!" David calls from the other room. "Do you want a drink? What would you like?"

Sodium pentathol. A Valium drip. Whatever you've got that will put me out for the next three days. "Scotch," she calls back. She takes a collapsing wheel of brie from the oven and burns her hand. "Shit," she mutters.

"Oh, my dear," Charlotte Watters says, breezing into the kitchen. "I can't imagine why I'm permitting you to treat me like a guest in my own house." Charlotte peers at the cheese. "Hmmm," is all she says, as if Katherine were serving disguised bat guano.

"Let me take that for you," her mother-in-law says, and carries the brie out of the kitchen as if she were in a hurry to get rid of it. At the door she stops. "Kitty, your getup, it's fetching. So bright! I thought it was the sunshine, but I can see now it wasn't." She shakes her head and is gone.

Katherine looks down at her red silk shirt and pants. Her face flames. She should have worn something more conservative. Suddenly the interviewer is back, sticking the microphone under her nose.

I: These people really get your goat, don't they?

K: Look at it this way. It's a better place than

most to have a sinus infection or break an arm.

I: That wasn't the question.

K: Well, David has always been my ally, but sometimes I'm not exactly sure of him. There's Tony, of course; he thinks they're all stuffy.

I: Unlike this hypothetical lover of yours?

"Knock it off," Katherine says to herself. Why do things hit her so hard these days? She's alternately full of lewd and wonderful longings for a person she scarcely knows, or moping around for a loss she can't put her finger on. Possibly she's cracking up.

"Kitty!" David calls.

"Mom! Mom!" It's Will.

"Is she still in the kitchen?" Bitsy.

"Coming," Katherine yells. These days there doesn't seem enough of her to go around. Maybe it's all this cleaning.

"Here you are," Bitsy says, coming down the hall. "Kitty, that color is simply gorgeous on you. With your hair . . ." David hands Katherine a drink, and she touches the icy glass to her cheek.

"Come," he orders. He takes Katherine's free hand and pulls her through the kitchen toward the back porch.

"We'll be right back," Katherine calls over her shoulder to Bitsy and Will.

"When do we eat?" Will asks.

"At eight-thirty," David tells him. "If you're hungry, have some cheese."

"Cheese? You mean, that thing's cheese? Yecch."

On the porch, David motions her to sit. In the twilit quiet Katherine feels self-conscious.

"What is it?" she finally asks.

"Listen," he says, "what's wrong with you tonight?"

"Me?" she says. "Nothing. Really."

"Well, you don't seem exactly welcoming."

She shuts her eyes against the sound of his voice. A loon cries near the shore of the lake, the noise enveloping everything in a primitive chill. Doesn't he know by now how she feels about his family? Doesn't he understand anything?

"It's only for a few days," he says. "Let's not mope."

Katherine is grateful that it's too dark for him to see her face. "I suppose you want me to go into my merry little tap-dance routine, something on that order?"

"Sure," he says. "Why not?"

Wearing the red shirt and cap of Skip's Bar, Robin positions himself under a drive so high that the ball catches the rays of the setting sun and, suspended in space, turns white. He moves backward, coaxing the ball short of the home-run trees, watching it turn dark and fall, hearing in advance the *whump* the ball will make when it meets his glove.

Before Robin's mitt encloses the ball, he knows that they're winners. He throws the ball toward the infield in a high curving arc, feeling a sudden extravagance of connections—with

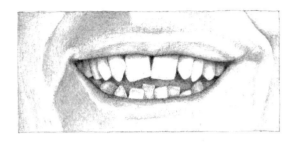

pitcher, ball, batter, bat, you name it. Anything, everything, seems possible.

More light hearted than he's felt in months, Robin heads in, stopping outside first base to kick up his heels. He accepts the congratulations of his teammates, then lopes on toward the just retired batter, hugging the dark-haired man, Ben Abruzzo, son of one of the Abruzzo brothers whose "Abruzzo Bros. Landscaping" adorns Ben's yellow shirt in white script.

"Son of a bitch," Ben growls. "I had that one figured for the trees. What happened? The wind come up?"

Robin can't stop smiling. "C'mon," he says, "I'll buy you a beer."

A few minutes later at Skip's Bar, listening to Ben's version of his split with Carol Ann, Robin wonders whether Ben's dark mood is due to leaving Carol Ann or to missing that home run. Could it be due to losing—as he hit the game's last ball—some momentum that Robin pulled down from the sky and turned into his own?

"It was a bad scene," Ben is saying. He sits sideways in the booth, his back against the knotty-pine wall, and seems to address the air.

"It kept coming back to the same thing—I think she wanted to get married." He shakes his head. "She had this *Father Knows Best* family in mind, you could just feel it. I finally go, 'You want me to hustle so you can play house, right?' And she clammed up. Then I go, 'Carol Ann, listen, I'm not ready for that,' and I'd be talking to myself. I began to think I was crazy. Finally I left."

Ben stares off toward the bar. Robin follows his gaze. He's aware his silence isn't exactly comforting.

"Well, anyway," Ben says after a while, "that's the deal on Carol Ann. I could do the romance bit, but the other . . . and the way she began to act like a deaf mute, well . . ." He shrugs.

Robin pours the last of the pitcher into Ben's glass. He's ready to leave.

"I'm not sure," Ben says, "but I think she took it pretty hard. If you see her at the barn or something, be nice to her."

Robin wonders briefly if Ben's idea of being nice to Carol Ann would include his going to bed with her. Maybe he'd been a fool not to. He also wonders about Constantina and Mars but doesn't ask. The last thing he wants to bring up is Carol Ann's visit to the barn the night before.

"Cheer up, Ben," Robin says. "Everyone will be okay. You'll find another girl." Ben doesn't say he already has.

"Sure," Ben says without conviction. Robin studies his face. Ben looks like someone from a cigarette ad, dark-mustached, handsome. His teeth are perfect.

"More beer?" Ben asks.

"No, I'd better get back. There's a new guy working at the stables. I should check."

"You and those horses," Ben says, extricating himself from the booth. "They're like your whole family, man."

Outside Skip's, the night is clear. A quarter moon hangs in the sky.

"Hey, that storm was a bitch," Ben says as they get into the truck. "Things really took off. How about that guy in the car?"

"The one who flew through the air?" Robin laughs. "Amazing."

"One of our greenhouse roofs was shattered," Ben says. "Is the barn's okay?"

"It's fine," Robin says. He doesn't mention the small hole in the roof he fixed this morning, or the mountain of stray vegetables he carted back to his neighbor at Mona Edwards's insistence. Nor does he mention the red Weber grill top not three feet behind Ben at this moment in the back of the truck. He had meant to drop it off on Carol Ann's porch earlier. He can't figure out how it made its way clear over to the Newcombs'.

"So how you doin'?" Ben asks as they head down Jefferson toward Ben's car.

"Not bad," Robin says.

"You got something new going?" Ben ventures.

Robin thinks, what the hell. "I met this amazing woman," he says. "Really incredible." It's a harmless diversion. "She lives up there," Robin adds, pointing toward the dark rise of Jefferson.

"Her old man must be rich," Ben says.

"I expect he is." Robin smiles. "He's a doctor."

"Hmmm."

"Of course, she's older than I am," Robin says.

"A lot?"

"Ten years, maybe more."

Ben misses several beats before saying casually, "No sweat."

"And she has two kids." Robin is into the swing of this now.

"Two kids? Man, is this some kind of joke?" Ben is nearly shouting.

Robin laughs. "It's nothing," he says, "just an idea." But something overtakes his amusement. Even joking about another woman feels like a declaration of freedom from Jannie.

"Listen," Ben says as Robin pulls up next to his car. "You watch yourself." He sounds concerned.

"Sure." Robin laughs. "You bet. You too."

Passing the Watters' house again, Robin thinks about Katherine Watters. She's attractive, sure, but mostly it's her life that appeals to him, all secure and rich and settled. The things a doctor gave her, what they've made of them together. He'd like that kind of life himself, prosperous and smart, *full steam ahead.* Lately his own life hasn't been going anywhere. Maybe Jake was right. It was time he paid attention to more than Jannie's absence.

Tonight this thought hits him like a revelation, as if a door suddenly flew open, revealing vistas he hasn't glimpsed in ages, chances he's almost forgotten. Unburdened, he parks his truck near the barn and gazes upward. The moon is lower now, the sky heavy with stars. He raises his arms heavenward in what begins as a stretch but becomes something more, so that for a moment he holds the night in his arms.

Then he jumps down from the truck and tosses his keys high into the air. He can't see a thing yet somehow knows exactly when to reach out and catch them. Left-handed too.

"Ju work by hand all the days?" the small brown man asks with great concentration. Through shooting pain, Harry tries to decipher his meaning by looking into the man's face but sees only an implacable round dish with what looks like the end of a thumb for a nose. Tinted glasses: what's keeping them up?

The effort momentarily takes Harry's mind off the massive coronary he seems to be having—has *been* having, as a matter of fact, for hours. By his reckoning, he should be dead now.

"I think what he means, Harry, dear, is if you do a lot of manual labor."

Harry groans and starts to shake his head. This hurts like crazy. He attempts to tell Irene to take the thermometer out of his mouth but produces only a prolonged moan. She pats his arm comfortingly.

The small brown man, Dr. A. Tolentino, according to his blue plastic name tag, doesn't bother to look up. He is writing away on a clipboard. Spanish? Chinese? Whatever the language, the man doesn't seem concerned that Harry is dying. Neither does Irene, whose widowhood Harry regards as imminent.

"Jour es-tomach hurt? Jour tum-tum, eh?"

Harry shakes his head wearily, wishing he was strong enough to choke the little bastard. His stomach, for chrissake!

"Ah. Jour intestines," the man pursues, "is okey-dokey?"

The pain on his left side is terrible, yet Harry grows calm. He is already dead, yes. This is hell; the devil babbles.

"I beg your pardon?" Irene asks pleasantly. Ever since this morning she has been unusually pleasant. She doesn't falter now. Probably just wants to give him a cheerful send-off.

The doctor turns to Irene, but his dark-tinted glasses makes it impossible to know what he's looking at. The little man repeats the

question, but Harry moves on, trying to lose himself in the institutional green wall. He wonders if his intestines *are* okey-dokey, all six—is it five?—miles of them. Probably not.

"Indigestion?" Irene suggests to the doctor. She pats her stomach.

"Jes?" he says, cocking his head worriedly. Then he makes a clicking noise, kind of a tut-tut, and hurriedly hands Irene a small metal pan.

I am a stranger in a strange land, Harry thinks.

"Oh, no," Irene says. "Not me." She smiles. The doctor smiles back, clearly confused.

Harry shuts his eyes. This is a test. They are all failing.

"He obviously wants to know something about your intestines, Harry," Irene says sotto voce. "Do you think I should tell him about your mother's diverticulitis?"

Harry looks at her. There is no one in the world who cares. His mother would have cared. But she has been dead for fifteen years. Gone. Perhaps he will see her soon, reunited at last. "Mother," he will say, "they treated me shabbily. No one ever loved me the way you did."

"Bowls," Tolentino nearly shouts. He seems very pleased with himself. "I es-pik of bowls."

The pain in his chest is suddenly more acute, yet Harry hardly notices this, he is so taken by the possibilities of this new conversational tack. He considers salad bowls, cereal bowls, finger bowls. Irene, obviously more resourceful, rises from the metal chair and questioningly gives A. Tolentino a graceful, if abbreviated, demonstration of bowling.

Is this the woman he's married to? Playing charades while he's dying?

The little man shakes his head.

Super Bowls, Hollywood Bowls, Harry thinks. Maybe this is some kind of game show they've walked into, not an emergency room. Toilet bowls? Where are the doddering old docs of his youth? At least they spoke a familiar language. Pipe bowls? Boll weevils?

"Bowels?" Irene ventures tentatively.

"Jes, of course. Bowls," Tolentino says rather sternly. Harry rolls his eyes at Irene. She takes his hand. "Don't worry," she says softly.

He's as good as dead. Why should he worry?

"Oh, I'm sure they're fine," Irene says reassuringly to Tolentino. She is acting as if this were the real world. "They always are," she adds.

She knows about his bowels? Harry is mildly shocked, having underestimated the powers of Mrs. Snoop. The things we learn living with people, he thinks. Their smells, their peculiar habits. Irene and the old Victorian water trick. Still turns on the faucet when she goes to the bathroom. He used to kid her about it. Of course, she would know when he took a dump.

Actually it was while he was sitting on the downstairs toilet dodging the painter who'd started work upstairs that Harry concluded that the sharp pains he was having probably meant curtains. He'd decided to clean up the yard, anyway. Make less of a mess dying outside. He wasn't absolutely certain he was dying then. Now he is. All day long, dragging branches around, he was simply testing the theory that you either die or get well. No question now which he'd do. But when?

The doctor—he is not really a doctor, it occurs to Harry, he's a waiter from the restaurant across the street, someone's houseboy—removes the thermometer from Harry's mouth. Harry glances down in time to see the man write the number thirty-seven on the clipboard. There it is in black and white; he's been dead for hours. His body temperature is close to freezing. Maybe he could request cryogenesis, is that the word? It would hardly be any trouble at this point, get a discount. Thaw him out when they have a cure for heart failure. Reincarnation.

He doesn't feel cold. He feels a little warm, as a matter of fact, maybe from being out in the sun all day, working hard at getting well or dying. He'd managed to do quite a bit for a dying man. Leave her with a clean yard, anyway. If not a son. Better off with a clean yard. Let the other go. She could sell the house, get out of town fast. Change her name to Nicolle if she wanted to. *Nicolle?*

"Come," Tolentino orders Irene. Irene doesn't bother to say good-bye but only turns and smiles. Harry watches their exit helplessly, his left side scalding. Painfully he shifts his gaze to the window for a second, while they linger in the doorway.

It is almost dark outside now. PARK flashes on and off in green neon. PARK. The word looks strange, as if he's never seen it before. PARK. It suddenly dawns on him that PARK spells KRAP backward. CRAP. All these years and he'd never

noticed. A dying man's revelation. What else has he missed?

With this unexpected insight Harry experiences a surge of resolve, what he takes for death's second wind. He turns his head to address all that's still visible of Irene in the doorway—one foot and ankle. She has lovely ankles.

"How about the cardiogram, Irene," he says as loud as he can. "Ask him when they do that. When I'm a corpse?" He has never stopped loving her ankles. He has always been loyal to them.

Tolentino pokes his little head in the door. He looks to Harry like an insect. "Ju also have shess pains? Es bery es-strange."

Sudden anger nearly blinds Harry. "That's why I'm here," he says, his face reddening. "Remember? My left side—or did that get lost in translation?"

"Harry," Irene scolds gently, coming back into the room.

At that moment a tall man in a pink shirt and bright patchwork pants breezes past Tolentino and Irene, all smiles. They should be sending the undertaker dressed in black, Harry thinks. Instead they send someone decked out like a clown.

"Sorry to keep you waiting," the man says. He smells of whiskey. First a dwarf, now a drunk. "I'm Dr. Atkins," the man in pink says, and Harry begins to relax in spite of himself. Atkins helps Harry lie down on the table and lightly feels around on his chest. Harry winces with pain. After a time Atkins stops and, turning to Tolentino, takes the clipboard out of his hand and reads. He sets it down on a chair and pokes Harry again. Harry sucks in his breath. He never knew heart attacks hurt like this.

"I see by your chart here you must be a neighbor of one of my colleagues," Atkins says, still starring at Harry's chest. "Dave Watters?"

For some reason Harry wants to cry.

Irene says, "Why, yes!" and sounds thrilled.

"How long have you been suffering, exactly?" Atkins asks Harry.

Fifty years, Harry thinks, give or take a few months. "Since this morning." Atkins must know Watter's wife, who, Harry realizes, he hasn't thought of since that morning. Clearly his life is drifting away. Death setting in. Atkins pokes again. "God." Harry groans.

"Boyohboy," Atkins says. "You really did a job here. Our new resident from—where is it you're from, Tolentino?" Atkins asks, not turning around.

Through blinding pain Harry hears Tolentino say something completely incomprehensible.

"Where's that?" Atkins asks bluntly and without much attention as he helps Harry to a sitting position.

"Feeelee-penus," Tolentino says. Atkins turns around abruptly. Irene looks wary. Something makes Harry think this is where he came in.

Irene's face brightens. "The Philippines. Of course. Bataan. Am I right?" Here we go again, Harry thinks.

"Jes! Jes!" Tolentino says enthusiastically. "My Een-gles . . ." He smiles sheepishly.

The Bataan Peninsula, Harry considers, trying to remain calm. For this MacArthur marched.

"Ju been going there?" Tolentino asks hopefully. Atkins looks appalled and shakes his head. Irene says, "No, I'm sorry, I haven't. Maybe someday, though."

"Ju look me up, jes?" the little man says. Jes, Harry thinks. Rich American widows. Jes.

"We'll just get a picture of this," Atkins says, turning back to Harry. "But Tolentino's diagnosis seems right on target."

Massive coronary. Why doesn't he come right out and say it? "Don't you normally?" Harry ventures. All eyes are suddenly on him. He feels uncharacteristically meek. "Don't you as a rule . . ."

Atkins leans toward him, his brow wrinkled. "Don't we as a rule *what?*"

Harry clears his throat and is overtaken by an excruciating stab of pain. "A cardiogram?" he whispers. "Don't you? Pains in the chest? Normally?"

"You have a history of heart trouble?" Atkins asks suspiciously. "I didn't see anything about that on your chart."

Do broken hearts qualify? If so, he qualifies. But Harry shakes his head. Medicine is voodoo. What difference if they speak English or not?

"Well, then," Atkins says a little too genially, "we don't usually take a cardiogram unless there's some indication. Not for a routine thing like this."

Routine? Of course. Someone dies every thirty seconds. Someone's born. In and out. Routine.

Irene smiles and takes Harry's hand. "It's a rib, Harry, a rib. They think you've broken a rib. Dr. Tolentino tried to tell you earlier." She studies his face and waits. Harry stares at her blankly. "A rib," she repeats.

"Ribs," Atkins amends. "I'd say two or three of them, anyway. It's hard to tell until we get an X ray."

What is this, Harry wonders, some joke to ease the blow? But no, no one's laughing. You don't die from broken ribs. "Ribs?" Harry asks incredulously. Everyone, even Tolentino, nods and smiles.

Then he isn't a goner? He isn't dying? A wave of relief so intense that he has to clutch the table passes over him. It's the sweetest feeling he's ever known. He was ready for the worst. He's always ready for that. He wasn't ready for this thing that now comes like a gift—a second chance.

"Sure," Atkins says, "Just a couple of broken ribs. We'll get you down to X ray and then we'll know about it. How in the hell, I'd like to know, did you manage to do this? There's no outward trauma, so I can tell you didn't bung yourself."

But Harry, newly resurrected, can't find words. He is having trouble refocusing. Not dead? Not dying?

"Harry." Irene nudges him gently. "Try to think."

Harry attempts to do as he's been told. Giddiness slows him down as he spot-checks the morning. When did the pain start? Before the toilet, he thinks. After Nicolle. (Nicolle?) After the painter with his . . . Then it hits him. The zucchini. So you want a mammoth . . . oh, no. Harry starts to laugh again, right there in front of the three expectant faces, but pain quickly turns his laughter into something more like strangulation. "Zucchini," he sputters, and then moans.

Atkins looks at him skeptically. Tolentino is thoroughly confused once more. It is left to Irene to get the message and translate. "Oh, Lord," she says, breaking into a smile. "Of course. Oh, Harry, I know now!"

"Did he say zucchini?" Atkins asks her.

"It's a long story," Irene says. "But Harry had a real laughing fit this morning." And she smiles like someone who enjoyed watching. "I think you had to be there."

"Beats anything I've ever seen, but I guess a good laugh could do it. Anything's possible in this business." Atkins shakes his head.

Harry concentrates on the doctor's every word, trying to fend off the mammoth zucchinis that threaten to push everything else out of his mind. He's afraid he'll burst if he starts laughing again.

"Tolentino," Atkins says, "what we've got here is a happy man."

"Jes?" Tolentino is lost.

To help him out, Atkins clutches his stomach and says, "Ha-ha-ha-ha."

Tolentino looks alarmed. Irene catches Harry's eye and winks. Not Irene. He must be hallucinating.

An orderly wearing a hair net joins the crowd

with a wheelchair. "X ray," Atkins says. "Take him away." He hangs the clipboard on the back of the chair and looks down at Harry. "I guess there's no need to tell a fellow like you to smile for the camera. Someday I'll have to hear the joke."

"Choak?" Tolentino says puzzedly, then breaks into a beatific smile. In an unprecedented burst of fluency he says, "Choak. I know choak! Ju are a choaker, right?"

Why not? Harry thinks, and smiling back, he bobs his head in a movement that starts a new fire in his upper body. He suppresses a cry and keeps on smiling, propelled from behind by the orderly.

As he's sped down the corridor, Irene's heels clicking behind him, his heart goes out to the little Filipino, to Irene and Atkins, to the orderly, to the whole world. Silently he blesses them all. Munificence surrounds him; he cures everyone in his wake. Harry the Healer. Born again.

V oices come and go. One stays, a faint echoing "now or never," but it means no more than another voice that persistently demands, "Ticket. Ticket, please. We must have your ticket."

Ticket?

He checks his pockets. No ticket there, nothing except a candy wrapper and some coins. His father's voice says something about a yellow leather ticket with a blue spanch across it. Spanch? Buddy doubts his father ever said that, forgetting how much he'd read to him.

Buddy doubts more than that, forgetting everything for a time, and is surprised to find himself sitting hunched under a dining room table. The light is fading. "Ticket, please." Where has he been? "Ticket, ticket, ticket."

The dining room floor is cluttered with bright objects—place mats and napkins, tablecloths, one of them red with green Christmas trees on it. Wrapping paper and ribbons lie in one corner amid shards of vases and serving dishes.

"Ticket, please. Ticket. Have you lost your ticket?"

The disorder around him is puzzling until he remembers he has lost something besides a ticket. Or hadn't found it. Emboldened by this fragment of memory, he ventures out from the safety of the table, oblivious to the absence of chairs, and proceeds on hands and knees across the chaotic dining room floor and into the kitchen.

He discovers that this room is also littered—with boxes and food, broken china, cans, pans. Rising to his feet, he picks his way to the sink. As he lowers his head to the faucet he sees a shattered jar oozing peanut butter. A jaunty Peter Pan leers up at him from the red label. He closes his eyes and drinks, grasping vague memories: things leaping off shelves, a heavy jar striking his foot. He had been looking for something. Peter Pan assaulted him.

"All children, except one, grow up." His father's voice again. Except one? Trying to make sense of this, Buddy stares down into the sink. Peter Pan slowly winks one round green eye, and Buddy is gripped by a fear that propels him out of the kitchen and up the back stairs.

"Ticket! Ticket!" The voice hounds him until he can no longer stand it, and he screams down the empty stairwell, "Shut up!" When he closes his mouth, he finds he has misplaced himself. Was he going up? Or down?

He chooses up because he is closer to the top. At the entrance to the second floor he hears a tiny, but steady, high-pitched electronic whine coming from down the hall. In dread, Buddy sidesteps into the room on his right and slams the door, leaning hard against it.

When he catches up with himself, he realizes he faces a wall covered with pictures of motorcycles—large photographs, posters, drawings—and at the center, above the bed, a poster of someone in a pink suit holding a guitar. No one he has ever seen, yet there's something familiar about the curled, pouting mouth, the half-closed eyes. Like Elvis, yes. Elvis, who blew up like a balloon and died.

Buddy shudders.

Shifting around, he spies a wild-haired, bearded creature, so gaunt and threatening that Buddy grabs a small lamp from the dresser and throws it at the stranger.

Glass flies around the room, and in blinding fear he flings himself through a door and slams it shut behind him. Something brushes over his face in the pitch-dark. He bats at it, inadvertently pulling the chain that turns on the closet light. In the sudden brightness he sinks to the floor and sobs, comforted by his own noises.

After a while he stops. He feels steadier.

Then a new fear bites hard: He is failing. But failing at what? What was it he was supposed to be doing? He's lost his place. Also his ticket, he remembers now. With that he recalls other things lost: a voice that held him close and said, "Once there was a little bunny who wanted to run away"; a slender knife in a leather sheath; his scalding light; so many things. His losses are numerous and unruly. They crowd for his attention. But what was he supposed to be doing?

He looks up at the light bulb in anticipation of an answer, but he can't concentrate and keeps forgetting the question. On the chance that he's being watched, he tries to look busy by fumbling around on the closet floor. His movements are heavy, but he goes on, anyway, mechanically passing his hands over a large box of crayons, a hammer, two yellow tennis balls. He clutches a small pair of shoulder pads and tosses them aside, only half noting the dirty pair of cleated shoes tied to them. While moving the shoes out of his way he touches something that doesn't belong and cautiously extracts from one shoe a worn-out-looking pack of cigarettes. He studies the front of the package. When he turns it over, he finds a blue pack of matches tucked into the cellophane. He knows there is some connection here he can't make.

Then, with a loud cry, he recovers not only the memory of his mission but of his earlier futile search for matches as well. As he does, he's consumed with purpose. He jumps to his feet, throws open the closet door, and, heedless of the slivers of mirror all over the floor, he dashes for the narrow stairs, passing the attic door at the small landing where the stairs become steeper, pulling himself up and up until he bursts into the small round room.

It's almost dark, but he's not afraid. He leans into the towering heap of dining room chairs and books and newspapers he now remembers assembling earlier. He lights the cover of a paperback near the bottom.

The cover takes the flame poorly, but he's undaunted. He strikes another match and lights the book's pages, watching them flame with a thrill of success. In the small flickering light, he stares awestruck as the pictures of smokestacks on the book's cover shoot real flames and then disappear along with the title:

TURES
ERRY
INN

Tossing the flaming book higher up the pile, he throws in more lighted matches until the whole structure begins to crawl with fire. Sooner than he expected, the heat and smoke force him to back down the steps. His face is almost on a level with the floor, and he gazes up at shooting yellow flames as they escape the pile to lick the walls. A pillow explodes with a hissing noise, carrying flames to a basket on a windowsill.

Buddy stands halfway down the steep stairs, rocking and waiting, dazed by his own power, nearly silent inside. He feels like a different person.

Flames scuttle across the ceiling. They take hold of something at the center with a loud pop, followed by a crackling shower of sparks: the light. He waits, rocking, and marvels as fingers of flame begin to outline each window, most of them shut tight, so that the room's glare, doubled by reflection, becomes immensely brighter.

A windowpane explodes, but Buddy remains on the stairs. He knows the fire can't touch him. Cured now, whole, unafraid—nothing can touch him. And it was so simple.

Part of the flaming ceiling crashes down, and a fountain of sparks rises up crazily from the room. Buddy shields his eyes and makes out night and a slice of moon where the roof used to be.

It is almost too hot to breathe, yet a memory stops him from leaving: The moon is eating the Earth. Some book he'd read said that. The moon feeds.

The flames are close to the stairs now, the heat more intense. Taking one last look at the miraculous fiery room, Buddy discovers his old friend Shiva dancing at the center, feet going like mad—double time, triple time. Go, man, go!

Then he is off, down the ladderlike steps, even faster down the rest, his feet slapping the wood as fast as Shiva's, feet he suddenly realizes are bare. Bare? This slows him down, and losing his rhythm near the bottom, he stumbles and has to grope his way down into the hall. Didn't he once have shoes? He turns in the direction of the door. It is so dark.

"Ticket? Ticket? Ticket, please, ticket."

He dares to take a breath and gets a noseful

of acrid smoke. With that, his blazing vision returns, and self-assured once more, he fishes in his back pocket as he heads for the door.

"Ticket? Ticket?"

He flashes a flattened candy wrapper. "I'm with the press," he says to the wall, and boldly steps outside.

Mona sits at the conference table in the Lethem Town Hall trying to look attentive. Her eyes are trained upward, as if she is considering some fine point in the discussion. In fact, she's counting the sheaves of acanthus on the molding.

An empty chair separates her from the members of the Lethem Environmental Council, who drone on earnestly. Already she's had to sit through a lengthy catalog of storm damage. She found herself unable to care about all the caved-in garage roofs and lost barbecue grills around Lethem. She has her own problems. Now the chairman, Frannie Tolland, has steered the discussion around to Dinky's Donuts' unsightly dumpster, one more thing Mona doesn't give a hoot about that night. She's only there because Frannie summoned her and she didn't have the guts to say no.

Dale Beavers guffaws loudly. He is buck-toothed and gives her the willies. He must have the same effect on Frannie, too, because she looks at him as though he's a fly speck and says, "Let's stick to the point." Mona has no idea what the point is, or even why she's been asked here. She's bored stiff, and every time anyone mentions Dinky's, her mouth waters for one of their deep-fried apple crullers.

Mona watches Frannie's dark hair swing against her cheeks. She always has a good hair-cut, a fact that confounds Mona. It's the only concession to style Frannie makes. She's a large, muscular woman, and with her deep bullhorn voice, she's positively intimidating. When she told Mona the LEVC needed her advice on a pressing matter, Mona, like a coward, hopped to.

The talk washes around her. She watches mouths as they open and close, and thinks how ugly they are. Considered apart from faces, they're actually grotesque. Mona notes that Buffy Renwick, who can't be forty, has vertical wrinkles above her upper lip. Too much sun? A secret smoker? Not that Buffy, who always shows up in old Levi's carrying the torch for the sixties, would care about wrinkles. Mona can hear her say wrinkles are organic. Well, Mona thinks, Dale Beavers's overbite is organic, too, and there's something obscene about the way his mustache sits on top of his lip. Ugh. Next to Dale, Molly Turner is flicking her tongue in and out like a lizard, in a weird tic. Mona can't see the two mouths to her right very well, but as the one closest to her opens and speaks, she notes a purplish stain in one corner. Did Frank Smeal have blueberry cobbler for dinner? Blueberry pie? Possibly cheesecake with thick, gooey blueberry topping? Mona's stomach growls softly. She skipped dinner.

She hears someone say "solid wastes." Between trying to make sense of that and watching the fine spray of saliva Dale Beavers send over the table, Mona loses track of the conversation altogether. Solid wastes? She makes a note on the pad in front of her to call Super Septic Service in the morning. Lower down, she doodles lines of interconnected figure eights, small, writing-size, in case anyone is checking.

"This whole recycling thing," Frannie booms, "is a darn good way to raise people's awareness about those problems. Face it, a dump just won't cut it anymore. Not in Lethem." Frannie's beginning to develop unsightly pouches under her eyes, and her left lid, in particular, sags. Maybe the poor woman doesn't know you can get things like that fixed. "Snip, snip, stitch, stitch," Dr. Spatzer told Mona last week. "In and out the same morning. A couple of black eyes for two weeks, then better than new." It costs an arm and a leg, and Mona didn't commit herself. Now, however, inspired by the sight of Frannie's drooping eyes, she makes up her mind. "Call Spatzer," she writes under the reminder about the septic tank.

"Picture it, Mona," Frannie says, and Mona snaps to attention. "Our green earth literally being buried in materials that could be turned back into themselves!" Mona doesn't dare show her puzzlement. Into *themselves?*

"We've got just so much space," Frannie continues. "Where do we put it all? Where in the world?" She pauses theatrically, eyes right on Mona, so that Mona thinks: Good gracious, if Frannie's asking me where to put it, I haven't the faintest idea. To escape this uncomfortable eye contact, Mona begins writing furiously, hoping to appear businesslike. She writes: caviar-filled new potatoes, roast leg of lamb with peppercorn crust, sauté of fresh green beans and ripe tomatoes, Bibb lettuce and vinaigrette. Mona stops, stumped by dessert, and racks her brain for something a little different.

"Everests of it," Frannie thunders.

"Continents of it, when you think of it,"

horrible Dale Beavers chimes in. Frannie looks down her nose at him.

Baked Alaska, of course! She hasn't had that in ages.

"Look," Frannie says directly to Mona, "besides violating our air and water and natural resources, we're probably deforming the planet. You get the picture, it's grim." She gives a little snort and shakes her head.

The only picture Mona gets is one of North America bulging, splaying until it meets England—Spain?—spreading west. Would Lethem wind up in the middle of the Atlantic, the Atlantis of the twenty-first century?

"We've tried to prioritize this thing, Mona," Frannie says, and Mona feels like she's being scolded. "We know you could make it work, right here in Lethem—our little corner of the world, heh, heh. Face it, you've got clout in this town."

Mona peers at her. Heads are nodding all around the table. She's not sure what Frannie wants. As for clout, well, Frannie's just trying to butter her up. Mona doesn't have clout, she thinks, all she has is perpetual motion, running around like a chicken with its head off.

"The energy angle's the hot one, naturally." Frannie says this as if Mona has expressed eagerness. "How many people in Lethem realize you get a seventy-four percent savings on energy when you recycle scrap steel?"

Goodness, Mona thinks. Should she care about this? Maybe Sam was right. Maybe she was better off before when she used to stay at home and wouldn't in her craziest dreams have attended a meeting of the LEVC. *Least* of all the LEVC. Of course she was fat then, a slob, but she was happy. And Sam stayed at home too.

Frannie passes Mona pamphlets and brochures. Mona hardly glances at them but stacks them neatly. The truth is, she muses, taking a book Frannie hands her and staring blindly at its cover, if she stopped flying around from one project to another, she would probably gain back every single pound she lost. Oh, woe, she thinks, it isn't easy staying thin, not with this appetite, anyway. It means always being on the go. (It means some other things, too, ones she'd rather not think about.) Constant vigilance, ready at the drop of a hat to banish from her thoughts the calming power of chunky peanut butter mounded high on a spoon; ripe Brie on salty corn chips; oily slabs of garlicky salami topped with Dijon mustard and a dab of mayonnaise; chocolate, almost any kind of chocolate. (She'll do Dale Beavers one better and start to drool if she isn't careful. Good gravy!)

"Listen, kiddo," Frannie says to her, "you could get this thing off the ground in no time flat. You've got the network, and we need your help. How about it, what do you say?"

Frannie stops and looks at Mona so expectantly that Mona has to fight the urge to run from the room. If only she had a better idea what Frannie wanted. She could shoot herself for not paying attention. Across the table, Frannie looms, larger and more threatening than she's ever seemed before.

"Well," Mona says, stalling.

"Can we take that for a yes, I hope?"

Best to get it over with. "Okay," Mona says, "Sure." What a wimp you are, Mona, she says to herself. What a perfect wimp.

"Super!" Frannie belts out, and the people around the table nod and smile. "Now listen," Frannie says. "We won't keep you. I'll get in touch with you later in the week. In the meantime take a look at this," and she hoists a bulging cardboard folder in Mona's direction. Mona clamps it under her arm, and hurries to the door.

Kay's red VW is parked at the curb next to a green trash container. Mona overcomes the urge to pitch everything Frannie gave her right in and drops it instead in a heap in the backseat. Why didn't she bother to listen? What in heaven's name has she got herself into now? Something to do with garbage. Garbage! "Jerk," she mutters to herself. "Sucker." The clock on the bank flashes 10:03/78°, and Main Street is quiet except for the usual crowd around Scoop's Ice Cream store. "Nitwit," she says, turning up Jefferson. What will Sam say now? Garbage!

Why can't she learn to say no? she wonders.

Why can't she learn to say N-O, No? Kay's done that for years, and look at her. Lovely things happen to Kay, like that Robin person. At the thought of him Mona flushes. The previous night at the barn she wanted to touch him—all that young, firm, muscular flesh, nothing sagging anywhere. Lord.

Abruptly Mona turns right. Crossing a narrow bridge full of chuckholes, she pulls up in front of the 7-11. The store is empty except for the checker, who's wearing earphones and boogying around in front of the gum. When she sees Mona, she jerks the earphones off. For appearances' sake Mona takes half a gallon of skim milk from the cooler. Then, on her way past the candy, she grabs a big bag of M&M's and, as an afterthought, a fried pie for Scott. She pays for her groceries and heads back to the car. The checker returns to her silent dancing.

Mona tells herself she's had a particularly trying day. The glass people crawling all over the house fixing windows, the pool company draining the pool. The tow truck she waited for all afternoon to take away her squished car never did show up. Then that ridiculous meeting. Garbage?

She sets the bag on the front seat and pulls out the sack of candy, ripping it open with her

teeth. By the time she turns back on Jefferson, her mouth is full of the sugar-coated discs. She resists the urge to chew. They melt and she tastes chocolate. Ooohhh.

Mona's world rights itself. Her indignation at having been railroaded into some dumpy job by Frannie Tolland vanishes. The empty, rusty feeling in her stomach disappears. She puts another handful of candy into her mouth, and glancing in the rearview mirror to find the street behind her empty, she thrusts her hand into the bag and tosses this handful out of the window. One for her, one for her conscience. She hears the candy tick-tick-tick as it scatters on the asphalt. The cheerful little noise makes her smile. Another handful of candy into her mouth, another into the street. By now the bag is nearly empty, and she feels much better. She captures a single M&M between her teeth and gently cracks it, awed by its power to soothe. That king who turned things into gold, she thinks; boy, did he miss the boat. If she had her wish, everything would be chocolate. Well, not quite everything. . . .

The urgent sound of sirens interrupts her reverie, and before she can make sense of this, two fire trucks zoom right past her. Rounding the bend of Jefferson behind them, Mona is stunned to see flames leaping off the Watters' roof. The VW plows into the curb; its motor stalls. Where Kay's round room should be, there is only a glowing, ghostly skeleton lapped by flames.

Mona stares as the flames rise and fall. She wants to believe it's not happening. The blaze is real, though; it's happening, all right. By the time she collects herself enough to start the car, the fire engines have reached the Watters' house from the alley. Firemen dash around the yard, tugging at hoses, hoisting ladders. The flames cower under a sudden stream of water.

Mona's stomach turns inside out. She remembers the fried pie and tears open the smooth, fleshy paper, devouring the soggy pastry so quickly, she inadvertently eats part of the wrapping.

She coughs, chokes it down, and with her eyes tearing, flings the candy bag and what's left of the pie wrapper into the bushes. Her tires squeal as she takes the corner of the alley.

Harry sits rigidly upright in front of the bedroom TV. Without the antenna that flew off in the storm, reception is muddled, the sound little more than a dry crackling. Shadowy shapes swim into view, jerked off every now and then in an electronic spasm that clears the screen. What follows is a moment of vivid, empty television blue, oddly soothing in its improbable color, like water in the Caribbean.

The jumbled images return, and Harry weighs the risk of getting up to fiddle with the dials. He'll wait for Irene.

The TV clears its throat again, turns blue, and in an odd lurch of time Harry collides with himself as a young Naval officer almost thirty years before. A fine morning breeze stirs the tropical air as he salutes some faceless dignitary over whose shoulder the Pacific glows palely. Strong and erect, Harry is on his way to a war (a conflict, they called it) that of course can't touch him. If someone were to tell him the deck he's standing on on that gentle morning would be nearly blown to fiery smithereens within the month, he would only laugh. He possesses the wonderful lunacy of youth: immortality.

This memory vanishes, and Harry is once more alone with the buzzing TV and the burning in his chest. His upper body feels like it's held in a vise. He wonders if the yards of wide adhesive Tolentino wrapped around him might be merely a diversion to take his mind off the real problem, two fractured ribs.

When he confronts his broken-down condition ("A fluke," Atkins said. "You couldn't do this again if you tried."), Harry is unnerved. What does it say about him that he ruined himself laughing? Or worse, that he gave himself up for dead?

Harry shifts his attention to the TV as the blurry pastel picture disappears and returns as a black-and-white negative, sharper and clearer than anything he's ever gotten with the antenna up. Fascinated, Harry follows three perfectly reversed figures as they bounce over the water in a speedboat. Abruptly this inside-out aberration is whipped off the screen, replaced by lazy, drifting horizontal lines.

"Now then," Irene says, bustling into the room carrying a tray. She hands him a tall glass of ginger ale. "Just what the doctor ordered," she says cheerily, and then adds, "Of course that's *my* translation." She laughs.

"Spare me," Harry groans, and takes a drink. He's parched. "Thanks," he says when he comes up for air. He's amazed to be able to swallow; what happens below his throat is anybody's guess.

"And I brought a sandwich in case you're hungry," she says, and sets the tray on a nearby table.

Unaccustomed to her helpfulness, Harry stammers his thanks. He's about to ask her if she can do anything with the TV when she moves toward his chair, undisturbed by the confusion on the screen. Gently she puts a hand on his shoulder. "Dear Harry," she says, and strokes the back of his neck. Harry is so astonished that he tenses momentarily. Then he takes her other hand.

"You've been . . . well, terrific," he says, and immediately feels self-conscious.

"You weren't so bad yourself," Irene answers.

"Not me," he says, thinking how strange and formal they sound. He wonders if she knows he thought he was a goner.

"Hush," she says, putting a stop to their awkwardness. "Relax." The two of them hold hands silently, staring straight ahead as if the mindless squiggles and jerks on the TV were the most riveting things they had ever seen.

"I love you," Irene whispers. Harry is so floored that he turns his head without a thought to the blazing pain this movement will exact from him. He's shocked to see her eyes full of tears. Irene continues to stare at the TV.

"I . . . uh . . . I," he starts. He's unable to continue for the welling-up inside him, a warmth so unaccustomed that the flames in his chest seem to have spread. "I . . . oh . . . Irene." *Love:* Why can't he say it? Out of shape for laughter, out of practice at love. Yet isn't love as good a word as any for what's come over him now?

"Love . . ." he tries. "Love you," he adds. The *I* never makes it.

"Shhh," she says, still not looking at him. "Shhh."

In the silence between them, life seems to pause. Who would have thought that the two of them would be trying to say these things? It's almost as if they slipped out of the present into a past he only faintly remembers. Still, he's wary.

"Change . . ." he says, on his way to delivering the idea that something so sudden might be merely a crazy accident.

"Oh, of course," Irene says, and darts toward the TV.

"No, no." He shakes his head.

She looks at him uncertainly over her shoulder. "Turn it off?" she asks.

"No. I just meant . . ." But he stops again. He's always thought that change, real change—if it were possible at all—would require a dizzying leap from one life to another. Now he's not so sure. Now all he knows is that he would like to leave behind the melancholy existence they've been leading together for so long.

She waits for him to speak.

He's been living as if he could willfully cut himself loose from her, from the past as well. He's been acting as if nothing were connected to anything else, least of all him to Irene.

But it's all connected, he understands now. Change wouldn't be a leap to something brand-new, but to something familiar, given their past.

"Harry?" Irene says, "Harry?"

He feels a sudden, intense curiosity about her. He's missed so much.

"Harry? Are you all right?"

Where has he been? "Ahh," he finally says. "Irene, forgive me."

"Harry, don't."

"There's so much I want to say, I just don't know how to begin."

The TV loops crazily behind her. She touches his cheek. "That puts us in the same boat," she says, smiling bashfully.

Harry smiles back. He pictures the two of them in some beat-up dinghy, or on *The African Queen*, maybe. He takes Irene's hand and wonders if he should risk kissing it. Would she think he was off his rocker?

Suddenly the room quivers, assaulted by the piercing whine of sirens. They both jump, Harry painfully all the way to his feet, Irene to the window.

"Oh, my God, Harry," she cries. "Look! The Watters' house is on fire!"

Harry moves as fast as he can to the window. Will this day never end? What next?

Almost on cue, as the noise of the siren fades and the fire trucks climb the Watters' drive, the sound of a familiar voice makes Harry catch his breath.

"Oh, Harry," Irene says. Her face drains of color.

My God, Harry thinks, remembering the meager craft he imagined them in. White water! The falls! S.O.S.!

The voice yells again.

"Up here, Buddy," Harry calls wearily. No bailing out this time, no escape.

"I'm home!" Buddy shouts at the top of his lungs. "I'm home!"

Harry takes Irene's hand and holds it tightly.

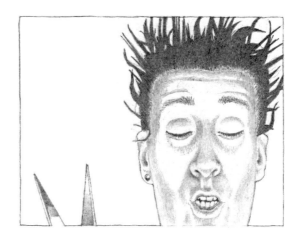

The beauty shop is the last place on earth she should probably be. But when Harry went to work after only four hours of sleep—all stiff and sore and bandaged like a mummy, poor thing—Irene decided to keep her appointment. Her hair didn't matter. Getting out of the house did. After last night it seemed haunted.

She's in a fog this morning, mellowed by her lack of sleep and the strain that preceded bed. She feels pliant and slow. Not being able to think very clearly is a blessing. If she was alert, she would be too nervous to sit still.

But Irene sits very still, moving only to stifle an occasional yawn. The room is all mirrors and light wood, airy and clean. Ordinarily she would find the spareness self-conscious, but today its simplicity strikes her as soothing. Irene has trouble sizing the place up in the mirror. Things are skewed and multiplied by reflection; people and objects aren't where they seem to be.

"Nikki?" the young man standing over her says. "Can I call you Nikki, or do people call you Nicolle?"

"I beg your pardon?" Irene says, snapping to attention. She almost forgot about him. In his bright flowered shirt and red high-topped sneakers, the young man looks bizarre, but Irene can't get worked up about that today.

Dark-eyed and slim-hipped, he has spiky coal-black hair, cut so it stands up from his head like a cartoon of someone who's just stuck his finger into an electric socket. There's a name for this unearthly style. Brute or something; thug?

"I was just wondering," the man says, "do people call you Nicolle, or, like, do you have a nickname?"

"Oh," Irene says, "just call me Irene." She's amazed to hear herself say this. As a rule, people call her Mrs. Newcomb.

"Irene? Wow! That's kind of different," he says, blessedly not pursuing the matter. The man is young, but he's older than Buddy. He's the Clarke half of the Lewis and Clarke Beauty Expedition, and he's carefully painting something foamy on her hair, then wrapping the strands in packets of foil.

"You're going to love this color," Clarke says. "It'll make you feel like a new person."

"How nice," Irene says, and then remembers: punk, not thug. Clarke wears a tiny diamond chip in one ear. She supposes he's gay, not that she has the energy for harsh judgments this morning. Gay, not gay, she finds herself thinking, what does it matter? Clarke probably never set fire to a house. . . .

"I did this to my wife's hair just last week," Clarke says. "She's mad for it. Look at her." He motions behind him to the receptionist, a pretty young woman with long shiny blond hair.

Irene is startled but manages to smile. "It's lovely," she says, and means it. "So natural." What does she know about anyone? What has she ever known to make her always so sure of things?

Clarke adjusts a piece of foil, one of dozens now. All of this seems slightly ridiculous to Irene, a vanity she shouldn't be party to. "Hair today, gone tomorrow," her mother used to say. But then look at *her* hair.

Clarke called this hair painting "flashing." Irene recalls when flashing meant something else—raincoats, unzipped pants. On her way to high school she often saw a tall man with an open raincoat. Day after day the two of them passed silently, he with his raincoat open and fly undone, she clutching her armload of books. After the first time she averted her eyes. She never mentioned him to a soul. In truth, she felt sorry for the man. Now flashing is something to do to your hair.

Clarke hums along with a tune on the radio. Between his humming and the gentle way he's touching her head, Irene's eyes begin to close.

She's so tired, she could be dreaming. Suddenly she's aware that Clarke has stopped working on her hair. Her eyes fly open to see him staring at her in the mirror.

"You've got good bones," he says, assessing her. Normally she would be horrified by such attention. She stares back. "Nice eyes," he adds, returning to work.

"Now, Clarke," Irene says, "Flattery—"

"Irene," Clarke says, interrupting, "after a while styles change, that's all. We'll get what's left of this old perm out of your hair. You just wait. By the way, are you married, Irene?"

"To a brick," she answers quietly before she can stop herself.

"To a *what?*"

"To a good man," Irene replies without hesitation, "a wonderful, solid, decent human being." This sounds like nothing Irene ever heard herself say. Why in the world is she telling such a thing to someone she doesn't know from Adam? Because she means it, she realizes. Where would she have been without Harry the night before?

"Gee!" Clarke says, "you really like him, I guess. Do you have kids?"

Irene stares off into mirrored space. Usually when strangers ask her this, she says no. "I have a son," she tells Clarke. "*We* have a son. He's twenty."

"Isn't that great," Clarke says. "I can't wait to have kids. They do the wildest things, they knock me out."

Irene tries not to think.

Carefully Clarke places a plastic hat that re-minds Irene of an old refrigerator-dish cover over her head. Then he escorts her across the room to a hair dryer. "This won't take long," he tells her. "Your hubby will fall in love with you all over again." He smiles and pulls the dryer over her head.

Irene realizes she can't wait to meet Harry for lunch, even if what they have to discuss isn't anything she's looking forward to. Maybe Harry will have figured out what to do about the Watterses by then. Warm air from the dryer cascades over her head. Her eyes close.

After a few minutes someone calls her name and taps her on the shoulder. "A catnap," Clarke says, feeling the foil packets. "Good for you!"

"Was I asleep?" Irene asks. She can't recall ever falling asleep in public before.

"Boy, I wish more of my customers were as laid back as you are," Clarke says. It's odd, Irene thinks, what she ordinarily would take for clumsy flattery, she finds rather enchanting this morning. Refreshed from her nap, she smiles up at him. In spite of the freakishness of his hair, there's a sweetness about him, Irene decides. Clarke strips her hair of foil and washes it, then takes her back to his chair in front of the mirror.

People bustle around them—all the cus-tomers smocked in pink, beauticians in vari-ous getups. A young woman to Clarke's left, working away with a blow dryer, seems to be wearing a Boy Scout uniform; the young man cutting hair next to her is dressed for the gym. Other people's children also wear dis-guises, Irene realizes. You can't tell who's who by clothes anymore. Even Buddy, in his Wild Man of Borneo getup, would probably fit right in. Except that Buddy . . . Irene shifts in the chair and wills the thought out of her mind.

Despite all the people around them, it seems to Irene that she and Clarke are alone in a bubble of quiet. He combs through her wet hair and begins snipping away, but Irene refuses to watch. Only hair, after all. How could it matter what happens to her hair?

"Do you like birds?" Clarke asks her after a few minutes.

Birds? "Why, yes, of course," Irene answers, as if this were a perfectly normal question. "Yes, indeed I do."

"I raise them," Clarke says, lowering his voice as if he's telling her a secret. "Tropical birds. Finches. Birds you never see outside—not here, anyway."

"How fascinating." People come up with the most peculiar things these days.

"The reason I mention it is you seem like an unusual person. Most people think it's a weird hobby, to tell you the truth. But then, not everyone's as easygoing as you are."

Easygoing? Deep down she's flattered, even though it's not true. Perhaps if she gave up sleep altogether, she could transform herself into a new person.

"A few days ago," Clarke tells her, "my Lady Gouldian finches had babies! You have no idea how thrilling it is!'' He sets down the comb and scissors and excitedly describes the hatch. He names other kinds of birds he owns, ones she has never heard of. He has parakeets too.

''Parakeets?'' Irene says, ''Why, I used to have parakeets!'' With an animation she didn't think she was capable of, she tells him about the parakeets she had when she was a girl.

''I just knew you were a good person,'' Clarke says, resuming his cutting. ''I mean, you have to be if you love birds. Next time you come, I'll bring you pictures of my birds. Would you like that?''

''Yes, yes I would.''

Clarke works on her hair for a while in silence. ''You know,'' he says, exchanging the scissors for a blow dryer, ''people kid me about my birds, even my wife, but I'll tell you, it's nice having something you can sort of control in life. Don't you think that's true?''

Irene looks up at him.

''You know,'' he says, ''things in cages, I mean. Even if you're only tricking yourself, it's a good feeling—protecting something, keeping it alive—and it doesn't hurt if it's only birds.'' He turns on the blow dryer. ''Nothing subtle about me,'' he says, and laughs.

Irene nods thoughtfully.

''I didn't mean to get heavy.'' Clarke shrugs. ''It's just, you know . . .''

''Of course,'' Irene says.

''Hey!'' Clarke exclaims. ''You're not watching what I'm doing to your hair, are you? I hope you're not worried or something.''

''I'd like to wait until you're done,'' Irene says. She can't tell him she's too tired to care about her hair or that holding her head up suddenly seems like a big effort.

''Well, it's going to be fabulous,'' Clarke says. ''Shut your eyes and I'll tell you when to open them.'' He makes a few more passes through her hair with a brush. ''Okay,'' he announces, ''open wide. Surprise!''

Irene hesitates. She's not sure she wants this interlude to end. But ever so slowly she opens her eyes. ''Oh, my lord!'' she cries when she looks in the mirror.

''Do you like it?'' Clarke asks hopefully.

''Like it?'' Irene is stunned.

''Well, listen, hey. I mean . . . look. If you don't, we can—'' He lifts the brush.

''Stop!'' Irene says, much louder than she intended. Clarke backs off. ''Don't touch it, Clarke,'' she adds in a more normal tone. ''Please. I love it.''

''Wow. I thought for a second there . . .''

''It's wonderful,'' she says. ''Wonderful!'' She's startled to hear herself sounding bosomy and thrilled, like a starlet on a TV talk show.

Clarke grins, obviously relieved. ''It's you, isn't it? It's the real Irene. A little geometric cut, and out of the chrysalis into a butterfly!'' He laughs.

The smartly cut golden hair is like nothing she's ever had, but it's what she's always dreamed of. There in the mirror is the Irene she's wanted to be all along. She has the oddest sensation, like she's finally met up with herself after all this time.

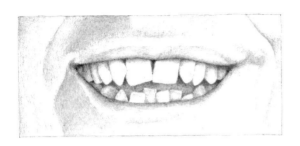

"Anybody home?" Robin calls. The front door is open, but the screen is locked. After a few minutes of waiting and ringing the bell, he decides she's not there. He leans the red grill top next to the door. As he heads for the steps he hears Carol Ann calling from inside the small house, "Who is it? Who's there?"

"Me," he says, walking back to the door.

"Just a second."

Robin waits, rocking on his heels. It's lunchtime, and his stomach is growling. He sits down on the top porch step and squints against the sun. Carol Ann's lawn has been recently mowed, and bees whine in the bushes by the porch. On the seat of his truck is a letter in a pale gray envelope, the first in weeks. He doesn't have to open it to know this will be more of the same. He had thought about throwing the letter away unopened, but he tossed it into his truck instead, as though it were a test of character.

His shoulders ache, and he hunches them to straighten out the kinks. Several drops of Mrs. Newcomb's paint have landed on the knee of his overalls. It's an odd color. Now, in the sun, it looks pink; in the house, it was almost violet. On the paint chip it seemed gray. When Mrs. Newcomb gets back from wherever she rushed off to this morning and sees her violet walls, she'll probably have a fit. At the moment he doesn't much care. A faint breeze rustles through the leaves of the sycamore on Carol Ann's lawn. The day is perfect. He wishes he were working outside today and not cooped up in a house.

"Oh, it's you," Carol Ann says. She is standing behind the screen door. Her straight, wet hair is making spreading damp marks on the denim shirt knotted at her waist.

"Hi," he says, getting to his feet. He figures it's best to act as if the other night never happened.

"You have paint in your hair," she says, opening the screen door. Her face is expressionless. What he's most aware of as she crosses the porch is the rising and shifting of her breasts under her shirt. Below her white shorts, her legs shine like they've been polished.

"I hope I didn't wake you or something," he ventures.

"Obviously not." She sits down in the spot he had just vacated. She leans her head against the wooden pillar and shuts her eyes as if he weren't there.

He stoops down next to her, not certain how to get her attention.

"So," she says without opening her eyes, "you changed your mind. You came to take me away from all this."

"Not exactly. I . . . uh . . ."

"Calm down," she says. "I was just kidding." Her eyelashes flutter as if she were going to open her eyes, but she doesn't. She lifts her chin higher toward the sun.

"Look," he starts to say.

"*You* look," she says, sitting up and opening her eyes. Rather wearily she says, "On the other hand, don't." She leans back against the pillar and closes her eyes again.

"Listen. The reason I came over is there by the door. You walked right by it."

She raises her head. "My God!" she says, getting quickly to her feet.

"Home at last," he says to her back.

"This is amazing." She picks up the grill top.

"I figured it had to be yours. I found it a couple of blocks away," he says. "Isn't that incredible? It *is* yours, isn't it?"

She doesn't say anything but takes the lid to the corner of the porch and sets it on top of the grill. He follows her, wondering why he bothered to knock in the first place. He should have put the lid by her door and left.

"It fits," he says, coming up behind her. "How about that?" A vivid fragrance surrounds her.

She looks up as if she forgot him. Then she turns away and says in a voice he has to strain to hear, "I'm sorry about the other night. I've been such a mess."

"Well," he says lightly, "you sure smell good!" He has a sudden desire to touch her.

"I should. I've been in the shower for almost an hour," she says, walking past him toward the door. She smiles suddenly and says enthusiastically, "Hey! You really brought my lost lid home!"

The way she says this, the words sound like the refrain of a bad country-western song, and Robin laughs, thinking of truck crashes, busted-up marriages, lost grill covers.

"You want some lunch?" she asks.

"Sure," he says, "I'm starved. I was on my way to town."

"Eat here," she says. "I promise not to jump you."

"Carol Ann . . ." he says.

The living room is cool and dark after the porch. He stops to adjust his eyes to the light and notices that most of the furniture is gone. Only the stereo, a lamp, and an overfull brick-and-board bookcase remain. Carol Ann watches him take in the emptiness.

"Be it ever so humble," she remarks. Her hair is frizzing out, growing bigger as it dries. It makes her look exotic.

"All of that stuff was *Ben's?*" he asks.

She nods. "Attractive, isn't it?" That's why I got so bent out of shape over that grill. I mean, I thought it would be nice to salvage *some*thing."

"That reminds me," Robin says, following her back into the tiny yellow kitchen and scooting into the breakfast nook. "Did you hear what happened over on Jefferson?"

"Hunh-uh," she says, taking things out of the refrigerator.

"You know the big white house up on the hill? The one with that funny little room on the roof?"

She nods and begins slicing salami.

"There was a fire," he says.

Carol Ann sets the knife down and looks at him. "You mean the Watterses' house?"

"Yeah," he says. "That's the one. The little room's gone, and I guess the whole place is a wreck. The Watterses are out of town, and their next-door neighbor, the woman I'm working for now, said it was wiring. But then I heard in town that the place was trashed. It's kind of weird."

"Trashed?"

"You know, vandalized or something, arson."

"That's terrible," Carol Ann says. "That's awful. One of their kids was in my class last year. Tony. Who would do a thing like that?"

He shrugs.

"God, you know, that really unglues me," she says after a minute. "That's somebody's *home.*" She finishes making the sandwiches and sets the plate and a glass of iced tea in front of Robin.

"Thanks," he says.

Carol Ann sits down across from him. Her face is troubled.

"Homes are different from what you and I have," she says. "For a while I thought we had one here, but look at it now. The furniture goes, and it might as well be a drop-in center."

He laughs, but she's right. "This is good," he says.

"Homes . . ." she says, and pauses thoughtfully.

"Huron," he intones, "Ontario, Michigan, Erie, Superior . . ."

"Oh, don't be so smart," she says. "You live in a barn, you're just passing through. Me, too, I guess, now. A real home is different."

"Yeah," he says. Then to temper this view, which he actually shares, he adds, "Don't romanticize the whole thing, Carol Ann. Homes aren't necessarily happy."

"Oh, that's brilliant, Robin," she says. "Brilliant. But the Watterses' is, I bet."

"They'll fix it, it's not ruined."

"I guess," she says. For a while he eats and she stares out of the window.

"Listen," Carol Ann says. "You want to hear how upset I've been? Yesterday I drove down to see Hart Crane's grave. Can you believe it?"

"You did *what?*"

"Honestly. I was feeling so morbid, I went to Garretsville and hunted up his grave."

"But, Carol Ann, he's not even there."

"Of course not," she says, "but a gravestone is. It reads, 'Lost at Sea.'"

"That's a nice way of putting it," he says. "Especially since the poor guy deep-sixed himself in a drunken stupor—where was it?—in the Gulf of Mexico?"

She narrows her eyes at him as if he were beyond the pale. "You know," she says, "sometimes you give real meaning to the phrase 'callow youth.'"

"I'm not so bad. I love Hart Crane, actually. 'How many dawns,'" he recites, "'chill from his rippling rest/The sea gull's wings shall dip and pivot him . . .'"

"Eat your lunch," Carol Ann says, but she's smiling now.

After another bite he asks, "Did you feel better after your little pilgrimage?"

"Yeah, I guess," she says. "You want an ice cream bar?"

"Sure," he says.

"How old are you, Robin?" she asks.

"Almost twenty-five."

"What are you going to be when you grow up? Do you think about that?"

He groans.

"I mean, is this day-laborer routine for real, or what?" She stands with her hands on her hips. This is the first time he's seen her look like a teacher.

"You make me feel like I didn't do my homework," he says.

"Come off it."

"Okay," he says. "What I want to be when I grow up is a millionaire cowboy with ranch holdings in three states. You know, cattle, an Arabian stud farm . . . oh, yeah, and a Porsche Turbo Carrera." He laughs.

"Come on," she says.

"It'll take a little financial planning," he adds. "I may have to win the state lottery, but, well—"

"Can't you be serious?"

"We're being serious?" He was afraid of that.

"Yes, we are," she says. "Yes, indeed."

"I'm not sure what I want to be when I grow up, Carol Ann," he says. "Frankly I'm not even sure I want to grow up, though lately it seems to have certain attractions."

She turns her back and begins putting things away.

"Actually, sometimes I think I might like to be a doctor." He has never said this out loud before. It gets her attention. "Do you think I'm too old to get into med school?"

"Are you still joking?" she asks.

"I don't know," he says.

"Tony Watters's father is a doctor," Carol Ann says. "A radiologist. Once Tony wrote in a paper that his father could see inside people. I liked that."

Doctors really *do* things, Robin thinks. They also make money. It would be a good life. Look at his grandfather. His grandfather's always wanted Robin to be a doctor but never pushed. Maybe he'll look into it. "Listen, Carol Ann. Did you mean it the other night when you said I was a phony?"

She turns and looks at him, a dish towel slung over her shoulder. "Oh, I don't know," she says. "Most of the time you seem to be someone who knows exactly what you're doing. It's very convincing, but I think lots of it is b.s. You're more like the rest of us than you seem—not really done yet, I mean."

He frowns.

"You know, like bread dough that's still rising or something."

He tries hard not to become defensive. Bread dough?

"You just put on a better show than most people," she says.

He's not sure he agrees, but the last thing he wants is for things to get heavy between them again. He squeezes out of the breakfast nook. "How much do I owe you for lunch?" he asks.

"You must think I'm crazy," she says. "One day I'm having a breakdown in front of you, and a few days later . . ." She lowers her eyes.

"Listen to you," he says, and takes her hand. It's so soft.

"Maybe you'll come back again sometime?" she says, pulling away. "I'll reveal yet another side of myself." They both laugh and walk toward the front door.

"You know," she says to him as he steps onto the porch. "I really was serious. You've got too much going for you to keep this up much longer. You'll begin to forget there's a whole world out there." She smiles. "Anyway, as my principal says, 'He who fails to plan, plans to fail.' The man's not a great brain, of course, but it's true."

"I'll think about it, Carol Ann. Really," he says. "You ought to make some plans yourself. You ought to plan to shop for furniture."

To his surprise she shakes her head, serious again. "I think I'm leaving Lethem," she says. "I'm trying to break my contract, and my lease too. A change is definitely in order."

"Are you kidding?" He's floored. "Where would you go?"

"New York," she says. "I've always wanted to live there. I've got a friend who works in a gallery in Soho. I can stay with her. I'll be twenty-eight next month, and there's nothing to keep me here anymore, not really."

"What about Minkie?" Robin asks. He can't believe Carol Ann would leave town just like that.

"I don't know. Maybe I'll sell her. Minkie's from a different life, anyway."

Robin feels like he's just been thrown a curve. After an awkward moment they say good-bye. He jumps into his truck, amazed by Carol Ann, and he waves, but she doesn't see him. She's busy picking blossoms off a hanging plant on the porch. Robin thinks of her in a different light: New York.

He backs out of the drive and toots the horn. Then he reaches for the gray envelope, and holding a corner against the steering wheel, he rips it into smaller and smaller pieces. He lets them fly out of the window a few at a time, watching in the rearview mirror as the letter he never opened flutters behind him in a trail of pale scraps.

Great, he thinks. Here Carol Ann's making plans to head for New York, and he's driving around Lethem littering.

Ye Old Cellar, neither old nor a cellar, but new and off the lobby of an office building near the Interstate, is so dark when Harry enters, he wonders if there's been another power failure. Large candles burn in ornate wall sconces. Smaller ones flicker on the tables.

Waiting to be seated, he makes out mock stone walls, tapestries, a drawbridge leading to the kitchen. The whirring of a blender issues from the bar. There hasn't been a power failure, after all, he thinks. The dark is someone's half-baked idea of a dining experience. First train cars and phony ship decks, then greenhouses, now a dungeon. What next? Gutted B-52 bombers? Merry-go-rounds? Construction sites? He speculates on entering a new line of work, restaurant decor. A little venture capital is all it would take. Endless marketing possibilities—barnyards; bank vaults; maybe a seasonal outdoorsy place, autumn leaves on the floor, later snow, after that spring flowers. Battlefields for a little history with your chow. Art galleries, feed 'em culture. Christ Almighty.

Why Irene chose this windowless, pitch-dark place for lunch is beyond him. He wonders if he heard her wrong. He tries to check the time but can't even see his watch. He'd feel better if Irene were here. He'd feel even better if someone turned on the lights.

Harry's bushed and his chest hurts, yet the pain dulls his state of shock over the previous night's events. When he hit the bed after carting Buddy back to Holly Hill, he didn't sleep, just lay there stunned by Buddy's latest. Harry can't bear to think about that, so he concentrates on his aches. His chest is wrapped so tightly, he has to stand at parade rest, like some joke dictator. All he needs is highly polished leather boots and a riding crop. Possibly a dueling scar. Him and Rommel? Goering? Did anyone ever stand as straight as the Nazis? Backs like plumb lines, but twisted souls. Inwardly, of course, he himself isn't as straight as he could be. The object of his own guilty conscience—the Watterses—seems too much to deal with.

The maître d' catches sight of Harry and nods. Harry says, "Two." The man gives him the once-over. "I'm expecting my wife," Harry adds. Even moving his lips hurts. Who would have suspected, he wonders as he follows the man to a table in a corner dark as a tomb, that your mouth is connected to your ribs? Yet here he is, living proof that everything connects, the anklebone to the shinbone, all the way up. One thing's for sure, he won't be laughing again. What could ever be funny after last night?

With great care Harry seats himself, only to be stabbed in the kidney by something sharp in the carved chair back. He resettles himself diagonally and asks the maître d' to send over a dry martini. Fast. Irene will probably make a fuss about the martini. Let her.

As he waits for his drink Harry sees someone waving to him from another table. He peers into the shadows and recognizes one of the bank's big customers, Zimmer, a cigar-smoking baldy who owns a chain of parking lots. With him is a woman who's a real looker, at least in the dark, young enough to be Zimmer's daughter. Harry nods back with a minimum of movement and sweeps his eyes over the room. Only then does he notice that most of the women in the restaurant are as young and well dressed as Mr. Park-O's companion. He seems to be in the midst of a bunch of high-priced call girls, which, come to think of it, would fit right in with the astonishing number of Mercedes outside. Irene is going to feel out of place here. He wonders if he shouldn't head her off, go somewhere else.

A tall, thin waiter with a lantern jaw the size of Frankenstein's wordlessly sets a martini in front of Harry. Harry takes a sip and reaches in his jacket pocket for the pack of cigarettes he

bought that morning. It's half gone. If he lights up now, Irene's sure to materialize. He'd even go for a drag on Mr. Park-O's cigar, he's that desperate. Where is Irene, anyway?

The waiter places two rolled-up scrolls on Harry's table. The guy's hands are as big as Harry's feet. Harry isn't hungry, and opening up a menu seems like too much work. He sips his drink and sucks on the swizzle stick. Around him, conversations rise and fall and silver tinkles pleasantly—as if eating in the dark were a normal, everyday experience.

Harry hates waiting and feels foolish alone when everyone in the room is with someone else. Sitting unnaturally upright, he's nearly overcome by a flock of disquieting thoughts. He extends his arm so his watch is in the light from the candle. Irene is twenty minutes late. She's usually so punctual, he can't understand it. He wonders if something happened to her. He downs what's left of his martini and signals Jaws for another. Krause probably wouldn't approve, but then for a number of reasons Harry's not too sure about Krause. Bad enough that he lost Buddy. Now, this morning on the phone, Krause warned him not to say a word about the fire to the Watterses. "Kevin's recovery could very well depend on all of us keeping our mouths shut," Krause said, and went on about extenuating circumstances and Buddy's need to act out his anger. "Lay low, Harry. Let things take their course," he advised.

Incredible as it seems, Buddy really set fire to their neighbor's house. Jesus, Harry keeps thinking, the place could have burned to the ground, people might have been hurt. On the phone with Krause, Harry persisted. "Aren't there some . . . ah . . . ethics involved in a situation like this?"

"Apply the ethics to your son," Krause shot back. "It's *his* life that's at stake, not your neighbors'. Forget your neighbors for now."

"But what if they find out who did it?"

"We'll cross that bridge when we come to it," Krause said. "Don't over-identify with strangers, Harry."

Strangers? Harry almost said. Strangers? My God, I was practically in love with that woman—her deep-red hair. But Krause would think he was crazy if he told him that. Besides, she seems to be fading from his mind. Harry can't quite recapture how he felt, as if he'd witnessed his infatuation with her on TV or heard about it secondhand. Where did it go? he wonders. How can someone haunt you one moment, and the next drift away?

"Harry," Krause said, as if Harry were a numskull, "these people have insurance. They're not poor. They weren't in any danger. Don't you see? The real victim is Kevin. Let me handle it my way. Confidentiality binds me to my patient. Now *that's* ethics. Kick up a fuss and it'll be Kevin who suffers. We don't want that!"

"No," Harry told him, "of course not. No. Kevin needs a courtroom like he needs a hole

in the head." The minute he said this, Harry realized that a hole in the head was about the only thing that hadn't been tried in the name of treating Buddy.

"Okay," Harry said to Krause, "it's your deal. I'll do whatever you say." That didn't make Harry's doubts disappear.

The waiter sets another martini in front of Harry and asks if he wants to order. "My wife's late," Harry offers. The waiter looks like he's heard this one before.

Harry checks his watch again to find it's almost one o'clock. Where is she? He contemplates accidents—Irene pinned behind the wheel of her car; run over in a crosswalk; lying motionless on a stretcher. He takes a drink of his martini and imagines lesser disasters: traffic jams; lineups in gas stations; Jehovah's Witnesses coming to the door just as she was leaving home. Why does she always let them in?

"Take some time off," Krause suggested. "Get away for a while. Kevin's safe now. You both need a rest."

"Doctor's orders?" Harry joked.

"Come now, Harry, you don't need my permission to get away," Krause responded humorlessly. The guy never lightened up. "Besides, you're not my patient," he went on. "Your son is. But you've been under a strain. Both of you."

Actually, at the time the idea of a vacation seemed appealing. Now Harry has fears about how he and Irene would get along without the cushion of everyday habits. Whatever happened the night before, whatever turning they seemed to take might be too fragile to hold up for long. Anyway, he thinks, maybe he only imagined that business with Irene. He's so exhausted, he's not sure he's thinking straight. Maybe nothing changed at all.

By now the martinis are beginning to work. One more, he thinks, and he'll forget to sit bolt-upright. He pushes the half-filled glass away and awkwardly unrolls one of the big menus. The heavy paper immediately rolls itself back up with a snap. Harry curses and tries again, anchoring one end of the absurdly large scroll under his elbow. He squints at the medieval script that would be nearly illegible under the best of circumstances. He runs his eyes over the menu, more annoyed by the minute. Why isn't anything easy? This is like trying to make out a foreign language, he thinks, reading COMEFTIBLES.

"Excuse me," a woman's voice says near his ear. He can barely hear her. Did she say, "May I join you?"

Harry glances up quickly to see golden-blond hair. "Sorry," he says, going back to the menu, "I'm expecting my wife." My God, he's being solicited right here in public!

"Please," the woman's voice says gently.

Harry shakes his head. "I'm afraid not," he says, talking into the menu. All he needs is for Irene to walk in and find him with a hooker. Out of the corner of his eye he sees that she's boldly sitting right down at his table. He sticks his nose further into the menu. Finally he clears his throat as menacingly as he knows how and lifts his head to speak. Something familiar about the figure's shoulders, the tilt of her head, stops him. He peers across the table into the face

framed by glittering blond hair. For a second he thinks he must be totally potted.

"Harry!" Irene says, and bursts into laughter.

"My God!" He's staggered. "It's *you!*"

She tosses her head. Her hair swings gracefully. "Of course it's me, you silly. Who on earth did you think it was?"

Harry is flabbergasted. Of course it's Irene, he can see that now, but what's happened? She doesn't look a thing like the woman he left behind that morning. In the restaurant's low light her blond hair makes her look like a cross between Doris Day and that woman on TV, Linda somebody-or-other. Evans. Yet it's not just her hair that's different.

"Harry," Irene says, "say something."

"You're . . . uh . . . you look gorgeous," he finally gets out. "I can't get over the change."

"Oh, Harry," she says, beaming, "do you like it?"

"Irene," he says, and painfully reaches across the table for her hand, "you look great, just great." What else can he say? You look great, but who are you? Not that he doesn't believe it's her, but part of him is having trouble absorbing this new glamour girl, part of him lags behind.

They hold hands across the table, and Irene chatters about her hair, obviously all wound up. He studies her closely. This new change is almost too much to digest.

The waiter appears, and to Harry's astonishment Irene orders a glass of white wine. "Bring him another one of these, too, please," Irene tells the waiter, pointing to Harry's half-empty martini. Dumbstruck, Harry stares while Irene unfolds the menu and bravely wrestles it to the table.

"Oh, Harry," she says, "they have fifh!" She pronounces the s like the f it resembles and begins to laugh. "But how about a firft courfe to start with?"

Can this really be Irene?

"And let's see, there's vichyffoise," she says with a heavy accent. "Or muffels, or look! pafta Bolognefe." Irene giggles.

As she reads through the entrées he gazes at her with stupefied awe. Their lives come crashing down, and here she is clowning around, looking like she just stepped out of a bandbox. Does she know something he doesn't?

"Chocolate mouffe," she reads. "Afforted cheefes. Oh, Harry, isn't this crazy?"

He nods. She looks prettier than he's ever seen her. He can't get over it.

"Harry. Now you listen to me," she says, catching him off-guard with her sudden seriousness. She stares deep into his eyes. He feels hypnotized. "This is not the end of the world."

Harry is astonished to find he believes her.

During the long drive home from Michigan, Tony listened to his new radio and rehearsed how bad the sight of their house would be. Somewhere west of Toledo, to a song he's forgotten, he saw the house—no house at all. That was scary, like traveling into the future to a time when they would all be gone.

Still, as they round the bend of Jefferson, Tony wills himself *not* to look. He has leftovers of a child's logic that what he doesn't see might not exist.

"Look at that!" his father says, pulling the car over to the curb. Tony clenches his fists. Oh, no, he thinks. Oh, shit. There's no changing it now, it really happened. He shuts his eyes tight.

"*No!*" his mother says.

"Jeez," Will pipes up, his head practically in Tony's lap as he cranes to see up the hill. Will's been crying almost all day long, acting like an incredible baby. At one rest stop his mother told Tony the carsickness medicine might be making Will carry on so.

"Why would anyone . . . ?" his mother begins, and Tony can no longer keep himself from looking. What he sees is better than some things he imagined, but still pretty bad. The round room is totally gone, and the nearest chimney is black with soot. A gutter dangles down to the porch, slicing a diagonal across the house, and pieces of the cornices lie scattered on the steps. He stares at the house and fights back tears.

"My God," his mother says, "it feels like we've been violated or something. It's terrible."

Tony doesn't know what she means, but he hears impatience in his father's voice when he says, "Come on, Kitty, let's not make this any more melodramatic than it already is."

Right then Will starts crying again. "Will, please," his father says, "we all feel terrible."

"Oh, let him cry," his mother says. "It looks worth crying over to me."

Halfway down the alley it does. "Look!" his mother screams. "Look there!"

His father slams on the brakes, and Tony looks where his mother is pointing on the river side of the alley. The swing set's gone! There are only splintered posts, barely knee-high.

"Jesus!" his father exclaims. His father hardly ever swears, and this is the first time today he's acted surprised. When the four of them hurriedly left his grandparents' house in Michigan that morning, and his mother was so worked up she was talking a mile a minute, his father kept saying, "Calm down, Kitty. Calm down." After he had said this four or five times, his mother said, "Oh, for chrissake, David. Just because *you've* been trained to be good in emergencies, don't expect the rest of us to be so cool. You're making me feel like an idiot. This is our life—*ours*, not some goddamn stranger's!"

Even though she wasn't talking to him, Tony felt the sting of her words and turned his radio way up. With the music blasting in his ears, he noticed his mother move far over, until she was practically sitting on the door handle. His father drove, looking straight ahead. The distance between them seemed wider than the car. Will huddled in his corner, either asleep or pretending to be.

They drove that way for some time. Finally the four of them seemed so alone, Tony pulled off his earphones and asked how many hours the trip would take from where they were. At least the question made them shift around in their seats.

"Maybe it launched itself into space," Tony

"It's not so bad," Tony manages to say. "Really it isn't."

Will looks at his brother with a blotchy-eyed, confused expression and stops crying. His father pulls away from the curb, and the car is suddenly full of a silence that feels like it could explode at any moment.

offers as he regards the stubs of the swing set.

"Just shut up," Will mutters. His hair is all messed up and his nose is red and peeling. He looks more freckly than ever.

Tony grabs his brother's arm and twists it. "You know what? You deserve a break today! Ha!"

Will socks him and pulls his arm away.

The car noses up the drive, and the back side of the house comes into view. It's worse than the front. Streaks of black are all over the white paint. Some of the upstairs shutters are gone; others hang askew. Suddenly, though it's not the house they're all gawking at. It's the yard. Tony sucks in his breath. The yard is a complete and total wreck! The big sycamore tree lies stretched across the lawn with its branches hanging over the ravine. Hundreds, maybe thousands, of limbs and twigs are scattered all over, and you can hardly see the lawn.

"What in the world . . . ?" his mother exclaims.

"Didn't Mona tell you about this on the phone?" his father asks, looking even more surprised than when he saw that the swing set was gone.

"She said something about a windstorm, but not about our tree. I guess she wanted to spare us."

His father shakes his head. "It must have been some wind." He stops the car in the middle of the drive and shuts off the motor. "We better take a look around." He doesn't move. Will has his feet up on the seat, hugging his knees as if he were trying to hide. Tony suddenly realizes why.

"The tent!" Tony exclaims. "I bet it's totaled. It's probably smashed to bits under that tree!"

Tony's sense of triumph is cut short as Will abruptly heaves himself into the door and flings it open like he's bailing out headfirst. For a second Tony can't figure this out. Then he hears the sound of splashing on the drive, and his brother gagging.

"I thought you gave him medicine so he wouldn't do that!" Tony shouts indignantly to his mother. She doesn't move. His father leads Will away, but she just sits in the front seat looking off into space. Finally she shakes herself and gets out of the car.

Reluctantly Tony joins her. The smell of smoke and burned wood hurts his nose. A path of splintered branches shows where the fire trucks drove over the lawn, and the enormous rhododendron bush at the corner of the house is flattened on one side. The flowers, which used to match the color of the house, look too white against the dark, sooty streaks on the wood.

"When I think of all the things that were in that round room," his mother says, "all that junk, all that past." She bites her lips. "Those picture albums and my old report cards. And those yearbooks, Tony, do you remember them? And those silly baby shoes of mine my mother had bronzed, and your tiny first pair of sneakers, and oh . . ." She looks sad.

Tony longs to be able to turn back the clock, or the world itself, like Superman did to save Lois Lane. He would give anything to have things back to normal.

His mother takes his hand and pulls him along with her into the front yard and up the porch steps. "Brother," she says gloomily.

"Really, it'll be okay," Tony tells her. "Honest it will." He desperately wants her to believe this so that he can too.

She looks at him curiously and breaks into a smile. "You're a swell person, Tony. I love you." She puts her arms around him, and his heart seems to leap out to meet her. He feels safer than he has all day.

Suddenly he has an inspiration. "A year from now this won't be so bad," he says. "A year from now it'll be different."

" 'Forsan et haec olim meminisse iuvabit,' " his mother says as they separate.

"What?"

"It's Latin," she says, "for what you kind of just said." She sighs. "Time rearranges everything, Tony. Our memories, even. It's crazy. It rearranges *us*."

Tony stares at her, but she pushes him on through the front door. The smell inside is so terrible, he tries not to breathe. The house is an incredible mess. Books and records and shattered plates lie all over the hall. The broken back of a dining room chair is wedged between the posts of the banister. The staircase wall is scraped and scratched. A roll of red-and-green Christmas wrapping lies unfurled in the dining room doorway.

"God, what a shambles!" his mother says as she steps over cans and broken bottles to get into the kitchen.

Tony just stands there in the hall. Amid all the stuff on the floor, candlesticks and silver and dozens of napkins, is his old tape recorder, its insides ripped out. He feels even creepier.

"Mom?" he calls. "Mom?" He hopes his mother was right. He hopes it with all his might. He hopes time rearranges this, and fast too.

"Ah, Kevin." Dr. Krause swivels his chair around. "You've slept." The small man arises and clasps Buddy's hands, finally releasing him in front of the couch. "Sit down, make yourself comfortable. I'm expecting a phone call any minute now, but it shouldn't take long."

Buddy falls to the couch, risking only a quick glance at Krause before lowering his eyes and pretending interest in the upholstery. Tonight, as always, looking at Krause raises certain problems for him, something about those watery, red-rimmed eyes tearing behind horn-rimmed glasses. Krause suffers from allergies and spends considerable time dabbing at his eyes, blowing his nose, coughing, clearing his throat. Buddy's first impression of Krause was that Krause was weeping for him too. All that sympathy, plus the doctor's smallness, makes Buddy want to do something for him; he's never known what.

"So," Krause says, "I'm sorry about what happened, Kevin. I'm deeply, deeply sorry you had to go through what you did." Krause's voice catches as he says this. Buddy's too nervous to utter a word. For a minute the room is silent, except for the faint hiss of Krause's humidifier.

"You know I feel responsible," Krause continues, "for whatever enabled you to walk out of here. Alex Clark—do you remember?—who was supposed to be with you that day? Alex is no longer with us. He slipped up badly, though of course in the end it's I . . ." Buddy hears the whispered zip of a tissue being pulled from the box, followed by muffled hacking.

Krause clears his throat. "I hope I'm making myself understood."

Buddy nods without lifting his eyes. He can't figure out what's going on. He expected one of those lectures his life has been full of; instead he's being given an apology. First his parents, now Krause. People are suddenly different, though maybe it's him. Things have been happening so fast.

"I'm afraid you didn't need to go two weeks

without your medication at this point. We have to make up for lost time."

Buddy knows lost time. "Three," he says to Krause. "*Three* weeks." He'd been pill-palming for a week before he split.

Krause shifts in his squeaky chair, then suddenly sneezes loudly. "Up to your old tricks, were you?" Krause says when he recovers. "Well, that's our fault too. I don't blame you for being angry."

Amazed he's still off the hook, Buddy raises his eyes, not to look at Krause but to watch the humidifier the doctor runs on all but the hottest days. Buddy tries to follow the vapor as it rises to the dark windowpane and becomes drops of water. He is concerned for Krause's wallpaper and woodwork, the upholstery he imagines must be dusted by a fine layer of mildew. During the past year he has often worried that the tweedy brown wallpaper would slide heavily off the walls and come flapping across the floor toward him in lumbering waves. He had a nightmare that the brown plaid drapes that hang limp and clammy at the window fell on him and he couldn't fight his way out from under them. Krause had his interpretation, of course, the usual blah-blah-blah. "Let's get serious," Buddy had wanted to say as Krause droned on. "You're going to destroy this room with that machine. Look at the rust on the wastebasket, the way the paint is peeling." But he kept still, afraid he'd hurt Krause's feelings and bring on a fit of loose, phlegmy coughing. Buddy feels a need to protect this slender, leaky man.

"Do you know how worried I've been, Kevin?"

This seems to require an answer. Buddy hesitates, then looks directly at Krause. "I guess," he says. Krause runs his fingers through his bushy gray hair. Krause's head is too big for his body, his hollow-cheeked face too wide. He's a snappy dresser, though. Tonight he wears pale gray linen pants, a brown cotton sweater, and soft leather loafers. The word is that Krause is a lady's man who's been married two or three times. Maybe that's why he runs so much. He runs every day for miles.

Without any warning, Krause propels his chair toward the couch and leans forward, coming so close that Buddy gets a whiff of cologne. He sits back as far as the low couch will let him, crossing his arms on his chest for protection.

"Where was it you wanted to go so badly, Kevin? Can you tell me?" Krause's voice is low, and his large head looks twice its size. Buddy wouldn't mind answering but doesn't have an immediate answer. He's diverted by Krause's curious eyebrows, which show the same renegade spirit as his hair. They bush out from the sides of his head like little gray horns, things on their way to someplace else.

"Home," Buddy finally says. Like many things he says to Krause, he has no idea where this came from.

"Home," Krause repeats, leaning back in his chair, and the two "homes" linger in the moist, heavy air.

"On the range," Buddy hears. "Where the something and the cantaloupe cook. Where

the chef combs his hair with the legs of a chair, and . . ." His father sings as he drives. Next to him, his mother smiles primly. Some private joke, but not for him in the backseat, not for Buddy, who's small and no part of this.

Just then the telephone on Krause's desk rings, jerking Buddy away from the backseat. Krause says, "Now then, this must be the call I've been expecting. I'll make it quick." Krause maneuvers his chair around to the desk, and Buddy regards its high green back, like the front seat he used to sit behind; him, an outsider, always afraid they'd forget him. Such surprise on their faces when they turned around to see him there, as if to say, "You! What are *you* doing here?"

Last night (could it have been only last night?) that same startled look had greeted him. His mother—or was it his father? For some reason he had trouble keeping them straight at first—said words he didn't hear, then ones he did: "That smell . . . oh, my God!"

"You must take a shower, Bud," and he was propelled down a hall and into a bathroom he'd never seen before where even the strong smell of new paint couldn't hold up against his own smells—sweat, dirt, most of all the bitter odor of smoke. He'd stepped into the shower and scrubbed himself down, remembering to wash his hair. This didn't take very long, probably because, as the horrified *O* on one of their mouths told him that when he came dripping out of the bathroom, he'd neglected to remove his clothes.

"Oh, no!" one of them exclaimed, and the

other said back, "He doesn't need that. Try to be calm." He was gently guided back into the bathroom where the kind voice, the one that had said, "Try to be calm," assured him he could do it and asked did he want company, did he want a hand? He was so rocked by that offer of help that something tight inside of him loosened, making new space. He gathered his strength and showered all over again, this time without his clothes, which were taken away and replaced by a polo shirt, khaki shorts, a pair of deck loafers. His father's clothes, the kind Buddy always made a point of not wearing.

His hair was too tangled and matted to comb through, so a pair of scissors with orange handles appeared. At the sight of them he couldn't get his breath. "That's the ticket," someone had said, and he breathed, allowing himself to be draped in a white bath towel. He was surprised he was letting the scissors near him. One of them groaned, the one cutting his hair, and kept saying, "This hurts like hell." Good-bye, hair, Buddy thought. His hair had been a long struggle.

After a while he began to feel docile, like a baby being turned this way and that. One of them produced a razor and foam. Everything was done so gently. Scraggly pieces of beard dropped into the sink.

"There!" someone said. "Don't you look nice." Risking a look in the bathroom mirror, he thought, who in the world is that? No one he knew. Yet *they* were there in the mirror, on either side of a stranger who wasn't bad if you went for the prepped-out type and who—this jarred him—must be him, Buddy. He was so amazed to think he might be this new person instead of the old one, he had to hold on to the edge of the basin.

"My!" one of them said, and the other one patted him on the back. "Not bad. Not bad at all." Confused as he was, he felt some change taking place among the three of them. The change had to do with more than clothes and hair. It made his other homecomings—those old disappointments, like jumping off a cliff and not flying but always falling, crashing— fade. Now, instead, he was almost soaring, and along with the two of them he admired his new self, astonished by the ease of it and by the feel of lips brushing his cheek. "Thank God you're home safe and sound." And he knew he was— him, pure and unblemished, cleansed of nightmare time.

He was taken downstairs, past strangely draped rooms where furniture was all jumbled together. His mother's housekeeping wasn't the same, and he felt better to see that she could be a regular slob like he remembered she had often called him.

"It's a neat house," he'd said.

"Why, Bud," one of them answered. There were tears in the voice, which must have been his mother's because he'd said, "Don't cry, Mom," and he was hugged in a gesture that caught him so off-guard that he almost returned it. Home. She'd fed him then, remembering, as if he'd never gone away and been someone else, what he liked to eat. Bacon and eggs and toast, with jelly on the eggs. And milk with ice in it, so cold that it made his head hurt.

His father came into the kitchen. He could tell them apart now, though he'd never noticed before how much the two of them looked alike. The same round-cheeked faces; his mother's colorless hair and his father's baldness; different shades of paleness, as if they were somehow fading together, making room for him. His father said, "Well, I talked to him. Everything's set on that end," and part of Buddy threatened for a second to leach away but didn't, because by then the three of them were sitting around the kitchen table, like a regular family, no one even yelling at him. Feeling safe again, he had said between mouthfuls, "I've never been here before. It's nice."

"It's your home, son," his father had said. "Remember that." He patted Buddy's hand. "Now listen carefully," he went on. "This is important for all of us." The sound of *all of us* warmed Buddy's insides, and everything else but right now seemed never to have happened. "It's essential that we get you back to Holly Hill tonight." Buddy felt himself take a nosedive. A sense of betrayal folded him. Where seconds before he'd been spread out clean and unafraid, he was now only a tiny inner package, scared. His mother touched his arm, "Wait, Bud." He barely heard her. Inside, he was running away so fast, he felt winded.

"Buddy, look." His father gripped Buddy's hand.

"Let go," Buddy said, and tried to pull away, but his father wouldn't let go. Oddly, in the sudden strength of the man, Buddy felt not a threat but something else: His father was keeping him from someplace he'd started to go but didn't really want to. His father was holding on to him for dear life.

"Not on your life, I won't let go," his father said, and hung on until Buddy knew it was all right.

"Harry, be careful," his mother's voice warned, and Buddy wasn't sure what she feared. Maybe him.

"Later, Irene. The damage is done." Buddy remembered sharp, hot fragments of something he thought was all gone. In a flash he realized his father knew everything.

"Oh, Jesus, I'm really sorry. I didn't mean . . ." It all seemed so far away, he could have been apologizing for a stranger's bad dream. He felt his father's grip relax momentarily, saw his parents' eyes shoot each other private questions, just like all those other times. He was fading, soon to become no one. *Don't let go,* he silently begged his father. *I'll do whatever you tell me to, just don't let go, don't leave me.*

". . . all busted and broken," his father was saying to him.

"That," Buddy answered, remembering the chairs, "but worse. I really screwed up." *Don't let go,* he kept wishing. *Don't.* He looked down at the hands, his father's and his own, locked in their curious handshake. His own knuckles were white, and for a second he wasn't sure who was holding on to whom. Just

to be safe, he said aloud, "Don't let go, Dad, please."

"The fire, Bud?" his mother asked hesitantly, as if she really didn't want an answer. He leaned toward his father for protection.

"Not now, Irene," his father said calmly.

"Did he think it was us? Did you think it was *our* house? Bud?"

"No, not yours. I knew that. I didn't think. I couldn't. I wasn't myself." How could he make them understand so his father wouldn't let go?

"You're safe with us, son, but you'll be safer at Holly Hill. Krause says—"

"You're going to take me to the police, aren't you?" There, he'd said it.

"No, Bud, no police. Believe me. Krause says

it's his fault. He's taking responsibility for whatever's happened. Are you with me, Buddy? Do you understand what I'm saying?"

Buddy nodded.

"You've got to trust us, Buddy. We can't go on, the three of us, being enemies any longer. We're in this together, and lately I've begun to understand that it's the only way we'll get out." Buddy knew that something was being said with their hands that meant more than words. But what? He'd been waiting so long for a sign from his people, and all he got were messages he couldn't rely on. He didn't understand who could be trusted to be who they claimed to be. He'd made so many mistakes.

Yet sitting there at his parents' kitchen table with moths flinging themselves at the screens, there rose in him the strangest idea: that here was where the chance of things was. Maybe everything could be looked at in ways he never dreamed, like those pictures they were always showing him, where he could see the two witches in profile but never the vase with handles. It was like he just caught sight of the vase.

"*Trust* you?" he said finally, and had trouble getting the words out.

"Who else is there?" his father said quietly. He kept a firm hold on Buddy's hand, eyeing him steadily, and Buddy knew there was no one and never had been, only voices that couldn't be counted on. Now he was alone, except for the two of them who'd been gentle with him. He never paid much attention to their kindness, or wanted their persistence all these years to count for anything. They'd been grim about it, but they'd stood by him. He often wondered what terrible things he did to deserve them; now it dawned on him, maybe they wondered the same about him.

"Maybe so," he said. "But I'm really in deep now." He feared they would send him to jail, to make sure he never hurt anything ever again. But hurt hadn't been the point. He wasn't sure *what* the point had been, but not that.

"Help me," he said, and heard his voice sounding high and far away. His father rose stiffly out of his chair and, without releasing Buddy's hand, moved toward him, pulling Buddy to his feet too. Then his father put his other arm around him in a strange one-armed embrace. Buddy wasn't prepared for this, nor for the tears streaming down his father's face. "Dad, Dad," he said awkwardly. "It'll be all right." He had never seen his father cry.

"Your father nearly killed himself today," his mother said dryly, and for a minute Buddy thought she meant what she said and was overcome with a sense of unexpected camaraderie. Then he understood from the way they both looked that that wasn't what she had meant. Still, some movement toward balance stayed with him.

"I thought I was a real goner," his father said, trying to smile. "You too," he added, nodding at Buddy. He blew his nose on a handkerchief fished from his pocket and adjusted his glasses. "Now here we both are. That's something." He smiled a little off-center smile and shook his head.

Buddy thought, He is talking to me like I'm not crazy, almost like he's not afraid of what I'll do next. But even if it were true, this couldn't last. He only felt safe because his father was holding on to him. When his father let go, he would be nowhere again.

But when his father let go of his hand to drive the car, and Buddy was sitting next to him in the front seat he still thought of as his mother's, Buddy found he really was still there. He didn't sink out of sight but only into half sleep that lasted all the way back to Holly Hill. And when his parents left, he hardly bothered with acting like they were abandoning him.

Seeing Krause again wasn't so bad. He made Buddy feel so welcome, it was odd. Standing next to the small man in his pin-striped bathrobe, Buddy felt like a giant, good enough that he could imagine he had just returned from a whirlwind two-week concert tour, all rave reviews. But no. He left; he came back. Something was over. Was it only a trip? He had dreaded the chewing-out he would get from Krause. Even now, as Krause hangs up the phone and turns around in his chair, Buddy can't believe he's escaped it.

"Forgive me," Krause says, moving his chair toward Buddy again, his little feet pedaling across the floor. "Always something."

"Sure," Buddy says. Maybe the medication is keeping him calm now. On this couch, in his laid-back state, he could be a guest on Merv Griffin, all cool and easy.

"I want to reiterate what I said last night,"

Krause tells him, and clears his throat. "I'm bound, as you know, by the confidentiality of our relationship." Krause removes his glasses and presses two well-manicured fingers to his eyes.

"It wasn't your fault, Kevin," the sightless Krause continues, "that you bit off more than you could chew. I'm speaking here of your freedom, of course." Krause replaces his glasses and pats his hair. "Nor was it your fault that you had a need to act out your fear of that freedom. It must have been terrifying." Krause pins him with a look so intense, Buddy squirms. Krause's eyes are enormous. In the past Buddy's often laughed when Krause came on strong like this. Now he just stares back into Krause's eyes.

"Face it, Kevin," Krause says. "You're no pyromaniac and never have been. A modest flirtation compared to the serious pathology." Krause pushes his chair backward a little. "We'll go into this later. Tonight I just wanted to make sure you know you're safe. You do know that, don't you?"

Buddy nods as if he believes this, suddenly remembering brilliant light.

"By the way," Krause says, standing up, signaling to Buddy their time is over. "Short hair gives you a whole new look. Very nice." He smiles. "You look like a different person."

"A regular guy," Buddy says, towering over him. "Maybe there's hope." That sounds like something his father would say. He has no idea how it came out of his mouth.

"Oh, there's hope," Krause says, moving closer to Buddy. "It's up to us, to you and me.

I can hang in there with you for as long as it takes. And *you*—if you'll just pay attention this time, you really can be"—Krause sneezes violently and makes a flying leap for the box of tissues—"free!" he says, coming out of it. "Free to be who you are without all this *junk* in your way." Krause looks up at him and nods slowly.

The idea that Krause could actually help him has never sunk in before. Now, incredibly, Buddy sees a glimmer of hope. He's torn between wanting to say this and something else on his mind.

He finally gives in to the latter. "Right here," Buddy says, gazing down at Krause and fingering a spot under his own nose. "A little . . . *you* know."

Krause swipes his upper lip with the tissue. It's gone. He smiles broadly. "There you go, Kevin!" he says, slapping Buddy on the back. "That's the spirit. That's the *caring* you we're going to see a lot more of, just wait! You're going to make it, believe me!"

High above Krause, the newly proclaimed Caring Buddy, self-appointed snot-spotter of Holly Hill, smiles, distantly aware that something seems to have been baked out of him in the dazzling light.

"Kitty! Kitty! Here, Kitty, kitty!" Carol Ann peers through the screen. The air is heavy and hard to breathe, and the day is too dark for eight o'clock. A good morning to turn up the air conditioner and go back to sleep.

felt hot and prickly under Carol Ann's bare feet. Now you seldom see hollyhocks anymore, she thinks, and the stories have all changed. Her grandmother has been dead for years.

She sets her mug on the table and goes back to the door to call the cat again. Except for a box of horticulture books and a frayed green toothbrush, the cat's the last vestige of Ben. The cat used to avoid Carol Ann, but has taken to sleeping at the foot of her bed since Ben left. For the past two mornings, though, it hasn't been there, and the food she put out yesterday wasn't touched.

Carol Ann wanders back into the kitchen, twisting the bottom of the oversize, faded blue T-shirt she filched from Ben. The front says, "I Ran in the Bellwood Sesquicentennial 10-K!" She never asked Ben if he ran in that race, wherever Bellwood is. Ben never ran at all when he was with her.

A terrible yearning for him comes over her, so acute that she closes her eyes against the sheer physicalness of it. She wishes he were still here, that nothing had changed. She thought she was getting better after Robin came for lunch yesterday. But later that afternoon when she went to the bank, she spotted Ben across the parking lot. Her knees turned to jelly. She sat there in her car watching him, her heart banging away.

He went into the drugstore and came out a minute later with his hand resting casually on the shoulder of a small wiry blonde who wore a suit and carried a briefcase. The blonde, at least from a distance, had the look of a washed-out urchin. Carol Ann couldn't believe this

She glances around the yard once more, then steps back into the kitchen where she left her coffee. Sipping, she stares out of the breakfast nook window onto the bed of hollyhocks. The red and pinks and violets are vivid in the flat light. She remembers when she and her grandmother used to make hollyhock ladies, tiny blossomy creatures with petal skirts who were always getting ready for the grandest balls. Clothespin princes in black-crayoned cutaway coats waltzed the hollyhock girls around and around as Carol Ann, and sometimes her grandmother, twirled them above grass that was Constantina. She needed to think of Constantina as someone perfect in all the ways she was not. She decided Ben was two-timing Constantina with the small woman on his way back to her, Carol Ann. This idea exhilarated her, and she backed out of the parking space with her hopes soaring. When she got home, though, she was shaken, she had to lie down. She knew it wouldn't work out like that. It didn't matter who the blond was.

Carol Ann now realizes she never liked Ben as much as she loved him. Recently she's begun to think maybe she didn't love him, she was just crazy about his body. Physically Ben undoes her. Even now the merest thought of his touch raises an alarming sensation in her chest—as if, of all things, her heart is on fire. Her feelings about Ben are so sharp, they obliterate her. Maybe the reason she felt better the night she threw herself at Robin was because with him she was more than a throbbing need. Rejected, she was at least herself. She'd said what was on her mind. With Ben she quietly absorbed everything.

When she finally came to her senses yesterday afternoon, she realized she never made it to the bank or the store. The whole botched day made her mad. She was acting like someone she didn't know, and this frightened her; she wasn't sure what to expect from herself next. She wondered how she could contemplate moving away, to New York of all places, if she were really this new, feeble person instead of her old reliable self.

To prove she could still function, she got up from her bed and called—not Robin, whom she thought of first—but a woman she taught with and hardly knew, an art teacher named Hanna. The two arranged to go to an outdoor concert that night. Carol Ann felt a little shell-shocked sitting on the same Hudson blanket she and Ben always sat on, in the same area of the bowl's enormous lawn. The orchestra played the overture from *La Bohème* and *The Grand Canyon Suite.* She watched the stars come out and permitted herself to believe her heart would never mend, a thought that seemed ridiculous in the face of the clear night and the promise it held.

This morning, with the world outside so gloomy, she no longer feels tragic. She's annoyed. The cat she never wanted in the first place, and which Ben should have taken with him, is gone, and now she's the person responsible.

Ben had found the kitten a year ago, under a bush in someone's yard. It was nearly dead when he brought it home. Carol Ann nursed it with a dropper, but the kitten grew up to be snooty. Though *she* was the one who fed it and changed its litter, Ben was the one it nuzzled up to.

Carol Ann doesn't know why Ben left the cat, if he thought it would be company or just forgot. But the more she thinks about this now, the angrier she becomes. Ben was as cavalier with the cat as he was with her feelings.

Outside, it suddenly begins to pour so heavily, she can't see her neighbor's house across the driveway. Something in the rain's terrific battering noise rouses Carol Ann to action, and before she knows it, she is dialing the number of the nursery.

The phone line crackles with static. Carol Ann can't believe what she's doing until she hears someone answer. Her stomach registers this with a long elevator drop, and she sits down, a little breathless.

"Abruzzo and Sons," a voice says through the static.

"I'd like to speak to Ben, please."

"This *is* Ben," the voice says, obviously no idea who she is. Carol Ann freezes. She doesn't know how to begin. She could hang up the phone and no one would be the wiser.

"Hello?" Ben says again. The phone line crackles dangerously. Carol Ann wonders if it's true you can be struck by lightning through a telephone receiver.

"Ben, it's me," she finally gets out. "Me, Carol Ann."

"Hey!" Ben says from a great distance. "Carol Ann! What's up?" His voice sounds hollow. She could be someone calling on business, no one at all. The roar of the rain subsides as the storm settles into a steady downpour. She watches rain rilling down the glass, blurring the colors of the hollyhocks. She takes a deep breath.

"Your cat ran away, that's what's up," she says, amazingly clearheaded all of a sudden. "I want you to come and help me find her, and then I want you to take her with you. I'm sure you didn't mean to leave her, anyway."

"*My* cat," Ben says, and sounds annoyed. "Carol Ann, she's *your* cat."

"*Mine?*" Carol Ann is flabbergasted. Who is he kidding? Already he's altered their history. "Let's not get confused," she says slowly. "The cat's always been yours, Ben."

A pause, and then, as if he's talking to a child, he says, "Well, if you need someone to help you find her, possibly I could come over later today. Just let me check." Before Carol Ann knows what's happening, he puts her on hold.

She's so astonished at the turn their conversation has taken, she pulls the receiver away from her ear and looks at it, as if the phone itself might be at fault. Sudden, fierce anger nearly bowls her over. She feels like she's been saving this up for years. In the time they were together, they never had a fight. She scarcely ever raised her voice. He was always getting his way, and she was always giving in, as if her feelings weren't important. Her scalp tingles as though someone is pulling her hair.

"I can't make it today," he says, coming back on the line. "I've got this appointment. Maybe tomorrow."

Carol Ann's head swims.

"You still there?" he asks, and sounds sheepish.

She opens her mouth, but what comes out is nothing she planned, nothing that seems remotely like her. "You fuckhead!" she screams into the phone. "You stupid, insensitive shit! I hate you!" She slams the receiver down and rushes to the back hall where she struggles into a pair of rubber boots and her red slicker.

She flings open the back door as the phone begins ringing, exactly as she knew it would, but doesn't pause. She steps out into the rain, skipping down the steps and striding quickly around the corner of the house. The phone rings and rings behind her. It stops for a second, then starts up again, becoming fainter the farther she gets from the house. After a few minutes she can't hear it at all.

She moves easily through the rain, as if it were her element and all she had to do was glide. "Kitty!" she calls. "Kitty! Here, kitty!" She feels cleansed and swift, more like herself than she's felt in ages.

Tony refers to the small red notebook he found behind the bathroom radiator as Exhibit A. The police missed it when they searched the house for clues and dusted for fingerprints, making a worse mess than was already there. He was really excited. He talked his mother into letting him Xerox the contents before he handed the notebook over to the police. Tony had high hopes of figuring out the notes and solving the mystery of who had set fire to their house. He imagined a headline: TONY WATTERS TRACKS DOWN ARSONIST. He imagined himself a hero on the six o'clock news.

But the notebook doesn't make sense. His mother helped him decipher the tiny, dense scrawl and told him to forget it, the notes were nonsense. Tony hates to admit she's right. He persists in thinking there's a code to uncover the writer's identity. By now he's read through the pages so often, he's memorized snatches. They haunt him—like the list of nonsense words he learned for a science experiment last year and was supposed to forget immediately but couldn't get out of his head for weeks.

On this rainy afternoon Tony takes the slightly out-of-focus photocopies and settles down at the desk in Mona's pink-and-white guest room. Every now and then a moist breeze lifts the white ruffled curtains. He crosses his fingers; maybe today he'll find something new.

He begins in the middle, skipping seven or eight boring pages on Vincent van Gogh. Tony reads.

> I propose to explode the myth of the supremacy of the psychomedical establishment by showing how it is possible to determine the nature and extent to which tissue disease and psychical organization are interrelated.

Tony frowns and goes on.

> Traditionally the avoidance of this connection can be traced to the destructive collusion between medicine and psychiatry, an arrangement that, if examined closely, reveals the root of all evil—*greed!* In their lust for wealth, doctors show contempt not only for patients but also for scientific inquiry.

Tony stares out the window. He tries to think of his father as a greedy person like Scrooge, but can't. His father may be serious and quiet, but he's not greedy. Come to think of it, since they've been staying at Mona's house, his father hasn't been as serious or quiet as usual. He's different somehow, more cheerful and talkative. Lately his mother's the one who's silent and sort of grim—almost as if his parents had traded places. Tony doesn't know what to make of this.

> I fully expect to be branded a maniac or brushed aside as a know-nothing. Even people of vision may be unconvinced for a while. But I am confident that my thesis can stand the test of time and personal abuse. Eventually I will be vindicated because my work bears the weight of *truth!* Given the challenge of my insights . . .

Tony skips several paragraphs.

> Thus I prepare myself. Within the next decade I will definitely claim my sphere of influence. When my treatise on van Gogh's retardation is completed and made public, it will alter humanity's understanding of experience for all time!

He flips impatiently over several pages of doodles, and a drawing of a bird that looks like a parrot. A balloon coming out of the parrot's beak says, "Hey, Buddy! Look under your seat!"

The whole thing stumps Tony. When he showed the notes to his father, his father said, "Don't ask me," but he did take them to a psychiatrist at the hospital, a friend of his, Dr. Shelby. Dr. Shelby told his father that the notes revealed a familiarity with terms you could pick up from almost any article on mental illness. The writer's interest in van Gogh wasn't surprising; for years people had been fascinated with van Gogh's art and madness. Dr. Shelby didn't think *retardation* was a term that would naturally come to mind when you thought about van Gogh. It sounded pretty far out to him. Of course, he couldn't attempt a diagnosis based on the notebook.

The poems might interest someone, Dr. Shelby said. He himself didn't know much about poetry. Tony's mother called the poems junk, but Tony sort of likes one of them, even though he doesn't really understand it.

A Riddle

I rhyme with heaven (also mud)
I'm old but always new
I'm all alone yet crowded by
The doubles I've been through

I'm homeless but I search for home
Through endless, blackened night
Where phantom paths of brilliant fire
Illuminate my flight

Look for me in shadow-land
Or when the moon flies by
Watch for me, wait for me
And tell me, who am I?

Tony thinks about this one a lot. He's gone over and over rhymes for heaven, but all he can get are seven and eleven. Mud rhymes with more things—spud and dud, flood, stud, thud. Also crud. Seven-eleven stud. He wonders, is that poker, or some greaser who hangs around a 7-11 store?

Tony stacks the papers together and turns off the desk lamp. He keeps thinking something will fly off the page and suddenly make sense, but nothing ever does. He can feel himself losing interest. So much for his dreams of being a big hero.

Things are weird, he thinks. Not just the crazy notebook but the fire and all—and staying here at Mona's where everyone is acting kind of strange. And even though he likes the rain, it makes things seem unreal. It's wet all the time, and dark. He wishes school would start, and longs for a normal life—like he used to have before the summer wrecked everything.

He switches on the small TV on the dresser. As he does, he hears someone banging pans around in the kitchen. Mona must be starting her daily cooking marathon. Ugh.

On the TV there's a rerun of *Leave It to Beaver.* Tony sprawls across the bed, propping his head in his hand, prepared to give all his attention to the program, but the back door slams and he hears his father's voice. What's *he* doing home so early? Tony thinks of calling down, but it's too much trouble.

The rain starts up again, and Tony watches TV, growing sleepier and sleepier. He dozes off, and when he wakes up, Phil Donahue is on. Half asleep, he hears Mona's voice at the bottom of the stairs, though he can't make out her words. Something peculiar in her tone jars Tony wide-awake. Silently he slides off the bed hands first, and turns off the TV. Then he steps out into the hall.

"I thought you and I were in the same boat," Mona says. She sounds sort of mad. His father's reply is muffled. Tony waits, listening hard, but their voices continue, too low for him to hear. He moves closer toward the stairs, then slips back into the room, afraid of getting caught, knocking down the wastebasket in his haste.

"Will! Scott! Is that you?" Mona calls. "Who's up there?"

"Just me," Tony yells back. Then, for good measure, adds, "I was asleep." He turns the TV back on.

In a minute his father walks into the room, his sport coat slung over his shoulder, along with his tie. "Tony!" he says, "what's up? Mona thought you went to the movies with Will and Scott."

"Naw," Tony answers. "How come you're here?"

"It's Wednesday." His father smiles.

"Oh, yeah, I forgot," Tony says. He wants to ask what's wrong with Mona but instead asks, "Where's Mom?"

"At the library, I guess."

Tony studies his father's face. It's a whole lot friendlier without the beard. He never liked his father's beard.

"I'm glad you're here," his father says. "Come over to the house with me and we'll see what the plasterers are up to. When they're

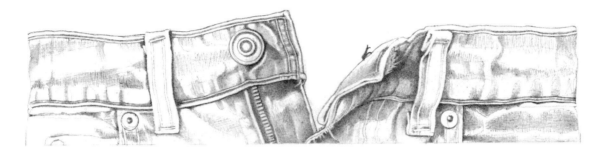

finished, we can move back in. The painters will have to paint around us.''

His father ambles down the hall into the bedroom he and Tony's mother share, and Tony follows, glad for the company. The smell of cooking drifts up the stairs. Tony dreads Mona's enormous dinners. It's like she's trying to smother them all in food. ''Food is love,'' his mother told him when he complained.

''She means well, Tony,'' his father said.

As far as Tony's concerned, food is food.

''I can't wait to get home,'' Tony says to his father's back.

''I know,'' his father says from the closet. ''This is kind of a strain on everyone, especially Mona. She's been working pretty hard to make us feel comfortable.'' Tony feels like this is something his father wouldn't say to Will.

His father emerges from the closet zipping up his jeans. ''Ready, buddy?'' he asks, clasping Tony's shoulder.

''You bet,'' Tony says. He feels like they're going someplace special, not just next door: him and his dad on a big adventure.

When Mona hears David and Tony clump down the stairs, she ducks across the hall into the bathroom. She can't bear to face David right now. Gazing in the mirror, she thinks how ridiculous her pigtails are, done up in red ribbons, how flat as a board she looks in her T-shirt. A real dish she is, some femme fatale! Lord, how resistible can you get.

Besides, no matter what David said, he probably does think she's off her rocker. But *touched?* Had he really said *touched?* And was that before or after she said . . . oh, God.

Smelling the sausage she left on the stove, Mona flies out of the bathroom, nearly falling over Penny, who is spread out in front of the door. Mona screams the dog's name. Looking befuddled, the dog slinks down the hall.

''Don't be so *sen*sitive!'' Mona yells after her, ''I'm sorry!'' Mona hurries to the stove and breaks up the sausage with a wooden spoon.

Don't think about it, she tells herself, and then, of course, thinks about it. She can't sort things out. For years she'd pegged David as quiet and aloof. She's always been a little scared of him. But lately, having him around every day . . . Lord love a duck, she thinks, she actually figured David for someone smooth and worldly underneath that cool exterior. Maybe it was her, maybe she came on too strong. . . . "Lunkhead!" she says aloud.

She drops ground beef into the sausage and stirs the mixture absently. Before she knows it, she's scattered meat all over the top of the stove and has to stop to clean up. Her mother always told her she was too neat to be a good cook. Her mother told her lots of things like that. Was that sort of advice supposed to get her into the twenty-first century?

"You numskull, Mona," she says. She tells herself to take it easy, but she's flustered.

Since the Watterses moved into her house almost three weeks ago, David's been sweet and cheerful, so helpful and attentive that she couldn't believe it. Between him coming on so friendly and Kay acting so far away and sullen, Mona began to think David really enjoyed her company. Things crossed her mind that wouldn't have entered it before. She should have let them to go to a motel like Kay wanted. Then none of this would have happened.

This afternoon David walked in the back door with a big smile on his face. "Hey, Mona!" he said in that darling way he had. "You look like you're getting ready to cook up a storm again. How about a break? You work too hard."

"Busy hands," she started to say, but couldn't remember what came next.

"Busy hands, my foot," he said, laughing.

He offered to go out for pizza or, better yet, take her and Kay someplace snazzy for dinner. "C'mon, Mona," he said. "You name it, I'll make reservations."

This threw her. "Don't be silly," she replied. Then she burst out, "It's like a fantasy for me, honestly. I never tell this to anyone, but I always wanted a big family. But Sam . . . well, Sam didn't, and that was that." She was astonished to find herself talking this way. "It's nice having you all here," she added. "I love cooking big dinners every night."

At that moment she had a powerful urge to tell him the secrets of her life. She was even ready to say that with him around her ravenous hunger was curiously quelled. But how would it sound if she told him he made her lose her appetite? He probably didn't suspect she had any appetite to begin with.

"Well," he said, "let's definitely take a rain check on that. You're terrific, and we appreciate it. Sam doesn't know what he's missing. Poor guy, I'd go crazy with all that traveling." David pulled a chair out from under the table and sat down, straddling it backward. The simple act nearly melted her heart.

"It must get pretty lonesome for you at times," David said, loosening his tie and pulling it off.

"Oh, David," she said in a rush, "you have no idea." The change in her tone caught her off-guard. Her heart began to race.

He looked at her steadily, his brow furrowed. "*That* bad?"

She nodded silently and turned her back. She was on the verge of doing something insane, and she knew it. She had no intention of stopping either. She filled the dishwasher with the lunch dishes, then flipped it on. All the while she was conscious of his eyes on her back.

"Gee," David said when she stopped making a racket.

"Gee?"

"I guess I don't know what to say."

"Don't say a word," Mona said. She turned around. "Just take me."

He looked up at her, confused.

"Take me," she repeated. She was suddenly lean and streamlined inside, instead of her usual blimpish self. She was beautiful. Passion and romance weren't just things you saw on TV or read about in books. They were right here in her kitchen. He was so sexy.

But David's face was all wrong. He looked lost. "Mona," he finally got out.

"I need you, David," Mona said.

Mona blushes at the thought and drains the meat. "You nitwit," she says, and launches into a béchamel sauce. She melts the butter while she peels and chops an onion. By the time she's finished, she's all tears and sniffles. She adds the chopped onion and half a cup of water to the melted butter, turning up the heat.

"Wow," is what David said then.

Mona grew patient. She watched David roll his tie into a neat little ball and examine it. "We're grown-ups, after all," she told him.

He stopped fiddling with his tie. He took forever to back out of his chair and replace it under the table. "Mona," he said when the chair was perfectly positioned, "I'm . . . uh . . . really touched. I'm not much good at this. In fact I'm lousy, but . . . well, I am, touched, I mean."

Touched? She tried to make the word fit. When she couldn't, she said, *"Touched?"* This came out much louder than she intended.

He nodded and looked worried.

"What is this 'touched,' anyway?" she said. "I want you. I lay it all on the line and you're 'touched'?" She racked her brain for another approach.

"Slow down, Mona," David said quietly. "This isn't exactly easy."

"You can say *that* again!" she said. "Is something the matter with me, David?"

He picked up the salt shaker and turned it this way and that. "No, of course not," he said, fingering the salt he had spilled.

She had never felt so bold in her life, but she couldn't quite get out the words. She screwed up her courage. "Then come upstairs with me," she said.

The dishwasher began roaring.

"Let's get out of here," David said, and went into the dining room.

Mona felt frantic. "You think I'm insane," she said, "I know you do."

"No," he said. He shook his head and went right on walking into the front hall. She tagged after him. "It's just that . . . well, I *am touched.*" He seemed to be talking to the floor. "I know how hard it must have been for you to . . . uh . . . talk like that, and I don't take it lightly, but . . ." He stood looking out the screen door.

"Listen," he said in the direction of Jefferson. "We can't, I mean, it wouldn't, well, it wouldn't be right." He cleared his throat. "You're a wonderful person and you're very attractive, and it's an . . . interesting idea, and I hope you know how fond I am of you, but . . ."

Mona knew only that her hopes were dashed. His back was to her, and he seemed to be testing the doorknob, twisting it back and forth, clicking the lock on and off. She thought she was going to scream.

"The fact is," he said, abandoning the knob and facing her, "the fact is, you're married. I'm married." He looked somber.

"Oh, don't be so square," she blurted out.

"But I *am* square," he said.

"No one would ever have to know," she said.

"We'd know," he replied gravely.

Mona sat down on a step and put her head in her hands. She felt like a fool. He came over to her and pulled her to her feet. Two steps up from him, she was the same height he was.

"Listen," he said, looking right into her eyes. His voice was firmer now. "I'm sorry to be so awkward," he said evenly, "but it wouldn't work. Really."

She put her head on his shoulder. "I'm so lonely," she said. "I had this pipe dream. I thought you cared. What an imbecile I was. I'm sorry."

"You're okay," he said gently, patting her on the back. "You are, Mona. You're the best. If Sam were home more, you'd be just fine."

"That skunk!" she said with unexpected venom.

"It's tough with him gone so much." David's voice was soothing, reassuring.

"It's terrible," she admitted. She pulled away and straightened up. "I thought I was doing okay, but the fact is, I'm beginning to think of myself as one of those single parents or something. I try to stay busy, but . . ."

"Maybe when this latest deal's over, he'll come home and stay home," David suggested.

"Fat chance!" she huffed. "You don't know Sam. He'll probably cook up something on Mars, as far away as he can get. Just watch!"

"C'mon, Mona. Don't be so hard on him."

"Honest to Pete, I don't think I can live this way anymore," she said. "I hate to admit it, but I've about had it up to here." She tapped the top of her head.

"Does Sam know how you feel?"

"It wouldn't make any difference, but no. Whenever he's here, I forget how bad it is when he's not."

"Don't you think you ought to sit down and tell him how you feel? Talk to him? Maybe he doesn't know," David urged.

"You're a fine one to talk about *talking!* I never see you and Kay talk. Why, I haven't even seen you two alone since you walked in this house!"

At the mention of Kay, David went back to the door and stared out. Mona was afraid she'd gone too far. "Well, maybe I just missed it," she said, "but sometimes you two seem like strangers."

After a moment of silence David said, "Things have been upsetting lately—the fire and not being at home. Kitty takes things pretty hard. She gets quiet. I try not to press her." He sounded forlorn.

"Maybe you should," Mona said. "Besides," she barged on, "she goes away just like Sam. She disappears like he does, only she never leaves home. I've watched her."

"*Kitty?*" David said. "Is that the way it looks?"

Mona nodded. "I guess that's why I let myself go to pieces just now. I thought you and I were in the same boat."

David looked like he'd seen a ghost.

"Maybe," she offered hesitantly, trying to soften things, "maybe you should . . . practice what you preach."

He nodded stiffly. "Thanks."

Funny. She started out to seduce him and he turned her down flat. Now she was sitting here giving him advice. Her big love scene, what a howl.

"You said a while ago we were grown-ups," David said. "It sure isn't easy, is it?" He seemed worn out.

"Oh, how would I know?" Mona said. "I just thought it was a nice idea. You're a very sexy man." Having said this, she felt tremendously relieved. She no longer had anything to hide.

"What can I say?" He smiled.

"How about 'nice try'?" she suggested.

This time he actually laughed. It was then that Mona heard a noise upstairs and leapt up, calling, "Will? Scott? Is that you? Who's up there?"

"It's Sherlock Holmes," David said when Tony yelled down to them.

"Oh," she said, "I'll shoot myself if he heard."

"Don't worry," David said, starting up the stairs.

"Dollars to doughnuts he was plugged into that radio," Mona said. "Let's hope." She grabbed David's hand and clung to it for a second before letting go. Then he was off up the stairs.

As she fills a large pot with water for the lasagna noodles, she scolds herself again for letting her lamebrained ideas get the best of her. How could she? She wonders if she really is lonely for Sam. These days she's out of the habit of even thinking about him; it's strange.

She slices mushrooms and tosses them for a minute in a little butter. Then she slips the noodles into the boiling water. Lately Sam's been home so little that when he is, he almost seems to be interfering with her life. Gad, she thinks, that's how far gone she is—treating her own husband like a visiting nuisance, mooning over her friend's husband, trying to get him into bed. She's been paying attention to all the wrong things.

The timer on the stove buzzes. Mona hoists the pot of water to the sink and drains the noodles. As the steam rises, she resolves that come hell or high water, she'll find a way to talk to Sam.

In a well-greased lasagna pan she arranges a layer of noodles. Over this she spoons béchamel sauce and the meat, continuing with layers of cheese until she has a neat casserole. She covers the dish with foil and writes in black marker across it: "375°/20 min." Mona marvels at how efficient she is in some areas of her life. In the ones that really count, forget it.

While she's cleaning up the kitchen, Mona hears Kay's car and looks up to see her running through the rain toward the back door. Mona's not in the mood to see Kay, of all people.

"What smells so good?" Kay asks coming into the kitchen.

"White lasagna," Mona answers. "An old recipe from Sam's mother."

"Well, it's too bad he's not here to enjoy it," Kay says, shaking her wet head.

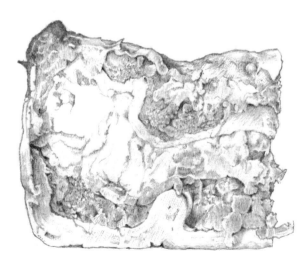

"Sam?"

"Of course Sam. Who else?" The way Kay says this, Mona realizes that everyone except her finds it odd that Sam's never home. This makes her angry—at herself and at him too.

"Oh, Sam!" Mona says disgustedly. "He gives me a pain where a pill won't reach!"

Kay looks shocked, but Mona's struck by how good it feels to say what's down deep in her mind and not bubbling safely along on the tip-top of it. People always call her frank, but that's only because she talks so much. Being honest is different from being a blabbermouth.

"What's the matter, Mona?" Kay asks, frowning. "What happened?"

"The matter is—" Mona says, and stops. She wants to get the words exactly right. "The matter is that no one seems to be paying attention to the right things. Not Sam, not me either. Oh, shoot!"

Kay appears stupefied. "What's come over you, Mona? What is it?"

"It's no big deal," Mona answers. "I guess I'm just tired of Sam being away so much."

"I bet you miss his sweet rolls." Kay laughs.

"Oh, for crying out loud, Kay!" Kay tries to make everything into a joke, but maybe she has a point. Sam's a wonderful baker with a knack Mona never acquired. It seems a lifetime ago, but she and Sam used to spend hours cooking together on weekends. Then she went on a diet, and Sam lost his best customer. Shortly after that Mona lost *him* when he decided to leave home in search of a fortune in fossil fuel. Standing at the sink with a scouring pad in her hand, Mona feels her mouth nearly water at the thought of all the fun she and Sam used to have.

"You seem upset," Kay says.

"You bet your library books I'm upset!" Mona drops what she's doing and rushes out of the room.

"Mona?" Kay calls behind her. "Mona? Do you want to talk about it?"

"No thanks," Mona says as she runs up the stairs. She has a vision of Sam in a big white apron, his Paul Newman eyes twinkling, flour on his nose. Here she went to pieces over David, when it was Sam she wanted all along. Sam, that lout. Sam of the rich, gooey, sticky rolls. Sam.

U nder the pretense of preparing for the upcoming semester, which doesn't start for a month and is the farthest thing from her mind these days, Katherine's taken up residence in a musty basement corner of the Lethem Public Library.

While rain poured out of the downspouts, Katherine worked her way quickly through Jane Austen. Today she's moved on to Henry James. Beefing up on the decorum of gentler times soothes her. Besides, as long as she's reading, she doesn't think much—except to bat away an annoying contagion of rain remarks, old saws, poems, snatches of songs. Frequently she finds herself intoning, "It's raining, it's pouring" or "Dr. Foster went to

Gloucester . . ." This drives her crazy. So does the weather. So do other things.

"Hear the whisper of the raindrops blowing soft . . ."

The minute she puts a book down, thoughts of Robin Hastings assault her— guilty, indecorous thoughts that keep going out to Robin and coming back to her like boomerangs. Out and back, out and back. It's dizzying, it's insane.

In her head, Robin is all mixed up with the fire—as if that's where her heated, if privately held, designs on him lead. Often it seems that she and Robin are in secret collusion, silent accomplices in some passion no less affecting for having nothing to do with real life. She hasn't even seen him since she's been back, yet she grows nearly breathless with longing at the thought of him, as if she's only at this late date been awarded a body. It's like waking up and finding she has wings. It also makes her wonder if she's losing her marbles.

Since my man and I ain't together,
Keeps rainin' all the time.

Katherine has tried calling Robin. She's called him from the chilly phone next to the deli counter at Tano's, and from the one that hangs over the magazine rack at the drugstore. JEALOUS HUSBAND NAILS WIFE TO CROSS, she reads as she dials. WOMAN, 54, GIVES BIRTH TO SPACE ALIEN. A MANIAC STOLE MY FINGERS.

Robin's never home when she calls, and she refuses to leave her name.

She feels bewitched or lovesick, possibly both. Certainly she's overwrought. Her back goes up at the least little thing. This morning she shook her fist at a driver who pulled out in front of her, then laid into a gas station attendant who made her wait. Yesterday she nearly decked the dry cleaner. She's civil, but barely, to people she knows. With her family she moves on tiptoe.

She imagines in Robin's silence a longing for her he simply can't face. He is staying away out of well-controlled passion, an overzealous moral sense. What else could it be? In the meantime the streets of Lethem seem jammed with red pickup trucks.

The rain it raineth every day . . .

It rains constantly. Dramatic downpours that plaster the leaves to the sidewalks alternate with interminable drizzles. There's been so much rain that the Dameron River, normally placid this time of year, rushes noisily over the falls with a roar you can hear for blocks. Even when no rain falls, the sky is slaty. Katherine's freckles have begun to disconnect; her tan is fading. The sun appears so infrequently, it gives the impression of showing up by mistake.

Most summer activities have been suspended. The country club pool has been taken over by toads and frogs, and Mona's is drained for repairs. The water in the Rec Center pool turned an alarming shade of emerald due to mutating algae, and the pool was shut down. The boys' baseball games are canceled and rescheduled, then canceled again.

Earthworms crowd the pavement; snakes turn up in unexpected places. Mona found one in her basement and bludgeoned it to death with a sponge mop. Katherine discovered another on the backseat of her car—a small garter snake coiled neatly on top of a pile of books. Will had to get rid of it for her. She refused to drive for several days. When it came to symbols, she knew her stuff.

Into each life . . .

Katherine feels she wears her bewilderment like she does her slicker—everywhere. She isn't the only one who's a mess. Her son, Will, complains fiercely about the rain and at night suffers bad dreams during which he shouts explosively, nothing anyone can make sense of. When he's wakened, he talks about ghosts and boogeymen. In the morning he refuses to remember.

Will woke Scott Edwards, who slept in the upper bunk, so often that Katherine finally had to move her son into Mona's tiny sewing room at the back of the house. She still hears him, but sometimes she isn't able to rouse herself to go to his side. Eventually he shouts himself back to sleep.

David blames Will's unusual behavior on the disruptions caused by the fire. He insists Will will be fine when they're back in their own house. Katherine isn't convinced. She

thinks something funny's going on with Will, but he won't—or can't—talk.

The world is puddle-wonderful . . .

In contrast, Tony's in excellent spirits most of the time and goes overboard praising the weather. Several times Katherine has spied him leaping around on Mona's drive, his upturned face to the rain, engrossed in some happy private communion with the elements.

But an irritating version of this same child likes to think he's hot on the trail of the person who set the fire. Despite the fingerprint dust the Lethem P.D. slopped over everything, Tony turned up the only real clues anyone found: several carefully flattened candy wrappers (not scrunched up as his or Will's would be, he pointed out); and a spooky tape of Bob Marley and the Wailers, which led Tony to bone up on Rastafarianism and Haile Selassie and accounts for his sometimes referring to the unknown arsonist as "Rasta-Man." He also found a small notebook, which he copied at the library before handing it over to the police. Katherine helped him decipher the writing, and it was so deranged, it made her queasy.

At lunchtime Tony often packs up a sandwich and goes over to his own house to play records for the carpenters—three young Amishmen with broad, red-cheeked faces framed by fringes of beard. All of them share the last name of Yoder but insist they're not really related. At noon the three Yoders sit on the floor and shout requests to Tony as they eat their lunches. They call him D.J., which pleases him and makes up for the songs they ask him to play, mostly old Beatles and Bee Gee tunes Tony regards as antique.

Come on with the rain, I've a smile on my face!

Mona says she's tickled pink to have company. She insisted the Watterses stay at her house and wouldn't take no for an answer. With Sam gone, grown-ups would be a real treat, she said. Mona spends a lot of time in the kitchen cooking enormous meals, treating food with all the reverence of someone involved in a crank religion, serving it with no thought to calories or portions. Katherine can't figure out what's come over her. She thought Mona forgot about food years ago. Not that she eats; no one eats much. Even the boys aren't hungry. Leftovers pile up in the refrigerator, periodically disappearing—into the garbage, Katherine assumes, though this wastefulness doesn't square with Mona's latest civic undertaking to set up a recycling center at the town dump. What next?

Yesterday Katherine returned from the library to find Mona fit to be tied, something to do with Sam's absence, a fact of life Katherine assumed she was accustomed to by now. Katherine tried to jolly her by making a joke about Sam's sweet rolls, but Mona left in a huff. Katherine let it drop. There was enough confusion in her own life without Mona's.

It's raining violets . . .

Like Tony, David claims to love the rain and seems unusually spirited these days, almost as if the bad weather and the fire and this stint at Mona's were things he's been waiting for all his life. Details that wore Katherine out to even think about—insurance claims, clean up, the new construction—seem to energize him.

Sometimes at night while Katherine sits with her eyes glued to a book, she hears David talking about their house to Mona with an enthusiasm that confounds her. He's never taken much interest in domestic things before. Not that Katherine's complaining.

With her David remains as quiet as ever, and for once she finds a measure of comfort in his silence. He can't, after all, read her mind.

Somewhere over the rainbow . . .

A week after the fire, Mona heard from someone she met at a garage sale that the Newcombs had gone to Maine for a vacation. Wasn't it romantic, the woman said to Mona, how Harry and Irene were staying at the same hotel where they'd honeymooned twenty-five years ago? Relating this story to Katherine, Mona added, "Even for them, that's kind of cute. Think of it, a second honeymoon!"

Katherine groaned. The idea of the Newcombs on a second honeymoon seemed indecent, though who was she to raise the subject of indecency when her own mind was operating like some porno cottage industry?

"By the way," Mona said, "I have a feeling she's going to get pregnant fast, like in a fairy tale or something."

"Irene *Newcomb?!*" Katherine nearly spit out a mouthful of coffee.

"Don't be ridiculous, Kay," Mona clucked. "Princess Di, who else?"

Raindrops keep falling on my head . . .

Even Katherine's sense of humor seems off. Face it, she keeps telling herself, this is only temporary. But she feels permanently out of whack.

"Ah, *there* you are, Fraulein Professor," Agnes Barnhouse, the loathsome head librarian, gushes in Katherine's ear. Katherine jumps a foot. "There's a handsome young man looking for you. Just thought I'd warn you!" Agnes winks.

Robin's finally found her, Katherine thinks. Well, she's known all along he'd come around if she gave him enough time. Torn between relief and panic, she's dismayed to see Tony coming down the stairs.

"Tony!" she says, "My God, it's *you!*"

"You were expecting John Travolta?" Tony asks smartly. He picks up her purse and riffles through it, clearly in need of money. Agnes Barnhouse laughs and laughs.

Buddy takes mental pictures these days (Snap!). Krause suggested this as a way to anchor himself firmly in reality. When he remembers to do it, Buddy believes Krause's silly game actually works. The things he takes the time to focus on (Snap!), he doesn't forget. It's like keeping a diary or filling an imaginary scrapbook.

(Snap!): AT THE BARBERSHOP. HICKTOWN, U.S.A.

"You new around here?" the barber asks. He eyes Buddy in the mirror, taking in Wilt with the same glance. Wilt is the strong-arm they send everywhere with Buddy these days, and he's the only person sitting in the row of chairs behind Buddy. Wilt doesn't talk much, but he keeps a close watch.

The barber snip-snips. The guy looks like a relic from *Happy Days,* with his graying, greased pompadour. Buddy figures he must be the owner of the lowered '57 Impala parked at the curb by the twirling barber pole.

"Yeah, I'm new," Buddy answers.

The barber whistles a snatch of a tune, then says, "You're not one of them from up at Holly Hill, by any chance?"

Buddy inspects his knuckles and weighs the pros and cons of answering no. Only yesterday he promised Krause he would try to be more truthful. Krause said he was only fooling himself, anyway. The trouble with listening to Krause was that all of a sudden Buddy had a lot to remember.

"I'm up there, yeah," Buddy says. The barber plays it cool, though there's an unmistakable stiffening to his back.

"I mean, I'm studying the place," Buddy adds in a low voice so Wilt won't hear. "Extra credit for a term paper I'm working on." This is not quite the truth, but close enough. Buddy's tired of people thinking he's crazy. Somewhere about the time of the fire, the appeal began to dwindle.

Oddly enough the barber believes him. "It must be a little weird hanging around with those nuts night and day."

"They're people too," Buddy finds himself saying calmly.

"I don't know. The ones I see in here, it makes you wonder." Snip-snip.

"Search your heart," Buddy says, amazed at himself. "Didn't *you* ever feel a little bit crazy?"

The barber pauses and considers this. "Got me there," he finally admits. "When my wife left me a couple years back for some kid who wasn't much older than our son, I kind of went off my rocker. Drinking didn't help." He chuckles ruefully. Snip-snip. "I finally gave it up and came to."

"The booze, you mean?" Buddy asks.

"Yep," the barber says. Snip-snip. And then in an altogether different voice he adds, "God answered my prayers."

"God answered your prayers?" Buddy puzzles the words out.

"He always does," the barber says. "By the way, take a look. You want me to go shorter?"

Buddy nods without looking. "What exactly did God say?" Buddy asks with some urgency.

"God?" The barber stops and looks Buddy straight in the eye. "God only says three things, didn't you know that?" Snip-snip.

"What three things? What are they?"

The barber clears his throat. "God says yes. Or no. Or wait," he informs Buddy somberly.

For some reason Buddy expected more.

"He told me no, so I laid off the booze," the barber continues. Then He told me wait."

"And?" Buddy asks eagerly.

"She came back to me cuddly as a kitten," the barber says, smiling.

"Happily ever after," Buddy says, thinking the guy's story is a real loser.

"Not quite." The barber chuckles. "Right off I busted her nose, and she divorced me. Got a new one now." He sounds proud.

New what? The barber's wife got a new nose? "New one?" Buddy asks.

"New wife. Young too. The old one took her busted nose and headed out west." Snip-snip, cool as a cucumber.

Buddy ponders this apparent victory for abstinence and sanity while the barber takes out the electric razor and buzzes up the back of his neck and around his ears.

"It does my heart good," the barber says expansively, "seeing young guys like you going back to the old styles. Damned if you aren't a dead ringer for G.I. Joe." The barber whisks

Buddy's neck, then removes the white cape. "Short enough for you?" he inquires.

Buddy doesn't answer immediately. He's fascinated by the peculiar sight of his scalp through his light hair—what's left of it. The more he scrutinizes himself, the kinkier he looks. All he needs now is a pierced ear.

"Thanks a lot," Buddy says, and tips the barber a dollar. "Buy yourself a Coke or something."

"Never touch the stuff," the barber says, making a face. "I'm a Seven-Up man, myself. No caffeine, it's bad for you." As he says this the barber lights up a Camel.

Wilt motions with his head. "Gotta split," says Buddy. "See you around."

Once outside, Buddy can't stand it. "That guy," he tells Wilt, "that barber. He was *crazy*, man!"

"Sure he was," Wilt says.

(Snap!): THE MAILROOM AT HOLLY HILL

Today Buddy's the lucky recipient of two postcards, a big haul for him. The first one has a picture of a lighthouse on it.

Dear Bud,
I wish you could see all the seabirds here. There are so many, the beach is alive with their squawks and peeps. Do you remember how we used to watch birds when you were small? Secretly I've always wanted to be one—a ring-billed gull perhaps, or a tern. Have you ever thought what kind of bird you'd like to be?

Love,
Mother

He has been waiting for a message, but can this be it? His mother a bird? Buddy frowns, then moves onto the second card, which has a picture of a lobster fisherman with an armload of buoys.

Old Buddy,
At the rate I'm eating lobster, I'll break another rib. But what a way to go! Speaking of eating, I hope you're doing plenty of that and have fattened up a little by now. Your mother (who sticks to lamb chops, by the way) is like a different person up here. It's doing us both good. Take care of yourself and we'll see you soon. All strength and love from your stuffed Pa.

Buddy rereads this one. Then, in answer to these epistolary curiosities, he imagines his own response:

Dear Mom and Dad,
Having a time myself. Are you really wonderful?

Love,
Buddy
P.S. Maybe a parrot, Mom, but I'll have to think about it.

On his way to the dining room for lunch, Buddy wonders who these people are, these new-sounding parents of his. Are they putting him on, or can he really trust them? If he prayed, would God answer? Would He tell him anything, or would He only laugh? For a moment Buddy contemplates the power of prayer, then abandons that in favor of digging into the mildewed-looking thing on his plate, Holly Hill's famous shit on a shingle.

(Snap!): LUNCH IN A NUTHOUSE

At Buddy's lunch table are seven people, including the ever-present Wilt, and Dr. Dingwell, a visiting psychologist who once was a student of Krause's. As far as Buddy's concerned, Dingwell didn't turn out too well if the written test he gave Buddy the other day is any indication. In the name of research, the test asked questions like, Which Would You Rather Do? (check one):

_____ Set the table
_____ Masturbate
_____ Lead a voter registration drive

Dingwell also tells such bad jokes that Buddy has come to believe that the man has, as Krause would say, insufficient self-awareness.

Directly across from Buddy is Mary Jean Schreider, who came to Holly Hill for treatment of anorexia. When she arrived, she looked like a dying stick and pushed her food around on her plate in a big, garbagey mess that was enough to kill anyone's appetite. She still carries around a bulging scrapbook filled with pictures of food, but she eats at mealtimes. She's gained a lot of weight—at least in places. On his return to Holly Hill, Buddy was amazed to find she'd grown tits. Though the rest of her is scrawny, these seem to get bigger every day. Buddy is keeping close track of their progress.

Mary Jean talks incessantly and without punctuation, mostly about her daddy's money or her daddy's this and that. Buddy doesn't know if she makes all this up, and he doesn't care. He is only interested in her expanding chest.

An older woman, Clarice, sits at Buddy's left. "I see what you're staring at," she hisses. "I watch you." Clarice has skin like an old grocery bag. Once in Big Group, she filled them all in on the details of menopause. Even in that crowd it seemed like bad taste.

"You should have seen mine," Clarice adds in her stage whisper, poking Buddy in the side with her elbow and spitting bits of scalloped potatoes all over his sleeve. "Those are nothing, take my word." Buddy wipes his sleeve with his napkin and ignores her.

He feels he deserves higher-class company than the people around him. If it weren't for the fact that on most days they make him feel like a walking advertisement for mental health, he'd refuse to have anything to do with them at all. Take Ronald, for instance, who's sitting next to Mary Jean. Ronald's totally fixated on time. Last week the battery in his watch ran down, and he had a screaming fit, jumping around and shouting that he was going to die. "If my *watch* stopped, I'm next!" he kept yelling. Someone finally went out and got him a new battery and he settled down.

"Kevin looks like an inmate of death row with that haircut," Ronald announces to the table.

"Shut up," Mary Jean tells him. "You're interrupting my story."

"Oh," says Nadine, a mousy girl whom Buddy has successfully avoided so far. "Is *that* who that is? Kevin Newcomb? I thought it was somebody new, some bald person." She peers at him through her thick glasses.

"Listen, Timex Head," Buddy says, addressing Ronald, "don't give me any shit."

"Now, now," Dr. Dingwell says, "let's not let our table talk degenerate."

"Tell us a joke, Dr. D.," Clarice urges. It's no secret that Clarice has the hots for Dingwell.

"As a matter of fact, I've got a good one today," Dingwell says, rubbing his hands together. "There was a farmer who lived way out in the country, and one day . . ." As if on cue, everyone but Clarice rises from the table and wanders away.

"I've got to go upstairs," Buddy says to Dingwell in an effort to be polite, but Dingwell scarcely acknowledges this, he's so wrapped up in telling his joke to Clarice. She's a little old for him, Buddy thinks, but they certainly deserve each other. Clarice's high-pitched witch's laugh follows him out of the dining room and up the stairs. Holly Hill is beginning to get on his nerves again. He has to keep reminding himself of the alternatives. Ronald wasn't far off when he said death row.

(Snap!): DIGESTING

In his room after lunch, Buddy experiences a sinking spell. Sometimes when he's tired or lonely or sick of the place, things don't quite hold. At times like these he still has fears. Lately he's been afraid that the furniture will fly off, with him on it. This fear has to do with his long-standing suspicion that gravity may be only temporary.

Krause has instructed Buddy to face his fears squarely and to share them with him. But if Buddy were to tell Krause his gravity theory, or how strange things sometimes seem to appear in the toilet, Krause would put him away for good. According to Krause, the trick is to learn what to pay attention to and what to ignore. As Buddy himself knows, he sometimes dwells on things that aren't exactly real.

But he's trying. Three days in a row, for ex-

ample, he's been convinced there was poison in the morning coffee but went ahead and tasted it, anyway. Isn't this progress?

Buddy's mind wanders, but he has it on a stronger leash these days. Sometimes he thinks of his condition as a dog he's walking that he'd be glad to dump or give away. "Woof woof," he remarks out loud.

Since he's been back at Holly Hill, he's taken up jogging with Wilt. This was Krause's idea, and it seems to calm Buddy down. Of course, he counts every footstep he takes when he runs, but that's about all he counts now. He is studying hard to be normal and is bent on imitating the actions of ordinary citizens in order to get the knack. To that end, he jumps up from his bed when he spots the plumber passing, and follows him down the hall into the bathroom.

(Snap!): A PLUMBER AT WORK

For a while the plumber pretends Buddy's not there, but then he turns around and gives him a funny look.

"Just watching," Buddy says to set the man at ease. And then, "You like your work?" The plumber begins pushing a snake down the toilet.

"It's work," is all the man says. The way he looks at Buddy over his shoulder isn't encouraging. Buddy has a sudden brainstorm.

"Hey! Did you hear the one about the Polack who stayed in the outhouse for so long, his friend began to get worried?"

"The one with the sandwich in his coat pocket?" the plumber says. "Yeah, I hear it at least a dozen times a day." Buddy's spirits falter as the plumber's snake rings against the porcelain.

Finally the man sits back on his haunches. "Listen, fellow," he says, "you got a problem? I mean, do you *like* being squeezed in this stall, just the two of us?"

This question throws Buddy. All he wanted to do was check out the guy's moves, him being a normal person from outside. Buddy steps back and leans against the basin. The plumber begins snaking again, flushing the toilet, ignoring Buddy. Buddy finally drifts off down the hall, feeling blue. But before he reaches his room, another bright idea hits him, and he walks back into the bathroom.

"I bet you didn't know there's a parrot in that toilet sometimes," Buddy says to the plumber, and waits for the man's reaction.

"You better believe I know it," the plumber says wearily. "Why the hell do you think I'm here?"

Buddy is astonished but somehow manages to say, "Well, I hope you get it. I never want to see that thing again!"

"I already got it," the plumber says, his head nearly in the toilet. He reaches back and pats his tool kit. "It's in here, fella, no sweat. I'm taking it home to my kids."

Buddy's eye twitches and he makes a beeline for his room. Talk about deranged, he thinks with alarm, talk about *non compos mentis.* Jesus. How is he ever going to learn to act

straight when everyone he meets seems crazier than he is? A dark cloud descends. His head is suddenly cold. There was no parrot, he's sure of it now. Positive.

"Pitch me some balls," Will asks his brother, who's sprawled on the bed in Mona's guest room watching TV.

"Later."

"C'mon. It's the first day in ages it hasn't been raining."

"Ask Scott."

"He's not here."

"Tough," Tony says.

Will waits for Tony to change his mind. "What're you watching?" he asks.

"Leave It to Beaver."

"What's that?"

"You remember," Tony tells him. "It used to be on a long time ago."

"Hunh-uh," Will says, and sidles into the room.

"Sure you remember. These are reruns of reruns of reruns, practically!"

"I don't."

"Well, *I* remember," Tony says.

Will works his way to the bed and is about to sit down when Tony says, "Don't. You'll mess it up."

"It's already a mess," Will observes, and sits gingerly on a corner. Tony pretends not to notice, and the two boys watch the program in silence.

"Who's that?" Will asks after a while.

"That's Beaver, dummy."

"Oh," Will says. "Then who's *that?*"

"That's his brother Wally."

"Wally?" Will asks.

"Beaver Cleaver and Wally Cleaver," Tony says impatiently. "Now will you please shut up."

"*Who* did you say?" Will asks. *"Who?"*

"What's the matter with you, anyway? Are you deaf?"

"Just tell me the guy's name again. *Please.*"

"Don't whine. You sound like a three-year-old."

"Come on, Tony."

"His name's Wally Cleaver. Now leave me alone."

"No!" Will says. "That can't be his name."

"Ask anyone. It's Wally Cleaver. I saw him a while ago on TV. He's big now. I mean, he's actually not so big. He's *old.*"

"Well, the Wally Cleaver *I* met doesn't look like that," Will says. "The one I met was real tall."

"What are you talking about?" For the first time Tony looks at his brother. "You didn't meet Wally Cleaver."

"I did too. I met him in the ravine."

"Oh, sure, Will, sure you did," Tony says with a snort.

"I *did!*" Will insists.

"Look, Will," Tony says, as if he's trying to explain something difficult. "It wasn't *this* Wally Cleaver. Whoever you met, it wasn't the *real* one. Anyway, that's not even his name. It's just a made-up name for TV."

"But that's what he *said* his name was," Will persists.

"He must have been kidding you. What did he look like, anyway?" Tony is sitting up now, not watching TV at all.

"He was real tall," Will says, "and he looked sort of like that friend of Mom's, that Robin. Except that he had real long hair like a hippie."

"When was this, anyway?"

"Before we went to Michigan." And then Will lowers his voice. "Cross your heart and swear to God?"

Tony nods.

"Okay. He asked me if he could use the tent. I mean, not that day in the ravine but the next day. That's why I didn't take it down before we left. He said he needed a place to stay, so I said okay. . . ."

Tony's eyes widen. "Wait a second, Will!" he shouts, leaping off the bed. "How do you know this wasn't the guy who started the fire in our house?"

"No," Will says very quickly. "No. He wouldn't have done that. I mean, he might have been, like, strange, but he wouldn't do that."

"But how do you *know?*"

Will says nothing.

"Listen," Tony says, grabbing Will. "Could you describe this guy to the police?" Tony is jumping up and down with excitement. "Could you identify him?"

"I guess. But it wasn't him."

"But how can you tell? He probably just said he was Wally Cleaver to fool you. Maybe he was an escaped convict or something."

"No," Will says stubbornly.

"Boy, are you dumb! Here you probably have the clue to the whole crime, and you're keeping it a big secret. Those were *his* matches we found in the tent—what was left of it, right? How come you didn't tell Mom or Dad?"

"Because they'd get mad, that's why," Will says very quietly.

"You want to go to jail?"

Will stares down at his knees.

"Well, *do* you?"

Will shakes his head.

"That's where you're going to wind up. For withholding evidence."

Will looks at his brother suspiciously.

"I'm not kidding. If you knew some stranger was in the tent while we were gone and you didn't say anything about it to anybody, then you're in deep trouble. You better go tell Mom right away. Maybe *she* can make the police go easy on you."

Will chews on his fingernail. "He was weird," he says. "He talked real loud and he didn't seem right. He told me some story about hiking across the country. Gee, I don't know." Will looks worried sick.

"You better tell Mom, and right away too!" Tony pulls at Will, but Will doesn't budge.

"You want to be a jailbird?" Tony asks. "Or go to the detention home and get your head shaved for lice?"

At this Will stands up. He looks very pale.

"Oh, jeez," Tony says anxiously. "Just don't puke, okay?" Tony pushes his brother out into the hall. "Just tell them what happened and maybe no one will even get mad at you."

"They won't?" Will asks in a small voice.

"No. And after, maybe I'll pitch you some balls. Okay?"

Will stares down at the floor. "Okay," he finally says, raising his head. The color has come back into his face and he looks almost normal.

"Of course," Tony says, "I can't absolutely guarantee you won't wind up in the slammer."

"The *what?*"

"Oh, forget it, Will. Just go on. Hurry up."

Katherine waits on her front porch staring out at the rain. Yesterday when she was grumbling about the weather, Charmaine said, "You got to fight against it, Ms. Watters. You got to *climatize* your mind."

Katherine laughed but Charmaine grew solemn. "Maybe we're fools not to be out there building an ark," she said. "Maybe this rain's a sign from You-Know-Who." She raised her eyes.

"Oh, Charmaine," Katherine said. "Really now."

But signs aren't lost on Katherine these days. Things are so haywire, she's taken to consulting her horoscope every morning like a ninny. "You are coming near an event that will definitely change your life," she read yesterday. "There could be an upswing in your popularity. Watch out for power plays. Be alert."

Alert, she considers, watching the rain. Lately she might as well be walking in her sleep. She's dazed, she forgets things. Twice she's driven through thunder and lightning to attend faculty committee meetings she might as well have skipped. She neglected to leave Mona's phone number with the English Department secretary or even to check her mailbox.

Katherine rearranges the porch chairs. She picks at the water-logged geraniums and paces around. Her hands are like ice. This morning her horoscope said, "Some prominent person may open the door to opportunity for you, but only if you handle your affairs more calmly. Concentrate on household chores. You can party later. Avoid imbroglios with a Capricorn."

The only Capricorn she can think of is Will. At least he's better. A few days ago Will and Tony burst into her room at Mona's with a crazy story about *Leave It to Beaver* and a stranger Will had met in the ravine. Will was scared, and Katherine drove him to the police station to talk to Detective Gerson. Unfortunately neither she nor the detective could make much out of Will's story about loaning the tent to someone who claimed to be Wally Cleaver and looked like Robin Hastings, but also like a hippie. Why not? Katherine thought. Anything fit these days when nothing did.

David gave Will a lecture about talking to strangers, and Tony kept asking his brother if he wanted his picture on a milk carton. Katherine told Will he should be more open; though she knew better than anyone that muteness and secrecy ran in the family. Will seemed relieved and began sleeping soundly again.

Suddenly the red pickup bursts over the rise of the drive. Katherine slips into the house and practices deep breathing. Lots of luck. Can she really have been looking forward to this moment? She, this wrecked, edgy person who can't think straight? Miraculously she manages to pull herself together and greet Robin almost casually when he comes to the door.

"Katherine!" He beams. "How was your vacation?"

She wasn't prepared for this. "Oh that," she says. "I nearly forgot."

The rain whips into a sudden frenzy. Both of them turn to look.

" 'Small showers last long, but sudden storms are short,' " she says, too rattled to keep her mouth shut.

"Katherine! That's great! You're amazing." He shakes his head, smiling. "Let me guess, *King Lear?*"

"*Richard II*," she answers. Won't he ever get this stuff straight?

Robin taps his clipboard restlessly. His neatly combed hair makes him seem older.

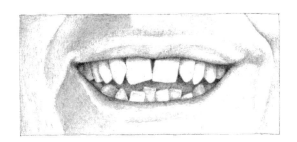

When Mona bumped into him in town and told him the Watterses needed a painter, he'd said he'd been away. This news perked Katherine up. She decided he wasn't avoiding her, after all.

"I hear you've been away," Katherine says.

"No," he says, "I mean, just for a couple of days." Her heart sinks. "When the Newcombs took off for Maine, I had some unscheduled time, so I visited my grandparents in Detroit, that's all." Katherine nods.

"But, Katherine," he says after a minute, "your poor house. It's really too bad. Have they found out who did it yet?"

"No," she says, "and they probably never will. But if you think it's bad now, you should have seen it before. It . . ."

He looks at her expectantly but she can't go on. This feels like work. Besides, he seems like no one she's ever met. Then she spots the gap between his front teeth and feels a distant pang of tenderness, for the remembered Robin.

"Well," he says, fidgeting with his clipboard, "I guess I'll just write up an estimate if that's okay."

She peers at him closely. Is this really the person she's been dying to see?

"Everything's guaranteed for a year," he says, "and Midnight Blue's fully insured. Our painters have plenty of experience. Really, you won't be disappointed. Normally the brand of paint we use . . ." He continues his sales pitch. Katherine feels lost.

"Midnight Blue?" she says.

"That's the name of my company. Didn't you know? After a horse I used to have."

"I see," she says, thinking she must have missed the point. In her current teenage incarnation she misses a lot of things.

The two of them go from room to room. She watches him carefully, trying to connect the Robin in front of her with the far more vivid one in her head.

Your romantic appeal will flourish later. For now, avoid thoughts of sex and the occult. Review any mining stocks you might own.

The person pacing off her walls and jotting things down is cute, Katherine thinks, but hardly the keen romantic figure of her fantasies. Seeing Robin today is like looking through binoculars and finding two images of the same thing. Against all reason, Katherine decides it's only a matter of time, or the right words, until she finds the correct adjustment so the images meet and become one.

"I missed you," she tries as they start up the stairs. Her voice sounds less jolly than she intended.

"I missed seeing you, too, Katherine," he replies.

Her eyes dart sideways.

"What's your sign?" she ventures when they reach the top.

"My *what?*"

"You know," she says, "your astrological sign?"

"Katherine!" He laughs uneasily, as if she has said something imbecilic. "Don't tell me you believe in that!"

"I was just curious," she replies.

"It's Capricorn," he says, and laughs again. Of course.

He gives her a funny look. "What's yours?" he asks.

"Aries," she says. The ram, she thinks, butting and hacking her way through life.

"My grandmother had this friend who was into all that," he says. "It turned out she was totally off her rocker."

Katherine refuses to defend the influence of heavenly bodies on human affairs. All she knows is what she reads in the paper. But how can she thumb her nose at astrology when at least once a week her horoscope fits her to a tee?

Proceed with caution. You are dangerously susceptible to flights of fancy and dreams of fast living. Don't be seduced by your rebellious nature, and don't expect money out of the blue.

Robin surveys Will's bedroom distastefully. His expression makes Katherine feel like she's responsible for the damage.

"You can't imagine how bizarre it is to have something like this happen," she begins, thinking that if she pours out her heart, Robin may come around. "I mean . . ."

"Don't worry," he says, interrupting, "A new mirror and a few coats of paint and everything will be good as new."

"It will?"

He smiles mysteriously and avoids her eyes.

"What's this room?" he asks as they walk into her smoke-darkened bedroom.

"My bedroom," she says. The phantom of her dreams, now here in the flesh, seems unruffled by this information. Of course, as a love nest the room doesn't make it. It's soot-stained and seedy. Robin takes a lot of notes.

They leave her bedroom and climb the steep steps to the cupola. It's been beautifully rebuilt. Except for being unpainted and smelling of lumber, it could be the original.

"Wow!" he exclaims, circling the small room. "What a view!" From here they can see the wind sliding sheets of rain across the river. She's imagined them in this room many times. They weren't staring out of any windows, either.

Rein in those daydreams. Come down to earth and tackle a job you can accomplish. Escape is not in the stars. This is a good time to look into tax shelters.

"The carpenters did a great job," he says. "The Yoders?"

She nods, but doesn't ask how he knew. Any minute now, she persists, he'll forget this charade of being all business. She'll relax. Yet even after they've gone through the whole house, nothing has changed. He's still nattering on about quality work; she's still perplexed.

At the front door he says, "You know, Katherine, you really should visit my barn one of these days. You'd love it."

She just stares at him.

"And oh! I nearly forgot! What I really want from you—he pauses; she holds her breath—

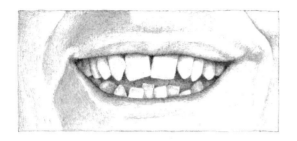

"is the name of the orthodontist Mona said you knew."

Orthodontist? She's been looking for romance, and he's worried about his teeth! She gives him the orthodontist's name, spelling it slowly. What she'd like to do is bean him. Instead she smiles.

After he leaves, Katherine sits on the porch and broods. Robin seemed negotiable only as a fantasy; she practically made him up. Thunder rumbles overhead, and a high wind makes the treetops sway wildly. Rain comes down in sheets, but Katherine hardly notices. She's thinking that when she met Robin, she seemed to be passing through an unpromising murk, she seemed to be fading away. At least then she was capable of coherent thought. Now she's like a revved-up teen queen and about as moronic. Had she secretly been yearning for mayhem all along?

She has no idea what to make of herself, but from the first Robin seemed to invite her to invent him and flesh him out. It dawns on her that maybe the neediness she senses in him is really her own. Maybe he's only a mirror.

Rain mists across the porch, and Katherine goes into the house where she takes out a bucket and begins scrubbing the kitchen cupboards. The sweaty work takes all her energy, so that after a while she stops puzzling over Robin and concentrates on scraping gunk out of corners.

When she's finished, several hours later, she feels better. Besides, the rain is stopping. Walking back to Mona's along the alley, Katherine spies a faint rainbow, the first one she's seen all month. She reminds herself she's seeing a reflection and refraction of the sun's rays through raindrops, nothing more, not a sign.

In the Edwards' drive, Katherine meets the Lethem dogcatcher, who's come to deliver Penny in his little white truck. He says he found the dog wandering around the high school parking lot. He doesn't smile.

Penny leaps out of the truck and jumps up on Katherine. The dog is dressed in a ragged Elvis Presley T-shirt and orange gym short, and looks ridiculous. The dogcatcher merely shakes his head, and Katherine doesn't bother to tell him that Will and Scott are responsible for Penny's getup.

"Down, Penny," Katherine says to the dog, whose breath seems worse than usual. "Down." Penny's an Aries, too, and gets carried away.

When the dogcatcher drives off, Katherine has a little chat with Penny. She scolds the dog for going so far from home, then tells her she's just seen Robin Hastings. "It wasn't wonderful," Katherine confides. She's amazed to find herself opening up, even to a dog. "Oh, Penny," she says, "I'm such a dope."

With that, Penny tears off across the yard

like she's chasing something Katherine can't see. She circles a pine tree and races back. Penny makes this circuit four or five times at full tilt. Suddenly one of her front legs gets tangled in the T-shirt sleeve and the dog halts. She limps pathetically over to Katherine.

"Look at you," Katherine says as she wrestles with Penny's muddy clothes. "Running around in circles like a dimwit!"

Penny bounds off toward the back door. Everywhere things glisten. Sunlight flashes off the grass, drops of rain spangle down from the trees. The sky is intensely blue.

On Mona's back porch, Penny claws the screen door and moans.

"Cool it, pal," Katherine calls.

Penny gives her the once-over and goes back to mauling the screen.

"Calm down, Penny," Katherine says, "For heaven's sake, you're home." Penny sits. She cocks her head and looks at Katherine thoughtfully. Then, Katherine could swear it, Penny smiles.

IV

The Lethem schools open for the year under a brilliantly clear sky. All day long, Mona's imagined the smell of new crayons and pads of manila paper—fresh starts from long ago that still make her a little giddy.

But that afternoon, as she brings her new Saab to a stop behind the middle school, she's watchful behind an enormous pair of sunglasses. Scott and Will, padded up for football practice, climb out of the car.

"Kay will pick you up at six-thirty," Mona reminds the boys. Spotting bright plastic on the backseat, she calls, "Scott! Will! Someone forgot his hat!"

Scott runs back to the car. "Helmet," he hisses. "How many times do I have to tell you it's not a hat? Now please, Mom, go home before somebody sees you." The door slams and he's off, his body rendered even skinnier by the bulk of the shoulder pads, the curve of the helmet under his arm.

"Thank God he's quick," Mona says as she pulls away.

Driving back home, Mona feels her eyes begin to water and dabs at them gently with a tissue. Except for tearing and a slight swollen soreness, all of which Dr. Spatzer told her to expect, the whole thing seemed easy as pie. She can't believe it was so fast and painless. Mona has faith in optimum results and plans to look like a new person soon, in time for the kickoff of the recycling center and the beginning of her exercise classes. Maybe not new, but younger, more attractive.

Home, she heads straight for the downstairs bathroom. She removes the gigantic glasses. What she sees in the mirror elicits a little moan. "Yuch," she says. An hour earlier her eyes were merely red and a little puffy, but not so puffy that she couldn't make out the teeny stitches across the lids and along the lower lashes. Now they're swollen and darkened with bruises. She has two enormous shiners!

"Oh, woe." She wonders if she should try more ice. She spent all afternoon with ice packs on her eyes in an effort to stave off exactly this. When Scott came home from school and found her lying on her bed with her face covered by an ice bag, she told him she had an eye infection and had to wear dark glasses for a week.

For some reason her son, who never really

looked at her, chose that moment to examine her intently.

"Jeez," Scott said, "it looks pretty bad. I mean, it looks really gross. Are you gonna be blind?"

"Good land, Scott." Mona yelped. "Of course I won't be blind!"

Now, in front of the mirror, Mona wonders if she *is* going blind, after all. "One in a million chance," Dr. Spatzer told her. "Far less than that. But, of course, I have to warn you."

Mona says to her mangled-looking face, "You are not going blind, Mona. Get a grip. You can see, can't you?"

Spatzer said her eyes would probably turn black and blue, but she wasn't prepared for anything this sensational. She decides she'll sleep all night long with the ice pack. If she were smart, she'd get it out right now, but she wants to do something that's a lot more important than her eyes. She takes one more look and briefly imagines herself decked out with a white cane and tin cup.

She leaves the bathroom and heads for the dining room table where a box of stationery and a pen lie waiting. After that afternoon with David Watters—which, strangely enough, hardly even makes her squirm—she promised herself that today, the day of her long-standing appointment with Dr. Spatzer, she would turn over a new leaf. She's determined to write a letter to Sam.

Mona seats herself at the table, pen poised above a sheet of paper, but after a while becomes restless. She planned everything except what to say. Mona props her head in her hand and thinks hard. She thinks and thinks. After ten or fifteen minutes she goes to the mirror again, but nothing has changed. She returns to the table and thinks some more, convinced there's a way to word a message that will make Sam pay attention. Should she tell him she's had it, she's through? Of course not. Should she tell him she's losing her wits without him? Never. She could just see his face when he read *that* letter. What wits, he'd joke. Ha, ha.

Listen, Sam, she imagines saying back. People take me for dumb, don't think I don't know it. But I'm not so dumb as all that. Either you get yourself home to stay, or else . . . Or else what? she wonders.

Mona considers writing something that will go straight to his heart and break it a little.

Dear Sam,
Someone once said that marriage is the road two people walk together and that love is the space between them. What happened to our road? Did we take a wrong turn? The space between us feels wide and a little empty. Oh, Sam, I love you. Come home.

She admires this sentiment for a few minutes, then rips up the paper. Not the mood she's searching for.

Mona racks her brain. It definitely has to be short. Sam's never liked long letters. He used to stop reading his mother's ten-page numbers after only a page or two. As she waits for a brainstorm, Mona feels her eyes cautiously. They seem a little sorer, but maybe she's imagining this.

Whenever she's talked to Sam on the phone lately, she's been careful to sound the same as ever, old cheerful Mona. She wants to spring something on him, surprise him into action. Whatever made her think she could do it in a letter, though? Who writes letters, anyway? Maybe a telegram would be better—that is, if they still have telegrams.

HAD IT STOP NORMAN THE VET AND I LEAVE FOR ACAPULCO TOMORROW STOP TOUGH LUCK SAM STOP. Come now, she thinks, this is getting ridiculous.

Just then a knock at the back door sends her flying out of her chair. Her sunglasses, she thinks frantically, where did she leave her sunglasses? In a panic, she races around the dining room table and is on her way through the kitchen when Kay walks in.

Mona ducks down behind the butcher-block island.

"Hi, Mona," Kay says casually, as if it were a perfectly ordinary occurrence to walk in and find Mona cowering in her own kitchen. "What's up?"

"I'm looking for something in this cupboard," Mona shouts, stretching farther into the deep space so that she is almost entirely inside. Pots and pans crash as Mona fumbles around in the dark.

"Come out for a minute," Kay says over the din. "I have to ask you something."

"Shoot," Mona orders.

"But you have to taste it first," Kay says. "What are you doing down there, anyway?"

Mona ransacks around for some excuse, but she knows she'll have to come out eventually. Damn, she thinks. She didn't want a soul to know about her little procedure. Now she's going to have to tell Kay. Ever so slowly she extracts herself from the cupboard and stands up.

"Mona!" Kay screams. "My God, Mona! What happened?"

"Now, Kay . . ." Mona begins. Kay looks horrified.

"Oh, Mona, what's wrong? Are you all right?"

"Kay, please, calm down! It's nothing."

"Nothing!" Kay shrieks. "You're standing there looking like you've just been mugged and you're telling me 'nothing'!"

Mona decides she'd better come clean and make it snappy. "It's just a little—uh—operation I had today," she tells Kay, "to, well, you know, remove the bags and lift the lids."

"You didn't!" Kay exclaims, all agog.

Mona throws up her hands.

"But you . . . you never said a word about it!" Kay sputters.

"I'm sorry," Mona says, and wonders why she's apologizing.

"Goodness," Kay says, and seems very flustered, "I just can't . . ."

"Really, Kay. It wasn't much. They look a lot worse than they feel."

"Why ever did you do it?" Kay asks. Mona thinks Kay's acting peculiarly dim-witted. "You looked fine before."

"Kay!" Mona counters. "Not around my eyes I didn't." She wishes Kay would go home.

"But you did!" Kay insists.

"Let's not mince up words, Kay. I didn't. I looked haggard."

"Well," Kay concedes, "you didn't look twenty-three, maybe. . . ."

"And I don't want to look twenty-three, either," Mona tells her. "I just want to look a little less saggy and wrinkled."

"I guess I never knew you were, well—" Kay stops.

"Vain?" Mona offers. Kay looks startled. "I'm vain, all right," Mona says. "Who isn't?"

"Hmmm," Kay hums thoughtfully, as if this were interesting information. Mona decides being all adrift doesn't suit Kay.

"Listen," Mona says, hoping to put an end to the discussion. "It's no big toot, right? It took forty-five minutes and I was gone from home for maybe three hours total. In a week or so I'll look fine, really I will." Why is she reassuring Kay? Mona wonders. "Now," she remembers, "what was it you wanted to show me?"

"Oh, that," Kay says. "I almost forgot," and she sets a foil-wrapped package on the counter between them. "Can you eat?" Kay asks as she opens the foil.

"Good gravy, Kay! Of course I can eat. I can always eat. But what is it? And by the way, when do you start school?"

"Not for almost three weeks," Kay says, pushing the package toward Mona. "These are supposed to be brownies," Kay says, making a face, "but something went wrong. I never made brownies from scratch before. You know how I hate to bake."

Mona takes one. The square is so heavy, it could be made out of lead. Carefully she nibbles at a corner, but the thing is as hard as a rock. Fearful she'll break a tooth, she nevertheless bites down with all her might and gets a sizable chunk. She chews and chews. This is the worst thing she's ever put into her mouth and has the consistency of a dog biscuit.

"Tell me they're awful," Kay says.

"They're awful," Mona says, still chewing, wishing she could spit the whole thing out.

Kay looks worried. "I can't figure out what's wrong," she says.

"Did you leave out the butter? The sugar? Did you bake them too long?"

Kay shakes her head. "I don't know. I wanted to surprise David. He said he had a craving for brownies. I guess I blew it."

"Where on earth did you get this recipe, anyway?" Mona asks, swallowing a little bit at a time.

"I thought it was Sam's," Kay says helplessly. "I mean, I know I'm not a baker, but at least I can read!"

Mona finally chokes down the mouthful of brownie, wondering if the thing floating around in her mouth is a nutshell or a broken tooth. "Well, it couldn't be Sam's," she tells Kay, and swallows whatever it is. Too late now. "For one thing, his brownies have a boiled icing, and they're soft, not chewy. I would say these are, uh, very chewy. For another, Sam never gives out recipes, not even to people he really likes. I mean, he doesn't even write them down. They're all in his head."

Kay has a bewildered expression again. "That's funny," she says. "I could have sworn I got it from Sam."

"Listen, kiddo. He won't even give *me* a recipe!"

Kay looks woebegone. "I guess I'd better go back to the mix that comes in the box."

"You could do worse," Mona tells her. "You *did* do worse."

"That's the story of my life these days," Kay says. "Everything's off."

"Oh, for heaven's sake, Kay. It's only brownies! Anyway, it's probably the paint fumes or something. Your house is all torn up too. By the way, how's that adorable Robin person?"

"Okay, I guess." Kay shrugs. "Actually, I haven't seen much of him. He sent over a crew of older men. He said they're experienced painters, but if you ask me, I think he got them at Manpower or picked them up at a city mission. They looked wasted, but I guess they can paint." Kay sighs heavily. "I've got to run. Tony needs school supplies, and then I have to pick up Scott and Will. I'm sorry I barged in. Let me know if I can do anything for you, promise?"

"You think this is crazy?" Mona asks, pointing to her eyes.

"Of course not," Kay says without much conviction. "By the way, who did it?"

"Spatzer," Mona says. "Do you know him?"

Kay nods. "He's supposed to be good."

"Let's hope," Mona says. Her eyes have begun to ache, and she wants to write to Sam before Scott comes home. Mona watches from the back door as Kay walks to her car, wondering when Kay's going to snap out of it. The fire seems to have flattened her. Maybe something else . . .

Hurriedly Mona goes back to the dining room table. She has less than an hour. The dreadful taste of Kay's brownie lingers. Wait, she thinks. Brownies! That's it! And picking up the pen, she writes quickly:

Dearest Sam,

I long for your brownies, your Mississippi mud pie, your caramel pecan rolls, your banana-nut muffins. Sometimes I think I can't go on without a taste of your fudge upside-down cake. I miss—oh, how I miss—your mocha cream pie, your chocolate cheesecake.

Mona's mouth is watering.

I was crazy to give up your toffee chocolate-chip cookies, your eclairs (swoon!), your coconut chocolate macaroons, your macadamia pie. I must have been out of my mind.

But oh, Sam, it's not just me. Our son will grow up thinking heaven is a Hostess fried pie! But it's not too late to get things cooking again. Come home and stay home. I'll grate your chocolate, I'll wash your pans. What is life worth, I'm asking you, without the things we love?

> *Hungrily, lovingly,*

Mona signs her name and puts the letter in an envelope, which she hastily addresses. If she hurries, she can scoot down to the post office and be back before Scott. The letter seems guaranteed to go straight to Sam's heart. She'll rest a lot easier once it's mailed.

Gingerly she puts on her sunglasses and goes out to her car. She realizes that if the letter works, she'll have Kay and her hideous brownies to thank. Wouldn't that be the limit.

At the end of the drive, Penny comes bounding out of the bushes. "There you are," Mona says. "Hop in." But as she reaches across the front seat to open the door, Penny barks and backs off like Mona's a stranger.

"Penny!" Mona scolds. "For Pete's sake, it's me!" Ever so carefully she raises the glasses so that Penny can see her face. Immediately Penny jumps into the passenger seat. Penny loves to ride in the car.

"Penny," Mona says to the dog, "cross your fingers this letter does the trick." Penny gives Mona a curious look as they zip down the alley and up the side street. At the corner, Mona executes a rolling stop, then peels onto Jefferson. Under the cover of dusk, Penny and Mona go tearing down the street. The dog pokes her head out of the window, ears plastered to her head, long snout pointed skyward, sniffing, sniffing. She's the absolute picture of bliss. Despite her watery, swollen eyes, Mona smiles, suddenly imagining scents—warm and fragrant from the oven—of her own.

"He loves you, Jenny," Calvin said with a look that riveted Jennifer to the sumptuous leather seat of the limousine. "Can you simply walk away from love?"

A mountain of grief seized her. She was unable to speak for the lump in her throat.

"The love of a good man is hard to find," he continued. "Divorce, my dear, regardless of what your sister says, means very little these days. In Lance's case—"

"Jennifer!" Jessica called impatiently, shifting her Louis Vuitton traveling case from hand to hand. "Please. We must hurry!"

"You also have a promising career in my business," Calvin added, taking Jennifer's hand. "Will you give that up too?"

Never had Jennifer been so tormented with doubts as she was at that moment.

"Jennifer!" her sister said sharply. "Come!"

Fearing another unpleasant flare-up between Jessica and Calvin Lundin, Jennifer pulled away from his reassuring, masculine grip. "I must go," she said. "I have given Jessica my word. But if, after three months . . ." Crystalline tears filled her eyes. She could not continue. Suddenly the three-month trial she had promised her sister seemed an eternity.

Calvin Lundin gazed at her, then turned away, and before Jennifer knew it, the sleek limousine had disappeared down the road.

"He's stubborn," Jessica said coldly, "like all men. You must pay no attention to him. *I* don't!"

In a matter of seconds the iron gate was opened by an immensely tall nun in a long gray habit, her feet bare in keeping with the rules of her order.

"I am Sister Bernina," the nun said ominously. "You will follow me."

Irene sets the pen down and presses her palms to her eyes. The twins give her a headache. Ever since her return from Maine they've been an intrusion in her life. She wishes she were done with them, silly girls. Ridiculous Samantha Egmont, heroine of *Winter Heat*, Irene's first romance, had never been so irksome.

Only this morning Irene received a letter from Ronda Michaels, her editor at Profile Romances. *Winter Heat* had been selected as a special bonus promotional item, Ronda wrote, and beginning in January, a copy would be packaged inside every jumbo-size box of Happy Trash Bags. "A big coup for your Nicolle!" she gushed. As if that weren't enough good news, Ronda continued, Profile wanted "Nicolle" to accept the enclosed invitation to speak at the Romance Writers' Convention in Albuquerque next March.

Irene is troubled. What began as a lark is turning into more than she'd bargained for. The Happy Bags didn't bother her—heavens, no. Nicolle Dundee could go winging her way into garbage cans all over the globe for all Irene cared. But how on earth could she, Irene, be expected to stand up in front of a crowd and pass herself off as Nicolle? Gracious, she'd have to go in disguise. As pleased as she was with her appearance these days, she was certainly no Nicolle. To impersonate Nicolle she'd need slinky dresses, spike heels, an enormous head of hair, jewels, the works.

Strange, Irene considers. Often these days it's hard to recapture what once seemed so wonderful about Nicolle. In the past year, Nicolle had sometimes been Irene's only friend and confidante.

But Nicolle is getting to be a problem, Irene thinks as she opens the medicine chest in the bathroom. She swallows two aspirin and glances briefly in the mirror, still pleasantly surprised by what she sees. Massaging her temples, she shifts her gaze to the window, blinking against the bright sunshine. There was so

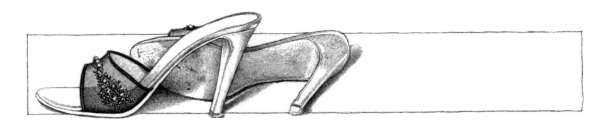

much rain last month that now, in September, the world looks as sharply green as June. How odd all this was—not only the weather but also the unexpected turns life has taken. She could purr with pleasure at the prodigious changes— Harry's attentiveness, Dr. Krause's encouraging reports. Some days she can hardly believe what's happened.

Back at her desk, Irene can't avoid Nicolle. In Maine it dawned on Irene (perhaps because of something Harry said) that Nicolle, she was the willing purveyor of foolish dreams. Lately that thought hovers uneasily at the back of her mind.

Yet no matter how fed up she is with Nicolle's giddy fictions, the spirit of that invented figure stubbornly hovers over Irene the minute she picks up her pen. Probably just as well, she decides, since she can't drop the twins in midstream. After all, she signed a contract. Besides, what she would do with her time if she didn't have Nicolle's throaty voice beaming in to her over some internal broadcast system?

Harry will be home for lunch in an hour. Irene smiles at the thought of what their lunchtimes involve lately, then forces herself to focus on the paper before her. From nowhere comes the heavy scent of Nicolle's jasmine perfume. The pen moves.

Sister Bernina walked quickly ahead of them, her uncovered feet oblivious to the rough gravel path. Jennifer, who had not visited the convent before, felt her eyes grow wide as they rounded a bend. There before them stood a gloomy, stone building, looking for all the world like an evil castle in a child's fairy-tale book. Her heart sank.

"I will show you to your rooms," Sister Bernina said, struggling with the heavy wooden door and ushering the twins into the building. Once inside, Jennifer's body was penetrated by a terrible chill. More than once her step faltered as the sister lead them down a long, damp, deathly silent corridor.

"Your room," Sister Bernina finally said, nodding to Jessica. Thanking Sister Bernina and giving Jennifer's hand a squeeze, Jessica turned aside quickly. "The past is all behind us now," she murmured. Then she was gone.

Jennifer's knees were shaking, yet somehow she managed to follow the sister farther on down the hall. With every step she took, the old building grew darker and colder. After what seemed like miles of walking, Sister Bernina pointed to a small door. "This is your room," was all she said.

With quaking hands Jennifer opened the small door to find a dim cubicle. "Sister," she was about to cry out, "there has been a terrible mistake!" But when she turned to speak, Sister Bernina had vanished.

With tear-stung eyes, she stood in the doorway gazing in disbelief at what she saw: a narrow cot, a small chest of drawers, a tiny table and chair. Above the desk on the stone wall hung a large wooden crucifix, and on the table lay a Bible, which felt cold to Jennifer's touch. She opened it at random, hoping to find some message of consolation, but the light in the room was so bad, she couldn't see to read. Frantically she searched for a lamp or a light switch but to her dismay found none. There was only a lone window, high above the cot and very small.

Suddenly panic overtook her. The walls of the room seemed to be closing in. Jennifer flew to the door, but its handle refused to budge. Trapped! her fevered thoughts told her. She was trapped!

A harsh sob racked Jennifer's throat, and she fell on the cold, unyielding cot, weeping as if her heart would break. "Lance!" her strangled voice cried out. "Lance!" But even as she called his name she knew that Lance Steel was lost to her forever.

"That's enough of *that!*" Irene says aloud, pushing back her desk and checking the clock, discovering to her delight that she has just enough time to fix a cheese soufflé for Harry. If she times things exactly right, the soufflé can be rising while . . .

K atherine sits cross-legged on the floor of her study, the morning sun warm on her back. The rugs are still at the cleaner's, and the painters have removed all the inside shutters. Most of Katherine's books lie in piles on the floor, waiting for the shelves to be repainted. Her desk is partly blocking the door. The study looks like a room someone's moving out of.

In front of her are two large stacks of printed sheets, one pink, the other green, along with several big boxes of envelopes already addressed. Mona commandeered Katherine's services to fold and stuff her flyers for Litter-Lifter Day. Who could say no to someone who looked as if she'd just staggered away from a bad bout in the ring?

Mona's a regular five-day wonder, Katherine thinks as she methodically creases pink sheets on top of green ones. Katherine used to believe people pitched in to help Mona because she seemed so flustered. This may be true, but Mona relies heavily on that twittery charm to get things done. Underneath her rattledness, something sturdy and able and quite *un*rattled drives her.

Take Mona's recent venture into eyelid surgery. What amazed Katherine most was that Mona decided a change was in order and then actually *did* something about it, just like that! Katherine herself was a person of little faith, but Mona was a true believer. She thought almost anything was possible, and for her maybe it was.

Katherine pauses in her folding to study one of the green sheets. Under the heading "Litter Lore" are facts about how long litter lingers before it decays and disappears. There's a time line with cute little drawings Mona did herself, and enough trivia to fill the gaps in several faltering conversations. Katherine, lately a mistress of faltering conversations, decides she could benefit from committing this information to memory.

A PAPER NAPKIN TOSSED ALONG THE ROADSIDE TAKES ONE TO TWO WEEKS TO DISINTEGRATE!

While this won't take anyone's breath away, who knows when it might come in handy?

Katherine likes the mindless work she's doing. She always suspected an assembly line was just her speed. These days she amazes her-

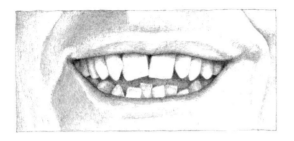

self by completing even the most menial tasks. Mostly she feels like a heroine in a Henry James novel, one of those women who knows too much and has to stuff her pocket handkerchiefs in her mouth to keep from spilling the beans. Her inner life is imaginatively hectic. She's cooking on too many burners. Yet from the store of sense left to her, Katherine sees that some small flaw has grown to gigantic proportions. Mooning over Robin Hastings isn't the point. It isn't even close.

She's long regarded herself as a person with prospects and a bright, bold future. What hit with a bang and nearly knocked the wind out of her lately is the realization that this *is* her future; she's been living it for some time now. Maybe other people understood you had to get it right the first time, but she'd been dallying with life as if it were a practice run or a dress rehearsal. This is it, all she'll ever have. And she wants *more*. She feels greedy, ravenous, hasty. She is working against the clock, after all.

And she pinned her hopes on Robin Hastings, a perfect stranger, little more than a child. Worse, she still believes deep down that Robin, in his heart of hearts, desires her, and

that some trick on her part can lure that desire out into the open. Often she feels like a character in a trashy novel.

A COTTON SOCK LINGERS FOR UP TO FIVE MONTHS!

Wasn't she the person who always said that after six months all men's dirty socks were the same? Wasn't she the one who scoffed at other people's broken marriages, their affairs and flirtations, as if, having witnessed them, she herself was above temptation? Well, she wasn't. She was a regular sap for a particularly heated-up vision of romance.

The telephone near her foot rings, and Katherine grabs for it.

"Sitting on top of the phone again?" Mona asks.

"Right," Katherine says. "I'm waiting for a call from the Pillsbury Bake-off judges."

"Ha, ha," Mona says.

"How are your eyes?" Katherine asks her.

"I went to see Spatzer yesterday. He said it was a gorgeous job. I told him it was a pretty cute trick, disguising my wrinkles with all these bruises. I don't think he thought that was funny."

"What did you expect? He's a doctor."

"Kay! Shame on you!"

"Listen," Katherine says, "forget Spatzer. I think you were brave."

"Oh, my God," Mona says. "If you think *that* was brave, you should hear what I've been up to this morning. Did you see *The Register?*"

"No, why?"

"Wait a minute, Kay. Somebody's at the door."

Katherine waits, stacking and folding. Her eye lights on this:

A WOOL MITTEN TAKES A YEAR TO FALL APART!

"Sorry, Kay," Mona says, returning. "I'm in a jam. I'll call you back later, okay? In the meantime think about this: Chez Mimi. Got it?"

"Chez Mimi?" Katherine asks. "That crummy restaurant on Church Street? You want me to think about Chez Mimi? I'm not sure I want to."

"Well, do it, anyway. I'll explain later. Think hard too. Now, toodle-oo." Mona hangs up.

Katherine puzzles over Mona's cryptic charge. Chez Mimi's a dump. It's ugly and the food is deplorable. No one can figure out how the restaurant's stayed open for as long as it has. There've been rumors of drug dealing, underworld ties. A shame, too, because the old Victorian house it's in could be a real knockout.

"There you are, Katherine! I've been looking all over for you."

Startled, Katherine pivots around. "Robin!" she says. In spite of her better judgment, her hopes surge. "I was just helping Mona out with her mailing for Litter-lifting Saturday," Katherine says, dithering. "I bet you didn't know that every man, woman, and child in this country generates three pounds of solid waste per day."

He looks interested.

"Or how about this," Katherine speeds on.

"Did you know it takes ten two-liter plastic pop bottles to make one polyester sport coat?"

"My guess is that wouldn't be virgin polyester, right? My guess is you wouldn't find one in Lethem, either. The coat, I mean." He laughs.

"Did you want me?" Katherine asks, rising to her feet. She manages not to flinch when she hears what she's said. Every other word she utters in his presence these days seems to be guided by the long arm of Dr. Freud. Not that it matters, of course; nothing she says seems to get his attention, anyway.

Strangely enough, he says, "Ahhhh," rather mysteriously and gazes at her dead-on for a long beat during which she holds her breath, careful not to bat an eyelash. She's not sure, she's never sure, whether he's coming on to her. Could he simply be thinking of what to say next?

"I wanted you to know I'll be here all day today," he says at last.

A PIECE OF ROPE TAKES FROM THREE TO FOUR-
TEEN MONTHS TO DECAY!

"Oh, that's too bad," she finds herself saying. "I was just on my way out." She hasn't the faintest idea where these words came from. She has, in fact, no plans at all. Could it be that she's wising up?

"I'm sorry," he says, and he really does look sorry. "I'd been looking forward to spending a little time with you."

Katherine thinks to herself, Hurry up. Hurry up and pick a face, pick a pose, pick someone to be besides your silly, adolescent self. All along she's tried too hard with him. One thing she hasn't tried is playing it cool.

"I guess that's the breaks," she says. "But I really must go." She smiles at him as adultly as she can and is astonished to find herself calming down.

"Well," he says, and appears crestfallen. Katherine wavers. There is something about his delicate wrists, his wide shoulders. "By the way," she says, "did you know a bamboo pole takes up to three years to disintegrate?"

He looks stymied. She laughs. "Litter Lore," she tells him. "Garbage gossip."

"Another time, maybe?" he asks hesitantly.

"Why not? It would be fun." Was she hearing right? she wonders. Had she just called this fun?

He brightens. "Listen, maybe you'd come out to my barn one of these days. You haven't ever been there, and I'd like you to see it. Would you come to my barn if I asked you?"

"Of course," she says, feeling herself begin to weaken. "I'd love to." Why on earth would she want to see his barn, though? Could he be getting at something here?

"I've really got to go," she says, pulling a stack of bills off the corner of her desk and stuffing them into a folder as though she has a date with the tax man.

"Well," he says, "I'll be upstairs if you come back, or, you know, if you need me."

She looks at him carefully, not sure she understands what he's said or what, exactly, he means. That's the thing about him: She never quite knows what he does mean, or who it is she's dealing with. At times like this he seems to possess vast, empty spaces just waiting for her to fill them up. The fact that he's the first man she's ever known who seems capable of turning her down flat is small potatoes compared to the inviting gaps she imagines in him: all that empty room, his eyes full of promises. Then again, maybe empty was just that: empty.

"You'll be fine," she tells him. "You've got your buddies." She raises her eyebrows slightly. "And Charmaine is around. Just follow the humming."

"Katherine," Robin says abruptly.

"What?"

A TIN CAN LASTS A HUNDRED YEARS!

"Did anyone ever tell you that you look like Jacquelyn Bisset? I saw her last night on TV, and it's really uncanny!"

Katherine takes this peculiar remark for a flattering intimacy, because he makes it sound that way. "Occasionally, yes, people say that," she says, veering dangerously close to witlessness.

AN ALUMINUM BEER CAN WILL STICK AROUND
FOR UP TO FIVE HUNDRED YEARS!

"You're really beautiful, you know, Katherine," he says huskily. "Especially for someone . . ."

"My age," she finishes for him, stung.

"No . . . that is . . . well, yes. But I really meant for someone with all those freckles."

Katherine cocks her head to one side and narrows her eyes.

"You're lovely-looking, Katherine, honestly!"

She thinks, My God, what's going on? Just when she'd counted him out, is he coming back? Or could this be only her imagination? From somewhere in the back of her mind an unexpected thought rockets: What he needs is a friend, but instead he's got me. This sobers her a little. Maybe *she's* the one who's not playing fair.

"Think of it," she says as she backs out of the room, clutching her folder.

"Think of what?" he asks her earnestly.

All those freckles could be yours, she wants to say. You could count them, one by one. "A Coke bottle," she says, hanging on to the remnants of her composure, "last indefinitely. Remember that the next time you pitch one. Watch," she says brazenly, looking him straight in the eyes, "Watch your discards."

"Oh, I will, Katherine." He smiles. "I will."

"Do that," she calls as she heads for the door.

Robin strides out of the Lethem Medical Building, grimacing at the pain in his mouth. It's a little after eight-thirty, sunny and clear, with the faintest chill in the air. Autumn. At this time of morning the town feels like it's been evacuated; half of its citizens off for the city and the work of the world.

Waiting for the light to change at Main and Jefferson, Robin sees a school bus round the corner.

"Hey, Robin!" a voice shouts from one of the bus windows. "Robin!"

He looks up in time to see Will Watters waving wildly. Robin waves back. As the sun shoots through the bus windows he notices Will is wearing the New York Yankees cap. His.

It's a mystery to Robin how his cap turned up at the Watterses' house. He doesn't remember leaving it, but maybe he did that week in July when he was there so much. Funny, but that week, when Katherine Watters somehow managed to tone down his dark, stirred-up inner life, seems like a strange dividing line in his summer.

Sometimes, though, Katherine confuses

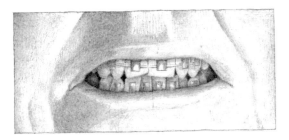

him. He doesn't know how to read her. Occasionally he's even imagined she needs him. But what could she possibly need with him when her life is so nicely spread out around her like some gorgeous picnic he hasn't earned the right to be invited to yet? He wishes he knew all the things she knows.

He pretends Katherine Watters's subliminal signals don't exist, which maybe they don't. He also pretends Carol Ann doesn't send him physically right over the edge. The old nose-to-the-grindstone. He pushes Katherine, who is married—and too old anyway—out of his mind. Also Carol Ann, who's leaving town. No future there. He has things of his own to tend to, and he's keeping his distance from both of them after what he went through with Jannie.

The first project on his list, his teeth, has begun. He feels his jaw carefully with his fingers. It's weird about the Yankees cap, though, he thinks. He found it on Will's dresser when he went into his room to paint the ceiling. He thought the cap was lost, but there it was—the paint smudges on the side, the rip in the label, the lopsided tilt to the beak. He put it back on the dresser, and later, when he asked Will, Will said he got it from a hippie named Wally Cleaver he'd met in the ravine. Robin laughed, but Will stuck to his guns. Will's brother, Tony, twirled his finger around his ear dementedly. Katherine came along and said, "I don't want to hear one more word about that damn hat!" Robin didn't press it. He abandoned his claim to the moth-eaten cap his grandfather bought him years ago at Yankee Stadium. The

way things wander out of your life when you're not paying attention troubled him more than the loss of the cap.

Crossing the street, Robin risks bringing his upper and lower teeth together in the gentlest of bites. He's nearly felled by the pain. Can this be worth it? Dr. Iris, the orthodontist Katherine recommended, seemed nice enough for someone who was obviously peculiar. At least he didn't propose pulling six teeth like the others. Iris said there was no need to if Robin could stand the pain. Robin thought, it'll be a snap until Iris installed a truckload of paraphernalia, all the while discoursing on bites, surfaces, and the integrity of the mouth.

The things people say to justify what they're doing, Robin thought. Dr. Iris talked on, some kind of eccentric advocate for the teeth. Oddly enough, Robin believed the man when he told him his teeth would soon be straight. Dissonance reduction, what else? He'd pledged two thousand bucks to the guy, after all.

Aspirin, Robin remembers. Iris said take aspirin for the pain if you need to, and Robin, who's taken a total of four or five aspirin in his entire life, makes a quick left into the Lethem Rexall and purchases a family-size bottle. He opens it on the spot and washes three aspirin down at the drinking fountain back by the drugstore phone booth, pausing in between gulps to scan the headlines of the tabloids: I DANCED AWAY FORTY POUNDS OF FAT! TEXAS WOMAN FRIES SACRED TORTILLA! JODIE FOSTER FINDS ANONYMITY AT IVY LEAGUE SCHOOL!

Out on Main Street, Robin decides his

mouth feels better. He takes off for the post office, remembering another walker with each long step he takes: his grandfather. The day he took Robin to Yankee Stadium and bought him the baseball cap, his grandfather was the tallest man Robin had ever seen. Yet only a few years later Robin was as tall as his grandfather. Now his grandmother has ordered her husband, the old doctor, to stop making house calls. Robin looks down at his feet as they move rapidly along the sidewalk and speculates on transmutation, metempsychosis, whether he will one day become his grandfather. Generations walking on, messages from the genes.

He arrives at the post office at a few minutes to nine and waits on the steps studying the faded Marine recruitment poster that's been there as long as he can remember. He's aware of his teeth only dully. Now his tongue seems numb.

A postal worker finally unlocks the door and lets Robin in. At the window, Robin says "Box seven, please," to the woman, and she winks at him as usual. While he waits, he considers the possibility that she may have a twitch in her eye.

"Thanks a lot," he says as she hands him his mail, afraid to risk a smile.

"Hey," the woman says with another wink or twitch. "You got yourself a mouthful, don't you, honey?"

Robin puts his hand to his mouth, surprised that the transparent plastic hooks, the rubber bands, and the wires are visible. "Yes," he says, "I guess I do."

"You'll look better," the woman says, all chummy and confidential. "I've always said to myself, why doesn't that boy get his teeth straightened?"

"You *have?*"

She nods knowingly. "A handsome fellow like you." This time she really does wink.

He thanks her for his mail and leaves the building fast. On the steps, he sorts through the pile—magazines, ads, bills, and something he didn't expect, a letter on her pale gray stationery, the first he's had since he ripped up that other. He decides to open this on the spot. She can't send him into tailspins anymore. In fact, sometimes he has trouble recapturing the version of himself that was so lovesick only a short while ago—as if it drifted away with his Yankee cap.

He reads, noting his calm.

Dear Robin,
I'll be home the first week in November. My Aunt Linda is finally marrying that nerd Tom. I meant what I said in my last letter, I really meant it. I love you; this has all been a big mistake.
Love, J

Robin gazes across the street at the windows of Tano's Shop-Rite, scanning the weekly specials plastered to the glass. It's like counting to ten or taking a deep breath. He reads the specials a second time, hoping to find a sign in the rump roast special or the toilet paper banner. No dice.

What we have here, he says to himself, is the *real* number one on the list. Forget teeth.

Suddenly the pain in his mouth returns. His whole head feels endangered.

For several miles the back road winds downhill through sun-dappled woods. As they leave Holly Hill behind, Harry feels some of the tension of his meeting with Buddy melt away in the warm September air. The soft breeze coming in the open windows smells faintly of apples. Now and then they pass a sumac that's gone crimson early, a maple turned golden yellow.

Harry ventures a glance at Buddy, sprawled across the seat next to him. He's put on some weight and is bigger than ever. His new crew cut, odd as it is after years of all that awful long hair, suits him well. He looks good, Harry decides, healthy. Yet Harry remains leery. Any minute now he expects Buddy to start up with his crazy, jarring talk.

Down in the valley, they follow the course of a narrow river where the sun flashes blinding diamonds off the shallows. The river swings around in a wide loop; they bump over it on a narrow bridge, then turn sharply to the right. Suddenly, without any warning, the road becomes a corridor of fiery color, blazing red and orange, copper, pink, deep winy purple. It's as if the trees on either side of them had burst into wild, hectic flames.

Harry catches his breath, breaking the silence in the car with a long, awed, "Ohhhh." The light under the trees is soft and rosy, as if an enormous pink shawl were being shaken over this small stretch of road.

Harry pulls over on the shoulder, forgetting everything except what's before him. After a few minutes he comes to. Glancing over at Buddy, he's relieved to see a wide-eyed look of amazement on his son's face. He was prepared to find Buddy staring at the floor, or even laughing at him.

"Brother!" Harry ventures. "When these red maples go, they really put on a show!" Even before the words are out of his mouth, he's embarrassed by the feebleness of his testimony.

Buddy stares and stares. He looks just like he did when he was a little kid. Something happens at the back of Harry's throat. The trees, the wide-open gaze on Buddy's face, the peculiar rose-tinted light. Harry shuts his eyes.

"Who would ever want to die?" Buddy says hoarsely. Harry's eyes fly open, and his spirits take a nosedive. Uh-oh, he thinks, here we go.

"Son," Harry admonishes gently, "don't." Meaning don't ruin it. Don't for once go into your screwball routine. Don't be what you are, a mental patient on an outing. Don't.

Buddy shrugs. "I don't think that's such a bad question," he says calmly. "All the times you think you should bag it, that nothing's worth it, then you see something like this. It reminds us."

"Reminds us?" Harry wishes he had kept his mouth shut.

"You know, like there's plenty to stick around for," Buddy says sensibly. "Sometimes I think it takes too much to get our attention, things outside of us in the world, I mean. Like we're all numb half the time. This''—and he nods upward at the flaming trees—"this qualifies as an attention getter. This is pretty sensational.''

Harry nods, flabbergasted by Buddy's speech, more coherent words at one time than he's heard from his son in years. Who can this be? he wonders. Where's the surly, truculent adolescent? The raving lunatic? The nearly blanked-out zombie he returned to Krause only six weeks ago?

"If you saw this on a calendar or something, you'd never believe it," Buddy says. "You'd think it was faked.''

They sit for a while longer. Finally, a little reluctantly, Harry pulls back onto the road, leaving the scarlet tunnel behind.

Gradually the woods give way to cornfields, a few of them already cut down for the winter. In one, a group of Amish farmers in overalls and straw hats are working around a contraption with two shoots going off to the sides like outstretched arms. Whatever it is—a combine? Harry speculates—it's drawn by two enormous horses. Next to it is a horse-drawn buckboard driven by a woman in a long black dress and a white apron. At the edge of this scene two small boys turn and wave, and like a normal friendly person, Buddy shoots his long arm out of the window and waves back.

"No idle hands there," Harry says.

"Did you know they have a lot of nervous breakdowns?" Buddy asks.

Harry thinks, please no, but he manages to say, "Is that so?''

"Yeah. I read a book about the Amish re-

cently. All the people who work in the kitchen at the Hill are Amish. The book was pretty interesting. They're against change, but it must be hard living in a society like ours.''

"They still don't drive cars," Harry says, trying to pitch in and do his part, "or have electricity or phones, isn't that right?''

"They're not supposed to have cars, but this book said a lot of the boys have them for a while. Their parents pretend not to know, and when the boys get it out of their systems, they give the cars up and join the church.''

"Sounds like they know their psychology," Harry says, and wonders if he and Buddy can really be having this casual, everyday conversation, or if he could possibly be imagining it.

They're stuck for a while behind a slow-moving Amish buggy with a brilliant orange triangle on its back. Halfway up a hill, the buggy turns off down a dirt road. Small Amish houses with one curtain at each window cluster together. At the top of the hill, Harry finds they're on the outskirts of a town. They drive by small manufacturing plants and a cheese factory, and the town begins to reveal its size.

"What is this?" Harry asks.

"Middleburg," Buddy says.

"Are you sure?''

"Sure, I'm sure. It's Middleburg. I know because a bunch of us were dragged here one day to see that cheese factory back there. Somebody's idea of an outing. Actually, it was okay.''

As Buddy is talking, Harry spots something he can't believe. "For chrissake, Bud!" he exclaims. "Look over there!" He stops for a red light, pointing ahead of them to a familiar brown brick building and a sign with golden arches. A hitch rail is crowded with Amish horses and buggies. "Can you believe that?" Harry asks.

"Well, I guess nothing says they can't eat Big Macs." Buddy laughs.

Harry jerks around and stares at Buddy. He laughed, Harry is thinking. He didn't snicker or snort or double over convulsively. Buddy laughed, just a commonplace, good-natured laugh.

They drive around a large village green, then in a few blocks they're out in the country again.

"Hey, Dad," Buddy says, "how about letting me drive?"

Harry's throat constricts.

"Seriously, Dad. I've got my driver's license with me. I never let it expire."

Expire, Harry thinks. "Now, Bud," he says.

"Listen, I'll be careful, Dad," Buddy tells him. "I wasn't such a bad driver before. That little accident I had, that could have happened to anyone. Even you said that."

Jesus, Harry thinks, remembering his silver-gray Continental being hauled away for scrap.

"Really, Dad."

"Sure, why not?" Harry says, and notes that he sounds like he means it. He pulls into the first driveway they come to and puts the car in park. Buddy bolts out of the door, and Harry reluctantly slides across the seat as his son assumes the wheel. For a time Harry forgets to breathe. Buddy backs out. Harry looks at the drainage ditch.

"Off we go!" Buddy says. There's not another car in sight. Harry clutches the door.

"Which way?" Buddy asks as they approach a four-way stop. Buddy brakes, and Harry watches a white pickup pull to the stop sign opposite them.

"Make a left," Harry says. Buddy flips on the turn signal.

"Should I wait for this guy or what?" he asks.

"Wait," Harry orders, but the driver of the pickup motions for Buddy to go. Harry shakes his head wildly at the driver, in an effort to communicate—No, *you* go. Buddy apparently misses this exchange, and suddenly Buddy and the pickup are both moving across the intersection, headed straight for each other.

Harry brakes, stupidly ramming his foot into the floor. Buddy steps hard on the gas, and the car skids around in front of the oncoming pickup, taking the turn so sharply that Harry's thrown into the door. Harry opens his mouth to yell bloody murder, the hell with Buddy's feelings. Inexplicably, however, he finds his lips clamping shut.

"Calm down, Dad," Buddy says, cool as anything. "If you're going to let me drive, let me drive. Two of us can't drive at the same time."

Harry's heart whomps insanely. "The person turning left always yields," he says pleasantly.

"But I got there first," Buddy says. "I thought—oh, well, you're right. I guess I should have let him go."

"No harm done," Harry says, marveling at his restraint. He sounds positively relaxed, when he's actually stiff as a board, his muscles tense. His ribs hurt as he clamps on the seat belt.

The marshland along both sides of this road is flat and colorless. It would make a watery, mucky grave. Buddy has the speedometer up over forty. Two cars whiz by, and Harry winces.

"Your foot, Dad," Buddy says. They slow for a sharp left curve. Harry looks down to see his foot working the nonexistent brake pedal. He tries to stop, but his foot has a will of its own. What he's doing with his foot is like what Irene used to do when she fed Buddy as a baby. She opened her mouth for him, chewed, licked her lips. "I guess I'm just trying to help," Harry says.

"Well, thanks, Dad," Buddy replies. "I appreciate that, but it makes me uneasy."

Uneasy, Harry thinks, nearly exploding. He's uneasy! And then calmly, "Take a left up here at this light, Bud." If he could pray, he'd be praying now. Blessedly, theirs is the only car at the traffic light, but Harry crouches like a coiled spring as they wait for the light to turn green.

"It feels good to be driving," Buddy announces cheerfully after he makes the turn. He flies over some railroad tracks so fast that Harry's head grazes the roof of the car despite the seat belt. He wills his mind to go blank and shuts his eyes, opening them after a short distance to see a giant wooden ice cream cone bending toward the road. Dear God, Harry thinks, don't let Buddy see that.

"How about an ice cream cone, Dad? I'm kind of hungry." Before Harry can answer, Buddy peels off the road onto the gravel in front of the ice cream stand, narrowly missing the enormous ice cream cone and screeching to a halt only inches from the plate-glass windows.

"Buddy," Harry says, nearly in tears, "Buddy, Buddy. You've got to put the brakes on *before* you get to what you're stopping for!"

"That was pretty bad," Buddy agrees. "I'm a little rusty. I guess you can tell."

"You just need some practice," someone says reassuringly as they get out of the car. "You'll be fine." Can this really be him talking, Harry wonders, or is he suddenly a medium for a kinder, more decent person?

"Can I help you?" a boy in a white cap asks from behind the window.

Jesus, Harry thinks. "Let's see now, Bud, what'll you have?"

"Oh, wow, Dad," Buddy says, slapping his head dramatically.

"What is it, son?" Harry expects the worst.

"I just remembered. I'm supposed to start lifting weights today with the Hulk at four, and after that I've got to go running. I probably shouldn't eat."

Harry attempts to process this information but can't. "Come again?" he asks, eyeing Buddy.

"Didn't I tell you?" Buddy says enthusiastically. "Krause said I could start doing weights today, and the Hulk—that's Wilt—he's going to show me how. We run together too. I started jogging my first week back, and now I'm up to four miles a day. I'm really getting into it. My knee's okay too." Buddy smiles.

Harry's mouth drops. Buddy a jock? Buddy, the kid who even when he wasn't half cracked thought exercise was opening the refrigerator door?

"Of course," Harry says, as if he has complete understanding of the situation, "you're right." To the boy at the window Harry says, "Thanks, anyway, but we've got to run."

"Ha ha," Buddy says, moving toward the driver's side, too fast for Harry. "That's good, Dad. Pretty corny, though."

Harry has no idea what Buddy is talking about. He steels himself and climbs back into the passenger seat. Only divine intervention will get them back to Holly Hill, but it's not as far as Harry thought, and within ten minutes Buddy is easing the car up the winding drive.

"Made it!" Buddy says, grabbing Harry's hand. "Gee, Dad, this was great. It's the best time I've had in a long time. Except for running, that is. I'm glad you came. *Really* glad."

Harry searches for a hint of sarcasm, a wrong note, but finds none. "Bud," he says, and notices their hands are still clasped together. "Bud, it's been wonderful. You seem . . ." Harry hesitates. "You seem good, son."

"Oh, I'm getting better, there's no question about it," Buddy says matter-of-factly.

"Your mother will be thrilled," Harry says. Immediately he's sorry. Sometimes Buddy reacts rather violently to the mention of Irene.

"Tell her I missed her, and I hope she'll come soon. Tell her I love her."

Harry swallows, nearly pop-eyed in disbelief. Buddy lets go of Harry's hand and slips out of the driver's seat. "Oh, and Dad," he adds, bending down, "give Mom a message for me, will you?"

"Sure."

"Just tell her this: a scarlet ibis or a kingfisher. Got that?"

"A scarlet ibis or a kingfisher," Harry repeats slowly. What kind of a message is this?

"Tell her I can't make up my mind. In fact, tell her a shearwater is also a real possibility."

"A shearwater?" Harry says as if it's a foreign word. "*Shear*water?"

Noting his father's puzzled expression, Buddy says, "You know, Dad. Shearwater." He puts his arms out to his sides and flaps them like a maniac. Harry stares. "The seabird that flies low between the crests of the waves," Buddy says. "Tell her I'm also leaning toward a shearwater."

Harry continues to look at his son blankly.

"Have you got that?" Buddy asks pleasantly, as if he'd made perfect sense.

"Scarlet ibis," Harry dutifully intones. "Kingfisher. Shearwater." He waits for an explanation, refusing to jump to conclusions.

"Don't forget to tell her," Buddy says

abruptly, backing off from the car. "And, hey, Dad, please come again soon." Then he turns and bounds up the steps to where Wilt stands like a waiting giant.

For a minute or two after Buddy and Wilt disappear into the house, Harry sits in the car. Scarlet ibis, he is thinking. Kingfisher. Shearwater. Slowly he slides over to the driver's seat and starts the car. Here he was all set to tell Irene that Buddy seemed a hundred percent improved. Now all he can see is the stricken look on her face when he delivers Buddy's crackpot little message. Scarlet ibis. Kingfisher. Shearwater. Sweet Jesus, he thinks.

Sam gently pulls the covers up and lights a cigarette in the dark. The hair on his chest shimmers. Mona snuggles up close to him. "Oh, my," she sighs, "that was just ducky."

"Ducky?" Sam chuckles.

"Well, it was," Mona says.

"Yep," he says, putting his free arm around her and pulling her closer. "I guess you could say that."

"I love you," Mona whispers.

"The Litter Queen," he says, and laughs.

"Oh, knock it off, Sam."

For a moment neither speaks, and Sam smokes quietly. Mona waits for him to say what she's longing to hear, but part of her knows there's no hurry. Sam's home, here in their bed for the first time in over a month. The Litter-lifting today went off without a hitch, and more people than she'd ever dreamed of pitched in. One more feather in her silly Lethem cap.

Sam may have noticed the bags under her eyes are gone, but he hasn't said a word. When he got off the plane early that morning he did say she looked fabulous. Someday maybe she'll tell him about Spatzer.

"I love you, kid," Sam says as he puts out his cigarette. This is the first time all day the two of them have been alone. After Mona rushed around with the Litter-lifting, they wound up having dinner at the Watterses'—not the gayest homecoming, with Kay so quiet and David gallantly trying to make up for her silences. Funny about David, Mona thinks, she isn't a bit embarrassed to see him. It's almost as if what went on between them that rainy afternoon happened to somebody else.

Sam switches on the lamp and reaches down, producing a large silver double-decker box of Belgian chocolates tied with a pink ribbon.

"Sam!" Mona squeals, and gives him a big kiss. She opens the box and picks out a piece that looks like solid chocolate but turns out to be some hazelnut concoction. "Darn," she says.

"Hand it over," Sam tells her. He pops what's left of it into his mouth. Mona selects one filled with a rich chocolate cream. But she tastes it from a distance. She can't remember ever wanting to spit out a piece of chocolate before. It's not the chocolate, she decides, it's her. Sam watches, smiling, enjoying what he regards as one of her great pleasures.

"Good?" he asks.

"Wonderful," she says, putting the lid on

the box. "But I guess I must be off chocolate or something. I don't know what's come over me." She doesn't want to hurt Sam's feelings. On the other hand, she wants to be honest.

"Don't worry about it," he says.

"Okay," Mona says, cuddling up to him again, wishing she had the energy to brush her teeth.

"I'm beat," Sam says, turning off the light. "Pooped."

"Me too." She sighs. She was hoping he would say something, anything, about what she's dying to hear. After the first letter, the one about food, he called to say he was coming home. But he hasn't mentioned her note about Chez Mimi.

"I've been thinking," Sam says, and Mona's ears perk up. To hide her sudden anxiousness she flops over on her stomach.

"What?" she says, trying hard not to sound too eager.

Sam begins doodling on her back in a delicate tracery that makes her shiver with pleasure.

"Tell me what I'm writing," he says, his finger light as a feather.

They haven't played this game in a long time, but "I love you" is easy. "Me too," she says happily. "Me too you."

"How about this?" he asks. With much concentration Mona pieces together "Let's do it."

"Keep it clean," she says. "Besides, we just did."

"Dope," he says. "That's not what I meant." He wipes her back like he's erasing it and begins again. "I'm home," he writes.

"Hmmm," Mona hums, thinking she's glad of that. Her eyes close, she's so sleepy.

"One more," Sam says. Half asleep now, Mona thrills to his touch, feeling along with it her own leanness under his hand. This time she misses whatever he writes altogether.

"Pay attention," he tells her, and she forces herself to wake up. *C,* she feels him write, *H, E, Z.*

Mona springs to her knees, suddenly wide-awake. "Oh, my land!" she gasps. "Are you saying what I think you're saying?"

"Yep," Sam says. "It sounds like it might be a good idea. I want to see the numbers, but, well, to tell you the truth, I'm sick of what I'm doing. All this racing around, I feel like I live in airports. I'll say this, though, it's made us some money, enough to take a chance with."

"Sam!" Mona cries. "Oh, Sam!" She throws herself on top of him and plants little kisses all over his face.

"Smothering me," he says, laughing. "Where will that get you?"

Mona can't hold on to him tight enough.

"Honey . . ." Sam says.

"Oh, Sam, I can't believe this! I'm so happy!" Sam pats her tenderly on the back. "Now tell me again," she says, "out loud this time."

Sam clears his throat. "Well," he says, "I think this Chez Mimi thing might be something like I've wanted to do with you all along. I thought you were too busy, I don't know, and I guess I got caught up in this rat race. I'm ready for something different. You must have sensed it."

"Oh, my goodness." Mona sighs.

"I went there today, as a matter of fact."

"To Chez Mimi?" she asks, surprised. "You did?"

"Yeah. I took Tony along. We had some god-awful omelets. They tasted like powdered eggs."

"Poor thing," she says. "I never meant for you to *eat* there!"

"Tony finagled his way to the basement, casing the joint, he said. He was funny. Anyway, he said the basement was dry. That's something. Actually the place seems in reasonable shape."

"It needs redecorating badly," Mona says.

"Oh, sure, but I peeked in the kitchen, and all that equipment is pretty new. Maybe it even works, who knows? I don't think the people who own it have the foggiest idea what they're doing. From the location, that place should be a gold mine, but here they are on the verge of bankruptcy."

"You really took Tony?" Mona asks.

"Didn't you say he's a regular Sherlock Holmes? Besides, I like the kid."

"He's a nice boy," Mona says. "But tell me more about Chez Mimi."

"Wait, I meant to ask you earlier. What's with Kay? She seems so down in the dumps."

"Do we have to talk about Kay right now?" Mona asks. Then, knowing how single-minded Sam can be, she says, "I don't know. She's not herself. At first I thought it was the fire, but now I'm not so sure. To tell you the truth I've been so busy lately, I haven't had time to try to figure it out. I will, though, just wait."

"She's always been pretty intense," Sam says. "One of those high-strung types, even though she pretends otherwise."

"Really, Sam! I never knew you'd studied her so closely," Mona says. "Hmmph!"

"Hmmph yourself." Sam laughs and strokes her hair. "I'll bet you've sized up David, haven't you? Anyway, about Chez Mim. You think we can set up a meeting with the real estate guy soon?"

"Tomorrow," Mona says.

"Good."

Mona finds herself all over him, and they are making love again, sweetly, joyously, like they've been practicing night and day for months. Who'd said, use it or lose it? Or has Sam . . . ? But Mona shoos that idea away. Nothing but what they're doing now matters. Sam's home at last.

Blinding sunlight glinted off the wing as the plane banked. Below lay the veil of adobe-colored smog that meant Los Angeles. Home, Jennifer thought, then remembered Los Angeles was no longer home but merely the first stop on their journey. She sighed, fighting off a wave of emotion she hadn't anticipated.

At least the convent was behind them. If they could make it through that long, dreary sojourn, surely she and her sister could accomplish what they had set out to do today. Bolstered by a sense of anticipation, Jennifer reminded herself that something good always came from life's trials.

Today the two of them were going home, really home. They had decided to return to New England and take up nursing careers. Jennifer could think calmly about Lance Steel now. After her months in the convent Lance was little more than a tender place in her heart, an old wound she would always carry with her. In time, she was certain, it would grow less painful. Of course, their relationship would have been impossible, forever overshadowed by Lance's tragic marriage and divorce, the divorce that resulted in his wife's institutionalization and terrible death. Jennifer could never build a life on someone else's unhappiness.

She banished all thoughts of Lance from her mind and reached for Jessica's hand as the plane bumped along the runway. They had only to pick up the few things they'd brought to California and catch their plane to Boston.

"Welcome to Los Angeles International Airport," the stewardess said. The minute the plane stopped, both girls were out of their seats. Mr. Lundin must know nothing of their brief stopover. He might try to persuade them to stay and cause a scene. The girls had agreed it would be easier to write to him when they were home at last.

The twins stepped into the crowded aisle. Time was of the essence.

"Dumb bunnies," Irene remarks to herself and blows her nose. She has a terrible cold, and her throat is so sore she can barely swallow. Fluttery and weak with a temperature of 102°, nevertheless she has propped herself up in bed so she can go on writing about these impossible girls. Irene blames her cold less on the chilly weather than she does on *Twin Hearts.* She's eager to be rid of the twins for good.

"Soup?" Harry says, poking his head in the doorway and beaming at her sweetly. He has new glasses and looks quite handsome. "Coffee? Tea? Juice? I'm at your service."

"Harry," Irene croaks, "you're such a dear." Abruptly she sneezes and falls back on the pillows, her eyes watering.

"Irene?" Harry asks, concern in his voice.

"Yes?" Irene answers feebly.

"Are you all right?" Harry comes over to the side of the bed and touches her shoulder gently. "Don't cry," he says softly. "Don't cry."

"I'm not crying," Irene says weakly. "It's this darn old cold." But then, suddenly, she *is*

crying, and what's worse, she's not even attempting to hold back her tears.

"Sweetheart," Harry says. He wraps his arms around her.

Dearest Harry, Irene thinks weepily. The thought of Harry staying home to take care of her touches her so that a wave of tears overtakes her. To her utter bewilderment she is weeping in Harry's arms, as if everything inside her has suddenly sprung loose. This feels horrible—no, it feels wonderful. She feels safe with him holding her.

Harry says, "Can you tell me what's wrong?"

The words spill out amid hiccoughing tears. "It's this stupid thing." She sobs, flinging her notebook aside. "It makes me feel dismal."

"There, there," Harry says.

"It's trash," Irene wails pathetically. "I know that's what you think, and you're right."

Harry rocks her back and forth. "Come now," he says. "You just have a bad cold."

"Whatever possessed me to write such nonsense?" She sobs into his shirt.

"Irene . . ." Harry scolds gently. "Don't be so hard on yourself."

Irene wants to stay in Harry's arms forever, but after a few minutes she pulls away and dabs at her eyes. "I guess crying won't do any good." She sniffs. "I've got to finish it, that's all there is to it."

"Of course you'll finish it," Harry says reassuringly.

Over Harry's shoulder, out the window, Irene spies a brilliant cardinal perched on a tree branch next to the house. The sight gives her a little more courage, and she blows her nose definitely.

"I didn't mean to fall apart," she says. "It must be this awful cold, you're right. But thank you, Harry. Thank you."

"Let me get you a drink of something," he says cheerfully. "You just stay put."

Irene snuggles down under the covers. Her tears were as unexpected as her suddenly blurting out what was on her mind. *Twin Hearts* seems vapid and silly, and the idea of Nicolle makes her feel a little foolish. Thank God she turned down the invitation to the romance writers' conference. The biggest problem with this Nicolle business, though, is that she can't imagine her life without a Profile Romance in it.

Lately Irene's begun attending an aerobic dance class just for fun, part of a workshop her neighbor, Mona Edwards, leads quite well, Irene has to admit. Irene loves dancing. In college, she was in the modern dance club, and though it seems strange now, for a while she seriously entertained dreams of going to New York and dancing with Martha Graham or someone like that. How different her life might have been, she thinks. Yet how different her life is today from what it was only three months ago. The change that's come over her and Harry no longer seems fragile or temporary but solid and real.

Still, much as Irene loves dancing, she can't dance all day long, and a future with Profile Romances is not what she wants, either. Nicolle and her stories seemed like the house Irene built around her loneliness, and even though things have taken a miraculous turn for the better, the question of how she could fill her days without writing still remains. Oh, dear, she thinks with a sigh as Harry returns carrying a tray with a bunch of zinnias and a tall glass of ginger ale on it.

"Thank you, Harry," she says. Harry settles into the rocker next to the bed.

"Feeling better?" he asks.

She nods.

Harry rocks back and forth for a minute, then stops abruptly. "Irene?" he says thoughtfully.

"Yes?"

"Irene, have you ever considered writing something else? Something serious?"

His words stop her in mid-swallow. "Oh, I couldn't," she says, coughing. "Don't be silly."

"Now just wait a second here," he says. "You're a good writer, Irene."

"Harry . . ." Irene protests.

"You always have been," he tells her.

"Oh, Harry," Irene says raspily, "much as I hate to admit it, the fact is, I have a junky mind."

Harry shakes his head. "Come off it."

"But, Harry," Irene says. All that's left of her voice is a whisper. "Deep down I'm really very shallow." She closes her eyes, pained by this admission.

Harry begins to laugh, and when Irene hears again what she's just said, she's laughs too. She starts to say, "It's true," but flies into a coughing fit.

"Now listen," Harry tells her when she's recovered. "There has to be some alternative to romances."

"Like what?" Irene challenges.

"Well," Harry says, taking her hand in both of his, "I suppose what comes to mind first is our own personal experience. Having a son like Buddy, I mean." He hesitates and then adds, "How we got through."

"Harry," Irene replies, "it's not over yet."

Harry hands her the half-filled glass of ginger ale. "Drink this," he says. "You need liquids." Then he leans back in the rocker. "It's not over yet, no," he says, "and I don't want to get our hopes up too high. But you have to admit he's enormously better. Plus, what Krause is telling us is more promising by a long shot than anything we've heard before."

Irene nods and blows her nose.

"And if Buddy's whole problem is really this adolescent psychosis Krause seems to think it is, well, then—"

"I'm afraid even to think of it," Irene says, interrupting. "I'm afraid if we so much as talk about it out loud, he'll get sick again. Poor child, he's been through so much."

"Look, Irene," Harry says. "Even if Krause is wrong, even if, well . . ." His eyes move around the room before returning to her. "You still have a lot to say, something that might be a consolation to other parents whose kids are in trouble. I know you could do it, Irene, I really do." He rises from the rocker and bends over her. "Think about it," he says softly.

Though Irene hasn't an iota of faith that she can handle anything weightier than the idiotic comings and goings of people like the twins, she nevertheless nods. "All right."

"Good," Harry says. "Now I'm going out to rake leaves before it rains. You sleep now. Put *Twin Hearts* away for now. Your job is to get rid of this cold." He kisses her lightly on the forehead. "Sleep."

Irene puts her arms around his neck and pulls him close, forgetting all about germs. "Thank you, Harry," she says. "Thank you."

"Hush," he says quietly. "I'll be out in the yard if you want me." For a split second Irene has an uncanny vision of Harry twenty-five years younger. That smile, the way he's standing. Then, for his benefit, she closes her eyes.

Oddly enough, after Harry goes, Irene feels a surge of energy. Her head seems clearer than it's been for days. What if he's right? she wonders. What if she really could do something worthwhile?

Suddenly she grabs her notebook and pen. She flips quickly to a clean page and, entirely without the aid of Nicolle, begins to write.

I remember a raw March day. Kevin was fifteen and had stayed home from school with one of the increasingly frequent colds he seemed to be having that winter. . . .

The story begins to pour out, details she hadn't thought she remembered, things she never wanted to face. I can't be doing this, Irene thinks, yet she writes on, astonished by the press of memories, the speed and rush with which they suddenly come back, almost too fast for her pen. Maybe this would be only for her and Harry: a recollection, a journal with hindsight. But it would be the truth, all that she could recover.

The words fly forth: the story she didn't believe she had it in her to tell.

Leaves shower down from the trees and rattle noisily against the house. Good-bye, autumn. Katherine's at home rereading *Tender is the Night* for a late-afternoon class, but something's wrong; the novel she's been so fond of for years seems soppy and sentimental today, downright silly in places.

Still, she's absorbed enough that when Charmaine pops her head into the room to say something, Katherine looks up in a daze, unable to separate herself from the book.

"I'm sorry?"

Charmaine shakes her head sadly. "The Hoover's up to its old tricks again, Ms. Watters. Phht! And me in the middle of trying to get those fuzz balls off the new carpet upstairs."

"What's wrong this time?" Katherine asks. Charmaine's only flaw is her tendency to administer rigorous endurance tests to the vacuum cleaner.

"The belt," Charmaine says mournfully. "But if you ask me, it's something worse than that." She brightens. "Maybe it's time to shop around for a new one. How about one of them deluxe Kirbys."

Katherine ignores Charmaine's familiar plea. "Listen," she says, "I'll run out and get you a new belt. Hold on. Have your lunch and iron for a while. I'll be back in a jiffy."

Charmaine mumbles something under her breath as she leaves, and Katherine arranges her lecture notes. Not that she needs them; not that she even needs to reread the book. By now random passages lodge stubbornly in her memory.

"Rosemary."

"Yes, Dick."

"Look, I'm in an extraordinary condition about you. When a child can disturb a middle-aged gent—things get difficult."

Oh, shut up, Katherine says to herself.

Katherine takes her purse and heads out the door. It's beginning to rain, and she throws on her slicker. The 7-11 is closer than anything else. When she gets there, she pulls two packages of vacuum cleaner belts off the rack and takes them to the cashier. As she waits in line,

Robin Hastings walks in the door. Katherine stares, still fogged from reading. Then her metabolism swings into high.

"Katherine," he says. He's wearing a red down vest and jeans.

"Robin." She feels suddenly unstable. She waves the belts around. "I'm on an errand of mercy," she rattles. "Charmaine goes through several dozen of these a month." She smiles feeblemindedly.

"Hey," he says, "are you busy?"

"Busy?" she asks, not sure how to proceed. "Sort of, not really, a little," she tries. "I have to teach a class late this afternoon."

"You want to run out and take a look at my barn?" he asks. "I've got a little while before I have to get back to work, and you're already halfway there. Besides, the stable's closed today, so it'll be quiet." His eyes seem to radiate invitations.

"Uh," she says, "well." Her mind races madly, springing to certain conclusions. This is it? Oh, hell, why not? "Sure," she says, attempting to ignore her mounting inner turmoil.

"I'll just get something for lunch and be right along. I won't be a second. I'll be right behind you."

He disappears down an aisle, and Katherine pays for the belts, dropping change all over the floor. Hurriedly she picks it up, wiped out by anxiety. When she pictured this moment in her mind's eye, she'd always been majestically cool and serene.

Somehow she manages to get to her car and start the engine. Sternly she orders herself to simmer down. She seems to have been reduced to a tremulous and disconcertingly sexy agitation, as if somehow her body had gotten a head start.

She whizzes out of the parking lot. She's about to commit an infraction of the rules and she's in a rush to do so. This is crazy, she thinks. No, it's not. For fifteen years of marriage she's been impeccable, true blue, pure and monogamous, at least technically. What can this possibly matter? The answering pang of conscience is nothing to the sensations of her quickened body. Scenes from her dreams bombard her. Ordinarily these panic her in the cold light of day, but now they're strangely comforting.

Part of her concentrates on keeping the speedometer steady. The last thing she needs is a ticket. Off and on it occurs to her she may not be thinking clearly. In between she feels extraordinarily lucid. In the rearview mirror she spots Robin's truck not far behind her.

> . . . Dress, stay crisp for him; button, stay put; bloom, narcissus—air, stay still and sweet.

Can it, she tells herself, glancing down at her sneakered feet, jeans, and oversized rugby shirt—not quite the right getup for an assignation. She smiles faintly. Why pretend to be coy? She's too old for that. From somewhere a voice cautions her not to expect too much, but she expects everything, all of it, each of her greedy dreams to come true.

The rain picks up, and the highway turns black and shiny before her eyes. Katherine flips on the radio and isn't surprised to find someone singing a love song directly to her. The song thrills her, then makes her feel helpless, like a teenager. She turns the radio off and, in the abrupt silence that follows, realizes she's scared. She tells herself that she's an enlightened, free-thinking person. *Who?* a voice asks, but Katherine muffles it.

She passes the town limits and then turns into the long driveway that leads to Robin's barn, slowing to a crawl over the rutted gravel. With every bump the car takes, she becomes more flustered. No scenario in her head has gone like this, and by now she thought she'd run through them all. Katherine bites her lip. What will he think of her? She hasn't slept with anyone but her husband for so long, maybe she won't even know what to do. She experiences a wave of light-headedness. Come now, she scolds herself. All she needs to do is pass out. For a split second that idea isn't unattractive.

Robin overtakes her and parks his truck next to the barn. She makes a stab at taking a deep breath but isn't entirely successful. Her legs are weak. She asks for strength but gets this instead:

> She was a compendium of all the discontented women who had loved Byron a hundred years before. . . .

Knock it off!

"Katherine!" Robin says. "Kay! Hi. You made it!"

She wills herself to stand, but he beams down at her so beautifully, she is in imminent danger of keeling over. Only the sight of his braces halts her slide. They make him look suddenly young and uncertain. She reminds herself of the authority of his shoulders, his arms. He seems bigger than ever, taller; then she notices he's wearing cowboy boots. *Cowboy boots?*

"We're getting wet," she says, looking into his eyes.

"Come on," he says, and taking her hand, he leads her into the dark barn. The smells are overpoweringly sweet and heady, and the first thing Katherine sees is a gigantic black horse moving restlessly in its stall. The air seems charged. She turns longingly toward Robin, who, now that they are inside, will certainly enfold her in his arms.

Her breasts crushed flat against him, her mouth was all new and warm, owned in common. They stopped thinking with an almost painful relief, stopped seeing; they only breathed and sought each other.

"I don't suppose someone like you would really be interested in horses," he says.

She opens her mouth, but before she can say a word, he is leading her down one long aisle of the barn and up the other, introducing her to each horse as they go. She is thoroughly dismayed, but at least she has a chance to re- claim the use of her legs. Robin is talking a mile a minute about how much he likes horses. She shoots him a mystified look, but he keeps right

on. She pretends amazement, amusement, whatever seems appropriate. After all, this is difficult for him, too, this about to be commit- ted . . . As if a hand had flown over her mouth, she refuses to think the word.

"Well?" he says when they've worked their way back to the door.

Katherine puzzles over what to say. She has just met several dozen horses. "My," she hears herself utter, "it's a big place. I had no idea." This sounds quite lamebrained.

"I want you to see my room," he says, smil- ing tensely.

Katherine gives him a significant look, but he seems not to notice. An alarm goes off in her head. She disregards this as he steers her through the barn office and into a room on the other side.

"Well, here it is, Katherine." He flashes her an impenetrable smile. She studies the small room, spare as a monk's cell—a bed covered with a dark, scratchy-looking blanket, a desk, a dresser, a long line of bookshelves under the two windows. The light is glaring and flat.

"Do you mind if I pull down the curtains?"
"Please do. It's too light in here."

Lay off!

"It's, uh . . . nice." She's nearly goofy with anxiety. He pushes her gently in the direction of the bed. Her heart bangs away like crazy, and she stops abruptly at the foot of it. Incredi- bly enough, Robin walks right up one of her heels and nearly knocks her over.

"Excuse me!" he says. His voice sounds odd.

Katherine tugs at the heel of her sneaker as he walks around her to stand at one of the windows.

"Look," he says, as if nothing had happened. "Look out there."

Bewildered, Katherine hobbles up next to him, her sneaker still half off. She sees a recently cut-down cornfield, woebegone and muddy in the rain. In the distance, a line of bare trees. The rain is coming down hard now, making a loud, clanging noise on the barn's metal roof.

"My Ohio fields, Katherine," Robin says. She twirls around, certain he's pulling her leg. Unfortunately he appears sincere. She grows calm, slow, as if she were having an out-of-body experience.

"Your. Ohio. Fields," she repeats in an effort to get the message. This is not going at all as she'd imagined.

"And beyond them," he says, "my dark woods."

Dark woods? What can this *mean?* Anxiously she looks behind her, checking the room again. It's a boy's room, not even cozy. Her mind veers off, stubbornly trying to right things.

"Isn't it funny and lovely being together, Dick? No place to go except close. Shall we just love and love?"

"Listen, Katherine," Robin says abruptly, "I've wanted to talk to you about something for a long time. It's been on my mind ever since we met."

Katherine gapes at him.

"I . . . uh . . . really respect . . ."

"It'll be all right, Robin," she hears herself say. "Don't worry."

"Well," he says, looking a little brighter. "Listen . . ."

She waits.

"I know you teach American lit and all, and well, tell me, what do you think of Hart Crane? I mean, I really think he's great, but I don't know much about twentieth-century poetry."

"Hart Crane!" Can he be talking about Hart Crane? Of course not, she's heard wrong.

"He's wonderful, isn't he?"

Katherine thinks she must be losing her mind.

"You do like him, don't you?"

"Like him?" In point of fact, she finds Crane's poetry unreadable, just what you'd expect from a long-winded drunk.

"I've always thought he was probably one of the most undervalued poets of the century, but then, like I said, I don't know a lot of poets. Tell me." He looks very earnest.

She smiles weakly and commands herself to monitor her tongue. "Hart Crane," she says slowly, "was a very . . . uh . . . interesting figure." She stops. "Of course, there are others—T. S. Eliot, Wallace Stevens, Robert Lowell." She goes on, sounding to herself increasingly like some joke English teacher. "Robert Frost," she adds. "Don't forget him."

"Could you make me a list, you know, like a reading list?"

"Oh," she says, "a reading list of twentieth-century poets?" Can this be happening? she wonders. Is this me? She wiggles her foot back into her sneaker.

"Thanks a lot," he says. "And now for the best part. I've been saving it till last."

For a second Katherine's stubborn hopes revive: He will take her to bed in this damp, chilly room. She will forgive him his taste in poetry, his horses, his youth, his braces, everything. She takes a deep breath.

Before she knows what's happening, he guides her across his bedroom and into the barn office. Her insides shrink as he switches on the desk lamp and leads her to a corner where there's a cardboard carton on the floor. Inside is a large white cat surrounded by pink, hairless kittens tinier than field mice.

"Ariel's babies," he says. "What do you think?"

Katherine stares at him dully. As he picks up one of the kittens she wonders if this can really be Robin, or if, by chance, someone is impersonating him badly. She modulates her voice as best she can. "You mean *this* is what you asked me here for?"

He looks momentarily puzzled, then smiles, but by now Katherine is tired of his smiles. They seem pasted on, as though all his charm had abandoned him and he was playacting. She hears herself sigh. Can this person who now puts the kitten carefully back into the carton, whom she is following out of the office, really have been the object of her wild fantasies?

They round a corner, and there in front of them is a sizable indoor arena. She pokes at its earth-covered floor with the toe of her sneaker.

"This is where everyone rides in the winter," he tells her.

"I don't understand you."

"You wouldn't believe this place when it's full," he says, as if he's answering.

The rain drums louder on the roof. "What is it, exactly, you had in mind, Robin? I mean, besides a reading list?" Her voice sounds small against the annoying racket overhead.

He looks at her for a split second, then turns away and points out a yellow golf cart used by the riding instructor, Horst. He tells her a story about Horst that she doesn't bother to listen to. He offers to show her the tack room and the hayloft. She refuses. He is merely showing off his house, she realizes, weirdly paying back some social obligation. It's her mind he's been after all along. Mind, she thinks. *What* mind?

"How about some yogurt," he asks her.

Katherine is suddenly annoyed. She hates yogurt. All she wants is to get out of this place. The smells alone . . .

"No," she says, "I'd better run. Charmaine's waiting."

"Really?"

"Well, I guess I've seen everything, haven't I?" She likes to be thorough.

"Do you like my barn, Katherine?" He seems so serious and eager, she can't figure out what he's doing. He might be laughing at her. He might know nothing, he might know everything. But she's tired of trying to read his mind.

Emboldened by frustration, Katherine says, "Well, it's a real barn, you can say that about it. There's nothing the least bit phony about it." She smiles fixedly, stopping herself before she can add that at least the barn doesn't promise things it doesn't deliver.

He gives her a look she doesn't attempt to interpret, then another smile. She has the sudden urge to wring his neck.

"I'll see you, Robin," she says wearily.

"Katherine! Kay!" He says this with such fervor, she whirls around.

"What?"

"I nearly forgot to tell you. Guess what I'm doing."

"I haven't the faintest idea."

"I'm going back to school in January, part-time, and pick up a couple science courses I need. Then I'm going to apply to med school. How does *that* sound?"

"About right," she says flatly.

"Aren't you excited for me? I mean, that I'm finally going to do something serious with my life?"

"You'll make a perfect doctor, Robin," Katherine says icily. "Good luck."

" 'Bye," he calls as she heads out of the barn toward her car. "And, Kay, listen! Thanks for coming! I can't wait for that list!"

She gets into her car without bothering to turn around and takes the drive slowly, avoiding the holes. She feels numb, not sure what's happened, or whether to laugh or cry. She's been such a fool, but at least she kept her mouth shut.

Once on the road, Katherine feels mortified, euphoric, ruined, saved. What went wrong? Did he find her unattractive? Old? Was he nervous? Did he—did anyone these days—have a high sense of morals?

A man can't live without a moral code. Mine is that I'm against the burning of witches.

Stop.

She sighs heavily and speeds up, struggling for clearheadedness as conflicting thoughts whiz-bang through her mind. Was he dense? Was *she?*

Then suddenly she knows he could never be the person she wanted him to be. The Robin she drove to the barn to seduce came right out of her head, after all. In her recurring pipe dreams he was pretty hot stuff. But horses, Ohio fields, dark woods, Hart Crane? And those smiles?

She can't deny that her pride is wounded. But then she stops to consider all she's been spared: the ghastly smells of the place, the glare in his creepy little room, making love to a person who worshiped Hart Crane (maybe David didn't read much besides medical journals, but Hart Crane?), the guilt, the complications.

For a long time nothing much had happened to her. Her marriage seemed like a still life where things never moved and were veiled in silence. She needed to believe she still possessed the energy for choices. And look, after

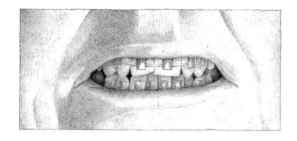

all, at all the crazy, steamy energy she had uncovered! She couldn't count herself out, not by a long shot; she could only admit she'd been unwise.

Go easy, she cautions herself. Don't get carried away. For once.

She knows she can either nurse her wounded pride or get on with things. She hates herself for being so levelheaded, but deep down she knows she can put Robin down as if he were . . . what? Well, a suitcase, perhaps.

And in her mind's eye she sees herself walking into an airport, shoving a bag—curiously, only a small overnight bag—into a locker. She tosses the key into a trash can and walks on down a long, long concourse. Soon she will be on a plane. Planes, after all, were always going somewhere. All destinations weren't the same. Maybe marriages, lives, were only as still and silent as you made them. She sees herself on the loading ramp, stepping onto a plane. She finds a seat and buckles up. The plane's motors stir, and it lumbers away from the gate. Finally she is airborne.

Oddly, this brings Katherine relief. Dragging Robin around, making him up as she went along, making him more than he was, more than he could be, had been a lot of trouble. He was so strange and flattering and flirty, but he wasn't the person she wanted or needed.

Suddenly, the sound of a siren jolts her from her thoughts. A police cruiser with its revolving red lights is coming up behind her. As she pulls over it occurs to her there may be a certain poetic justice at work: a ticket for her ridic-ulous excursion into the fast lane, why not? She catches herself smiling.

"What's the hurry here?" the policeman says. "Is there some kind of emergency? Is something wrong?" Katherine debates with herself for only a second.

"Wrong, yes," she says. "I have *got* to get home. I've been nearly frantic."

"Say," the policeman replies, cocking his head, "aren't you the one who had the fire in your house? On Jefferson?"

"Yes," she answers, willing to milk this for all it's worth. "So much has happened."

"You were going almost twenty miles over the speed limit," he says sternly.

Katherine arranges her face to look stricken and waits.

After a lengthy pause the policeman says, "Okay. I'll let you go this time. But you'd better watch it."

"Thank you," she says, and sighs heavily. Today she could take up sighing as an occupation. The policeman nods curtly and returns to his car. Saved again.

Katherine rolls up her window. Looking carefully all around, she pulls the car onto the road and slowly heads home.

Will and Scott dash down the alley, shopping bags full of candy knocking against their legs. They are dressed in green paper operating-room smocks and matching elasticized hats that Will's father brought home from the hospital. They've shoved their rumpled white surgical masks down around their necks. Penny lopes along next to them. On her head is taped a doll's nurse cap with a red cross on it, and bouncing around her neck is a plastic stethoscope. They are headed for the Newcombs' house, their last stop of the night.

Earlier the boys agreed they would see what the Newcombs gave them before deciding how they would trick them. They have almost a whole can of shaving cream left. They run across the Newcombs' lawn and barrel up the steps to the front door. Penny flops down on the porch and attacks her stethoscope as the boys yell, "Trick or treat!" and pull the masks over their faces.

Mrs. Newcomb opens the door so fast, she must have been hiding behind it. "Now let me see . . ." she says slowly. "Who do we have here?" Mrs. Newcomb is putting on a big act, and Scott starts to laugh. Will jabs him with his elbow, and both of the boys shuffle around while she pretends not to know who they are.

"Why, I haven't a clue in the world!" she says, sounding terrifically phony.

Will figures this could go on all night, so he says, "It's us, Mrs. Newcomb, Scott and Will."

"I *thought* I recognized those freckles!" Mrs. Newcomb smiles. Then, of all things, she winks at Will.

Scott snorts, and Will bites his lip.

"Harry!" Mrs. Newcomb calls behind her. "Harry! Come see who's here."

"Jeez," Scott groans under his breath. Will peers behind Mrs. Newcomb, but all he can see is a table with a bunch of flowers and a photograph in a silver frame. Everything else is in shadows.

"Look at our neighbors, Harry!" Mrs. Newcomb exclaims. "Aren't they cute!"

Will concentrates on his sneakers. He doesn't dare look at Scott.

"Well, well," Mr. Newcomb booms, "a house call. It's been years since doctors made house calls!" He chuckles.

"And just look at that, Harry. Isn't the dog adorable?"

Will thought Mrs. Newcomb hated Penny. He and Scott are going to die of boredom before the Newcombs are through. He can't understand why they're being so nice.

"By God, a nurse!" Mr. Newcomb says. "A redhead too!" He moves a little to the side, giving Will a straight shot at the photograph. It's a picture of a man with blond hair, wearing shorts and a T-shirt with a number on the front. Something about him strikes Will as familiar. He's right on the verge of knowing who it is when Mr. Newcomb steps back and blocks his view.

"It's Nurse Penny," Will informs the Newcombs, trying to speed things up.

"She's a real dog," Scott chimes in. This is about the hundredth time tonight Scott has said that, but Mr. Newcomb laughs and laughs like it's the funniest thing he's ever heard.

"A real dog," he repeats. "Ha, ha, ha."

Will leans around so he can see the photograph. Just like that, it hits him. The hair in the picture's a lot shorter, but he recognizes everything else. He doesn't get it, though. What's a picture of *him* doing in the Newcombs' house?

"Come now, Irene, let's not keep these boys waiting," Mr. Newcomb says.

"Maybe you'd like to come in and have a glass of cider," Mrs. Newcomb says. "It's so warm out for Halloween."

The boys exchange wary looks. "Naw," Scott says. "We'd better not."

"Not even a little glass?" she says, like she's very disappointed. "Why, I don't think you boys have ever been inside our house."

Scott shoots Will a desperate glance. All Will can think of is the witch in "Hansel and Gretel" luring the poor little kids into her house. It's funny, though. Mrs. Newcomb doesn't exactly look like a witch the way she used to. She looks sort of normal, in fact. He'll never forget how she looked that day last summer, wandering around in her nightgown or whatever it was, calling into the trees like a ghost or a crazy person. He still gets the creeps thinking about it.

"Our moms will be mad if we're late," Scott says.

"Yeah," Will adds, "but thanks, anyway." Mrs. Newcomb reaches around the corner and produces two giant candy bars, the really big ones. Will's eyes nearly pop out of his head.

"Here you are, boys," she says, giving them each one.

"Awesome!" they say in unison. "Gee, thanks!"

"A special treat"—Mrs. Newcomb smiles—"for our very good friends. I've been waiting all night for you two to come. I'm so glad you did."

Will stares at her, no idea what to make of this.

"And, oh, wait . . ." She disappears, and Mr. Newcomb says to Will, "Everything back to normal at your house?"

"Hunh?" Will asks.

"Your house," Mrs. Newcomb says. "All fixed up, is it?"

"Yeah," Will answers. "Yeah, it's fine."

Mrs. Newcomb comes back carrying a big bone in a plastic bag. "We had a steak tonight," she tells Will and Scott. "I bet Nurse Penny would love the bone." Will feels suddenly like he's missed something. Is this the same woman who used to call the dogcatcher on Penny every other day?

"Gee, thanks," Scott says.

Penny begins leaping crazily all over the Newcombs' front porch. The little nurse's cap sticks tight to her head, making her look amazingly dumb. Will grabs for Penny's collar and holds it tight. "Thanks," he says. "Thanks a lot!"

"Come back again, boys." Mrs. Newcomb smiles.

"That's right," Mr. Newcomb says. "Drop by anytime. Good to see you."

The Newcombs stand in the doorway, and the boys take the walk instead of cutting across the lawn. When they reach the driveway, Scott takes the bone out of the plastic bag and gives it to Penny, who trots on ahead of them, carrying it proudly.

"I don't get it," Scott says. "How come she was so nice?"

"Beats me," Will answers.

"I guess we'd better not . . ."

"Yeah . . ." Will agrees. There's no way they can prank the Newcombs now. Mrs. Newcomb was so different. Still, he feels a little cheated or something. "Hey!" he says, remembering the photograph. "Did you see the picture on the Newcombs' table?"

"What picture?"

"Oh, there was just this picture," Will replies. "I thought maybe you saw it."

Reaching the bottom of the Newcombs' drive, they find Penny sprawled in the middle of the alley, happily gnawing on the bone. "Come on, Penny," Scott says, taking the bone and holding it high above his head. "You want to get run over? Let's go!"

At his own driveway Will peels off, saying only " 'Bye." He has a sense that they've just been fooled but can't quite find the words to talk about it. Anyway, what can you say after someone gives you an enormous candy bar like that?

"See you tomorrow," Scott calls over his shoulder.

All by himself on the darkest part of his drive, Will quickens his pace. He wonders why Mrs. Newcomb put on that big act. Grown-ups could be really strange. On Halloween, kids were supposed to play tricks on people. He hoists the shopping bag over his shoulder as his house comes into view. Sometimes it was hard to know who people were.

He walks across dead leaves and goes up the back stairs into his house. His mother and father and Tony are just finishing dinner.

"Hi, Will," his father says. "You got a lot of loot there."

"Yeah," Will answers. "And look what Mrs. Newcomb gave us!" He holds up the candy bar.

"My," his mother says, "I didn't realize she was such a fan of yours. Or maybe she's recruiting for the local dentists."

Tony narrows his eyes. "It probably took her a long time to inject every one of those squares with arsenic," he says.

"Tony!" his mother says.

"And guess what?" Will says, ignoring Tony. "Guess who Mrs. Newcomb has a picture of in her front hall?"

"Who?"

"Just guess."

"Idi Amin Dada?" Tony says, and smirks.

"Phyllis Schlafly?" his mother says.

"I've got it!" Tony slaps his forehead. "John Belushi!"

"Mrs. Newcomb has a picture of Robin Hastings!" Will announces.

"Right," Tony says. "They were having this big love affair, see . . ."

"Robin *Hastings?*" his mother exclaims.

"Well," Will says, "I *think* it's Robin. Only with real short hair."

"You sure it wasn't David Bowie?" Tony asks. "I bet Mrs. Newcomb's really into him.

Jeez, Will, what a dork! Now hand over that poisoned candy bar.''

''Let's take a look at all this candy, Will,'' his father says, spreading a piece of newspaper on the floor. He begins laying Will's candy out in neat little rows.

''Here,'' Tony says, coming up to Will and whisking the candy bar out of his hand, ''I'll take that.'' Before Will knows it, Tony is off up the back stairs. ''This is just reeking of poison, Will!'' he yells. ''But don't worry, I'll save your life!''

Will's parents look at him. He can tell they're waiting for him to chase after Tony, but he just shrugs. ''He can have it,'' Will says, and begins helping his father.

''That's very nice of you, Will,'' his mother says.

Just then the word Will's been searching for comes to him: *bribe.* That's what the candy bar felt like, something some slimy man would give you to get into his car so he could kidnap you and you'd never see your family again. Because by the time they found you, you'd be

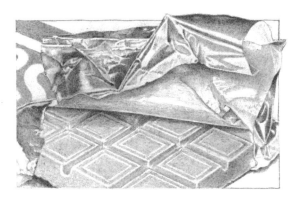

hacked up in little pieces and dumped in a freezer.

Well, Tony can have it. Besides, maybe it *is* poisoned, after all.

''. . . and then Chipper—oh, God, it was incredible—Chipper drowned! Can you imagine what a massively traumatizing thing it is to see a Lab drown? He went right through the ice and never came up.'' Jannie takes a drink of beer, then flops down on Robin's bed, her slightly grimy suede boots on his pillow.

''I guess it was around then,'' she continues, ''that my father took off with one of his secretaries. Myrna or Myra, I can't remember. This past summer when he came to California to see me, he told me that he and this secretary were actually married for about six weeks!'' She scratches her leg and in a low voice addresses the blanket. ''My mother went into her room and started this marathon crying jag. Did I ever tell you that? Every once in a while she'd come out and go, 'Things will be fine, Jannie. Just be a good girl,' and then she'd shut herself up in her room again. Thank God for third grade, is all I can say. At least I had someplace to go. It's weird, though, I can't remember eating any-

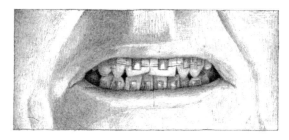

thing for weeks, except for some gross chocolate cereal. Oh, wait!'' she says in a voice full of discovery. ''Wait a minute! Just now I remember eating a lot of gaggy bananas. I bet that's why I despise . . .''

Robin sits motionless on the floor, feigning attention as Jannie reworks the narrative of her childhood, much of which he's heard before, though never with this Valley Girl twist. What's happened to her in California? Had she always talked this way?

In their darkest versions these renderings of Jannie's early years seem to touch on every form of misery in the twentieth century. They used to catapult him into tailspins of empathy, but tonight he's having trouble even looking alert.

''Of course, my mother has always been this amazing bitch,'' Jannie says.

He no longer knows what point she's working toward. They first met at a *Ghosts* cast party someone dragged him to. Jannie had played the maid. She was dressed all in black and wore four or five silver earrings dangling off one ear. He found her exotic and artsy. All the women he'd known up to then were field hockey players or went out for crew.

Almost immediately Jannie began telling him stories about her awful home life. He felt genuinely sorry for her but was so mesmerized by her throaty voice, what she said hardly mattered. He liked it best when she read poetry aloud.

Not until he saw her play Rosalind in *As You Like It* did he decide he was in love with her. Later he conceded that maybe it was Rosa-

lind he'd fallen for. Possibly he liked Jannie best when she was somebody else.

''Then she married this creepy broker, Whitehall. Did I ever tell you about him? Whitey, she made me call him. I mean, Whitehall was his *first* name, and he was possibly the biggest zero in history. The thing I remember about him, he had this incredibly perfect Brooks Brothers wardrobe, and he'd sort of crouch over whenever I came near him. I finally figured out he was pro*tect*ing himself. I mean, he was afraid I'd get his clothes dirty! And by then my father had dumped this secretary, and *he* started hanging around the house. . . .''

A sense of impatience propels Robin to his feet and over to the window. In the dark he can see only his own reflection and, behind him, hers. Jannie doesn't miss a beat. He peers blindly out of the window. He doesn't want to think harshly of her. After all, if it weren't for Jannie, he might be an intern in the Zimbabwe investment division of Citicorp like one of his old roommates, or a broker worried about his clothes like Whitehall. At least she'd saved him from that by cajoling him into coming back to Lethem with her. She wanted some little theater experience. Only later did he learn she believed that by returning to the place where the crimes against her childhood had been perpetrated, she could somehow right them.

In Lethem those first weeks, he'd felt like a fifth wheel, and he was soon as deeply in debt as he was in love. He'd had to scramble, which wasn't much fun. They were supposed to be living together in a rented place on the out-skirts of town, but Jannie would often retire for days to the comforts of her father's house, leaving him on his own. Frequently during that period he'd been penetrated by cold, sweaty nightmares. These may have been the result of a diet heavy in ketchup and crackers cadged from Bell's Restaurant, or of having been forced to reinvent manual labor after a spell of relative ease in New Haven. But when he was new to Lethem, Jannie was all he had and less than dependable. Mostly she raced around spending her father's money, unable to fathom why Robin wasn't keeping up.

"Oh, God, do you remember," he hears her say. Exhaling so that he steams up the glass, Robin forces himself to tune back in. ". . . the night I stole the horse from here?"

Robin turns away from the window and searches her face in vain for the way it used to look. Nothing seems the same, though of course he recalls chasing her through the dark streets of Lethem, both of them on horseback. He started after her angrily, but the chase soon took on the aura of some eighteenth-century romance, or at least cowboys and Indians. By the time the Lethem Police intervened, he and Jannie were indignant. That time she was mad at him because he'd moved in to manage Abruzzo's stable, though by then she didn't need a reason to fly into one of her rages.

He remembers other tirades and messy scenes, dramatic crying fits, and reconcilia-tions, some of which actually lasted for several weeks. But he can't recapture his tolerance for all that. She's no longer the person he'd loved with such all-forgiving passion, or maybe he's not the same person who'd loved her.

"What's the matter with you tonight, Rob? You're acting kind of out of it." She looks over at him so carelessly when she says this, she might not be seeing him at all.

"Wait a second, Jannie," Robin says. He wants time to collect himself. He walks around the bed and goes into the bathroom, shutting the door behind him. Leaning on the cold por-celain sink, he peers into the mirror. His teeth are on the march, less ragged-looking every day, but it isn't his teeth that interest him now. It's the lines at the corners of his eyes. He looks older, like he's been somewhere.

On the other side of the door, Jannie lies on his bed, reminding him that time doesn't stay put. Yet even with that he feels clearer about things than he has for a long time. The thought skids into his mind that this has something to do with Katherine Watters. He's taken pains to avoid thinking about her, but when he does, he knows it was Katherine who somehow gave him a chance to be himself. He met her at a time when he needed solid ground, and she was kind enough to let him poach on hers. In among all the little unexamined messages he imagined darting in the air between them was a strange kind of safety that gave him time to catch his breath, take hold of himself. She put things in perspective.

Jannie calls his name, and Robin flushes the toilet, wishing she would disappear. He doesn't relish what he's about to do.

"You've got to hear about this thing my friend Phoebe is into," she says as he steps back into the room. "I thought you'd like fallen in or something. Anyway, she's living with these two guys, and one of them is this flitty computer person Barry, and the other one, well, he's this brilliant physicist, but he's well, like . . ."

Robin stands with his back against the door and wonders who it is she thinks about when she thinks of him, who she's seeing, whether he's as foreign to her now as she seems to him. That afternoon when he told her about his hopes for medical school she scarcely heard him. He might as well have been talking about an errand he had to run.

"Listen," Robin says suddenly, "I can't do this."

". . . and in the meantime she had this totally freaked-out thing going with—" Jannie stops and regards him as if she's surprised to see him. "Can't do what?" she asks.

"This," he says. "Us."

"What?"

"This won't work, Jannie," he says quietly. "Things are different."

"Don't be crazy," she says, sounding ready to dismiss the subject.

"I'm serious," he tells her.

"You're a big drag tonight, Rob," she says. Then her voice softens. "Come on over here." She pats the bed.

He shakes his head. "No."

"Is this your idea of a joke?" she says, sitting up.

"No," he says quietly. "No joke."

"There's somebody else, isn't there?" Her voice sounds shrill.

"No," he says. "No one."

"I know!" she says triumphantly. "I know! I knew the minute I saw her. It's that woman you waved to today. The one with the hair."

"Jannie . . ." Robin says.

"You always were trendy, weren't you? It's just like you to be on the cutting edge of some soap opera fad. The older woman. Jesus!"

Robin concentrates on the wall.

"You shit," she says in a low voice.

"I'm not going to fight," he says steadily. "If that's what you want, you better go."

"You're asking me to go?" Her voice rises precipitously.

He nods.

"You're asking me to leave this cruddy barn?"

In the past she was always the one issuing ultimatums. Now she seems astonished that he's capable of a simple request.

"Yeah," he says. "I'm sorry things worked out this way."

"Oh, sure. Right," she says angrily. "Of course." And then, as if there were a third person in the room, she announces, "He's telling me to leave, which is really fascinating, since we all know he'll be coming after me in five minutes."

"Shut up, Jannie," Robin says, amazed by how sincerely he means this.

"You goddamn bastard!" Jannie shouts, leaping off the bed and stomping over to the door. "You lousy, phony bastard!" She grabs her suitcase off the chair and flings open the door, slamming it so hard after her that the wall shakes. Robin waits and, after the first loud crash in the barn beyond, decides to follow. Once when she was throwing a tantrum, she threatened to let all the horses out.

He emerges from the barn office to find her far down the aisle, throwing everything she can get her hands on. When she sees him, she screams, "Just go ahead and see what a miserable life you have without me! Just go ahead, what the hell do I care?" She heaves a feed bucket in his direction, then pitches a coiled hose so that it unravels like a long orange snake coming for him. A shovel flies through the air, a pitchfork, a rake.

The horses move around nervously in their stalls. Robin doesn't say a word. Finally, with nothing left to throw, she upends a tack box and runs out of the barn, directing her farewell to him—"Fuck you!"—over her shoulder. A second later he hears the screech of his pickup's tires on the gravel. The truck will be at her father's house in the morning in some kind of shape. He has no intention of going after her now.

He holds his breath until everything grows relatively still and only the uneasy snorting and pawing of the horses remains. Then automatically he begins straightening the debris along the cluttered aisle. After a few minutes of interior silence, what descends on him is nothing he expected: "Nevermore, Nevermore"—the phantom refrain of Poe's raven, to whom Jannie had once been unreasonably devoted. This refrain seems completely unconnected to him, the raving of a vestigial voice, possibly lunatic.

He shakes his head at the weirdness of things and begins sweeping up.

"Precisely!" Ram Gupta exclaims ecstatically. "Things differ from themselves. You're right, they do indeed!" Katherine's eyes widen in perplexity. Did she say that?

Whatever she said, she smiles sweetly. Ram (Ramesh S. Gupta, known to everyone as Ram, and to some, though never to his face, as Rami

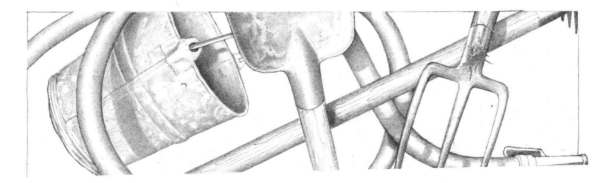

the Swami) has long been a professor of English at Erie College and is currently chairman of the department. Tenure, Katherine's own, is on her mind whenever she talks to Ram these days. At the moment she is also concentrating on keeping her eyes open. She was up half the night grading papers, all but one lousy, and that one surely lifted from something she couldn't quite place. She leans against the wall as Ram rambles on, the subject of his discourse (if she is following him at all) de-forming in a minor poem—something about a dead spouse—by the obscure seventeenth-century poet Bishop King.

"I would contend, then, that the overreaching analogy in this case . . ." Ram carries on, but Katherine doesn't bother to keep up. He'll continue without her attention; he always does. And the meticulously constructed paragraphs flowing from his mouth as if he were reading aloud will stop only when he's finished. To stay awake Katherine concentrates on the man's nose which, relatively speaking, is enormous. Ram reminds Katherine of a character from the comics and she often falls into a cartoonish mode around him.

Primitive little monosyllabic balloons think their way up from her head. Ram's declama-

tions make her feel tongue-tied and dopey. This may have something to do with his elegant Anglo-Indian accent.

"And, of course," Katherine hears him say, "by the very act of doubling back on itself, the poem cleverly reveals the gap, the fissure, the seamless hole. Aha!" Ram smiles with deep satisfaction, having, unlike Katherine, carefully traced his deconstructive convolution.

"Ram," she says, "you must let me read your article."

"But of course, my dear. Just as soon as it's properly typed. I welcome your comments. So often you see things that others miss. I would consider it a great honor if you would take the time to read it."

"I'd love to," Katherine murmurs, and attempts to sidle out of his intense, dark-eyed gaze.

"By the way, Kay, your classes are going well, I hope?" Ram has impeccable manners.

Invariably Katherine winds up wondering what's really on his mind.

"Oh, yes. Fine, thanks."

"We must have lunch sometime soon," he tells Katherine. His eyes make a discreet scan of her body: an innocent mannerism or lust?

At that moment Ram's secretary summons him to the phone.

"Do forgive this untimely intrusion," he says with a smile. "I'll check my calendar and get back to you before the day is out."

"Wonderful," she says as he moves off through the outer office. Katherine takes from her mailbox a glossy film schedule, a set of directives about the new library computers, and a handwritten invitation to an upcoming department sherry hour for one of Ram's structuralist pals.

Katherine hurries down the stairs to the basement of Darke Hall and unlocks the door to her own office. Sunlight, coming through large deep-welled windows, lies in squares on the threadbare Oriental rug she'd carted from home. Katherine drops her mail into the basket next to her desk, adding to the accumulation of unread and half-read mail.

She sits down at her desk and stares up at the gilt-framed engraving on the wall, a nineteenth-century rendition of three ethereally beautiful women entitled *The Three Graces.* Splendor, Mirth, and Good Cheer, items conspicuously missing from her life at this moment. She saw the engraving at a house sales years ago and thought it quaint. Now she's tired of those blank, lovely stares. Oh, hell, she thinks, she's tired, period. Six weeks into the quarter and already she's suffering a fatigue she associates with finals time. Her nights are riddled by disturbing dreams in which she wanders through steep mountain passes or labyrinthine library stacks. Frequently she is chasing a man, not Robin Hastings. It's someone tantalizingly familiar but too slippery for her, too evasive. In these dreams she is totaled by need for this mysterious figure, by desire and outright lust.

But she can never catch him.

What is going on in my life? she inquires of the graces. The ladies in the engraving gaze out at her, sweet but decidedly aloof.

Katherine yawns and toys with the idea of a quick nap before her next class. The overstuffed chair, from the same house sale as the graces, beckons. She's about to move when the phone on her desk rings.

It's David. He seldom calls her at work, and the sound of his voice snaps her out of her funk. David announces that his sister, Bitsy, finally had her baby, a little girl, early that morning.

"Have they put the kid on a horse yet?" Katherine inquires.

"Kitty," David says, "give poor Bitsy a break, will you?"

"Oh, all right," Katherine says, relenting. "A pony?"

"Guess what they named her?" David asks.

"Buffy? Muffy?" Katherine tries.

"Nope," he says, refusing to be baited.

"Heather? Melissa? Jessica? Jennifer?"

"They named her after you," David says.

"After *me?*"

"After you, Kitty. They named her Katherine."

"They did? Well. How nice." She says this without a trace of sarcasm, startled to find herself so touched.

"My mother's pleased as punch," David says. " 'What a wonderful role model this little girl will have!' she said. She thought it was especially nice because we don't have a daughter."

"You mother said *that?*"

"See?" David says, "Things can't be so bad if they're naming babies after you."

"*Bad?*" Katherine asks. He's noticed.

"Maybe *bad* isn't the word," David says. "But do you think you can go on not talking to me forever?"

Her husband's question startles Katherine. Can this really be old see-no-evil, hear-no-evil David?

"Kitty?" David says, "are you still there?"

"Only partially."

"Tell me about it, will you?"

"David, I can't talk. I have a class."

But David, always so respectful of distance and silence, won't let it drop. "Then later," he says. "Don't you think it's time?" He sounds concerned and genuinely curious.

"Well . . ."

"I just figured you'd like to know," he says. "About the baby, I mean."

"I'm flattered," she says, trying to sound breezy. "Really, I am. I'll call Bitsy as soon as I get home."

"I thought you'd get a kick out of it. By the way, why don't we go out for dinner tonight, just the two of us."

"Dinner?" she inquires, as if he had suggested something exotic.

"Dinner," he says. "I'll make reservations."

"W-well," she stammers, "I mean . . . if . . . well, sure."

After she hangs up the phone she wonders if he plans to interrogate her, though that wouldn't be at all like him. If he does, what will she say?

She glances up at the three graces, and then, seeing the time, gathers her things for her next class. As she does, there's a light tap on her door. "Come in," she calls.

Ram Gupta enters her office. "I hope you will forgive me for intruding," he says, "but your phone appeared to be busy."

"I was on it," Katherine volunteers.

"Certainly. However, to continue our conversation of some minutes ago, I would be greatly pleased if you would have lunch with me next Thursday. Would your schedule permit that? Say about one o'clock?"

Katherine pulls out her calendar. "That would be fine, Ram, just fine."

"Good, then," he says, rubbing his hands together. "I'll be looking forward to it. After all, 'The bread I break with you, my dear, is more than bread,' to borrow a phrase from Conrad Aiken, who, to give him his due, had his moments, few and far between though they were."

Katherine nods and watches Ram step back out. He seems to bow ever so slightly—or is that her imagination? The prospect of having lunch with him brings on an attack of yawning.

She takes her books and walks out of the office. On the way up the stairs she finds herself thinking she has a namesake now, a baby. Her step grows lighter. Suddenly she feels wide-awake.

"Well, here it is, kid," Sam says to Mona as he unlocks the door to Chez Mimi, officially theirs as of twenty minutes ago. "Should I carry you over the threshold?" he asks. Without waiting for an answer, he tosses her over his shoulder fireman-style.

"Sam!" Mona yells, pounding on his back. Coins and keys fall out of her coat pockets.

He sets her down inside the door and kisses her. "No fair," Mona grumbles. "Nice, but no fair." She retrieves her things from the floor as he ambles over to the windows.

This is the first time Mona's seen Chez Mimi empty. The cold, dim restaurant smells of garlic and stale cigarettes. A layer of filth coats everything—the fake wood paneling, the woodwork, the dreadful red-and-black flocked walls. During all the negotiations she never realized how grimy the place was.

"Lord, Sam," Mona says. "It's a dump! What in the world have we done?"

But Sam just laughs. "All the place needs is some sprucing up, and we've known that from the start." Gingerly he lifts an ugly red drape. Dust flies out.

"Sam," Mona wails, "this is the slimiest place I've ever seen."

Sam inspects the drapery rod above him, then yanks it. The drape thuds dirtily to the floor. Plaster cascades over everything.

"Not bad," Sam says, gazing out of a window that hasn't been washed in years. "At least there's more light." Methodically he begins pulling down the drapes. Dust billows up along with plaster. Mona sneezes and wonders if Sam's lost his mind.

"Hey," Sam says, halfway down the wall of tall, narrow windows. "This is fun."

"Sam, stop it, will you?" she pleads. "Oh, I could just brain myself for getting us into this mess!"

"Phooey," Sam says, struggling with the last drape. Already the place is less dismal, but Mona only sees more flaws. A neon beer sign hangs askew; the acoustical ceiling is gray with soot. She could just weep, yet Sam seems to be having the time of his life. Now he's ripping the wallpaper.

"Look!" he says, "this stuff comes right off." Plaster is coming off with the wallpaper in big chunks. "I figured these walls had had it," he says.

"Sam," Mona says soberly. "I think we've made a terrible mistake. I think we should go right back to the bank and tell them. No one will ever be able to fix this. We'd be better off setting it on fire!"

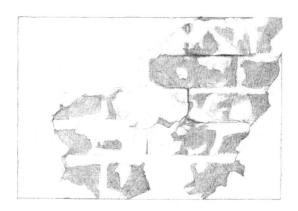

"Maybe you could scare up the guy who did Kay's." He laughs as he drags a chair over to the wall.

"Listen," Mona says, "I just wish you'd stop laughing. This isn't a bit funny!" She watches him chink the plaster off with his pocket knife. Soon he's made a spot big enough to see the brick walls through.

"Stand back," he says. Mona jumps as a big piece of plaster crumbles to the floor.

"Sam, listen," Mona says, trying to get his attention. He starts poking at a ceiling panel. "We were babes in the woods. The only thing holding the place together is that ghastly wallpaper!"

"Natch," Sam says, prying loose an acoustical panel and tossing it across the room. Mona peers up into the hole. The real ceiling's at least three feet higher.

"You mean, you knew all along it was this bad and you didn't tell me?"

"It didn't take an Einstein to call this, sweetheart," Sam says, stepping down from the chair. "Hey," he says, taking her face in his hand, "this is going to be terrific."

"Terrific? Have you lost your marbles? Me and my bright ideas. It's like once more into the drink or something!"

Sam looks puzzled.

"Brink?" she tries.

"Breach," he says. "It's into the breach."

"Well, whatever it is, we've done it. Give me strength."

Sam stoops down and rips up a frayed piece of gritty red carpeting. Underneath a smudge of yellow linoleum shows through. He scrapes at the linoleum to reveal crummy-looking wood. "Aha!" he says. "I knew it was down there. Oak!" He looks triumphant.

Mona bites her lip.

"Look," Sam says, abandoning the floor. "This may be bad, but already it beats slogging around oil fields." His narrowed blue eyes make Mona's heart lurch. "It beats flying all over peddling natural gas shelters too. Hell, Mona, at least now I'm home, and I have a good feeling about what we can do with this place. I have since the first day I saw it."

Mona puts her arms around him and leans into his sweater, which smells of something comforting and leathery. "You're not mad?" she says into his sweater, and gets a piece of wool in her mouth. "You're not just giving me a line with these high hopes of yours?"

"Take it from me," he says, kissing the top of her head, "this is going to be great. Hell, it's going to be a breeze!"

"Breeze?" she says incredulously. What the place needs is fresh air, she realizes. She flings open the front door. A cold wind sweeps in. She opens one of the balky windows. While she's doing that, Sam opens the others. Fresh air floods the room, so that even in her coat Mona shivers. But her spirits lift with the chilly November air, and the old house, seedy Chez Mimi, suddenly seems to perk up, as though the cold were driving away the bad spirits of the place.

"Sam, hey," Mona says. "If all this plaster is falling down, you know what we could do?"

He nods. "Brick walls," he says. "Right?"

"Yes!" Mona says, "Oh, maybe this is going to be okay, after all." She pictures the room without the flocked wallpaper but with lovely, rough, pinkish brick walls. She sweeps away the carpeting, the phony paneling, the mounds of filthy, rotting drapes. She imagines wood floors, simple pine tables and chairs—the kind she could pick up at auctions and barn sales— flowers, candlelight. The smell of freshly baked bread would drift out of the kitchen.

"I think I've got it!" she says, her teeth chattering. Antique quilts here and there on the walls. Things hanging from the exposed beams—dried flowers, baskets, some of the funny old toys she's picked up over the years. She's brimming with ideas.

"Oh, I can't wait!" she says. "This really is going to be fun! But until this minute I couldn't see it. Now I see *every*thing!" She takes Sam's hand.

He cocks his head and looks at her. "You know something?" he asks.

She shakes her head.

"I dote on you," he says, smiling.

"Now listen here," Mona says, "don't get all mushy. We have work to do!" She begins closing the windows, slamming them down hard. Behind her, Sam laughs.

"Does this church remind you of an airplane hangar, or is it just me?" David asks Katherine.

"I was thinking a gym," she says, eyeing the painted cinder-block walls and steel girders. A large metal sculpture over the pulpit looks like a tribute to Commerce or Justice, possibly Space.

Organ music swells; a hush falls over the church. David takes Katherine's hand, and she looks down at their intertwined fingers. For a second their hands seem foreign, body parts she's never noticed before.

Heads turn, and up the aisle sweeps Annie, one of David's radiology technicians, on the arm of her father. She dwarfs him. Annie's a peach—efficient, cheerful, good at what she does. Large. In her spare time she lifts weights. Even David was surprised when she told him she was getting married. "I didn't know she went out on dates," he told Katherine. Now Annie rustles by them, powerful and a little pale in a vast white dress. Her dark hair's been done up in corkscrew curls, which bounce happily.

"She doesn't look so bad," Katherine whispers to David.

He gives her a peculiar look. "Not for someone who bench-presses two hundred," he says.

The groom's a C.P.A. named Fred, who from

a distance looks like Woody Allen. Fred waits solemnly. He moves to make room for Annie and trips over a step, recovering at the last minute with the help of his best man. The minister herds everyone in place. Katherine's afraid she's going to get the giggles.

The minister reads. He reads from Pope and Shakespeare, from the Bible. He reads other things Katherine can't identify: song lyrics, poems. He doesn't speak of matrimony; he skips God. This is a Unitarian church, after all. Phrases such as *joyful fellowship,* and *loving spirits* drift over the packed pews like puffs of smoke. A man with a video camera keeps blocking the view.

The minister launches into Kahlil Gibran. "Let there be spaces in your togetherness," he intones. Katherine turns to David and rolls her eyes. In response, he arches his eyebrows goofily and lets his tongue loll in the corner of his mouth. Katherine nearly laughs out loud. Ordinarily he would be elbowing her to keep still.

"And now," says the minister, "Annie and Fred would like to say a few words to all of you." Katherine tenses as the bride and groom turn to the wedding guests. They are holding hands and look like Mutt and Jeff. Somehow it doesn't help that Annie's peach-gowned bridesmaids are almost as large as she is. One of them is pregnant, to boot.

"I met Annie at the bowling alley," Fred says, sounding quavery. Katherine digs her fingernails into her palm. "We happened to be there the same night, and I didn't know how to keep score." Several people laugh uneasily. "It was love at first sight," he adds, pushing his dark-rimmed glasses up his nose. Annie looks beatific, as if she doesn't have any problem believing someone could fall in love with her. "I knew from the first that it would come to this," he says, and grins. "Well, let's say I hoped it would."

Katherine's eyes widen. She isn't up on current wedding protocol. Possibly this routine has replaced getting married in a field at sunrise. At least everyone's wearing shoes.

"I want to personally thank each and every one of you for sharing this moment with us today," Fred goes on. "We won't let you down, believe me."

Fred turns to Annie and smiles encouragingly. She clears her throat.

"We met like Fred said, at the bowling alley," Annie says nervously. "I know a lot of you probably didn't know I bowl. I mean, you think I'm at the health club all the time, right?" She seems to be getting into the swing of things. Katherine looks over at David. He's listening attentively. "Well," Annie says, "I was subbing for my good friend Amy." She points to her pregnant bridesmaid and waves. "To tell you the truth," she resumes, "when I met him, I thought, who's this guy? He doesn't even know how to keep score." She pauses and smiles. "Believe me," she says, "he knows the score now! Anyway," she continues, "this is the real thing. I've waited all my life for a man like Fred."

The church is hushed. Katherine wishes Annie would hurry up and finish.

"We're going to have a wonderful life,"

Annie says. "We're going to do ourselves proud and have a whole lot of fun. And I'm going to teach Fred to be a power lifter. Already I've got him spotting for me."

"He's planning to grow," Katherine whispers.

This time David says, "Shhh."

"Anyway, I guess that's all I want to say," Annie says, "except thanks a lot for being here with us."

The bride and groom turn back to the minister, who seems tickled by their performance. He reads what he tells the assembled guests is a Navajo prayer.

Katherine sneaks a look at David. He seems completely absorbed.

Rings are exchanged. The minister speaks softly to the bride and groom, then booms out a passage from Rilke. It urges loving the distance that exists between two human beings, "which makes it possible for each to see the other whole against the sky."

"Whole against the sky" isn't bad, Katherine thinks, afraid to look at David, not sure what she'll find.

Annie and Fred walk down the aisle beaming, stopping to speak to people here and there. When Annie spots David and Katherine, she leans over and hugs them both.

"Annie," David says.

"Dr. W.," she says. "Was I great or what?"

"You were the best," David says warmly.

Finally the guests stream down the aisle, chatting animatedly.

"Hmmm," Katherine says.

"No smart remarks," David says to her.

"They were terrific, I loved it." In the crush of the aisle he pats her rear affectionately.

Outside, the moon is a perfect circle. "I'm still glad we got married by a justice of the peace," Katherine says as they head for their car. The wedding reception is miles away.

"I'm just glad we got married at all," David says, looking sweet and boyish and sincere.

"Sure," Katherine says.

"Well, I am," he says, and seems very serious.

"What's come over you?" she asks.

"Gratitude." He sighs, then smiles. "Sheer gratitude." He opens the car door for her with a great show of gallantry.

"That Annie." Katherine laughs. "She really got to you."

"A lot you know," he says, slamming the door.

"Tell me the truth," she says when David gets into the car. "What *has* come over you?"

"You," he says dreamily, pulling her toward him. She expects a kiss but instead receives a chorus of "There'll Be a Hot Time in the Old Town Tonight" hummed in her ear, zany and loose-lipped so it sounds like a tuba.

My, Katherine thinks. My.

The annual Lethem PTA rummage sale seems tackier than usual to Mona. She's anxious to find Kay and leave. She climbs into the stands and scans the high school gym for Kay's red coat, but the gym is crowded and red coats are everywhere. People spot her and call up greetings. She waves and smiles. It occurs to her that at the rate she's going, she'll soon have a whole new set of creases around her eyes. Oh, what the heck, she thinks. The fact is, she smiles often these days.

Mona hops down and takes another turn around the packed gym. Finally she steps outside. The November wind is biting, and the sun flickers in and out between fat, bluish-gray clouds. As Mona buttons up her coat and pulls on her mittens, she hums the snatch of a vagabond tune that's been with her all day. After a minute or two a group comes out talking and bundling up. Kay brings up the rear.

"There you are!" Mona says. "I thought I'd lost you!"

"Let's get out of here," Kay mutters.

"Wasn't that the absolute pits?" Mona says. "Worse than ever."

Kay shakes her head. "I don't know why, but it stuns me to see an acre of gently worn polo shirts. And what was all that brushed aluminum junk? There was a table full of it." Kay pulls on her hood and thrusts her hands into her pockets. "Where do people find that stuff?"

"At other rummage sales, where else?" Mona says, and laughs.

They cut across the lawn and Kay stops abruptly in front of the high school. "Where did I park?" she asks, looking all around. "This is the second time this week I forgot where I put my car."

Mona giggles. "We walked, Kay, don't you remember?"

Kay gives her a startled look. "You're right," she says.

"It feels good to walk," Mona says. "Even if it is cold. Boy, am I sick of driving. Last week I drove nearly four hundred miles, and I never left Lethem!"

The two of them pick up speed as they pass the rec center, Mona working hard to match her steps to Kay's longer stride. The pool is sorry-looking, drained and dirty and full of leaves. Mona thinks how fast the seasons have changed this year. The sun breaks through again, and Mona fishes around in her purse for her sunglasses.

"Did you see that woman fly off the handle in there?" Mona asks. "I think it was over a teapot that was already spoken for. Who was she, anyway?"

Kay groans. "Sally Something-or-other," she says. "Fortunately I've forgotten her name. In my former life I occasionally played doubles with her. She called bad lines. Once, when I was pregnant with Will, she told me she never sweat because she kept her weight down. It was all I could do not to sock her."

This is more words at one time than Mona's heard Kay speak in months. "That probably explains why she's all dried up and pruny-looking," Mona says. "Her pores don't work."

They shuffle through a pile of leaves. The sun disappears abruptly and the wind picks up. The trees look scrawny and bare, but Mona finds the whole scene invigorating. Every day there's something new.

"You didn't buy anything, did you?" Kay says.

"Just these," Mona admits, pulling a handful of lacy white doilies from her purse. "Every restaurant needs doilies, don't you think?"

Kay gives Mona one of her skeptical, raised-eyebrow scowls.

"I know, I know." Mona laughs. "But nothing matches, anyway. Besides, it was a civic gesture."

Kay shakes her head.

"You know," Mona says a little dreamily, "Princess Di really looks elegant pregnant."

"Oh, Mona," Kay says, "don't romanticize it. Anyway, how old is she? Twenty? Twenty-one?"

"Maybe you're right," Mona says. "Gee, you should have seen me when I was pregnant. I looked like a ship in full frigate!" Then, sensing something wrong, she stops and grabs Kay's arm. "Wait. Is *that* what I meant to say?"

"I think you meant you looked like a frigate under full sail." Kay smiles.

"Well, I looked like a slob. Brother!"

Kay nudges Mona with her shoulder, indicating they should take a shortcut around the cinder track that surrounds the football field.

"They're tearing this all up in the spring," Mona says as they start around the track. "Did you hear? It's going to be one of those all-weather deals for you nuts who jog."

"David started running," Kay says. "Isn't that amazing?"

"I know," Mona says. "I saw the two of you just the other day. At least you'll get your money's worth."

"You look wonderful now," Kay says in a conversational sideswipe that gives Mona a second's pause.

"Do you really think so?" she says when she gets her bearings.

"You look better than I've ever seen you," Kay says. "You look fabulous."

"Dr. Spatzer and his magic stitches," Mona says.

"You overrate Spatzer," Kay says in the good-natured, grumpy voice that Mona's missed lately. "You're happy and it shows. Sam's home and you've got your restaurant in the works, and face it, Mona, things really have changed."

"You look pretty spiffy yourself," Mona ventures. It's true too. Kay looks healthy again: the dark shadows have disappeared from under her eyes and her cheeks have filled out.

Kay throws up her hands. For as long as Mona's known her, Kay's shied away from talking about herself. She pulls these little disappearing acts, clowns around, or changes the subject.

"But you *do*," Mona insists. "You look grand."

Kay stares down at her feet and, in a voice so quiet that Mona has to strain to hear, says, "Sometimes it's hard to believe that the person who lived through the last four months was me. Maybe it wasn't. I really had the pins knocked out from under me. That crazy fire . . ." She trails off into silence.

"It was that kid, too, wasn't it?" Mona says.

Kay shoots her an astonished look. "Oh, him." She sniffs.

"You have these interesting little intervals, Kay. And he's . . . well, he is darling."

"Could that possibly be interludes?" Kay inquires loftily.

"Intervals, interludes," Mona says. "Don't try to change the subject." She can't remember their ever talking this way before, and she doesn't want to lose it.

"My big romance," Kay says, and bites her finger, "it was nothing, trust me. The strange thing is, though"—and Kay stares off into the distance—"that when I discovered it *was* nothing, I expected to be just the same old person I was before. Instead I seem to be, well, different. Something happened. The world seems kindlier, somehow, more hopeful." Kay stops in front of the boarded-up ticket stand. "But why am I telling you this?"

"Because I'm interested, Kay, and besides, I was worried about you."

"You were?" Kay says as they begin walking again.

"And how's David?" Mona asks, pressing. Kay seems surprised by this question.

"David? He's weird—for David, I mean. He's sort of loosening up. I'm not sure what it is. He's . . .'"

"Oh, Kay," Mona can't help saying, "he's one of the dearest men ever to come down the pike! Really." Mona's own grateful heart extends to her neighbor and seems for a moment to spread gently over the whole town. She wants everyone—especially Kay—to be as happy as she is.

"Well," Kay says, "he's different. . . . I don't know."

"Life is so strange," Mona says. "You never know what to expect."

"Yeah, and nothing is ever quite what it seems at the moment," Kay says.

The two women turn up Jefferson, but after a few steps Mona stops. "Yikes! I forgot I told Sam I'd go downtown and pick up some of these thingamajigs for him." She reaches into her pocket and shows Kay what Sam had given her.

"Sure," Kay says. "Why not? I'm freezing, though. Let's walk fast."

Mona and Kay reverse their course and, carried down the hill by what feels like their own speed but is actually the incline itself and the wind gusting at their backs, begin to go faster and faster until finally both of them are running. They run all the way down to the railroad tracks. A wave of elation grips Mona, and in the brisk air she feels light-footed, light-hearted, free as a bird.

"Whee!" Mona says when they've crossed the tracks and have slowed to a walk. "That really felt neat. Maybe *I'll* try the new running track."

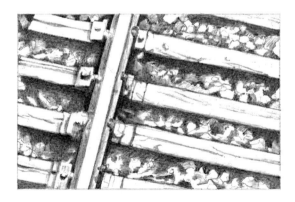

"Forget it," Kay says. "You draw such big crowds, they'd have to hire a traffic cop." Then she smiles. It's a smile so lovely, so much the essence of Kay—all flickering with color and her sublimely lovely blue eyes—that Mona can't help reaching over and hugging her.

"Oh, Kay," she says, "I'm glad you're back."

Kay rolls her eyes. "Yeah. For a while there I thought I was going to wind up making ashtrays out of little tiles in some loony bin."

"A crack-up," Mona says thoughtfully, and nods her head. She always thought *she* was the only person with ideas like that.

Kay looks at her. "A crack-up?" she asks, as if she didn't hear correctly.

"Oh, probably everyone goes on the fritz once in a while," Mona says. "There have been

The dog people wouldn't wish things on.

moments in my life I wouldn't wish on a dog. But I suppose they always teach us something."

Kay stares at her curiously.

"Oh, I'm deep." Mona laughs. "You didn't know that, did you?" Kay is still looking at her, searching her face, and Mona has the odd sensation that only now, after all these years, are they being honest with each other, speaking from the heart or at least someplace close to it.

"'Deep,'" Kay smiles. "Nobody says that anymore. Nobody *is* that anymore. You are, though—deep, I mean. You're a fooler."

Mona smiles back, and what she says next is nothing she intended. "I love you, Kay. Maybe now we can be friends instead of just neighbors."

"Mona," Kay says, "you're really something. You know everything, don't you? You always have."

"Of course I don't," Mona says, squeezing Kay's arm. "But I've got a few things in my information tank."

"Data bank?" Kay asks.

"Oh, you know what I meant."

"Me and who else?"

Laughing, they head across the street toward the hardware store, recently remodeled to look like something from the set of a gunslinging Western. As she steps on the curb Mona stops in her tracks.

"Oh, my stars, Kay!" She gasps. "Get a load of that!" In the parking lot on the far side of the store, Robin Hastings is standing next to his pickup talking to a woman. Mona thinks for a minute she must be imagining things, but when she looks at Kay, Kay's eyes are nearly popping out of her head.

"Quick!" Mona snaps, pulling Kay onto the store's front porch. "Lordy, that gave me a start! For a minute I thought she was you!"

"It's the hair," Kay says.

"Face it," Mona says. "I can tell from here you're much better looking." Mona peeps around the corner of the porch. "Oh, my God, Kay! Here they come!" She pushes Kay inside the store. "Pretend to be shopping," she orders.

"Calm down, Mona," Kay says. She takes Mona's arm and directs her to a teenage clerk.

"Listen," Mona says to the boy, "whatever this is, I need fifty of them, and on the double too. Please."

"Nuts," the boy says.

"Nuts?" Mona exclaims. "This is a nut? I thought nuts were those other dohickeys."

The boy takes the nut out of Mona's hand and disappears just as the little bell on the door jingles. Winking at Mona and putting his finger to his lips, Robin Hastings sneaks up behind Kay and covers her eyes with his hands. Behind him, Kay's look-alike, who looks less like Kay up close, lurks around the dish drainers wiping her nose.

"Robin Hastings," Kay says offhandedly. "Won't you ever get the smell of paint off your hands?"

Robin drops his hands and Kay turns around. "Seriously," he says, "how did you know it was me?"

"Oh, you never fooled me," Kay says, flashing him a brilliant smile.

Only then does Robin remember his friend.

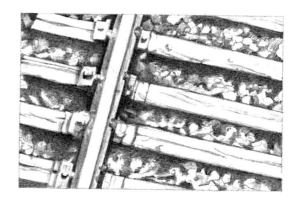

He introduces her to Mona and Kay, but the red-eyed young woman is apparently incapable of shaking hands or looking directly at them. She ducks her head and shreds her Kleenex. Either the girl has a dreadful cold or has been crying, Mona thinks as she pays the clerk and says good-bye. The bell on the door tinkles pleasantly as she and Kay step outside.

Neither says a word until they recross the railroad tracks. Then Mona bursts out, "My land! What a perfectly charming person. I wonder where he dug *her* up?"

"Interesting hair, you have to admit," Kay says.

"Well, a lot of good it does her."

Kay shrugs.

"I guess she can always put him through medical school."

"Doing what?" Kay asks. "Blowing her nose?"

"Oh, Kay," Mona says, "you know the young these days. It's different than it was twenty years ago. In one bed and out another.

It's probably just one of those purient relationships."

Kay stops. "Mona," she says patiently, "it's prurient. There's an *r* in there. It comes from the Latin 'to itch.' "

"Itch? Oh, I like that," Mona says. "Now listen, Kay, will you teach me how to talk?"

"Which language?" Kay asks, then bursts into laughter that rises up sparkling in the cold, clear air. Mona grabs Kay's arm, and together they climb the hill, battling the wind. The tune Mona hummed earlier resumes.

"I still think this was a lousy trick to pull on the boys," Katherine says to David after Tony and Will excuse themselves.

"It probably scarred them for life," David agrees.

"With my luck they'll wind up on someone's couch over this evening," Katherine says. " 'That's what kind of mother we had,' they'll be saying. 'She couldn't even bother to cook a turkey on Thanksgiving.' "

"Such a load of guilt," David says. He seems immoderately at ease tonight.

"Listen," she replies, leaning closer to him, "there's a little voice inside me that says *mothers* are supposed to cook on Thanksgiving, not country clubs. *Least* of all country clubs." She lets her gaze wander around the large dining room full of other families. Elaborate chandeliers sparkle softly.

"Well," David says, flicking his wineglass so it makes a silvery ping, "the boys weren't complaining. Anyway, it doesn't do them any harm to get dressed up and mind their manners now and then."

This sounds to Katherine like something David's mother would say. Even so, it's not a bad point. Her protests are largely idle.

A white-coated waiter pours more coffee into their cups. "Now the boys get their swim," David says, "and we can have an after-dinner drink in peace. It's a good deal all around. Of course," he says with a laugh, "I have certain . . . ulterior motives. I've got you all to myself." He reaches across the table and puts his hand over hers, an unexpected gesture that causes Katherine to eye him a little suspiciously. She casts around in her head for a distraction, but her mind seems blank. Finally she says, "About that after-dinner drink?"

"Sure," David says. "Let's go back to the bar." He takes a last sip of coffee and signs the check. The dark little bar is empty except for the bartender. David guides her to a corner table.

They sit down, and Katherine props her chin on her hand. "The Pilgrims wouldn't approve," she announces, eager to fill the silence between them.

"Probably not," David says, slouching comfortably in his chair. "But they might have been better off with a little booze. Maybe then we wouldn't be stuck with this load of Puritanical guilt. That is, *you* wouldn't. I myself seem immune to it." He laughs and orders two cognacs from the bartender, who has stepped silently over to their table.

"That's just because you're so good," Katherine tells him when the bartender has gone. She says this jokingly but means it. Under the table she slips one shoe off and puts it on again.

"Good doesn't count if you're a moron," David says, catching her off-guard. "I've been a moron."

Katherine stares at him. "A moron?"

The bartender sets their drinks down and disappears.

"Well, maybe not a moron," David concedes, "but for a long while there I wasn't paying much attention to anything but my work. I guess in the back of my mind I expected the rest of life to take its course."

"Like an illness?" Katherine asks, picking at her cocktail napkin. As much as this newfound voice of his unglues her, it also makes her curious.

David sips his cognac and wrinkles his brow.

"I don't get it," she says. "What's happened to you?" She rolls the scraps of her napkin into a ball.

"I'm not sure," he says.

"Did it have something to do with the fire?" she asks. Under the table she slips her shoe on and off, on and off.

"I suppose," he says slowly. "The fire, yes. Staying at Mona's too. It was like getting outside of our life in a funny way. Mainly, though, you."

"Me?" She pretends great interest in her brandy snifter.

He nods.

"I haven't been at my best lately," Katherine says quickly. Suddenly she can't locate her shoe.

"Kitty," he says in a way that makes it impossible for her not to look at him, "who has been? The point is, we got through it okay. And I don't know, something sort of jolted me awake."

"I wonder what."

He doesn't answer but looks off toward the bar thoughtfully. Talk to me, Katherine finds herself pleading. Tell me. Under the table she discovers her shoe and slips it on.

"I guess it hit me," David says, "that you don't necessarily have to be by yourself to be alone."

This remark disarms her.

"I don't think I ever really allowed myself to make much of . . . well, love," he says, looking straight at her.

Katherine has the terrible sense that she's in over her head.

"I tried to keep the lid on things like that," he says. "Feelings . . ." He stares down at his glass. "Maybe I was afraid," he goes on, "and I guess in my business you learn fast—to keep your distance, I mean." He shifts around in his chair. "I can see now, though," he says after a moment of silence, "that what might work okay in one part of my life wasn't doing the other part much good. Distance, holding back . . ." He shakes his head.

Katherine takes a big swallow of cognac. It scalds her throat and heats up her insides. Even if she knew what to say, she couldn't speak now.

"I guess you begin after a while to think it has something to do with marriage." His voice is low and intense. "That marriage—please don't laugh when I say this, Kitty—somehow cancels out passion."

She, who is close to stupefied, laugh? Did he really say passion?

"Now I think that was convenient rationalization." David ducks his head, and when he looks up, he's smiling. "Living with me has probably been about as thrilling as a hospital menu."

Katherine feels thoroughly perplexed, but even so, she can't help smiling: this man, her tongue-tied husband, talking like this. She knows better than anyone that it can't be easy.

"All I mean to say," he goes on, "is this, Kitty. I love you." And in the way he looks at her he somehow forces her to feel the weight of his words down to her bones. She experiences a peculiar stirring in her chest, yet she's not sure whether to trust herself. Didn't her recent little fantasy prove she wasn't trustworthy?

"I'm baffled by you," she finally says. "The way you're able to *talk* all of a sudden."

"Oh, Kath," David says, looking into her eyes. "I've *always* talked to you in my heart. Really I have."

The little candle on their table makes everything blurry. Then Katherine realizes her eyes are on the verge of overflowing. She blinks back her tears and faces him as steadily as she's able. With David she's accustomed to being businesslike about matters of the heart. Yet here she is feeling awed and a little panicky.

"Do you *know* how much I love you?" he asks, as serious as she's ever seen him.

Again the room shimmers.

"If you love me," she says, "give me a Kleenex."

"Take this," he says, handing her his napkin.

"It's true, though," David says, not letting up. "It's always been true. I've just been . . . scared."

Katherine feels flattened. His words have the force of years behind them, all the time they've spent playing it cool and safe. Just because you don't say things, she realizes, doesn't mean you're not saving up. She waves her hand helplessly. "I don't think I can talk."

"At least you're not cracking jokes." He smiles.

"You don't like my jokes?"

"I love your jokes, Kath," he says. "But sometimes your jokes . . . well, face it, sometimes your jokes have a way of deflecting things."

Katherine nods in bewildered agreement, visited by an image of herself as some kind of guerrilla, bent on chaos, striking confusion in the hearts of the innocent. How many times has she blithely dispatched David into silence?

"I've been a shabby person," she says quietly and with genuine distress. She is thinking of more than jokes. She is thinking of the ardent interior life she has never shared with David and, with a pang, of her foolishness over Robin.

"Listen, you're the best person I've ever known."

"You must know some real jerks," she says.

"Katherine," he says, "I *adore* you. I have ever since we met. But nothing I was able to say ever seemed adequate. Now . . . oh hell, now

I'm just saying it. It seems a lot simpler, more honest. I love you.''

She stares at him. He looks peaceful, like he isn't waiting for an answer. David strokes her hand gently. ''You haven't been yourself for a long while,'' he says. ''I've always counted on you to be charming for two, to be, you know, gay and abandoned.'' An apologetic smile flickers across his face.

Katherine looks away. ''I guess *abandoned* slices both ways, doesn't it?''

''You've seemed . . . almost haunted, Kitty. I haven't known what to do to help you.''

Her hands are folded on the table; both her shoes are on. Haunted, she considers, thinking how ghosts overrun lives. She wants to tell him she's weary of being haunted, tired of fantasies. She needs someone real. She doesn't want to be alone anymore.

''Say something, Katherine,'' David urges.

Suddenly it hits her: The person she's been chasing in her dreams is David. *He's* the one who eludes her. She sits bolt upright. ''Maybe ghosts are where you turn when you can't get what you need,'' she says quietly. ''I think I've been chasing after you every which way, I just didn't know how to get your attention.''

''Well, you have it now,'' he says.

''I feel like I've fallen through a hole,'' she says.

David smiles.

''I've never seen you like this,'' she says. ''It . . . kind of dazzles me. But it frightens me, too, if you want the truth.''

He puts his hand on her leg.

''I've always been so smart,'' she says, trying not to be distracted by his hand moving up and down her leg. ''I've always known everything. Now I don't know much at all. I don't know what's going to happen next.''

''Anything can happen,'' he says.

''Well, it's scary for an emotional cretin like me.''

''That makes two of us.'' David smiles. ''Maybe we can bungle along together.'' His eyes hold hers. This is even more disconcerting than what he's doing to her leg.

''Yes,'' she says, feeling breathless.

Just then the boys burst into the room. With them is a boy about Will's age whom Katherine's never seen before. All three are dressed to the nines and have uncombed, wet hair.

Katherine tries to pull herself together as Will introduces the stranger. David speaks with the child for a moment, but Katherine is making such an effort to appear normal, she scarcely listens. Finally David hands Tony a

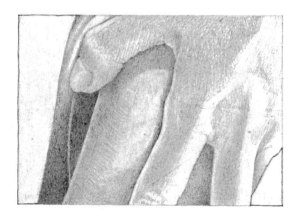

comb and the boys leave in a noisy tumble. "Five minutes," David calls after them. The room falls silent again.

"St. *What* was the name of his school?" Katherine asks as she gathers up her purse.

David shrugs. "St. Vlada's of the Infarcted Heart? You think I was listening? I have more important things on my mind."

Katherine shakes her head. "*You* make the jokes from now on."

In the long hall that leads to the front door, David pulls her close and says, "How about we go out to the car and neck? We have three or four minutes."

Katherine steps back. "Why, you're *wooing* me," she says. "You really are, aren't you?"

"You got it." He laughs. "Can you take it? I mean, what have we got to lose?"

"Plenty, buster," she says without even thinking. "Plenty."

H arry sits in the downstairs bathroom with his trousers around his ankles. He's attempting to speed-read the pile of typewritten pages Irene had given him before she went grocery-shopping. After a few minutes he sets the stack down on the rug and sighs for the sports pages.

He craves a cigarette, though he hasn't touched one now for . . . three months, twelve days, some odd hours. Harry the human calculator, ex–nicotine fiend. If he had a cigarette now, he'd smoke it. Of course, Irene would

sniff it out. Irene, who for all her new, sweet coyness, is more adamant than ever about breathing pure air into her firmed-up body. A dancer, his wife. What next?

Well, he reflects, she has a nice bottom for a woman her age, nice other parts, too, which Harry now explores on a regular basis in ripe, pleasurable sex, so good that it seems to be what he's been waiting for all these years. Who ever would have suspected better sex after a quarter century of marriage? No more rushing to get it over with, and certainly nothing he thought he'd ever reach with Irene. Like long, slow excursions into lush dreams.

Harry, all alone, nevertheless grows almost shy at the thought. He wouldn't have missed what's going on for the world. Irene's startlingly passionate advances take his breath away. The feats they accomplish! Harry the student, grateful beyond words for his wife's instructive flowering, and floored by the emotions that frequently overcome him. Sometimes at the thought of her his interior seems to grow warm and expand, as if there were a sunlit garden blooming inside him. Harry, beloved: the last thing he had expected.

Harry wonders what he and Irene will do when Buddy comes home in a few days and they lose their privacy. He envisions them furtively meeting at local motels. Nooners. Irene might go for the added drama, a hint of risk, like having an affair without the guilt. She puts these younger women to shame, he thinks, though largely on the basis of conjecture. He's been just about true-blue through all the tough times. Just about. There was Julie—what? Five years ago? Barbara, the top-heavy teller. Mostly sex was the farthest thing from his troubled mind.

Strange, he thinks, how it took the sight of his neighbor's long, freckled legs to revive him. He wonders what she would say if he told her that: The idea of you brought me a little alive.

Harry muses on favors received from strangers, people who change our lives without ever knowing it. No way to say thank you. If you tried, you'd be locked up like old Buddy, who would soon be locked up no longer, Dr. Krause having pronounced him cured. Interesting, Harry thinks, that Krause refused to take the credit. "Sometimes these things simply disappear with the end of adolescence. A little late in this case, but we're lucky here." Lucky, maybe, Harry thinks. He'll keep his fingers crossed and lock up the Mr. Clean just to be on the safe side. Buddy, the mental patient, about to become plain old Buddy, the undergraduate.

Harry has hopes, cautious to be sure, but this time things feel different. Something to do with Buddy coming on like common sense itself, all straightlaced and serious. A little earnest for Harry's taste, but consider the alternatives. Healthy mind, healthy body, that's Buddy, who's now training for a marathon. Have to hand it to the kid, he finally stuck with something. Winning that race in Middleburg in October gave him the biggest boost he ever had. Then another and another.

A natural-born runner, who would have ever suspected? After three wins Krause counseled Buddy to throw away all medication, take up something called interval training. Coach Krause, a runner himself for years, which explains the man's gaunt look, his amazing slimness.

Can life really come together like this? Harry wonders as he unreels the toilet paper. Is he a fool not to be holding his breath? You imagine the world has ended, and then suddenly one day you find yourself thinking the good times are just beginning. Accidents, flukes, they can't *all* be bad ones, though once he didn't think so.

Harry rises and flushes the toilet. Nothing lasts, of course. Carpe diem. Besides, who is he to quibble with the future? Hang loose, as Buddy would say. Don't get heavy, as he also would say—heavy being, as Harry only now realizes, the opposite of light. Which is what he feels like: light, lighter.

He zips his pants and gathers the stack of typed pages from the bathroom floor. The idea of Irene writing romances still doesn't thrill him; he persists in finding something sleazy about the impulse. Still, it's her choice, not his. "This one is about twins," she said. "I hope it works. Twins are unheard of, but, oh my, doesn't *everyone* secretly long to be a twin? Didn't you, Harry?"

"God, no," he replied. "Not me. Always been too much of me as it was." Buddy wanted to be a twin, Harry recalls as he rinses his hands. Look where it landed him. Maybe someday Harry will be able to convince Irene to write something worthwhile.

Harry remembers to mop the vanity after he's turned off the water. Adult standards of cleanliness and order, Irene says, and they please her, so why not? Besides, even he has to admit this is the middle class they're assigned to: bathrooms as neat as if nothing went on in them, clean underwear in case of accident, RSVPs, thank-you notes. Form, manners—civilizing influences. Harry glances in the mirror and considers himself briefly as the Emily

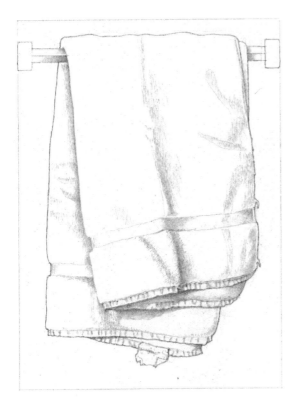

Post of the eighties. He smiles and starts to leave the bathroom, remembering at the last minute to turn off the fan. What a lot of people he is: lover, husband, father of the about-to-be regular kid down the block. (Also holder of noble superstitions. He knocks on the doorjamb.) Keeper of secrets—from his lavishly freckled neighbor—not only lust but also fire. "Let's be practical, Harry," Krause told him. "Some things you have to put aside. Kevin's through with all that. He's come around, he's cured. You're his father, believe it. I'd wager my life on it." Well, Krause's life should be good enough for Harry. The man's as old as he is and lays it on the line every day by running eight seven-minute miles.

Harry heads toward his den to finish Irene's story, which he knows will have a happy ending. This doesn't offend him as it once might have. Happy endings are what Harry's striving for now. Happy beginnings and middles too. Life imitating not art, but romance. A good joke, but what the hell.

Harry reflects, as he settles into his easy chair, that life imitates a number of things. He sees life most vividly these days as a trip through unexplored territory where you never know what's coming next. The trick is staying light on your feet, not dwelling on next but sticking to now. Maybe one day he'll get it.

Harry regards for a moment the snowflakes that are lazily drifting down outside. A little reluctantly he turns to Irene's manuscript, taking care to read every word, though he often finds himself wanting to skip. Half an hour later, when he hears Irene's car coming up the drive, Harry races over the final pages.

Jennifer took aim and tossed the bouquet gaily into the air, watching closely as the beribboned lilies of the valley sailed toward her sister, Jessica. Aided by a nudge from Calvin Lundin, Jessica caught the flowers to the delighted murmur of the assembled guests.

"Well," Calvin announced, loud enough for all to hear, "it looks like Jessica will be our next bride!"

"Don't be foolish," Jessica replied sharply.

"Ah, well, my dear," he said. "No harm done," and as the wedding guests looked on in horror he took the bouquet from her hands and proceeded to pull it apart.

"Whatever is he *doing?*" Jennifer whispered to Lance. "Why is he making this unpleasant scene at our wedding?" But Lance merely held her tighter. "Wait," he said quietly. "Watch."

"For you, my dear Jessica," Calvin said as the stunned crowd stared. Ceremoniously he handed Jessica the largest part of the divided bridal bouquet. "And for me too," he added, hastily shoving what was left into his lapel. "Of course, I have forgotten one little matter." He chuckled and turned to Jessica. "Will you marry me, Jessica? I love you deeply."

After a moment of shocked silence the guests buzzed with amazement. Tears sprang to Jennifer's eyes as the full significance of Calvin Lundin's words struck her, tears of sorrow, for how hopeless his question was! And how she dreaded the volley of words her sister would surely unloose on him for committing this terrible blunder.

Incredibly Jessica's expression softened.

She no longer looked confused, and to Jennifer's bewilderment she did not seem angry. "Thank you," Jessica said to Calvin Lundin softly. "I should be honored indeed." Having said that, she reached over and kissed him on the cheek. "Cal," she said a little louder now. "Cal," she said, and smiled, "I thought you'd never ask."

Jennifer caught her breath. "See?" Lance said. "Everything works out for the best."

"But—" Jennifer stopped. The heart's secrets overwhelmed her. Tears filled her eyes once again. "Oh, Lance," she said. "You knew it all along! How happy I am for Jessica, but what a surprise!"

Gently Lance led Jennifer down the steps and through the smiling crowd toward her sister. For a second the two young women, mirror images of one another, though dressed very differently today, stood gazing at each other, then embraced.

"I never dreamed . . ." was all Jennifer could say.

"And that is all *I* did," Jessica said. "It seemed too much to ever hope for after everything we've been through."

"I'm so thrilled!" Jennifer exclaimed. "So thrilled for both of you!" And releasing her sister, she threw her arms around Calvin Lundin. "Will wonders never cease?" she asked him. "What joy you've brought into our lives!"

"It was nothing, dear Jenny," Calvin said. "Following your heart is as easy as falling off a log." His eyes twinkled.

"Falling off a log!" Jessica repeated with uncharacteristic merriment. "It's quite bumpy too! Bumpy but . . . wonderful." She snuggled cozily into Calvin's arm.

At that same moment Lance pulled Jennifer to him in an embrace that said far more than words ever could, and she found herself quivering with joy. "Happy endings," she finally said to Lance. "Aren't they sublime?"

"Happy beginnings," Lance countered, looking deep into her eyes with a love that burned right through her. Then, still gazing at her adoringly, he raised her hand to his lips. Jennifer no longer needed to pinch herself to know it was true. They had entered, all four of them, the kingdom of love at last.

THE END

The kingdom of love? Harry ponders this phrase for a moment, then thinks, Oh, hell why not? The kingdom of love.

Buddy explores Lethem on foot, running routes he traveled beforehand by car, carefully checking the odometer. He is growing familiar with the distances, all of which begin at the bottom of his parents' driveway in the alley, where a chill sweeps off the river and the trees look like X rays of their leafy summer selves.

Today Buddy's making a six-mile loop that starts off easily down Jefferson and across the tracks, continuing on to Main Street, where he turns right. Cold sunlight, hardly more than a glare, filters down from a remote December sky. The temperature he recorded at seven-thirty in his running journal was seventeen degrees. Two hours later it isn't much warmer. In his navy blue running suit, cap, and gloves,

Buddy is comfortable. Only his face feels the splintering cold.

Traffic in the center of Lethem is light in the lull between morning rush hour and the opening of stores. He runs across the bridge and for a second is surrounded by the billowing cloud of steam sent up by the Dameron River as it dashes over the falls. Emerging back into the watered-down sunlight, he notices that the trees on the riverbank are covered with a brittle coating of ice. Flashing and chattering in a sudden breeze, the trees have a spooky beauty.

Buddy takes in everything he sees. Each day he spots something new and unexpected: today the fragile, ice-covered trees; across the street, a leather shop he hadn't noticed before; ahead of him, a phone booth on the corner of Route 442 and Main that lists precariously like a drunk.

He'll come back to town later today, as he's done every day since he got home, and walk around slowly; look hard; investigate the stores, brightly decorated for Christmas; treat himself to a thick chocolate shake. Something in him requires that he lay claim to this place—the smells, the faces, the way the town looks and sounds. For the first time in years he knows he is somewhere.

Passing the leaning phone booth, Buddy races the traffic light, and before he knows it, he's halfway up Moss Hill with the incredible steepness that forces him to lean so far into it, it's almost as if he's defying some natural law by not pitching onto his face. Today he conquers the hill easily, not even breathing very hard when he reaches the top. From there the extension of Main Street stretches out before him, hill after hill like a gentle roller coaster, which he rides in small spurts upward and in flying descents.

Buddy moves swiftly past houses set far back from the road, past what's left of airy Easter hemlock forests, past barns and empty pastures with jagged split-rail fences. By the time he reaches the end of Main Street where it butts into the redbrick road, he is running effortlessly, caught up in the almost trancelike state he loves—movement, icy air, his mind and body fused into peaceful harmonies he never dreamed existed before he began running. Nevertheless he's alert—for cars, uneven bricks, objects of roadside interest: a patch of ice in a drainage ditch; a noisy scattering of crows in a field; a sheepdog chained in someone's front yard that barks fiercely twice and then stops. He is a funnel through which everything flows, a moving eye. He is a hoarder of sights, making up for lost time.

At some point on the gradual incline that continues for almost two miles, Buddy recalls the edge of a thought he had in the night. Lying in bed, in the first room he can ever remember feeling he belonged in, he realized something that made him turn over and sleep more safely. He'd realized that he and his mother and father all moved in some of the same mental spaces, with enough memories in common to have dreams that might converge on the same dream sites. Newcomb geography. Sleeping minds merging as the cold blew in his open window and he resettled himself under his mound of blankets. They share more than the house.

A red pickup passes, veering into the oncoming lane to avoid him, and Buddy is drawn back into the day, night thoughts dispersing like seeds he's broadcast. Sun glints off a storm door that someone opens to shake out a mop; it illuminates a bright red mailbox with evergreen boughs wound around its post. He hits another downhill and gains steam. He wonders where it comes from, this new swiftness of his, the vast energy that propels him through the sharp cold like an arrow.

He swoops across High Street and takes a left down through the bag-factory road. A man in shirt sleeves peers out at him from an upper-story window in the aged, jerry-built building where they make bags for dog food, bags for seed. Buddy raises his hand in greeting. Then he recrosses the river on the new bridge, climbing with the riverbank, all concentration. At last he bursts over the top of the hill and is back on Jefferson.

Checking for cars, he races across Jefferson and moves steadily uphill, still easy, not a twinge from his knee. Later he'll go to the weight room at the health club his father recently joined. Later he may also swim. In the back of his mind Buddy toys with the idea of tackling a triathlon. First he'll have to see how the March marathon he's entering goes, and whether he's any good at bicycling. Who knows what can happen with this momentum?

As he passes, he steals a glance at the white house with its porches and small, round room on top. There's a large Christmas wreath on the door, and the house looks cheerful, as though the fire had never happened. Buddy can't remember much of what went on there, and he no longer tries. It wasn't him—not this him, anyway. He claims the act but feels no guilt. It's over now. Yet in the way a dream can change you, the house changed him.

He sprints down the street that leads to the alley. His kick is good; he's got plenty in reserve. Joined by an Irish setter and inspired by this new companion, Buddy races to the mailbox. He presses the timer on his watch and jogs on, slower and slower, the dog still by his side. At the end of the alley he turns and walks back to the driveway where he checks his watch: 38:59. He lets out a whoop, and the dog jumps up and licks his face. The dog's breath is hideous, but Buddy hugs the animal, anyway. After all, he's just set a new personal record for that hilly six-mile course. What's a little bad breath?

"Go on home," Buddy tells the dog. Giving Buddy a forlorn look, the dog turns and lopes off down the alley. Buddy strolls up the driveway, past the garage and the frost-silvered lawn. Ahead of him, two squirrels tear across the grass and scamper up into a tree, tails flying out behind them. These days things he never would have noticed in his previous life fascinate him: wonder everywhere he looks. He removes his cap, and his sweaty-wet head feels immediately icy. The cold lays a stillness over the world. Buddy takes the steps two at a time and enters the warm house, home at last.

Wearily Mona climbs onto a barstool and puts her head in her hands. She heaves a big sigh.

"Listen, sweetheart," Sam says from behind her, "don't fret. This is going to be fine. I can feel it right down to my bones." Mona raises her head in time to see Sam walk around the bar and light a cigarette. She could brain him for being so easygoing.

"Bones!" she huffs.

He leans his elbows on the bar so that his face is close to hers. Even in the low light his turquoise eyes are piercing.

"Sam," she says, resisting his eyes. "Here I'm suffering from a terminal case of heebie-jeebies, and you look like someone who just swallowed a handful of sleeping pills."

He merely continues to gaze at her. Mona makes a small clucking noise and lowers her head. "What time is it, anyway?"

"Twenty of eight," he replies.

"What if no one comes?" she says. "What if no one shows up—"

A voice from the kitchen interrupts. "Mona, help!" it says. "Come quick!" The kitchen door bangs shut and Mona groans. It's Hunter, the chef that Sam hired away from a fancy restaurant in the city. "Oh, great," she says, raising her head. "What's wrong with our temperamental little friend now?"

"I'll go," Sam says.

"Not on your life you won't," Mona says. "First he flunked the chocolate, now who knows? I could just wring his neck!"

"Whoa, babe, go easy on him," Sam says.

"Ha!" she says as she slips off the stool. "I'll just tell that little twerp he better knuckle down," she says, sputtering. She heads for the kitchen like a bullet.

"Mona," Sam calls, "don't clobber him, he's all we've got."

But Mona keeps right on walking.

"Just be your sweet, adorable self," he says.

"Very funny," Mona says as she flings open the kitchen door.

I'm not sure what to wear," Carol Ann says.

Don't wear anything, he wants to say. He is lying on top of the rumpled bed in his new suit. She is standing in the middle of the room in her tiny white pants; a blue ribbon threads through the lacy band that cuts across her abdomen. He can't believe he actually notices this when he's staring at her breasts all the while.

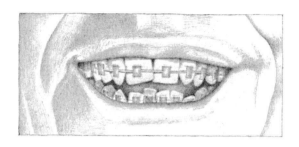

She kneels down and riffles through her suitcase, working around her breasts like they don't exist. This kills him, the way she's so casual about them.

"Let's not go," he says. "I can't even remember why we were going."

She doesn't look up. "Fresh air," she says, pulling things from her suitcase. "We can't stay cooped up in here all the time."

If this is cooped up, then it's the only state he aspires to. She has this incredible power he can't explain.

He closes his eyes and aims for self-hypnosis, a trance, anything to help him cool out. With his eyes shut he's aware that her perfume fills the room. He hears a silky rustling, other disconcerting noises. Abruptly he swings his legs over the far edge of the bed and sits up with his back to her. He contemplates his shoes.

She goes into the bathroom humming. He remembers how she surrounded him and feels her breasts again, sweeping and sweeping across his chest as she rose and fell. He lost track of himself entirely. The earth didn't move; it simply fell away, leaving him floating in space.

This is dangerous, he tells himself. What is he doing?

Water runs, something metallic clanks against the basin. A hanger falls on the floor.

He thinks he should stand up now, move around, at least mimic the actions of someone in charge, but his mind's crowded with her. They were a perfect fit. He never realized she was so tall.

She walks back into the room and stands in front of him. She is wearing a red dress, black stockings, black heels. Her hair, much shorter now, is still darkly wild.

"You look great," he says, "even dressed. It's amazing."

"Thank you," she says, and smiles.

"Listen," he says, taking her hand, "we really don't have to go."

She makes a face and heads for the closet. All he wants to do is bury himself in her, never come up for air.

"Really," he tries again as she puts her arm into her coat. He can't stand it the way she's covering herself up, going about her business as if he weren't ready to fall down and swoon.

"Are you okay?" she asks. "You look kind of pale."

"Pale and wan," he says, barely able to smile. "Lovesick."

She has her hand on the doorknob. She's laughing. "We'll just take a breather. It'll do us good."

He watches her open the door. He thought he knew something about women. He doesn't know a thing.

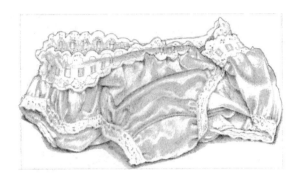

Tony watches from the bathroom door as his mother pencils brown stuff around her eyes. "Will and Scott wanted me to ask one more time why we can't come," he says.

"I told you before," his mother says. "You're all too short."

"I'm not so short," Tony says, moving closer to the mirror. "Look, I'm almost as tall as you are, and you're wearing high heels."

His mother turns away from the mirror and stares at him. "Gee," she says, "you really have grown. I didn't realize you were so tall." After a second she goes back to the mirror.

"So why can't *I* come?"

"Because you weren't invited," she says. "And you're baby-sitting. Anyway, you don't drink enough."

"Mom!"

Now she's doing something to her eyebrows. "You comb your eyebrows?" He can't believe this.

"Katherine!" his father calls from downstairs. "Are you about ready?"

"Coming!" she calls back.

"Personally," Tony says, "I don't care about some party with a bunch of old fogies, but Scott and Will feel really left out."

"They'll get over it," she says, touching her hair. "Feed them Christmas candy. Better yet, slip them some of that wretched fruitcake your grandmother sent. Play your new Trivial Pursuit game." She turns out the bathroom light.

Tony glances out of the window and sees snow. "Why couldn't it have snowed for Christmas?" he asks no one in particular. He follows his mother and finds her waiting for him in the hall with her arms outstretched.

"Well?" she asks. "Do I look okay?"

"Yeah," he says automatically. Then he looks at her. "Hey," he says, "you're really pretty!" He's always known it, but this is the first time he's ever seen her quite this way. "Really, Nee, you are!" He hears the surprise in his voice and right away knows she'll probably come back with one of her wisecracks.

Instead she says, "Thank you, Tony," and leans over and kisses him on the cheek. Her perfume is always the same sweet, flowery smell. It smells like her and like memories of her at the same time. Weird, he thinks as he rubs at his cheek and they start downstairs, even noses remember.

"Mona!" You've absolutely *transformed* this place!"

"It's terrific. Wow!"

Mona scurries around, greeting her guests in a flurry of pecks on the cheeks and hugs and handclasps. Earlier she was so jittery about their pre-opening party, she thought she'd collapse. Now, surrounded by familiar smiling faces, she feels calm.

"But this place was so tacky. Just *look* at it now!"

"Can you believe the change?"

"Aren't those quilts on the wall wonderful! The colors are divine."

Oohs and aahs wash over her as she artfully channels people toward the back, working the crowd, pulling names out of nowhere. She drops in and out of conversations, introduces strays, urges food and drink on everyone.

Someone takes her aside. "Tell me," he says, "wherever did you get the idea to take the walls down to the brick like this? It's the perfect touch."

Mona decides not to go into the saga of removing the ghastly flocked wallpaper and watching the plaster beneath fall off in chunks.

"Sam and I just thought it might be nice." She smiles. "I'm so glad you like it."

"Say, Mona! Yoo hoo!" someone else calls. "What on earth is this fabulous stuff I'm eating?"

Mona whisks over. "That's pesto mayonnaise on Sam's black bread," she says.

"It must be habit-forming. I've already eaten half the tray. What did you call it?"

"Pesto," Mona says. "The guacamole of the eighties." She flashes a smile.

Mouth-watering smells waft from the trays the waitresses are passing, and mingle with the heady scent of evergreens. The room ripples with laughter and talk. Mona spies Sam next to the bar and slips through the crowd to his side.

"How're you doing?" he asks.

"Dandy," she says. "I'm sorry about earlier. I was wound up higher than a kite."

Sam grins. "I told you we had a hit on our hands. People are making reservations like crazy!" He squeezes her shoulder, then heads off across the room. Mona stands taking in the whole scene until someone taps her on the arm.

"Irene Newcomb!" she exclaims.

"Mona, dear."

"Don't you look fantastic!" Mona says. "See? All that aerobic dancing's done wonders for you. Now, where's that Harry? I want to be sure and say hello."

Irene hesitates for a second, then leads Mona to a corner where Harry Newcomb stands against the wall. "Nice job," he says, shaking her hand and smiling stiffly.

"And this is our son, Kevin," Irene says, nodding to a young man next to Harry.

"Son?" Mona gives Kevin a quick once-over as he takes her hand and mumbles hello. He's tall and thin, with very short blond hair, a kind of rawboned, unsmiling version of Robin Hastings.

"Irene!" Mona says. "I had no idea you had a son!"

"Yes, and he's at home with us now, isn't that nice? In fact," Irene goes on, "he's starting back to college in a few weeks. Erie College."

"He is?" Mona says. "Then he *must* talk to Kay!"

Harry Newcomb stares at her blankly.

"Kay Watters," Mona explains. "You know, our neighbor. She teaches there."

"Kevin's quite a runner," Harry Newcomb announces as if he didn't hear her.

"Good gravy!" Mona says, attempting to smooth things over. "I sure hope it's catching! Just look at my husband over there, Kevin, smoking like a chimney. We've got to do something to get him in shape. Maybe one of these days you'll come over and light a fire under him!"

Kevin's face falls, and his father looks unnerved. Irene laughs a little too merrily. Mona wonders what on earth she said.

"Sure," Kevin finally gets out. Deciding she's barged into the middle of something, Mona excuses herself and hurries on. No time to worry about the Newcombs now.

For a moment she surveys the crush around the food-laden tables where people are stuffing themselves like crazy. Feeding others does her heart good, the no-cal thrill she's always searched for. She watches the mayor of Lethem's wife wolf down two strawberry tarts, one after another. Better her thighs than mine, Mona thinks. These days she's made her peace with food. Sometimes she even forgets to eat.

"Try this," someone says. "It's scrumptious!"

"Gawd, I don't know what to eat next," Frannie Tolland thunders.

"Mona," someone says, "your hair is all cut off! Don't you look darling, like a little China doll."

Mona dodges into the kitchen to check on

Hunter. Hunter's a terrific cook, but he's suffering first-night jitters. All day long he's been in a snit.

"I ordered the cucumbers without seeds," Hunter says through the great crop of mustache on his upper lip. "Look at these waxy things. Who checked them in? What am I supposed to do with them?" Hunter sulks.

"Stuff them," Mona says. Hunter looks insulted. "You know," she says, "like in tomatoes?" Hunter's mustache twitches, and he shows her the whites of his eyes.

"Maybe I could slip them into a perfection salad," he says, snarling.

"Come now, Hunter," Mona says, trying hard not to lose her composure. Hunter stares at the ceiling. "Oh, heck," she says, "everything else is so great, who cares about cucumbers, anyway?" She pats his arm, and Hunter grumps. "That's the spirit," Mona says.

Coming out of the kitchen, Mona gazes around the crowded room, all awash with color and shimmering candlelight. Enormous bunches of red tulips are placed here and there, a touch of spring against the snow piling up at the windows. The people in the room look happy and lively. Everything is exactly the way Mona imagined it would be, only better because it's real.

"I just love it here," someone says.

"Now, finally a place to eat in this town besides Bell's."

"Why, Robin Hastings," Mona exclaims, "you're all gussied up! I hardly recognized you."

"It's new," he says, touching his lapel. "Is it okay? I'm masquerading as a respectable person." He gives her a big smile. Maybe it's the light, but he looks less like the real Robin than a handsomer, older double of himself, Mona thinks. What a hunk, though, good night!

"And this is Carol Ann Drumley," Robin says, introducing Mona to a tall brunette with an impressive bosom. The two of them look like they just got out of bed or were about to jump in.

"Of course!" Mona says. "The famous Miss Drumley. I've heard about you from Tony Watters. I thought you'd moved away, though."

"I did," Miss Drumley replies pleasantly. "To New York. I'm just back here visiting my horse." She gives Robin a loaded glance, and Mona thinks: Bully for him. This Drumley's a big improvement over that redhead with the runny nose.

Just then Mona spots Kay. "Kay!" she calls. "Look who's here!"

Kay drifts across the room, radiant in a black dress. "My," she says to Robin, "don't you look snazzy!" Robin laughs a little awkwardly and is rescued by Miss Drumley, who asks Kay if they ever found out who set fire to their house.

"No," Kay says. "Only that it was a real amateur."

"You don't ever worry," Robin asks, "that this . . . uh . . . amateur might come back?"

"Not really," Kay says. "Anyway, we're all hooked up to one of those fancy security systems now—you know, burglars, fire, ice, the works. Of course, we manage to set it off accidentally almost every day," Kay says, and laughs. "But, well, once burned . . ."

"Gee, I hope *I* can get in if I come to see you," Robin says.

"Oh *you*," Kay says. "You're safe. Who could be safer?"

Just then Frannie Tolland descends on Mona and buzzes something in her ear. "I'll call you about it soon," Frannie booms as she walks away.

"Good grief, Mona," Kay says. "I saw that woman the other day in Tano's, and she was wearing a big Greenpeace button. You're such

a wow at getting things done, she probably wants you to save the whales."

"I'm announcing my retirement from public life," Mona says. "As of now."

"You heard it here," Kay says, joking.

"Right." Robin laughs. "Should we hold our breath?"

"These two are perfectly hopeless," Mona confides to Miss Drumley, then darts off.

Mona floats around the room, carried by a wave of good wishes and appreciative smiles. As the evening moves on and the laughter and talk grow louder, Mona glides from here to there, guided by a charmed automatic pilot: her perfect-party self. Suddenly it's late. People begin collecting their coats.

"What a fabulous place!"

"When do you open? I can't wait to have dinner here!"

"Right after the first of the year," Mona says. "Do come back." She presses a box of matches into an outstretched hand. "Our phone number."

The small gray matchbox reads:

NO PLACE LIKE IT

17 Church Street
Lethem, Ohio
555-4200

"Terrific time," someone says, squeezing her hand.

" 'Bye, Mona, thanks. We're coming back just as soon as you open."

"January fourth," Mona says. "See you then!"

"Thanks, and by the way, Happy New Year!"

The reporter from *The Lethem Register* pounces on Mona. "Mona," she says, "this is wonderful! I'm calling it 'a labor of love.' Do you think that sounds right?"

"I do," Mona says. "That just about hits the nail on the head."

"Hell of a place," the mayor says. "Just what the town needed. Good for you!"

Mona smiles and smiles. Finally she ducks out of the stream of departing guests and sidles up to Kay.

"I lost a lot of mail," Kay is saying to the Newcombs' son. "I had it all in a basket in my office, and the janitor must have decided it was a wastebasket, because one day it was empty!" Kay laughs. "So I didn't get it, Kevin, but I hope you'll come and see me when you're back in school and tell me what your letter said. Your son," Kay continues, turning to Harry Newcomb, who looks to Mona even more out of sorts than he did earlier, "he was one of the . . . well . . . more imaginative students I've had." Harry Newcomb nods distractedly and helps Irene into her coat.

"Did you know about *him?*" Mona asks Kay when the Newcombs have gone.

"Kevin Newcomb?" Kay says. "You mean, did I know he was *theirs?* Heavens, no! I had him in freshman English a couple of years ago. To tell you the truth, he sort of gave me the willies, but he seems okay now. I thought maybe drugs, but I guess he just had to grow up. He's taller than I remember."

"Well, *I* think it's peculiar we didn't even know they had a son," Mona says.

Kay shrugs. "What's peculiar?" she asks Mona. "I mean, everything's peculiar when you think about it. Eloise Schmidt came up and said you told her Sam's chocolate cake was bio-degradable! Honestly, Mona. Did you say that?"

Mona frowns. "Isn't it?" she asks.

"Polyunsaturated," Kay says. "I bet that's what you meant."

"Of course it is," Mona says. "See? You understood."

Kay laughs. "And speaking of peculiar, did you check out all the Ultrasuede in this place tonight? Enough to upholster a jumbo jet!" Kay says. "I'm going to rescue David from your pal Frannie. She seems to be recruiting him."

Mona sails over to the door to join Sam in his good-byes.

"Thanks for coming."

"Watch the driving!"

"We loved having you, come back soon."

Cold air sweeps in from the vestibule. Mona cuddles close to Sam.

"Happy?" he asks her during a lull. His blue eyes take her in indecently. It's his eyes that do it, always, she thinks.

"Mmmm." She sighs. "As a clam."

"Some clam." He winks.

The three of them head for the car, huddling together against the icy wind that swirls the snow in blinding eddies. In a matter of a few hours the world has turned white and ferocious.

By the time Buddy has brushed off the car windows, they're nearly covered over again. Harry motions him inside where the heater is going full blast, and Buddy squeezes in next to Irene. Cautiously Harry pulls out of the parking space, great gusts of wind sweeping snow across the windshield so that visibility comes and goes. To Harry the churning blizzard is nothing compared to what he's just been through.

"Well!" Irene says a little too cheerfully, "what a delightful place! I'm sure it will be a great success. We must go back for dinner soon."

"I was flabbergasted, Bud," Harry blurts out. "I had no idea you . . . uh . . . knew her."

Irene delivers an elbow to Harry's side, its impact muffled by layers of clothing, but a message nevertheless.

"Yeah," Buddy says, "but I didn't *know* I knew her. I mean, I just never made the connection."

"Of course not," Irene says calmly, "But, Bud, when you did, you handled yourself beautifully."

"It wasn't so hard," Buddy says matter-of-factly. "She's nice."

Nice! Harry almost explodes as he fantails onto Main. Somehow he manages to right the car just as it appears they're going to wind up in the front window of the Lethem Department Store.

"Be careful," Irene cautions.

Harry grunts, turns the heater down, and peers around at the center of town. Snow is everywhere—sweeping down from the sky, rising up from the ground, rendering the storefronts ghostly and pale, the streetlights almost invisible. All along Harry worried about taking Buddy with them, but Irene insisted. What were they supposed to do, anyway, lock him up? Besides, who in his right mind could have predicted that Buddy knew their neighbor?

"I'll tell you," Harry growls, "it's the last thing I was prepared for."

"Harry, dear," Irene says gently, "no one's ever prepared. We just do the best we can. And Buddy was magnificent—you were, Bud."

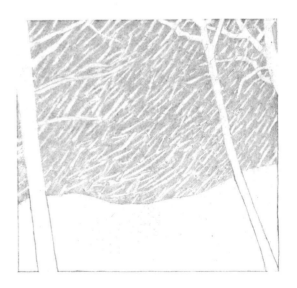

"Was I really okay?"

"You certainly were," Irene says, jabbing Harry again.

A car passes them going sideways, and Harry slows to a crawl. He hates to admit this, but ever since Buddy came home things have been out of whack—as if there were a guest in the house cramping their style. Irene's grown quieter, more reserved. Maybe the honeymoon was over, kaput.

Irene's elbow jars again, wanting him to speak to Buddy. Well, the kid rose to the occasion, no doubt about that. After all, what difference does it make if he, Harry, wasn't prepared? It sure as hell wasn't the first time.

"You were great, Bud," Harry says. "Your mother's right. You were just fine. In fact," Harry continues, amazed by a sudden excess of emotion, "I should have told you that right away. I'm proud of you, Son."

"Really, Dad? Gee."

"You bet I am."

"Thanks, Dad," Buddy says, and Irene nudges Harry once again, more tenderly this time. Elbow talk—they're getting good at it. Maybe things weren't as bad as he thought; maybe they were just pausing, readjusting.

The wipers clank-clank, wands of solid ice. Snow slides across the windshield in veils. Turning onto Jefferson, Harry drives largely by memory. Only intermittently can he make out anything besides billows of white.

"Jesus," Harry says indignantly, "this is one helluva storm. The weatherman didn't say a word about it on the six o'clock news."

"Don't sweat it, Dad, we're almost home."

Irene says to Buddy, "Your father likes a little too well to know precisely what's coming next. This, of course, assures him a measure of daily desperation." She laughs good-humoredly.

"Dear Harry," Irene says, patting his knee affectionately. "We love you, anyway, don't we, Bud?"

"Sure we do," Buddy pipes right up. "Our own desperado. Every family needs one."

Buddy making wisecracks? That's another thing Harry wasn't expecting. The kid's been so earnest lately; good for him. Harry feels his prickliness begin to vanish. Irene's right. The things she knows about him are amazing. Besides, they were back in touch. Who could tell where elbows might lead?

The car slips and slides around the corner of the alley, plowing steadily like a tank through the drifts of snow. Concentrating hard, Harry guns up the drive. The tires spin, whining, then catch, and the car lurches forward. Miraculously—spinning and lurching—Harry manages to drive almost all the way to the house.

"Goodness," Irene says, "I thought for a minute we weren't going to make it."

"Yeah," Buddy says, reaching over and clapping Harry on the shoulder. "Nice going, Dad."

"We try," Harry says. He's bushed by his efforts. "We may not be perfect, but brother, we try."

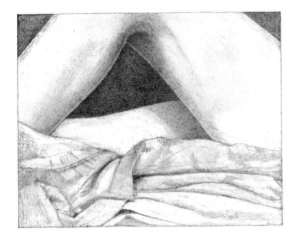

They sleep now like a pair of spoons, they make love at odd hours. It's as if neither of them ever had sex before, certainly not with each other.

She tells him, "But I used to think we had a pretty nice sex life."

"Maybe too nice." He laughs.

"Too married," she says thoughtfully. "How does that happen?"

There are times when they both seem a little stunned, like they don't know what hit them. He looks dazed and dreamy and soft-eyed. Her color is perpetually high. Sharing some mutual hunger, they astonish each other with wordless, heart-stopping messages.

"This is mad," she says to him one cold night when they've managed to pull the sheets off the bed and lie tangled in quilts.

"Maybe you'd rather watch the late movie," he whispers.

He touches her all over, electrifies her. She charts his body inch by inch. Everything is hot and mysterious.

"Do you think we've lost our minds?" she asks him early on the morning of New Year's Eve day when they both happen to be awake.

"I hope so," is all he says.

Suddenly she is galvanized into a lust that bewilders her. In the dark she reaches inside of him as the two of them climb higher and higher. They ascend into air so rare, she can scarcely breathe, like they're working toward a summit, high, high. They explode brilliantly in unison.

He says her name, but she's too blown away to answer. She strokes soft skin, for a split second not sure whether it's his or hers. She holds him as they both fall back asleep.

She dreams that she's lying in bed with him just as she is. When she wakes again, the transition between sleeping and waking is perfectly seamless.

Tony rolls off his sled and lies in the snow, staring up at blue sky and fat white clouds. The speeding clouds spread, drift apart, take on new shapes before his eyes. Here on the ground the snow makes everything quiet and still. Yet far above him, the high winds of the sky shuttle the clouds around fast.

He hears the hiss of sled runners coming

closer and closer, and raises his head long enough to see his brother headed straight for him.

"You better turn that thing, stupid!" Tony shouts. At the last minute Will does, then stops several feet away. The world falls silent again.

"What are you doing lying there?" Will asks.

Tony points to the sky.

Will rolls off his sled onto the ground next to his brother. "What?"

"Watch how the clouds move," Tony says. "See the way they're only like themselves for a minute and then change into something else? Look at that one there." He points. "It looks like an elephant."

"No," Will says. "It looks like a map of the United States."

"Hey! Now it's a tank. There's even smoke coming out of the gun."

"A *tank?* It looks like a giant snail to me."

Lying in over a foot of new snow, the two of them gaze upward while the shape—the tank or the snail—grows small in the middle and splits in two.

"Now it's a rhino chasing a camel," Tony announces.

"No, it's not. It's a truck with a little car behind it."

"You must be blind," Tony says, but by then both clouds are only wispy memories of themselves.

"Are you gonna sled down the hill again, or are you just gonna lie here?" Will asks.

"It's crummy sledding, the snow's too deep," Tony says. "Hey! I know! Let's make angels!"

Will groans.

"Listen," Tony says, "we could make a row of angels all along the side of the hill. It'd be neat."

"Angels are for babies," Will grumbles.

They leave their sleds near the sidewalk and climb halfway up their front yard hill. "I'll start at this end, you start at the other," Tony directs. He trudges off to the right, Will to the left.

Tony picks his starting position, turns around, and falls backward. He raises and lowers his arms several times until he's sure the wings are good and deep. After that he kicks his feet apart, making a skirt. The snow is heavy and hard to move.

When he finishes this one, he gets up carefully, leaps to the right and falls down again. He repeats this perhaps a dozen times until he meets Will almost perfectly, their mittened fingertips touching.

"Look!" Will says, pointing upward.

"Where?"

"Up there. It's a big fat rabbit."

"Hey, for once you're right," Tony says. The two boys watch as the rabbit moves eastward, its ears finally disappearing, then its head.

"I'm cold," Will says. "I'm hungry too."

"Yeah, let's go in. I'll make pancakes. You can help."

"Excellent," Will says.

The boys grab their sleds and start up the hill. Will runs on ahead, but Tony stops to admire the ragged line of angels guarding the house. Glancing up, he's surprised to see his parents, in their bathrobes, high above him in the round room waving at one of the windows.

Tony gestures to the angels, and his mother claps her hands and smiles. His father grins and then steps back, but his mother stays by the window, squinting against the sunlight, running a hand through her hair. Her bathrobe seems whiter than the snow. After a minute she begins waving again, and from something in her expression Tony knows that what she's waving isn't hello, or I see your angels.

She's waving I love you, she's waving her love.

As he raises his arm to signal he understands, a snowball smacks him on the head and showers snow into his mouth and eyes, down under his collar.

"You dick!" Tony screams at his brother.

"I'm starving," Will shouts, "and you're standing there waving. Hurry up!"

Tony drops to his knees, forgetting everything except the smooth little ice ball he's making, just the right size to slip down Will's shirt.

ALICIA METCALF MILLER lives in Chagrin Falls, Ohio, with her husband and three children.

ANN MCCARTHY'S work has appeared in *Esquire* and *The New York Times*. Her most recent book is *Midnight Mouse, Her Life and Times, Part One*.